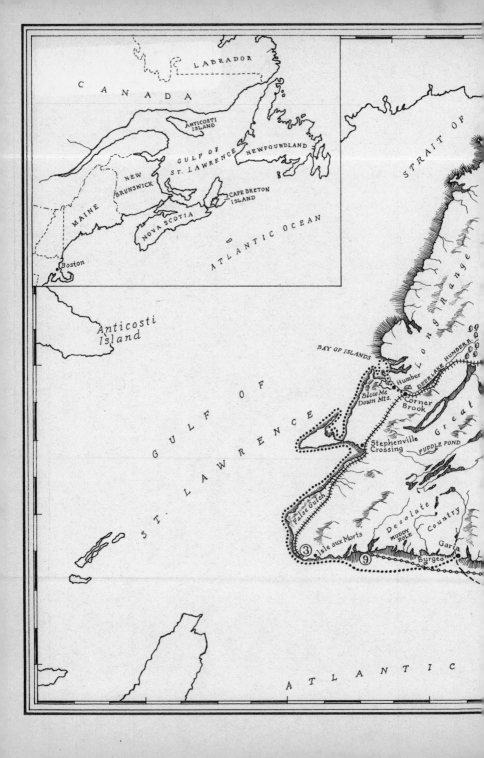

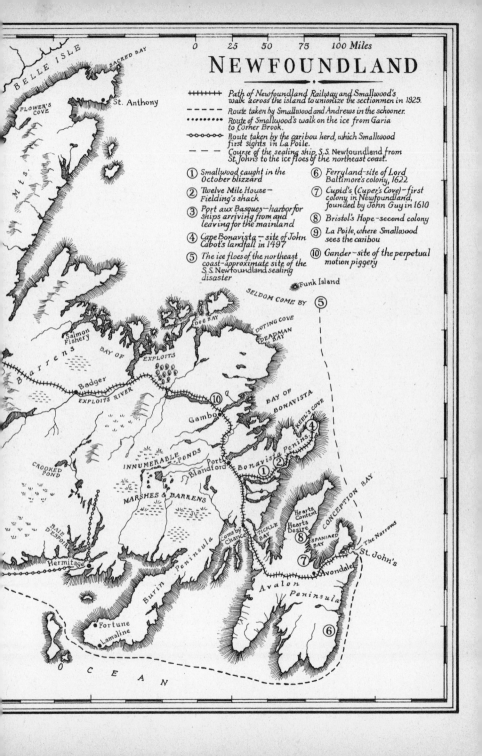

NEWFOUNDLAND

0   25   50   75   100 Miles

++++++ Path of Newfoundland Railway and Smallwood's
       walk across the island to unionize the sectionmen in 1925.
- - - Route taken by Smallwood and Andrews in the schooner.
•••••• Route of Smallwood's walk on the ice from Garia
       to Corner Brook.
-o-o-o- Route taken by the caribou herd, which Smallwood
       first sights in La Poile.
- - - Course of the sealing ship, S.S. Newfoundland from
       St. John's to the ice floes of the northeast coast.

① Smallwood caught in the
  October blizzard
② Twelve Mile House –
  Fielding's shack
③ Port aux Basques – harbor for
  ships arriving from and
  leaving for the mainland
④ Cape Bonavista – site of John
  Cabot's landfall in 1497
⑤ The ice floes of the northeast
  coast – approximate site of the
  S.S. Newfoundland sealing
  disaster

⑥ Ferryland – site of Lord
  Baltimore's colony, 1622
⑦ Cupid's (Cuper's Cove) – first
  colony in Newfoundland,
  founded by John Guy in 1610
⑧ Bristol's Hope – second colony
⑨ La Poile, where Smallwood
  sees the caribou
⑩ Gander – site of the perpetual
  motion piggery

BELLE ISLE

SACRED BAY

FLOWER'S COVE

St. Anthony

Mts.

Funk Island

SELDOM COME BY

DOTING COVE

DEADMAN BAY

DOG BAY

⑤

Salmon Fishery

BAY OF EXPLOITS

Barrens

Badger

EXPLOITS RIVER

⑩

Gambo

BAY OF BONAVISTA

KEEL'S COVE

④

Bonavista Penins.

CROOKED POND

INNUMERABLE PONDS

Porte Blandford

② ①

Come by Chance

MARSHES & BARRENS

TICKLE BAY

Hearts Content

Hearts Desire

⑧

SPANIARD BAY

CONCEPTION BAY

The Narrows

St. John's

⑦

Avondale

BAIE D'ESPOIR

Hermitage

Burin Peninsula

Avalon Peninsula

Fortune

Lamaline

⑥

O C E A N

Acclaim for

THE COLONY OF UNREQUITED DREAMS

"Transforms the forlorn territory of Newfoundland into a fabulous terrain of tragicomic struggle and loss. . . . This prodigious, eventful, character-rich book is a noteworthy achievement: a biting, entertaining, and inventive saga— brilliant."
— Richard Bernstein, *The New York Times*

"Wayne Johnston is a brilliant and accomplished writer, and his Newfoundland—boots and boats, rough politics and rough country, history and journalism—during the wild Smallwood years is vivid and sharp."
— E. Annie Proulx,
author of *The Shipping News* and *Wyoming Stories*

"A novel of cavernous complexity that nevertheless doesn't overwhelm the reader, who can repose in pure narrative without second thoughts . . . [an] eloquent anti-epic."
— Luc Sante, *The New York Times Book Review*

"This splendid, entertaining novel is both a version of *David Copperfield* transposed to twentieth-century Newfoundland and an evocation of vanished ways of life in a place caught in tumultuous political changes. Rich and complex, it offers Dickensian pleasures."
—Andrea Barrett,
author of *The Voyage of the Narwhal* and *Ship Fever*

"Evokes not only the beautiful, unforgiving subarctic terrain of Newfoundland but also the spirit and people of Smallwood's times."
—*The Wall Street Journal*

"Comical, compelling . . . in the figure of Smallwood's soulmate-nemesis, Sheilagh Fielding, Johnston has created a boozy, prickly, lancet-tongued seductress who could hold her own against Dorothy Parker."
—*Chicago Tribune*

"Gorgeously written. . . . Immensely readable. . . . Imagine that John Irving wrote a novel about the life and times of Franklin Delano Roosevelt, but focused less on FDR's politics and more on an unrequited love affair with a fictional female journalist—then you'd have some idea of what Wayne Johnston is up to."
—*The Seattle Times*

"Charles Dickens would have greatly admired Johnston's style and humor. . . . And the old master would have envied the vivid scenes Johnston draws of Smallwood's impoverished boyhood."
—*Houston Chronicle*

"Brilliantly realized. . . . There's an epic quality to *The Colony of Unrequited Dreams*, and it may well be referred to, before long, as the quintessential Newfoundland novel."
— *The San Diego Union-Tribune*

"*The Colony of Unrequited Dreams* has many things: irony, humor, satire, history, romance. It shows what a very talented writer with a great story to tell can do when he sets his mind to it."
— *The Denver Post*

"Johnston writes about Newfoundland like Joyce wrote about Ireland, creating literary gold out of a coarse, common place. . . . Throughout the book Johnston's writing never fails either the grandeur or humanity of his subject."
— *Book*

"*The Colony of Unrequited Dreams* is an indispensable masterpiece. It reshapes and animates history with luminous verisimilitude. Every page of Wayne Johnston's stunning novel displays the highest regard for his reader's intelligence and for the art of writing itself."
— Howard Norman,
author of *The Bird Artist* and *The Museum Guard*

"Johnston reminds us that politics, for all its squalor, is fit material for passion and suspense—and even so, he's smart enough to let a love story run off with his exceptional book."
— Thomas Mallon,
author of *Dewey Defeats Truman* and *Henry and Clara*

WAYNE JOHNSTON

THE COLONY OF UNREQUITED DREAMS

Wayne Johnston is the author of a memoir, *Baltimore's Mansion,* as well as five novels, *The Story of Bobby O'Malley, The Time of Their Lives, The Divine Ryans, Human Amusements,* and *The Colony of Unrequited Dreams,* which was nominated for the Giller Prize and the Governor General's Award in Canada. Born and raised in Newfoundland, Johnston now lives in Toronto.

BOOKS BY WAYNE JOHNSTON

The Story of Bobby O'Malley

The Time of Their Lives

The Divine Ryans

Human Amusements

The Colony of Unrequited Dreams

Baltimore's Mansion

THE COLONY OF
UNREQUITED
DREAMS

THE COLONY OF UNREQUITED DREAMS

WAYNE JOHNSTON

ANCHOR BOOKS

A DIVISION OF RANDOM HOUSE, INC.

NEW YORK

FIRST ANCHOR BOOKS EDITION, MAY 2000

Copyright © 1998 by Wayne Johnston

All rights reserved under International and Pan-American Copyright
Conventions. Published in the United States by Anchor Books, a division
of Random House, Inc., New York. *The Colony of Unrequited Dreams*
was originally published in hardcover by Knopf Canada in 1998.
Originally published in hardcover in the United States by Doubleday,
a division of Random House, Inc., in 1999.

Anchor Books and colophon are registered trademarks
of Random House, Inc.

All of the characters in this book are fictitious, and any resemblance to
actual persons, living or dead, is purely coincidental.

The Library of Congress has cataloged the Doubleday edition as follows:
Johnston, Wayne.
The colony of unrequited dreams / Wayne Johnston.
—1st ed. In the U.S.A.
cm.
Smallwood, Joseph Roberts, 1900– —Fiction. 2. Newfoundland—History
—Fiction. I. Title.
PR199.3J599C65   1999
813'54—dc21
99-19144
CIP

Anchor ISBN: 0-385-49543-9

Author photograph © Jerry Bauer

www.anchorbooks.com

Printed in the United States of America
10 9 8 7 6 5 4 3 2 1

For seven women of St. John's:

Claire Wilkshire, Mary Lewis, Lisa Moore,
Sue Crocker, Mary Dalton, Beth Ryan
and Ramona Dearing.

The history of the Colony is only very partially contained in printed books; it lies buried under great rubbish heaps of unpublished records, English, Municipal, Colonial and Foreign, in rare pamphlets, old Blue Books, forgotten manuscripts . . .

—D. W. PROWSE, *A History of Newfoundland* (1895)

Prefatory Note

From the early 1600s to 1825, the island of Newfoundland was ruled by a succession of British governors who lived in Newfoundland only in the summer months. Although the other regions of British North America confederated between 1867 and 1871 to form the country of Canada, Newfoundland was not given even colonial status until 1825. From 1855 to 1934, Newfoundland was a "self-governing" colony of Britain with a parliament that, although elected, still owed and pledged allegiance to the mother country. During those seventy-nine years, its measure of self-government inched slowly towards an outright independence that never came. In 1934, its parliament was suspended by Britain, and for the next fifteen years Newfoundland was ruled by a handful of British "commissioners." On July 22, 1948, in a referendum on confederation with Canada, Newfoundlanders voted by the barest of margins for confederation. The leader of the confederate forces, Joe Smallwood, was acclaimed the first premier of the province of Newfoundland. The induction ceremonies took place, in Ottawa and Newfoundland, on April Fools' Day, 1949.

The Colony of Unrequited Dreams

I

—◆—

THE BROW

They had been friends and fellow students at Oxford, and in quite a natural way, as one pawns off a worthless horse on a friend, so Sir William sold a large portion of his grant at a very high price to Lord Baltimore.

—D. W. PROWSE, *A History of Newfoundland*

The Boot

Dear Smallwood:

You may not know it yet, but I am back in St. John's. Six months since Confederation. The past is literally another country now.

I remember, it was in New York, I think, you once suggested that I do as Boswell did with Johnson and keep a running tally of your life. Even now, knowing you as well as I do, it seems hard to believe that you meant it, but you did. And you were so offended when I laughed.

I walk as far as I ever did, though it takes me longer. The past is a place I visit on Sunday afternoons. Things I cannot remember when I have been indoors a week come flooding back.

I look up at the Brow, which separates the city from the sea, and think of you. What is the name of the river, I asked my father when I was five, that runs between the city and the Brow? The Waterford? he said. No, the big river, I said. By which I meant the harbour.

I go to the west end, where the coal piers and the car barns used to be. I like to remember what used to be where something else now stands, or what used to be where there is nothing now. The pastime of the old, and I am not yet fifty. Did you know that you can tell from where the mansard roofs begin how far the fire burned in 1892?

I walk along the waterfront and watch homesick fishermen from the Portuguese white fleet play soccer on the pavement of the apron, their ball bouncing off the steel hulls of ships and landing in the harbour.

I have been remembering the city, Smallwood. In 1900, there were forty thousand people in St. John's. If it had grown at the pace that other cities that size have grown at since, there would be half a million people here. Even now, no one thinks of it as a place from which nature has been crowded out.

But how different it used to be, Smallwood, this city, yours and mine. More yours than mine, you would have said back then. I came from what your father called the quality, you from what my father, more fondly than you might imagine, called the scruff.

Animals were everywhere. The smell and sound of them was everywhere. Cows, goats, chickens, horses, dogs.

Goats wandered about at will the way cats in cities do today. If they lingered long enough in one neighbourhood, they were designated "lost" and were "claimed" by someone. But it was a rare goat who would stand for being tethered, so they more or less remained common property. Everyone milked them. For children, to go out milking was not much different than to go out picking berries. It was a common sight, children chasing goats down Water Street with buckets in their hands; children in winter thirstily gulping warm goat's milk from tin cans.

I was afraid of the crossing sweepers, boys wielding birch brooms who hung round intersections waiting for people to cross the streets. They walked backwards in front of my father and me, heads down, furiously sweeping the dust or snow, clearing a path for us. My father, once we reached the other side, would give the sweeper a penny, sometimes more, depending on how poor he looked. The same boy would then sweep another pedestrian back across the street on the very track that he had swept for us, redundantly sweeping it again. That it was just a disguised form of begging I didn't understand. On the same downtown street, we might be swept across like curling stones half a dozen times by the same fierce-faced little boy, who I felt was picking on my father and who, to my indignation, did not sweep a path for anyone who was not well dressed.

What I miss most are the horses. The sound of the city changed gradually as the horses were replaced by cars and the streets were paved.

I remember the sound of a lone horse clopping past the house when it was dark outside. The double plumes of steam that issued from the nose of every horse when it was cold. It seems now that they vanished overnight, that one morning I woke up and there were cars instead of horses in the streets.

In these same streets I saw women twirling parasols and walking arm in arm with men in tall black hats. And children, with their bare legs mud-bespattered, hop-scotched between the potholes. And men gingerly rolled casks of port the size of steamrollers from Newman's, where it was aged in mine-like cellars, to ships that sailed to Boston and New York, where the expatriate quality drank it with their meals. My father drank one glass of Newman's port a day.

The wooden water tanks set out at intervals along the streets, where people wearing hoops from which buckets hung went to get their water. I would watch in wonder as some hoop-wearing woman staggered by bearing half a dozen pails of water.

The smell of the salt fish. I miss that, too, though I could never stand the taste. The first few hundred feet of land beyond

the harbour is no longer spread with cod, nor is cod stacked
storeys high in the premises of Harbour Drive as it used to be.
Some of the streets were arched over by fish-flakes propped up
on mast-like stilts, on top of which salt cod was laid out to dry
and beneath which, in the shade that reeked of brine, people
took cover from the rain while the traffic passed.

The harbour. I loved the harbour as only a child to whom it
was nothing more than a place to walk could love it. I remember
how the harbour looked when it was crammed with bare-masted
schooners and steamers with four smokestacks whose mainmasts
were so tall they had to be brought in from other countries.
There are only steel ships now, and from time to time a tall ship
for the tourists and the young, with gleaming sails and polished
pine, looking nothing like the tall ships of the past.

There were so many schooners that when their sails were
down, the harbour was a grove of spear-like masts.

After it rained, the schooners would unfurl their sails to let
them dry, a stationary fleet under full sail, the whole harbour a
mass of flapping canvas you could hear a mile away. How high
those sails were. If they had not been translucent, they would
have cast a shadow in the evening halfway across the city.

Instead, in the evening, in the morning, the sun shone
through the sails and cast an amber-coloured light across the
harbour and the streets, a light I have not seen in twenty years.

Water Street was paved from end to end with brain-jarring,
axle-cracking cobblestones. It was the only paved street. The rest
were mere dirt roads, with potholes so large and so enduring that
some were given nicknames. The main streets were occasionally
tarred in summer to keep the dust down and, in theory at least,
to prevent the creation of further potholes. On dry days, dust lay
like bloom on everything. If there was no wind, a yellow cloud
of dust formed above the city. You once told me that your father,
looking down from the Brow, always noted the appearance of
that cloud with glee, as he did the fact that when they tarred the

streets of St. John's, the reek of oil was such that even the quality could not leave their windows open.

The city smells. Tar and dust, horse manure and turpentine, the hybrid hum of fish and salt and the reek of bilge-water. The smell of coal that was burned in factories and forges and the boiler rooms of ships. The city sounds. The grinding of the wheels of the streetcar as it struggled up the hill to Rawlin's Cross.

The parrots squawking in the rigging of the schooners from Jamaica and Barbados that came loaded down with rum and left likewise with salt fish.

I remember the shrieking hordes of sea gulls that hovered above the tables of the men who cleaned the fish on the side-streets, the "coves" between Water Street and Harbour Drive, the gulls swooping down and plucking at the fish guts while the men still held them in their hands.

My father, being a surgeon, cleaned his own fish, denying he did so because uncleaned fish cost a little less. I remember once he lugged by the gills with both hands a cod so long its tail dragged and left a trail of slime behind us on the sidewalk. He barely made it to the carriage, and when he laid the cod on the paper he had set out, he measured it at four feet long and said it must have weighed a hundred pounds. "More than you," he said. I looked at the cod, lying there in the carriage with its little beard-like chin barbel and black spots on its skin as big as eye-balls. "There's just the two of us," I said. "We can't eat all that." "We're not eating any of it," he said. "It's for the hospital."

I used to enjoy the slow descent of evening on the city, watching from my bedroom window the clapboard houses fading as if their light came from within and, after seeping slowly from them one last time, would not return. Every day it looked like that. And every day there were a thousand other such sights, a tedium of wonder that exhausted me.

It was like that, Smallwood. Not three hundred years ago but twenty. One generation.

In this journal I write to people as if I am bidding them goodbye, as if they are asleep in the next room and will read what I have written in the morning when I'm gone.

It is impossible to fix exactly in time when something happened, and sometimes impossible to remember how life was before it did. This was our city when we were still in school. This is what it looked and smelled and sounded like.

But how it was before what happened between us, how it felt before we met, we can no more recall than we can how we felt when we were born.

───────────

I AM A NEWFOUNDLANDER. Although up to the age of forty-six I would have been voted by those who knew me to be the man least likely to warrant a biography, one has been written.

My mother believed my birthdate, Christmas Eve, 1900, predestined me for greatness. One day before Christ's birthday. One week before the new century. I was the first of thirteen children, the last of whom was also born on Christmas Eve, when I was twenty-five years old. "Thirteen," my father said, "a luckless number for a luckless brood."

No one called my father Charlie. Everyone called him Smallwood, which he hated because, I think, it reminded him that he was a certain someone's son, not self-created.

After accomplishing the rare feat of graduating from high school, my father set out for Boston with high hopes, but came back destitute. He had then worked for a time at the family boot-and-shoe factory, "working under the old man's boot," he said, referring to my grandfather and the giant black boot with the name Smallwood written on it, which hung suspended from an iron bar that was bored into the cliffs about ten feet above the water at the entrance to the Narrows, so placed by my grandfather to advertise to illiterate fishermen the existence of Smallwood's Boots, a store and factory on Water Street, where a smaller but otherwise identical boot hung suspended from a pole above the wooden sidewalk.

My father hated every minute he spent beneath the Boot, partly because he had to work under his father, who had predicted he would come back to St. John's from Boston with "his tail between his legs," and partly because he believed business to be the least dignified way on earth to make a living. He found a job that at least allowed him the illusion of self-sufficiency, that of lumber surveyor, his daily task being to walk about the decks of ships docked in the harbour and tote up the amount of wood on board. He walked about the cargo holds, tapping on the cords of wood with what he called his toting pole, which was also so-called because he tied his lunch and other sundries to it and in the morning set out for the waterfront with it on his shoulder. It was a stick of bamboo of even width that he often carried with him even when not toting anything, using it as an oversized walking stick, though, because of his mane of hair and bushy beard, it gave him the look of some staff-wielding prophet.

He spent most of his meagre wages on bottles of cheap West Indian rum, which he bought from foreign sailors on the dock. When drunk, he wandered about the house, cursing and mocking the name of Smallwood. He had been told by someone, or had read somewhere, that the name was from the Anglo-Saxon and meant something like "treeless" or "place where no trees grow."

"It wouldn't have been a bad name for Newfoundland," he said.

He could be flamboyantly eloquent when drunk, especially when the subject of his speeches was himself and the flagrant unfairness of his fate. "I should have stayed in Boston," he said. "What in God's name was it that made me leave that land of plenty to come back to this God-forsaken city, where my livelihood depends on a man famous for nothing but having hung a giant black boot at the entrance to the Narrows?"

We often went to the boot-and-shoe store on Water Street. My grandfather, David Smallwood, was a short, bright-eyed man who always wore a tailcoat at the shop and had a beard so long he had to pull it out of the way to see his pocket watch. He had a scraping, servile way with customers that made me feel a little sorry for him. He was, I suppose, born to keep shop. I could not see my father running about, shoehorn in hand, as my grandfather did, fetching boots for people to try on, kneeling down and holding people's feet while he fitted them for shoes. (My father said the old man's hands always smelled of other people's socks. My mother said his wallet smelled of other people's money.) As a customer walked up and down, trying out a pair of shoes or boots, my grandfather would walk beside him, turning when he turned, stopping when he stopped, in a kind of deferential mimicry, eagerly looking now at the customer's face, now at his feet.

The one thing we were never in need of was boots and shoes, for we got them from Smallwood's for next to nothing. It was easy, in our neighbourhood, to spot the Smallwood children; we were the ones wearing the shabby clothes and the absurdly incongruous new footwear, conspicuously gleaming boots and shoes for which we took no end of teasing, especially as we were all fitted for them at the same time.

My father did not avail himself of the special family discount, but instead went for years wearing the same boots and shoes, and when he absolutely needed new ones, bought them full price at a rival store called Hammond's. It is an image that stays with me, his worn tattered shoes, his patched and repatched knee boots, set aside from ours in the hall, in a token gesture of protest. We were always well-heeled, he was always roughshod; it set him apart from us in a way we children found funny, though my mother said it was disgraceful.

To my father, the Boot was like the hag; he would have boot-ridden dreams that when recounted in the light of day seemed ridiculous, but that often kept him up at night, afraid to go to sleep. He would tell me about them, tell me how he had dreamed about the Narrows boot swaying in the wind on the iron bar like some ominously silent, boot-shaped bell. At other times, it was a boot-shaped headstone.

When one day my mother told him there was "more booze than boots" in those dreams of his, he laughed and went around repeating it all afternoon as if in tribute to her wit. That night, however, he stayed up late and announced that having run out of "the usual combustibles," he was about to burn the boots.

"Go ahead," my mother said, thinking to call his bluff, "there's plenty more where they came from." And so he went ahead and did it, built himself a roaring blaze and kept it going all night long with boots, each time announcing which pair it was he was consigning to the flames. "I'm burning Joe's knee boots now," he said. "Now I'm burning Sadie's shoes, the ones with the brass buckles."

"I'm telling Mr. Smallwood," my mother said, once the smell of burning leather made its way upstairs.

All that remained of our footwear in the morning was a heap of charred soles in the fireplace. He had even burned our slippers, which we left by the stove so they would be warm when we came down for breakfast in the morning. The only boots he had spared were his own, in which he had left for work by the time my mother got up. Luckily, my mother kept her slippers beneath her bed. Slipper-clad in mid-December, she walked all the way to the store on Water Street. A great bundle of boots and shoes and slippers was delivered to the door that night. My father came home late, penitently close to sober. He took Sadie on his lap and told her he was sorry he had burned her little boots, which got her crying, though she had spent the day quite happily, if house-bound and barefoot, as glad as the rest of us to get a day off from school no matter what the circumstances. He sat all evening on the sofa with a chastened, sheepish air about him, staring into the fire.

My mother was always predicting his imminent disappearance. She had never known a drinker not to run, sooner or later.

He would up and leave us someday, she was certain, she said; it would not be long now, she had seen men like him before, he was showing all the signs.

"One of these mornings you'll walk out that door and that will be the last we'll ever see of Charlie Smallwood."

"Maybe I will," my father said, which got us youngsters bawling.

"I won't be pining for you when you're gone," my mother said.

After we went to bed, he would start singing "It's a Long Way to Tipperary" and every other song of departure he could think of.

"I'm leaving, Minnie May, do you hear me? First thing in the morning."

"I hear you," my mother said. "Tipperary, first thing in the morning."

"Twilight and evening bell / and after that the dark / And may there be no sadness of farewell / When I embark."

"There won't be," she said.

When he wasn't drinking, he sat about the house in chastened silence, now and then vowing that he would never drink again. "I've had my last drink, boy," he said to me. "I've learned my lesson. You'll never see Charlie Smallwood take another drink, no sir." He would concoct grandiose money-making schemes and enthral us with stories of how rich we would be someday because of him. He went out briefly on the steps and looked wistfully at the sky above the city as if he had just returned home after years away, as if he knew his sobriety would not last, for he was too far gone to stop for good. The suspense when he was sober was unbearable, for I knew that he would go back to drinking and the only question was when. Truthfully, the house did not seem right when he was sober, nor did he seem to know what to do with himself, but would wander around as though in imitation of sobriety, as if not entirely sure what it was that sober people did.

We were forever changing houses, forever being turfed out of the ones we were renting and moving on to even shabbier establishments. All I remember of the houses we lived in is a succession of attics and basements, for these, whether empty or cluttered with objects discarded by strangers, all seemed unique, whereas the houses themselves all seemed the same once the furniture was put in place, our furniture, which went with us from house to house like parts of our essential selves.

I came home from school one day to find the entire contents of our house on Gower Street piled atop two horse-drawn carts at the reins of which were men I had never seen before. My father was at the reins of a third, in which there were hampers of clothing and the smaller bits of furniture. My mother and the younger children had found what room they could among the clutter. It was the first I knew that we were moving, and I thought I had caught them in the act of leaving me behind. It was all my mother could do to convince me that they had not been about to leave without me, but on the contrary, had been waiting for me and would have waited forever if they had to. "You're my little lad," she whispered to me so the others wouldn't hear. "You're my little lad, you know I wouldn't leave you."

We set out, our little procession of three carts, the horses' hooves clopping on the pavement. I had no idea where we were going, and we drove for so long I began to wonder if we had a destination or if my father was merely looking for a place to pitch the tent my mother had often predicted we would wind up in someday. They sat side by side, my parents, not speaking, though I could tell she was mortified at the spectacle we made, pretending not to notice the stares of strangers as we rode along, a dispossessed, disfavoured family with all its belongings on display.

For some reason, the rule was that the longer we spent in transit, the worse our new house and neighbourhood would be. This day's seemingly unending journey convinced me we had hit rock-bottom and, socially speaking at any rate, I was right. "Where are we going?" I said. They didn't answer. I played a game with myself. I would pick a house I liked the look of up ahead and tell myself we were going there, and when we passed it by, I would pick another house and concentrate on it, as if I could thereby influence our fate. But we passed so many houses that looked promising that I sat down with my back against the cart and closed my eyes.

After a while, I felt the cart begin to climb a slight gradient and stood up to find that we were on the bridge crossing the Waterford River, not far above where it flowed into the harbour. We were headed as far from the favoured part of town as it was possible to go, to the south side, the "Brow" of which my mother often spoke as though it lay in outer darkness. It was the least desirable, most scorned of all the city's neighbourhoods; the home, even those brought up like me had been led to believe, of people one step up from savages, the dregs, the scruff of society, a kind of company town whose single industry was crime. A Pariahville of ironically elevated bottom-dwellers.

We drove along the base of a cliff so steep and high the cart was almost always in the shade, then began to make our way up the winding road that climbed the cliff. Our house, bigger and better maintained than the one we had left, affordable to us because the reputation of the neighbourhood kept prices down, was at the very top, in a saddle-like depression of the ridge on the height of the Brow so that, from the front, you could see St. John's and from the back the open Atlantic. From its front windows, the view of the city we had been deemed unworthy to live in was affrontingly spectacular. You could see all the way from Mundy Pond to Signal Hill, and below the Hill, the Narrows and the cliff-face and the Smallwood boot.

I mention this house over all the others because, perversely, as if to spite the city that had spit them out, my parents wound up buying it. My father called it a double-decker because there was a deck on front and back, which would allow us, he said, to escape whichever of the two prevailing winds was blowing, the onshore east wind, which blew when it was stormy or foggy, and the west wind, which in winter made the sunny days so cold. The east wind would not have been a problem had the house been built in the lee of the Brow, but whoever had chosen the site had preferred the double view to being sheltered from the wind. My mother expressed doubts that a house so situated could withstand the kind of wind we got from time to time, but my father said the fact that the house was twenty years old was proof enough for him that it could.

We had not been living there a week when there was an onshore storm with winds well above hurricane force. As I lay in bed, I felt the whole house shift in its foundation. I imagined it toppling end over end down the Brow and landing upright in the Harbour, bobbing about among the ships until someone climbed aboard and found us dead. When a gust subsided, the house would slowly right itself, creaking like a ship whose hull was rolling. Once, the house lurched more than usual and there was the sound of cracking boards. My parents came running from their room and got us out of bed (there was a boys' room and a girls' room, two in one, three in the other) and into our coats and boots, then told us to go back to sleep on the kitchen floor. It was my father who fell asleep, however, for he had gone to bed drunk, and we who kept vigil, wondering how we would survive outside if we had to leave the house.

The larger of the two decks, the one that faced the city, was built out over a steep slope and supported by stilts that forever needed shoring up. The other deck faced the ocean. My father, when he was drinking, whatever the time of year, would pace back and forth through the house from deck to deck after I had gone to bed, sometimes forgetting to shut one door so that, when he opened the other, the wind tore unimpeded through the house, through the funnel of the corridor that ran from deck to deck, eerily howling and causing all the closed doors in the house (closed by my my mother in case this very thing might happen) to rattle loudly in their frames.

My father would go out on the front deck at night and alternately extol and curse the city across the harbour, one minute

bemoaning our exile from it and the next bidding it good riddance, one minute declaring it too good for us and the next declaring us too good for it. He had found the ideal stage for his
soliloquies of rage and lamentation, for the nearest house on
either side of ours was two hundred feet away, out of earshot of
even Charlie Smallwood's booming voice. He declaimed from the
front deck as though the whole city below and across the way
were listening, as though the lights along the Southside Road were
footlights and the dark mass of the city the unseen gallery hanging
on his every word.

Down below, St. John's looked like the night sky, the lights
that marked the neighbourhoods like constellations of stars. There
was Buckmaster's Circle, Rawlin's Cross, the Upper Battery, the
Lower Battery, Amherst Heights, Waterford Heights, Barter's Hill
and Carter's Hill, the Hill of Chips, Monkstown, Cookstown,
Rabbittown, all with their distinctive patterns of lights. We had, at
one time or another, lived in almost all these neighbourhoods; it
was our history down there, spelled out in lights. My father
pointed them out to me once in reverse order, counting down to
Amherst Heights.

He would roar in triumph when the lights were put out in
some house across the way, as if he had done it himself, as if, in
the face of his blustering eloquence, the people who occupied the
house had admitted their defeat and gone to bed.

As she lay in bed one night, my mother provided a subversive
commentary like some parody of exhortation, his mocking congregation of one, undercutting him, deflating him, audibly piping
up whenever he paused for breath or gave in to sobbing self-pity
and loudly blew his nose into his handkerchief.

"I am a Newfoundlander, but not St. John's born, no, not St.
John's born," he said.

"You're a bayman and you always will be," my mother said.

"We're not good enough, it seems," my father said. "We are
baymen, a brood of baymen among a sea of townies."

"Shut up and go to sleep," my mother said. "Even baymen have to sleep."

"This is what I must endure," he said. "To be spoken to in this manner by a shameless Huguenot named Minnie May."

On the front deck, he ranted and raved against mankind; his enemies; the Smallwoods; his father; his brother, Fred; my mother. But on the other deck, which faced the sea, the object of his wrath was more obscure. God, Fate, the Boot, the Sea, himself. He started out like he might go on for hours, but soon stood staring mutely out to sea, the sea he couldn't see but knew was there, as if the sheer featurelessness of the darkness he faced had stifled him. Stuck for words, he looked up at the sky as if in search of inspiration, planning to let loose his fury on the moon or on the stars, but the sky was almost always dark.

"They should have called it Old Lost Land, not Newfoundland but Old Lost Land," he roared, with a flourish of his hand as though to encompass the whole of the island, then held his arms out to the sky like some ham actor beseeching God's forgiveness.

Fielding's Condensed
History of Newfoundland

PREFACE

Our friend, Miss Fielding, has asked us to introduce in a few words the important history on which she has for so long been engaged. Although there is really nothing for us to do but conduct her down to the footlights, and then to retire with a bow to the audience, we are honoured by and humbly accede to her request.

We find happily married in Miss Fielding's *History of New-foundland* two virtues that in other such works are not on so much as speaking terms — we mean brevity and comphrehensiveness. She does in twenty pages what Prowse could not manage in eight hundred. Nor does her argument need bolstering by numbers, photographs, footnotes or illustrations.

But as Miss Fielding has erected her *History* not on the ruins of others but on fresh ground, let us follow her example.

We can think of no more sincere way to recommend her book to the reader than to express our humble hopes, not only that our own exploits will warrant a chapter in some revised edition, but that we may be among those rare few upon whom she confers her *imprimatur*.

Lest we, in our acknowledgement, set to bickering the very virtues in her *History* whose blissful co-existence we find so remarkable, we hereby take our leave and hold out to the reader a volume that we know will at last secure for its author and her country the fame that they deserve.

The Right Hon. Prime Minister of Newfoundland,
Sir Richard Squires, P.C., K.C.M.G., K.C.
St. John's, March 1923

The Feild

M Y DELIVERANCE FROM life at my father's came when I was twelve. The new bane of my father's existence, his brother, Fred, who became manager of the family boot-and-shoe factory when my grandfather retired, offered, at my grandfather's urging, I'm sure, to send me to Bishop Feild College, a private school attended by the children of some of the city's better families. The idea was that I, the oldest of the family, would drag us Smallwoods out of poverty by one day getting the kind of job you could get only with a diploma from "the Feild." My father declined the offer, saying that he would not be known as Charity Charlie, that Methodist College had been good enough for him, and dismissing Bishop Feild as "a training ground for snobs." He claimed to know a man who had sent his son to Bishop Feild, only to have that same son, who was with a group of his schoolfriends, pass him in the street one day as if he didn't know him.

"I will not be snubbed in public like poor Baker was," he went around saying for weeks. This became the subject of his midnight soliloquies.

"Don't leave me, boy," he roared while he stomped about on the deck. "Don't leave me in my dotage, I beseech you."

"You're thirty-nine years old," my mother said.

"Do not forsake me, boy, I beseech you," he shouted. "Will you leave me, boy, will you leave your poor father and me in my condition?"

I tried to explain to him that Bishop Feild was barely two miles from where we lived. "It's not like you won't be seeing me for years," I said. "I'll come to visit every Sunday, and I'll be back home at Christmas and in the summer." But he would not be consoled.

"You'll never come to visit," he said. "Once you get in with that crowd, you'll never come to visit. You'll be too good for me, too good for Charlie Smallwood; you'll be like Baker's boy, snubbing me in public. This is the start of it, now, someday soon they'll all be gone — Marie, David, Ida, Isabel, Sadie."

"Sadie is six months old," my mother said.

"They'll all be gone and, God help me, I'll be left alone with Minnie May Devannah, with no one to keep me company in this God-forsaken city, on this God-forsaken rock, but an Irish Huguenot named Minnie May."

My mother prevailed, however, and I went to Bishop Feild with Fred Smallwood one sunny morning in September, walking away from the house with my suitcase in my hand while my mother and brothers and sisters stood on the steps, shouting and waving goodbye, my mother weeping freely, my father nowhere to be seen at first, but then the upstairs window opened. He had been sleeping one off and had been awakened by the shouting from below. He leaned out the window in his undershirt, running his fingers through his hair. Suddenly, with my father looking at me, I felt very much the dandy in my short pants and stockings and my gleaming white Eton collar, which looked impeccably starched though in fact it was made of celluloid so it could be cleaned with a wet cloth and would not need laundering. Up to now, I had dressed as all boys did on the Brow, like a little man, in a tattered peaked tweed cap, a half-length coat and woollen trousers, my unparted dark hair slicked back from my forehead. I had the eyesight of someone who'd been reading books by bad light for twenty years. I wore glasses, behind the almost opaque lenses of which my eyes were tiny blue beads.

"Are you off to Bishop Feild, boy?" he said, grinning sheepishly.

"Yes," I said, my voice quavering.

"Will they take good care of him, Fred?" he said.

"Oh yes, Charlie," Uncle Fred said. "They'll take good care of him, don't you worry." There was something in Fred's voice that made me feel sorry for my father and resentful of Fred, a dismissive tone I did not think he should have used in front of me. I felt like a traitor, abandoning my father's camp for Fred's, and was acutely aware of how badly my father came off in comparison with his brother, who was even better dressed than usual that day in his waistcoat and his vest and his gleaming top hat. I was ashamed of not having woken up my father to say goodbye. I walked a few steps away from Fred and looked up at him.

"I'll be back this Sunday," I said quietly, pointedly excluding Fred from the conversation. "I'll see you on Sunday."

He smiled down at me. "All right, boy," he said. He clasped his hands, for a moment hung his head between his arms, his throat convulsing as though he were about to cry or be sick. Then he looked up and smiled again. "I haven't been everything you might have wanted me to be," he said. "But I promise you this. I'll be a better father to the other children than I was to you."

"OK," I said, determined not to cry. "I'll see you on Sunday."

I walked with Fred to his two-horse carriage and we climbed up onto the plush leather seat.

"Be careful with those horses on the hill, Fred," my father said. Fred smiled and nodded.

We started off down the Brow towards the city. My father kept up a steady stream of promises of self-reform to me and admonitions to Fred as we made our way down the winding gravel slope. Long after I could make out what he was saying, I could hear my him shouting, until at last he either stopped or we passed out of earshot.

Bishop Feild, named after himself by the Church of England bishop who founded it, was a Tudor-style brick building at the corner of King's Road and Colonial Street. It was modelled on the English public school, with students advancing through forms rather than grades. Sons of outport merchants, doctors and magistrates stayed at the dormitories, while the students from St. John's went home after school.

A series of stone steps led up to the turret-crowned entranceway of the main school. On either side of the steps were a pair of almost identical mature oak trees, oaks as large as oaks could get on the east coast of Newfoundland. You could see the harbour and the sea between the Narrows, and feel and smell the wind when it blew off the water, as it seemed it always did.

I was the only townie boarding at Bishop Feild, which marked me as odd right from the start. It had been decided that I would board at the Feild, to reduce by one the number of children my mother had to care for and so that the sight of me, a Feildian, would not be a constant provocation to my father. I was not about to explain my circumstances to the other dorm boys, who spoke of how much they missed by having to board at school, and who were so well-to-do that, to them, life at Bishop Feild seemed unbearably rough and they couldn't wait to get back home. To me, the relatively Spartan accommodations at Bishop Feild seemed luxurious, so much so that I felt guilty about living so high while my family was still stuck in its dreary existence on the Brow.

The three fireplaces in the dorm were kept burning all night long, an unheard-of luxury. Each of us boys took turns replenishing the fires with coal in the middle of the night. About every three weeks it was my turn to be the "scuttler," as we called it, but even that I didn't mind. As I fed the fires, I would look down the line of beds at the dozens of boys sleeping cozily beneath their blankets, marvelling that it was not so cold that I could see their breath, as it was in the house on the Brow at night for ten months of the year.

As for the food, I vowed I would never mention it to my father, who managed once or twice a month to snare a few rabbits in the woods behind our house so we could have our meal of meals, rabbit stew, our only fresh-meat meal. My mother sometimes cobbled together "shipwreck" dinner or jig's dinner, boiled cabbage and potatoes and salt beef, along with pease-pudding made from peas boiled in a cloth bag. Mostly we ate salt cod and potatoes. My father often came home with a board-stiff plank of salt cod beneath his arm. Even after days of soaking, the fish was so salty I was never able to eat more than a few forkfuls of it. The potatoes, boiled in the same water to save coal, came out the yellow colour of the cod and tasted not much better. When we had flour, my mother made damper dogs, or toutons as my father called them, balls of dough fried in lard on a skillet. In the spring, my father would buy seal flippers at dockside, and my mother, after soaking the flippers for days, casting off the oily water every morning for a week, made flipper pie.

I had my first taste at Bishop Feild of food that was neither pickled nor preserved with salt, nor cooked in the same pot with food that was either pickled or preserved or food that did not to have to be boiled for days to be made edible. At the Feild there was fresh meat but never fish, fresh or otherwise, for though many of them were salt-cod merchants, the fathers of the boys at Bishop Feild would have considered it an abomination that their sons be served salt fish. There were bowls of beef and vegetable soup, steak and kidney pie, on special occasions slabs of roast beef and fat-browned potatoes in thick gravy and treacle-drenched suet or trifle for dessert.

I arrived at my new school even thinner than was warranted by my degree of malnutrition. It was as if my body, because it received so little food, had altogether lost the knack of absorbing nourishment. My forearms were of the same thickness from my wrists to my elbows, my legs the same thickness from my ankles to my knees. There was a slight thickening in my upper arms and legs, but not much, which is why I always wore an undershirt and longjohns, even in the summer.

There were three factions at Bishop Feild. The elite faction called themselves the Townies, though one did not qualify for membership simply by being a townie. The Townies were Prowse-picked; Prowse, who eventually went on to be the captain of the school, was the grandson of Judge Prowse, who had written the eight-hundred-page opus, *A History of Newfoundland*. He did not feel the need and was never called upon to explain his often arbitrary, seemingly random picks. Many was the townie who believed he deserved to be a member of the Townies on the basis of his social standing but was passed over by Prowse.

The second faction, known to the Townies as the Baymen, called themselves the 'Tories because they stayed in the dormitories. The 'Tories were more democratic than the Townies. To be a 'Tory, you had to stay in the dormitory, that was the lone requirement except where I was concerned. Their leader, a huge boy named "Slogger" Anderson because of his prowess with a cricket bat, declared that despite being a dorm boy, I could not be a 'Tory because my family lived in town. This was all right with me. They seemed to me an odd lot. They spoke with such heavy accents that they were all but incomprehensible, and their parents seemed to have scoured the Old Testament in search of their names: Azariah, Obadiah, Eliakim.

Outcasts and misfits at Bishop Feild eventually settled for one another, falling into a third faction cruelly called the Lepers. They were a close-knit group, the Lepers, kindred misfits who were at once shunned and regarded with a kind of patronizing affection by the other boys. For a while it seemed that I was destined to be one of them, until Prowse, exercising his God-like, arbitrary powers, and knowing, no doubt, how much it would irk those he whimsically excluded, invited me to join his group, an invitation that I, of course, accepted.

Prowse, though in the Lower Third, was one of the school's best athletes and had risen to his present status partly by beating the school boxing champion, a Sixth Former named Croker. He was also at the top of the Lower Third academically and was a favourite of the masters, who seemed to think that the presence at Bishop Feild of a boy of his quality somewhat mitigated the terms of their existence. He had eyes like those of the judge, whose photograph comprised the frontispiece to A History of Newfoundland, bright blue eyes, all the more startling because his hair was jet black and his complexion dark. He was taller than most of us and displayed a relaxed, self-confident posture and demeanour, as if he knew you would agree with him that everything that came his way was no more than his due.

I had often seen him standing amidst his Townies with his feet widely planted and his hands behind his back, smiling and listening as the others carried on in efforts to impress him. While standing so one day, he looked about the playing field and caught my eye, stared at me. I was in dread of what he had in mind for me and could not believe my good fortune when he off-handedly informed me that I could join his group if I wanted to.

Bishop Feild had a sister school named Bishop Spencer, an all-girls' school that backed onto the Feild, separated from it by an iron fence at the end of our playing grounds. At lunch-time and after school, the boys of the Feild and the girls of Spencer would meet at the fence, talking and teasing. But there was one girl who would go up onto the street and come back down on the Bishop Feild side of the fence. This was forbidden, but she would stay out of sight of the mistresses of Spencer and the masters of the Feild.

She seemed to be a kind of honorary member of Prowse's group, a visiting wit, his Spencer counterpart, or so his manner in her presence seemed to say, though the instant she was gone he was making jokes about her. "Old sculpin-puss," he called her, which made me wonder if he had ever seen a sculpin, for I found her quite appealing. He also called her old good-for-a-feel Fielding, always grinning knowingly when he was asked how he knew what she was good for.

Fielding was considered something of an exotic for having estranged parents. Her mother lived in New York, her father, a well-known doctor, in St. John's. This was almost never mentioned, not even in her absence, but it was common knowledge. The boys of Prowse's group gathered round whenever Fielding — her name was Sheilagh Fielding, but no one, not even the girls of Spencer, called her anything but Fielding — showed up on the grounds.

"How are things at Spencer, Fielding?" Prowse said one day.

"Much as they are here, I should think," she said. "Except for the classes in embroidery and needlework, of course, but we hope to have them soon." We all laughed.

From a distance, even with no one standing beside her by which to gauge her stature, she looked like a fully grown woman and carried herself like one; a well-off, disdainfully composed woman, out to take the air, walking exaggeratedly erect, pointing at this and that with her purely ornamental silver-knobbed cane. That she was just thirteen was easy to forget. She wore full-length dresses tightly belted at the waist, with flounced sleeves and tight lace collars. Close up, however, the elegant look she affected did not come off, partly because of her size — not even the clothes she wore could conceal the fact that she was athletically built, large-boned — and partly because of her almost perpetual expression, which was at once self-ironic and humorously scornful of others. Only rarely, and for no apparent reason, did this expression vanish and her face relax, and she would look, suddenly, tenderly, wonder-struck. I was always on the lookout for this sudden, fleeting transformation, this other Fielding, who for an instant would peep out from behind her veil of scorn.

She wore her dark hair, which looked as if it would otherwise have hung down to her waist, pinned up to show the long, furrowed nape of her neck and her pale white throat.

I saw her first in early fall and would, for the rest of my life, whenever we met, remember what the day was like, the sad, sweet smell of September in the air, a west wind and white caps on the water of the harbour, the silver undersides of the leaves showing as the gale moved through the trees. And Fielding like something that was part of, and would vanish with, the season, a girl as I had never noticed girls to be, a girl with goosebumps on her arms and strands of black hair blown forward round her face, one strand always wet, for it would catch between her lips. Fielding in the fall of 1912.

One day when Fielding was present, Prowse read aloud John Donne's "To His Mistress Going to Bed":

License my roving hands, and let them go,
Before, behind, between, above, below.
O my America! my new-found-land!

"Oh, my America, my New-Found-Land," Prowse said, leering at Fielding. She seemed embarrassed and, blinking rapidly, looked about as though in search of something, pulled that rogue strand of hair from between her lips.

"What might you be staring at?" she said, stepping towards me, her two hands on her cane, which she planted on the ground in front of her.

"Your name is Smallwood is it not?" she said. I nodded. "Not much meat on your bones, is there?" I shook my head, suddenly aware of how I must look with my clothes flapping from my skinny frame. "Henceforth," she said, "because you are so skinny, you shall be known as Splits, which in Newfoundland means 'kindling' and puns, quite nicely, I think, on the two halves of your absurd last name, Small and Wood."

The boys laughed. I could think of nothing to say. I hoped she was finished with me. The smell of salt water was in the air, the wind onshore, a beckoning from the world beyond the cloistered confines of the school.

"I've heard your uncle sponsors you," Fielding said, "because your father is a good-for-nothing drunkard."

Again, I was speechless.

"What does Uncle do?" Fielding said.

I felt light-headed with recklessness, my heart pounding. Who cares, I thought, who cares; I don't belong here anyway.

"My uncle is in boots," I said. "Except when he's in shoes and socks."

The boys laughed.

"Very funny," Fielding said, pursing her lips, one shoulder twitching nervously. She looked me up and down. "And what in God's name does your *father* do?" said Fielding, as if she could not imagine what sort of man might be responsible for the existence of a boy like me.

"He lives with his wife, who is the mother of his children," I said.

The boys went "Ooohhh" and Fielding blushed. Prowse clapped his hands together once and doubled over, not so much at what I had said, it seemed, as at this colliding of two worlds that he had engineered.

"Do you know something, Smallwood?" Fielding said. "You — you are —" I, we, waited for the *coup de grâce*. Her colour deepened. She looked away from me, blinked rapidly. The group, excepting Fielding and me, erupted in laughter at her frustration, throwing back their heads, doubling over with their hands on their knees, Prowse clapping me on the back in a kind of mock-congratulatory fashion, as if he had no doubt that despite my good showing, Fielding would soon make short work of me. I tried to assume a kind of "there's plenty more where that came from" look.

Suddenly, on the verge of tears, the muscles of her face fighting, her chin blotched red and white, she turned and, without a word, marched off in the direction of Bishop Spencer, holding her skirts clear of the ground, her cane in one hand, head down. A great cheer went up. A few boys, like pack-emboldened dogs, followed her shouting "Boo-hoo" but keeping a cane's-length distance between them and her. Prowse and another boy hoisted me on their shoulders and carried me about the pitch while the other boys followed behind. I had, I realized with dread, slain Fielding, whom the boys had obviously long thought was in need of slaying. Afraid of her, they had disarmed her by making her one of them, settled for being entertained by her, or pretending to be. I had slain Fielding, for now at least. I had done it by using the forbidden facts of Fielding's life, which no one had ever dared use as ammunition against her, assuming she would respond with the full fury of her wit, all the vitriol that her manner seemed to say she was holding in reserve. But she had turned and run.

Word of the "good one" I had got off at Fielding's expense soon spread throughout the school. "Did you hear what Smallwood said to Fielding?" one boy asked me, not knowing I was Smallwood. Everywhere boys repeated it to one another, everywhere little groups erupted in guffaws. "He lives with his wife, who is the mother of his children," Prowse kept saying. "An example to fathers everywhere."

For two days after our encounter on the playing grounds, Fielding stayed away from the Feild — the word from Bishop Spencer was that she did not come to school — a fatal mistake on her part. Had she been capable of wryly smiling through a day or two of teasing, her standing among the Townies and my standing at the school might not have changed much. But the two days she stayed away so magnified her humiliation that she could never live it down. When she came back, she rejoined Prowse's group, but she was diminished in stature now, if not one of the rank and file, then certainly not among his favourites, following Prowse and the rest of us about in sullen silence as if she dared not speak up for fear of provoking an allusion to her parents and thereby losing what little dignity she still had left.

One rainy Sunday, Fielding followed me when I headed out from the school grounds for my weekly visit home. She must have known my weekend routine and have been waiting outside the gate for me. She had an umbrella, as I did not, and made no effort to conceal herself, just hung back a couple of hundred feet, stopping when I stopped, walking when I walked. "What do you want, Fielding?" I shouted at her, hoping to cajole her into talking to me and perhaps even some sort of truce. It seemed to me that she was taking my fluke victory in our exchange of repartee far too seriously, that there was no reason we could not become friends and she could thereby regain her standing in the group as its presiding wit, which I was certain she deserved more than I did. I also felt guilty, for I knew that I had spoken cruelly, no more so than she had perhaps, but cruelly nonetheless, and the memory of her looking away from me, the expression on her face as she struggled to compose herself, stayed with me. She had been oblivious to the precariousness of her status among the Townies. To them, she was a prodigy of her gender, but they could have no real affection for her, or any compunction about setting upon her the instant a crack in her armour was revealed. She had achieved a certain fame by flouting the established order but had also thereby forsaken its protections and its privileges. I felt sorry for her, despite her unprovoked attack on me.

"What do you want, Fielding?" I shouted again, in as friendly and inviting a tone as I could manage at that volume.

She said nothing, however, just stood there with her hands on her cane, now and then looking at me.

I realized she wanted to see where I lived and I thought about trying to give her the slip or just walking aimlessly around until she got fed up and went away, but, figuring that sooner or later she would find my house, I headed straight for home. Fielding

followed me through town, gloating, it seemed to me, at my saturated state. It was October and the rain was cold, driven slantwise
by the wind. Horses struggled up the slopes of the city, their
hooves emerging from the muck with a series of sucking plops,
their undersides and rumps spattered with mud. All the yellow
water was running downhill and pooling on Duckworth Street
and Water Street and Harbour Drive and overflowing into the harbour, the edges of which were cloudy, puddle-coloured. The world
seemed turbulent and volatile, inciting Fielding to this foolishness.

I walked across the bridge and up the hill to the Brow. Every
time I looked back, there she was, plodding up the slope with her
umbrella, picking her way among the puddles until she saw that I
had stopped, at which point *she* would stop, looking grateful for
the rest. Even from that distance, I could see that despite the
weather, she was out of breath and flushed from her exertions, not
used as I was to climbing the Brow. I walked up the front steps of a
house that, though it was no mansion, was far superior to ours and,
as silently as I could, put my hand on the door knob. I looked down
the hill. There was Fielding, expressionless, sullenly staring at me,
but not fooled. She waited and, humiliated, I crept down the steps
and resumed my journey home. Fielding followed at the same distance as before. This time, I went straight to our house and, once inside, peeked out through the curtains. Fielding, as if she thought I
might somehow still be bluffing, stared a while longer, then, satisfied that she had seen my house, started down the hill again.

On the playing grounds the next day, Fielding spread the
word among the Townies that I was a "Brow boy." "He doesn't
live in town. He lives in a shack on the Brow," Fielding said con-
temptuously. "He tried to fool me my by walking right up to the
door of another house. My God, Prowse, you should see the place
he lives in. I'll take you there if you like."

Everyone looked at Prowse, who stared at Fielding.

"What did you do, Fielding," Prowse said incredulously, "follow Smallwood home?"

"No," Fielding said, "I ... I just —" She looked at Prowse, her blue eyes blurred with tears. Then she turned her back and, in a comic replay of her first retreat, marched off, skirts hiked, towards the road.

Among the other Townies, I was not so much well-liked as feared. The fallen Fielding was a constant warning to them of what might happen if they crossed me, and consequently I came to enjoy an undeserved and, after Fielding, unproven reputation as a counter-punching wit who, though he would not pick on you, would give better than he got if picked upon himself.

I was one of only a few boys who actually wanted to be at Bishop Feild. It was considered proper to be openly scornful of the place. Almost everyone at Bishop Feild had a chip on their shoulder about having to attend. For the well-to-do boys, being sent to Bishop Feild meant either that their parents were not quite so well-to-do that they could send them to public schools overseas or else that the boys were so academically unpromising there would have been no point in sending them.

A lot of boys made up stories about what they were doing there. A boy named Thompson claimed there was a rule at Eton that no more than two brothers from any family could attend and, as two of his brothers were already there, that let him out. "There are other schools, of course," said Thompson grandly, "but when you come right down to it, they're really no better than Bishop Feild, so why should my father waste his money?" This story was scornfully dismissed by most, but Thompson stuck to it.

Some claimed they were not long for Bishop Feild but would soon be moving on to Rugby, Sandhurst, Harrow, St. Wulfric's, Gordonstoun. "In any good school, it's really only the Fifth and Sixth forms that count," a boy named Porter said. "Another year at Bishop Feild and then, thank God, I'm off to Harrow. I'll never have to see you lot again."

Certainly none of the masters, most of whom were itinerant Englishmen, wanted to be there. Almost to a man, they had either tried unsuccessfully to find a place at some public school in Britain or some colony more highly prized than Newfoundland, or had had such a place and, for one reason or another, had been let go. The Feild was like some sort of Mecca for the oddly named. Among the masters there was Beadle Wagstaff, Ikey Samson, Polly Bernard, Askew Pridmore, Tasker McBain, Arthur Onions and a Frenchman who always introduced himself as Adolph E. Bernard, stressing the *E* as though there were some other Adolph Bernard that he was concerned he might be mistaken for. They seemed fated by their names to a kind of failure-induced eccentricity, though perhaps their eccentricities came first. Rumours abounded about their supposedly shady pasts, about why they had been dismissed from their former jobs and, though Eton- and Oxford-educated, had wound up in Newfoundland.

Most of the masters were wittily scornful of Newfoundland, delighted in itemizing its deficiencies and the many ways it fell short of being England, and were forever sending up local customs and traditions. They found the winters unbearably oppressive; the number of canings went up dramatically once the snow set in. Like the boys, they went to great lengths to make it clear that they were not long for Bishop Feild, that they had wound up there because of some fluke or temporary set-back and would soon be moving on.

The headmaster was a man named Reeves, a veteran of the Boer War who always walked about with a blackboard pointer tucked like a swagger stick beneath his arm. He had been too long at Bishop Feild to believe, or get away with pretending, that he would ever leave. He called Newfoundland "the Elba of the North Atlantic" and told us his job was to undo the damage done to us by more than a decade of living there. His job, he said, was not only to educate us, but also to civilize us, for it was plain to him that underneath our "imitation finery," we were nothing more than savages descended from the "dregs of England." (He did go back to England upon his retirement a decade later and is said to have shouted, as his ship was sailing through the Narrows, "Goodbye, Newfoundlanders, you're dirtier than the Boers.")

We were taught next to nothing about Newfoundland, the masters drilling into us instead the history and geography of England, the country for which they were so homesick that they acted as if they were still there, denying as much as possible the facts of their existence. Every day in Lower Third history, which we took from Headmaster Reeves, we started class by drawing in detail a map of England. As the year went on, we got better and better at it, Reeves having us compete to see who could draw an acceptable likeness the fastest.

The masters accepted the verdict of the boys as to who was in and who was out. They had spent all their lives in public schools and had carried over with them from their student days a desire to be liked by the right sort of boys, whose favour they courted by openly showing their distaste for boys like me. As for Prowse, he was a favourite of the masters. He could do no wrong in their eyes, and when he committed some minor offence like arriving late for class, he grinned sheepishly at them and they grinned back, as if he was the kind of plucky, likeable rascal they wished they had been at public school.

The masters never seemed to know quite what to make of me. They seemed unconvinced that my popularity would last and were therefore unwilling to commit themselves. They did not mind the presence at college of a few of what Reeves called the great unwashed. Our being there, far from undermining the class order, was a reminder of its existence. But there seemed to be an unwritten rule that for us, only a kind of small-time, limited success was possible. We could climb to the top rung of our little ladder, but we could not switch to the larger ladder the others were climbing, as they likewise could not switch to the ladders atop which the masters stood.

Sometimes I caught Reeves looking at me, sizing me up as if he was wondering if I understood this, wondering what I imagined I was doing, hobnobbing with the likes of Prowse. I think it was in an unconscious effort to assure him, or perhaps to fool him into thinking, that I knew my place that I became class clown — no amount of success was wholly legitimate that came by way of clowning; a clown who got the highest marks in school was still a clown. Like Shakespeare's Fool, I was able to get away with saying almost anything. It also gave the masters a certain latitude with me.

In class, at least, Reeves could be the kind of engagingly cynical teacher boys find entertaining, a teacher easily diverted from his lesson to hold forth on the universal awfulness of things, especially things as they were in Newfoundland as opposed to England, and as they were everywhere now as opposed to how they used to be.

"Get Reeves going," Prowse told me as we were filing into class.

I started by asking him what he had against living in Newfoundland. "What have you got against Newfoundland, sir? Don't you like it here, sir? It's not so bad once you get used to it. Do you miss merry olde England, sir? It must be lovely there this time of year. What does your wife miss most about it, sir?" Reeves, knowing what I was up to but loathing teaching as much as we loathed being taught, pushed back his chair, put his feet up on his desk and his hands behind his head, threw back the sleeves of his black gown with a flourish and, tapping his pointer/swagger stick on the desk as if he were counting out the stresses in a line of poetry, began.

"The worst of our lot comes over here, inbreeds for several hundred years and the end-product is a hundred thousand Newfoundlanders with Smallwood at the bottom of the barrel."

"And you as my teacher, sir," I said.

"How many brothers and sisters do you have, Smallwood?" Reeves asked.

"Six, sir."

"My God," he said. "What are your parents trying to do, start their own country?"

"How many brothers and sisters do you have, sir?" I said.

"I am an only child," Reeves said.

"Your parents must be very proud of you, sir," I said. "Your having got such a superb posting as Bishop Feild, I mean. Have they been to visit lately?"

Reeves's previous posting had been in India, where, he swore, the students spoke better English than did Newfoundlanders.

"We understand each other, sir," I said, indicating my classmates. "It's you we can't make out."

On and on we went, Reeves smiling all the while as if it didn't matter if I got the best of him, as though he was holding in reserve some trump card he could not be bothered wasting on the likes of me. He never cut me short by invoking his authority or threatening to punish me for disrespect. He was far beyond believing that character-shaping was possible or even desirable.

Like most cynics, he seemed to have contrived his own disillusionment by starting out expecting more from the world than he knew it could deliver. There was still the faintest trace of the youthful idealist in him, though, and it was that which made him dangerous.

"There is no poetry worth reading after Tennyson," Reeves said. "There are no novels worth reading after Dickens," as if, in an age of mediocrity, individual failure such as his was excusable, inevitable. Not just Newfoundland, but the New World in general was a cultureless outback, he believed, though for Newfoundland he reserved his greatest scorn.

"It's not that I'm blaming you," he said. "It's not your fault your so-called country has no culture."

He read aloud Keats's "Ode to a Nightingale" and Shelley's "Ode to the West Wind" and asked us what there was in Newfoundland to equal those. He held up a copy of *David Copperfield* and asked us what there was in Newfoundland to rival that. "It takes thousands of years to make a great culture, a great civilization," he said.

"Prowse's grandfather wrote a great book," I said. "It's called
A History of Newfoundland."

"A history of Newfoundland cannot be great," Reeves said,
"because there is no greatness in Newfoundland. I have not read,
and will not read, the book you speak of, of course, but I have no
doubt that it is a well-researched, competently written chronicle of
misery and savagery, full of half-educated politicians and failures-
in-exile like myself and their attempts to oversee and educate a population descended from the dregs of the mother country." He looked
at Prowse as if to say, "Not even for you, Prowse, not even for you
and your book-writing grandfather will I make exceptions."

"Think of it," he said, "many of you are descended from people who couldn't even make the grade in Ireland, a country of bog-
born barbarians, or in Scotland, whose culture peaked with the
invention of the bagpipes. My God, it boggles the mind. If you lot
are the elite of Newfoundland, what must the rest be like? Smallwood here we may think of as the riff-raff's shining star. Try to
imagine someone in comparison with whom he would seem to be
a shining star. No, the mind balks, it is beyond imagining. The riff-
raff are out there, we know by extrapolation from Smallwood
that they exist, but luckily for us, we cannot picture them."

At the end of my first year, I was eighteenth of nineteen in the
Lower Third. My mother took it in stride. "They've all got a head
start on you," she said. "You'll catch up. And remember, even
with all his advantages, one boy finished lower than you did.
Imagine how he feels." I was not much cheered by the thought
that it was especially humiliating for a boy to be judged inferior to
me. My "character" mark was forty-five out of five hundred, the
lowest, not only in the Lower Third, but in all of Bishop Feild.

My father denounced this as a slur on the name of Charlie
Smallwood. "Character," he said. "They wouldn't know character if it smacked them in the face." He said it was obvious that
they measured a boy's character by how rich his father was, by

how fine his clothes were. What mark had they given Baker's boy, he wondered, who had snubbed poor Baker in the street?

"If you think of God as five hundred, then forty-five is not so bad," my mother said.

"God?" my father said to her. "What has God got to do with it? Is God enrolled at Bishop Feild?"

Numbers haunted him and he could not get these particular numbers out of his head. My first night back on the Brow, he played around with them every which way on a piece of paper at the kitchen table, adding up columns of figures with his pencil, dividing, calculating percentages, pouring himself glass after glass of rum. He was still at it when I went up to bed.

"Forty-five out of five hundred," he roared. "Forty-five out of five hundred, nine per cent. Four hundred and fifty-five marks missing. Two hundred and five marks short of barely passing. Can you imagine the gall? I suffer from a ninety-one per cent character deficiency. Ninety-one per cent of my character just isn't there."

He called out to me from the bottom of the stairs. "It is not you who has been judged, boy," he said. "It is your father, your poor father. I want you to tell Headmaster Reeves that I have judged his character to be fifteen out of five hundred. No, no, that's too much. Tell him I have judged his character to be absent altogether. Zero. Null. That's his mark for character from me. Tell him that as far as I can tell, he has no character at all."

Marks for school subjects were assigned by the teachers who taught them, but Headmaster Reeves judged the character of every boy in the school, so I had expected a low character mark, if not one quite so low, for my "interview" with him had not gone well. (Each of us went to see him near year's end for our character interview.) He said I had a tendency for "romancing," by which he meant day-dreaming. The other teachers reported to him that I was often caught at my desk staring at lists of names I had composed that had my own name at the bottom. Convinced, for instance, that I would myself write a history of Newfoundland as Prowse's grandfather had done, I compiled this list of Newfoundland historians: Judge John Reeves, The Reverend Lewis Amadeus Anspach, The Reverend Charles Pedley, The Reverend Philip Toque, The Reverend Moses Harvey, Judge Daniel Woodley Prowse, Joseph Robert Smallwood. I compiled a list of Newfoundland's prime ministers, a line of succession that ended with me: The Right Honourable Sir Joseph Robert Smallwood, K.C.G.M., P.C., M.H.A. Reeves assured me, laughing at his own cleverness, that no one as "benighted" as me would ever "be knighted."

I read a lot of books that Reeves deemed to be improper, that is to say books written by non-Englishmen. I read *The Last of the Mohicans*, *Huckleberry Finn* and *Moby Dick*.

At the time of my interview with Reeves, I had heretically been attempting a book not even written by someone who spoke English, *War and Peace*, a copy of which I had got as a Christmas present. I fancied that I would one day write a book that did for Newfoundland what *War and Peace* had done for Russia, a great, national, unashamedly patriotic epic.

"You're a great reader, aren't you, Mr. Smallwood?" Reeves said. "Always going about with extracurricular books beneath your arm. And what books they are, too; big books for a boy your age. Every time I see you, I say to myself, There goes little Smallwood, another load of books beneath his arm. What's he up to, I wonder, what's he thinking? I tell myself that in a way, it's a good sign, all this extra reading. He must be confused, he must be searching for something in those books. He's no ordinary young man, he doesn't take things at face value. He wants to know, what's the expression, he wants to know what makes things tick?"

This was one of his favourite rhetorical devices, to pretend to be groping for some phrase, to be unschooled in the ways and expressions of the world, so preoccupied was he with more important things.

"I was like that once. I used to ask myself, what are they called, the Big Questions. I fancied I could understand the answers."

He looked at me as if he was waiting for me to agree or disagree with this assessment of myself. All I could think to do was raise my eyebrows.

He performed a series of ironically dismissive gestures: adjusted his glasses, smoothed his moustache, put his hands on his hips.

"You've got a book there now," he said. "Let me see it." He held out his hand.

"*War and Peace*," he said in a tone of weary amusement, as if he had so often countered its claims to greatness that to do so again would be a waste of breath. He moved the hand that held it up and down appraisingly, then shrugged. He held it out at arm's length. "Perhaps the greatest novel ever written by perhaps the greatest novelist of all time," he read, laughing slightly. "Oh my, oh my, oh my. Now, Mr. Smallwood, you probably read that, 'The greatest novel ever written,' and you say to yourself, Imagine if someone said that about a book of mine. That's it, isn't it?"

He spoke this last sentence in a sympathetic tone, as though he was inviting me to confide in him, as if to say I need not be embarrassed about owning up to it, here was my chance to get it off my chest, to unburden myself; as if to say he knew what it was to labour under such prideful illusions as believing oneself to be destined for greatness.

"Leo Tolstoy," he read, "1828–1910. So where is Leo perhaps-the-greatest-novelist-of-all-time Tolstoy now, Mr. Smallwood? Can you tell me that, where is poor old Leo now?"

"Right there," I said, pointing at the book. He raised his eyebrows in mock acknowledgement of my quick-wittedness. Then he reached again into the desk and came out with a large, leather-bound edition of the Bible, which he placed side by side on the desk with *War and Peace*. He bent slightly forward over the desk, extended his hands like a merchant displaying his wares or like a magician inviting you to see that his props were exactly what he said they were.

"Well?" he said, looking up at me with a kind of canny smile.

"Sir?" I said, pretending not to know what he was getting at.

As if my reaction had confirmed some hunch of his, he put the Bible back in the drawer and handed me my *War and Peace*.

"You're planning to write the great Newfoundland novel, is that it?" he said. "*War and Peace* by Leo Tolstoy. *Fish and Chips* by Joey Smallwood."

He stood up and turned his back to me, looking out the window.

"Pride goeth before a fall, Mr. Smallwood," he said. "I was myself once full of pride. And pride is the greatest of all sins, the sin over which the first war was fought, the sin because of which Lucifer and his rebel angels were driven out of heaven and cast into the pit of hell. I want you to remember that. You can go now."

Fielding's Condensed
History of Newfoundland

Chapter One:

LANDFALL

We intend our history to be the story of the island of Newfoundland since the geological formation which bears that name first rose above the surface of the sea....

The earth's crust cools ...

John Cabot discovers the island on June 24, 1497. He believes he has found Cathay, now known as China, to find a shortcut to which he had set out thirty-five days before. He returns to England and tells King Henry VII that he has found the land of the Grand Khan and will surely find the Grand Khan's kingdom if Henry will finance a second expedition. The king agrees. Cabot leaves for Newfoundland and is never seen again.

In 1534, Jacques Cartier circumnavigates Newfoundland, proving it to be an island, which he manages to convince his crew is as great an achievement as doing what he set out to do, namely, discover a passage to the East Indies. This explains his later remark, inscrutable to many, that the quality he prizes most highly in a sailor is gullibility.

In 1583, Sir Humphrey Gilbert, the half-brother of Sir Walter Raleigh, sets out in search of a passage to the Orient, but settles for claiming Newfoundland in the name of Queen Elizabeth I. Upon leaving Newfoundland for England, he takes with him a piece of turf and a small twig, symbols of ownership which, unlike him, remain afloat when his ship sinks in the mid-Atlantic.

Judges

ONE OF MY FATHER'S most prized possessions, for all the scorn he heaped on Newfoundland, was his copy of *A History of Newfoundland* by Judge D. W. Prowse, published in 1895. It was one of the world's great histories, he said, though he doubted it would ever be so acknowledged outside of Newfoundland.

He was as awed by Prowse's prowess with numbers, his tables, graphs, charts and columns of statistics, as he was by Prowse's prose, which had the conviction and lucid eloquence of court decisions, judgments rendered and explained, effects painstakingly traced back to causes. It read like some great argument written to confound appeals to higher courts, though the argument was often lost amid the mass of detail. It was, as Prowse confessed in his foreword, not complete, it could not be at even ten times its eight hundred pages, for the instant he finished writing it a moment of history went unrecorded and even in what was written there were gaps, implausibilities, unsatisfying explanations and conjectures, though he believed that all of the latter were at least theoretically correctible and the only impediment to the perfection he had set out to achieve was time and the availability of documents. Four centuries of island history were encompassable, the judge believed. A Hansard-like transcription of our past could be set down, if only there was time.

To me, it was as if the *History* contained, not a record of the past, but the past itself, distilled, compacted to such density that I could barely lift it.

My father revered the *History*, not so much because it justified the ways of Newfoundland to the world, or because it denounced England for its three-hundred-year exploitation of Newfoundland, though that it did both he greatly appreciated, but because it was the concrete product of a man who had succeeded in doing in life the thing he considered most worth doing.

"Do you really think my grandfather's *History* is a great book?" Prowse asked me after class one day, just before the Christmas break in Lower Fifth, two years into my stint at Bishop Feild.

"Yes, I do," I said. "My father has a copy. He thinks it's a great book, too."

"Oh, really? Would your father like to meet my grandfather, do you think?" Prowse said, flashing me that smile that always accompanied such displays of unasked-for generosity. "He could autograph your father's copy of his book."

I told him I would ask my father that Sunday when I went home to visit.

My father seemed almost terrified at the thought of meeting the judge. "No, no, my God, no," he said, as if I had made some dreadful blunder, pacing about the floor of the front room, shaking his head, worried that Prowse might already have arranged the meeting and the judge might be expecting him. I assured him this was not the case, but asked him why he did not want to meet someone whose work he so admired.

"I don't know why," my father said. "I don't want to meet a man like that, that's all I know."

"Meet not the judge lest ye be judged," my mother said.

"Here," he said, handing me his copy of the *History*, "you go with young Prowse to see the judge and have him sign my book. Tell him Charlie Smallwood says hello."

Nine years before, in 1905, the judge had begun revising his *History*, not just to include the years that had passed since the publication of the first edition, but to correct the many mistakes that had been brought to his attention and the sight of which set down in print kept him awake at night, and to take into account new documents that had come to light, documents ages old of which there seemed to be no end.

I walked with Prowse to the judge's large old house on Military Road, followed him up a set of stairs to a study where we found the judge all but buried in the detritus of scholarship, his desk a chaos of maps and charts, the crude, curiously blunt and rounded maps of primitive cartography, the floor littered with massive volumes, colonial registries and Blue Books. It seemed the walls were made of books; on top of the shelves books were piled until they touched the ceiling; slats of light came shining through the piles of books that blocked the window. "Grandpa," Prowse said after knocking briefly on the door, "this is Joe Smallwood, a friend of mine from Bishop Feild."

The judge seemed pleased to be interrupted. He swung around in his chair and, smiling broadly, held out his hand for me to shake. I made my way among the books scattered on the floor and took his hand. "Pleased to meet you, sir," I said.

"Pleased to meet you, boy," he said. He looked in good-natured confusion at Prowse, then shook his head and looked back at me. The house was cold; he was dressed in a buttoned tweed overcoat and red scarf, the latter just discernible through his long white beard.

"Joe's father likes your book," Prowse said, "and Joe was wondering if you would sign a copy for him."

Prowse opened my father's copy of the *History* on the desk in front of the judge, and the judge, as if indulging some delusion of ours, shrugged and grinned and signed his name in the place Prowse pointed to with his finger and beneath that wrote four lines that I could not make out.

"You follow that advice," he said, tapping what he had written, "and you won't go wrong."

I nodded.

"Who did you say owns this book?" he asked me.

"My father," I said.

"That rascal," the judge said, and for a second I thought my father had been afraid to meet the judge because they had met before. Prowse winked at me and shook his head. The judge looked around the room. "I'll never get it done," he said in the cheerful manner of someone who merely wants to impress upon you the scope of his ambition and really has no doubts that he will succeed.

"You know what I would do if I had the time, boy," he said to me. "I would write about one man, like Rousseau did, like Boswell did, one representative Newfoundlander. And do you know who that representative man would be?" I shook my head. "Cluney Aylward," he said, leaning back as if the better to see if I shared his view that Cluney Aylward, whom I had never heard of, was a representative Newfoundlander. "He was a great man," the judge said. "A learned man, of course, foremost in his field, a scholar, but a man of the people, too, a leader the likes of which we'll never see again. I would follow him around and write down everything he said and did and everything other people said about him."

"Joe and I had better be going, Grandpa," Prowse said, and again the judge looked confused, shook off his confusion, grinned indulgently. "Remember, boy," he said. "The question is, What has made us what we are and what will be our fate? That is the question I wrestle with every day, here at this desk." Then he bade us goodbye.

"Who's Cluney Aylward?" I said when we were downstairs. "There is no Cluney Aylward," Prowse said, grinning broadly. Then he explained that the judge, because of a stroke his family believed had been brought on by his exhaustive labours on his book, thought he was back working on the first edition of *A History of Newfoundland*, a delusion that not even showing him a copy of the first edition inscribed with his own name could shake for long. It was years since he had done any real work on the revised edition, though he went every day to his study and wrote page after page of illegible scrawl that his family had long since stopped trying to decipher. He had filled hundreds, thousands of pages with this scrawl. It was as if the judge were writing in some language that no one else could understand, a language of his own invention, the only one in which he could properly complete his book; as if he had advanced in his art to the point of inscrutability and now was writing for no one but himself. He did not know he suffered from this agraphia but rather believed he could still write and *was* writing as he moved the pen across the page.

As for Cluney Aylward, though the judge, humoured by his family, would go on for hours about his accomplishments, his stature as a Newfoundlander, there was no record anywhere of a man by that name. He was apparently a stroke-inspired fiction.

"And you know when you said 'my father,'" Prowse said, "and he said 'that rascal'? He thought you meant my father. He thought you were me. I don't know who he thought I was today."

I was angry with Prowse for playing such a trick on me and on his grandfather, but mostly I was in a panic as to what to tell my father. I thanked God he had declined to come and tried not to think of the scene that might have taken place if he had. I opened the book to the title page. Here was my father's *History*, defaced by the author himself.

"I can't bring it back to him like this," I said. "You can't make out a word of this, not even a letter, what will I do?" The signature, though illegible, was signature-shaped at least and, appearing below

"D. W. Prowse" on the title page, could, Prowse supposed, pass for a signature, but the rest, he contritely admitted, was a problem for which he was to blame. He'd ask his father to help, he said, though that would mean letting his father know he had done something he wasn't supposed to do, namely, bring people to the house to see the judge, his condition being something they were trying, not very successfully, to keep secret. Luckily, it was still several days before Sunday, and Prowse told me to leave the book with him and he would figure out what to do with it. I reluctantly went back to Bishop Feild without the book, leaving it in Prowse's hands and wringing a promise from him that he would do no further damage to it.

Two days later, on Friday, he brought it back to school with him and gave it to me. There was a "translation" beneath the judge's scrawl that read: "For Charlie Smallwood. I was glad to hear from your son that you enjoyed my book so much. He and my grandson are great friends at Bishop Feild, as you and I might have been had we gone to school together." Also, there was a note addressed to my father, signed by Prowse's father, explaining that the judge suffered from a palsy so severe that his handwriting was illegible to all but his closest relatives.

"I hope your father wasn't too upset with you," I said.

"Not too upset," Prowse said, ruefully rubbing his backside and grinning. I was greatly relieved, though I worried that Prowse's father might have laid it on too thick and that my father would now relent and ask to meet the judge.

On Sunday, I brought the book back to my father, who at first seemed greatly pleased with the dedication.

"Not condescending at all, is it?" he said. "He sounds as though he means it. 'Friends as you and I might have been had we gone to school together.' A very kind thing to say. A very gracious thing to say."

My father sat throughout my visit with the book open on his lap, staring at the dedication while I darted nervous looks at him from time to time, praying he was not becoming suspicious. He started asking me questions, which, I was certain, I would give myself away in answering.

"Did you tell him Charlie Smallwood says hello?" my father asked. I hadn't, but I assured him that I had.

"What's he like?" my father said.

"He's very old," I said, as though that were a trait the judge had carried with him all his life.

"Very old," my father said, nodding, as if this conformed nicely to the image of the judge he had already formed.

"His hands shake pretty badly," I said, "and he has a long white beard."

"He never said anything about the Boot, did he?" my father said. "Did he make the connection between the name Smallwood and the Boot?" I assured him that the judge had not mentioned the Boot. "What did he say?" my father said. "Tell me everything he said."

"He didn't say very much," I said. "We didn't stay long. He was pretty busy."

My father went out on the deck after I had gone to bed. When I heard him I got up and looked out the window at him. He stood with his hands on the rail and spoke as if the judge were standing just below him. "Friends. As you and I might have been had we gone to school together. You old bastard. You wouldn't have given me the time of day."

The next day, I spoke to Prowse on the playing grounds before the first bell. "That inscription. And that note you included with the book," I said. "The note to my father. Did your father really write those?" I thought I had recognized the handwriting as Prowse's, but did not tell him so.

"To tell you the truth, I didn't show my father the book," Prowse said, looking hangdog. "I would have told you, but I wasn't sure how you'd react. Anyway, he would have killed me for bringing you to see the judge. So I wrote the inscription and the note myself. No harm done, I hope."

"Oh, no," I said. "No."

At the mid-year evaluation of the following year, I was second of sixteen, first runner-up for the Knowling Scholarship, which Prowse won, largely on the strength of his whopping grade of three hundred and eighty-five out of five hundred for character. "Everybody knows you should have won," Prowse said. He said he and the other boys were thinking about starting a petition, asking that the Knowling be appealed, but I talked him out of it for fear of getting into trouble.

All my marks had gone dramatically up, except my mark for character, which had stayed at forty-five. Its being not only so low, but also fixed, never-changing, was the point. It could not change, Reeves seemed to be saying; my other marks could go up or down, as the case might be, but my character, my fundamental self, would stay the same. I might as well have had forty-five stamped on my forehead. I was what I was, my character was my fate and my fate was forty-five.

Two days after the mid-year evaluation was released, my father showed up drunk at the college gates, roaring to be let in. It was late afternoon in mid-December and the Townies had already gone home. The 'Tories rushed to the windows to see what was going on.

"Who is it?" Slogger said, but I had recognized my father's voice right off. I ran out of the dorm and across the field, to shouts of mock encouragement from the bay boys.

"It's Smallwood's old man," I heard someone say. "He's absolutely pissed. Go get him, Smallwood, go get him. Ask him if there's any left for us."

"Headmaster Reeves," my father roared, shaking the bars of the gate. "Whoremaster Reeves, Charlie Smallwood would like to have a word with you, Whoremaster Reeves. Let me in. Or perhaps you would like to join me, sir; we could have a little chat right here outside the gate. It won't take but a minute, sir, I assure you. It concerns my son, you see, my son whom you have judged to be unsuitable, an honest mistake, I'm sure. Perhaps you would better understand him if you spent some time with me, perhaps then you would see him in an altogether different light."

By the time I reached the gate, the porter, a little old fellow named Antle who stayed in a hut by the gate to monitor the comings and goings of the boys, was beside himself. He wore a sod cap and, as if he had never left the Feild after graduation, a school blazer bearing the crest of Bishop Feild.

"Be quiet, sir, be quiet," Antle was saying, standing well out of reach of my father's hands, wringing his own. "If you don't be quiet, they'll have the 'Stab on you."

"I have friends in the constabulary," my father said.

"Go on home, father," I said. "Go on home now."

"*Joe*," my father said, as if the last person he had expected to run into at the school was me. He looked like he'd come straight up from the waterfront, for he was wearing his coveralls with the row of pencils in the pocket and a pair of black, salt-stained leather boots, and he had his toting pole in his hand. He was bareheaded, his hair sticking up like he had just removed his stocking cap, though there was no sign of it.

"Go get Headmaster Reeves, Joe," he said. "Tell him your father, Charlie Smallwood, would like to have a little word with him." At the word *little*, he made a motion with his thumb and index finger not very far apart.

"He's not here," I said. "He had to go to a meeting somewhere. Why don't you just go home?"

"WHOREMASTER REEVES," my father shouted, throwing back his head, eyes closed as if the better to hear himself, the better to revel in the sound of his own voice. The boys at the windows of the dorm were in hysterics. "You tell him, Charlie," Slogger shouted.

"Hello, boys," my father shouted. "You're all good boys, all suitable, I'm sure. But you're no better than my Joe, I don't care what Whoremaster Reeves says, you're no better than my Joe. He's got some backbone, Joe does. WHOREMASTER REEVES."

He grabbed the bars of the gate and shook them again. "Charlie Smallwood is no good, chop him up for firewood," he said, further inciting the 'Tories. I turned and looked at the head-master's residence. I had lied about Reeves not being there, but there was no sign of him at any of the windows. Antle looked beseechingly at me.

"The 'Stab will be here soon," Antle said, on the verge of tears. "The headmaster won't stand for this; he'll call the 'Stab for sure."

"I don't care about the 'Stab," my father said.

"What will the headmaster think?" Antle said. "Oh my, oh my."

"I'll go out and talk to him," I said.

"Oh, no," Antle said. "Oh, no, I'm not allowed to let you out. And if I open the gate, he'll come in. I can't open the gate."

"Open the gate," my father said.

Without giving Antle a chance to go through the motions of trying to stop me, I climbed the gate and dropped down on the other side to a burst of applause from the boys. I took my father by the arm and tried to turn him around, but he wrenched himself free and made a grab for Antle through the bars of the gate, barely missing him, then tried to poke him with his toting pole.

"The 'Stab — " Antle said, all but falling down to elude my father.

"I'll stab the 'Stab," my father said. "And I'll stab you while I'm at it."

My father put one boot up on the lowest horizontal bar. "If he can climb out, I can climb in," he said. He tried to hoist him-self up but could not get a purchase on the ice-coated gate with the other boot and, even as I was putting my arms around his waist to keep him from going any farther, he fell backwards, knocking both of us to the ground. A great mock cheer went up from the dorm, though with the wind knocked out of me and the back of my head smarting from where it had hit the ground, I was only half-aware of it.

"Are you all right, Joe?" my father said, getting up on his knees, staring down at me, his toting pole in his hands as if he had felled me with it. "Are you all right? I didn't hurt you, did I? You hit your head, let me see."

"I'm all right," I said.

On his hands and knees, he stared at the snow-covered ground and shook his head.

I managed to stand up and, grabbing him under the arm with both hands, helped him to his feet.

"Let's go home," I said. This time he was compliant, allowing me to drag him away from the gate but at the same time shouting over his shoulder.

"I'll be the judge of your character someday, Reeves," he said. "Judge not lest ye be judged. The boot will be on the other foot someday. Do you hear me, Whoremaster Reeves?"

I led him towards home. After a while, he stopped hurling imprecations over his shoulder and, as he often did after such an outburst, became quite remorseful.

"I'm sorry, boy," he said, his head down as he shuffled along, his toting pole in one hand like a spear. "I've gone and made matters worse, like always. That's all I ever do is make things worse. I'm no good, Joe, I'm no damned good and that's the truth. But you are, boy, it's not right what they're doing to you, it's just not right."

"Never mind," I said. "We'll go home and have some soup. I'll tell Mother they let me have a night pass and I met you on the way home."

"Good enough, boy," my father said, "good enough. God bless you, Joe, you're a good boy. The best of the brood. And what a brood it is. That's one thing that I'm good at. There's nothing more potent than booze, you know."

The next day, when I walked into class a few minutes before the bell and took my seat, a hush fell over the boys. No one said anything, though some of them had been at the windows of the dorm the day before. At lunch-time, I joined up with the Townies on the playing field. Prowse, though I was certain he had heard, said nothing about what happened, and the other boys followed his lead. I told them Reeves had gated me a "whopping dollar," as Prowse called it, for leaving the grounds without permission.

"I'm not going to pay it," I said.

"If it's a question of the money — " Prowse said.

"He didn't fine me because I left without permission," I said. "He fined me because my father called him 'Whoremaster Reeves.'" Prowse and the others, who I was sure had already heard this from the 'Tories, laughed.

"You're probably right," Prowse said, "but — "

"I'm thinking about quitting," I said.

"Don't be a fool," Prowse said. "You'll be quitting over nothing. Boys here have been caned so badly they couldn't walk for days."

"He knows I'd rather be caned than fined," I said. "He knows what a dollar means to me. He wants me to go to my uncle and ask for it and humiliate my father."

"I told you," Prowse said. "If it's a question of the money, there's no problem. We'll take up a collection. Reeves will never know."

I shook my head bitterly.

"If you quit, he'll say that he was right about you all along," Prowse said. "You're not the only boy he's got it in for, you know. A few weeks from now, he'll be picking on someone else and all this will have blown over."

In the end, I relented and let them pay my fine. I didn't say a word about it to my father.

After we got back from Christmas break, the masters informed us that we were all to go, one by one, to Reeves's office. Throughout the day, we took turns. When one boy came back, the boy who sat behind him left. The boys who came back looked terrified and ignored all whispered questions as to what was going on. When it came my turn, Porter, who had just come back, said Reeves had said I should wait until last. I looked across the room at Prowse, who had not yet had his interview. He shrugged. The interviews went on until it was Prowse's turn. He grinned and winked at me as he left the room, but when he came back he did not look at me. Finally, the next-to-last boy came back to say that Reeves would see me now.

When I entered his office, Reeves stood facing the window that overlooked the grounds, ominously tapping it with his swagger-stick pointer. The back of his high-shaven neck was flushed a livid crimson. It was for some reason the only part of him that went red when he was mad, and I had never seen it redder. He was wearing his tasselled mortarboard and his headmaster's gown.

He turned around, looked at me through his small round spectacles. He thrust out at me a piece of paper, then withdrew it when I reached for it.

"What is it, sir?" I said.

"What is it, sir," he said. "I'll tell you what it is, sir, as if you don't already know, sir. It's the letter you wrote to the *Morning Post*, sir — "

"No, sir, I didn't — "

"It's the letter you wrote to the *Morning Post*, which thank-fully was read first by a friend of this school and sent to me and which reads as follows — you may recite along with me if you wish:

To Whom It May Concern:

The masters at Bishop Feild do not treat us properly. They
keep most of our meal money for themselves and with what's
left they buy the cheapest food that they can find. We are
always so hungry we cannot concentrate on our work. Then
they tell us we are lazy and cane us for making mistakes.
They make us buy our notebooks at the school and charge us
twice what they are worth. Also, our dormitory is always
cold, as there is never enough coal to go around. Three boys
had to leave school for good last year they got so sick. Everyone is always coughing. One boy got bitten by a rat....

"It goes on and on. A pack of malicious lies. It's signed, 'Yours
Sincerely, The Boys of Bishop Feild.'"

"I didn't write that, sir," I said. "It can't be in my handwriting."

"It isn't in anybody's handwriting," he said. "It's composed
with words and letters cut from books. 'Our dormitory is always
cold.' You gave yourself away there, Smallwood. The letter is
postmarked St. John's during Christmas vacation, when the only
dorm boy in St. John's was you."

"But — "

"Can you imagine, Smallwood, how much damage this letter
might have done? Imagine what a time the Catholics would have
had with it."

"But I didn't write it, sir; I swear."

"Are you telling me that someone else did?"

"I don't know — no, sir, I don't know who wrote it. What did
the other boys say?"

"Never mind what they said."

"I didn't write it, sir. Anyone could have put that bit about the
dorm in just to get me into trouble."

"That's just like you, Smallwood, to try to put the blame on
someone else. Get out of my sight." I stood there, staring at the

letter in his hand. "*Get out!*" Reeves said, smashing his pointer on the desk.

Prowse called a meeting of all the boys, Townies, 'Tories, Lepers, on the athletic grounds that afternoon. Eager to hear what Reeves had said to the others, I showed up early, stood in the shelter of the entrance to the gym, facing the harbour. Beyond the Narrows, the water was as black as slate. The metallic smell of an approaching storm was in the air. Snow eddied across the open field and down the unpaved icy length of Bond Street. It would be so dark by five o'clock that the snow as it fell would be invisible. Finally, the others began to arrive, hands stuffed in the pockets of their overcoats, heads bent to keep their caps from blowing off.

It turned out that Reeves had tried to get each of them to admit that I had written the letter, claiming that he had already been told by one of the students that I had and that he was merely seeking confirmation of my guilt. Prowse demanded that each of the boys swear an oath, bare hands on their hearts despite the cold: "May I die this night if I wrote that letter." Everyone, Slogger and the other 'Tories, the Lepers, the Townies, me and finally Prowse, swore the oath.

Then Prowse revealed that Reeves had threatened that unless he was soon told who had written the letter, he would mark them all so far down for character that the diploma they received upon graduation would be worthless.

"You did this, didn't you, Smallwood?" Prowse said, suddenly turning on me, putting his face to within an inch of mine. "You were the only dorm boy in town over Christmas."

I felt sick to my stomach, as though at the memory of some warning I had been too proud to heed. "I didn't write any letters to anyone," I said, staring at him.

"You've got to tell us if you did it, Smallwood," Prowse said, turning up his collar as the wind blew a gust of snow across the field. "It's a good joke, really it is, a great joke, but it goes too far."

"I'm not going to admit to something I didn't do," I said.

"There's a lot riding on this for some of us, you know," Prowse said. "We can't afford to be marked down."

"But I can, is that it?" I said. "Someone might have put in that bit about the dorms to frame me."

"Are you accusing someone?" Prowse said.

"No one in particular," I said. "I can't think of anyone that smart."

"The evidence points to Smallwood," Slogger said. "We'll have to tan his arse until he confesses. You might as well confess, Smallwood, and spare yourself a caning."

I looked appealingly at Prowse.

"We've got to do *something*, Smallwood," Prowse said, almost sheepishly. "Look, I don't know if you did it, but we've got to do *something*."

"I did it. I sent the letter."

We turned and there was Fielding, her cane planted in the snow in front of her, her back to Spencer. She must have gone up on the road and come down on the Feild side of the fence, then marched across the playing grounds unnoticed to us, unheard because of the wind.

"I did it," Fielding said. "It was me. I did it to get back at Smallwood."

I looked at Prowse, who seemed almost at the point of panic he was so confused. It was a crucial moment for him and he knew it. Everyone looked at him.

"What shall we do with her, Prowse?" Slogger said.

Prowse looked at me, and for a second, I thought he was going to overrule Fielding's confession with one of his own. "She'll — she'll be expelled," said Prowse. "That's enough."

"Not for me it's not," Slogger said. "I say we flog her bare arse."

"I say we let her go," said Prowse.

"What's the matter, Prowse?" Slogger said. "Afraid of what Reeves will say?"

"I'm not afraid of anything," Prowse said. He grabbed Fielding's cane away from her so quickly she almost fell forward into the snow. "Quick," Prowse said, "before someone sees us."

With the rest of us following, several of the Townies hustled Fielding into the manual-training centre, where woodworking was taught but which at that time of day was empty. They bent her over a saw-horse. Prowse made to raise up her coat and dress.

"*No*," I said.

"You're really going to do it, Prowse?" said Slogger. "I mean, I can't believe you would even flog a girl at all, but you're going to flog a girl's bare arse?"

Prowse looked uncertainly about. From where I stood, I could not see Fielding's face. Two of the Townies had their hands over her mouth to keep her from making any noise, though she was not struggling. Slogger laughed, doubled over, as did some of the other 'Tories.

"My God, Prowse," Slogger said. "You should see — you should see the look on your face."

"I *was* going to do it," Prowse said. "But if you lot — but only if everybody did it. That way there'd be no tattle-tales. Just her word against ours." He cocked his head at Fielding. "We could say she made it up. Just like she made up that letter to the *Morning Post*."

The Townies, having followed his orders to drag Fielding inside to be flogged, had no choice but to back him up or else lose face themselves. "I'll do it if everybody else does it," Porter said. The others murmured their assent.

"Come on, boys," Slogger said, laughing again. The 'Tories followed him from the training centre. Then the Lepers left, leaving only us Townies, and Fielding bent over the saw-horse.

"Let her go," Prowse said.

When the two boys holding her released her, she stood up but did not turn around to face Prowse and me.

"Go on, Fielding," Prowse said. "It was just a joke, that's all. If you tell anyone — Here, take your cane and go." Fielding said nothing. I could not see her face, but I was certain from the way she stood that her eyes were closed.

"Give it to me," I said. Prowse looked at me, shrugged, handed me her cane. He and the Townies filed out, snickering, whispering.

"Fielding," I said. "Why — Why did you — "

"Please put the cane on the floor and leave," Fielding said. Her voice quavered. She sniffed as if she might be crying, but she did not bow her head. "Go, Smallwood," she said. "You'll have your revenge. Just leave me be."

"Why did you — "

"I told you, to get you into trouble."

"No, I know. I mean why — Why did you confess?"

"For lack of better sense," she said. Now I was certain she was crying. "Please go, Smallwood. Don't say another word, just go."

I left. Outside it was almost dark and the snow had started. It was drifting, funnelling up between the buildings. The 'Tories were in the dorm, the lights of which were on. The Townies were nowhere to be seen, gone home most likely. I stood in the lee of the gym, waiting for her to show. I knew this was exactly what she didn't want, someone watching as she left. She appeared at last, looked around as if to see if the coast was clear. She set off, gloved hand on her hat, long skirts swishing as she scuffed her buttoned boots through the snow. How strange that she had for so long harboured that grudge against me, waited three years for revenge. I remembered the day she followed me to see where I lived. I could well imagine what her house looked like. I vowed never to set eyes on it. Suddenly, she struck out with her cane, in full stride struck and struck again, furiously wielding it machete-like as if she were hacking herself a passage through the storm.

When the Townies told Reeves that Fielding had confessed, Fielding was called to the office of the headmistress of Spencer and expelled. I was called to Reeves's office the next day. "I'd expel you, too, Smallwood, if I had any proof," Reeves said. "I know you had *something* to do with it." Apparently sure enough of himself where I was concerned that he knew he could get away with it, Reeves told me that next year, I would be in the Lower Sixth (Commercial), a class for those judged to be unsuited for going on to university. A couple of weeks later, convinced that for me Bishop Feild was a dead end, I dropped out.

Far from being gleeful, Reeves seemed almost disappointed, at least at first. I think he had been looking forward to watching me plod pointlessly through the Commercial Class. I didn't offer an explanation and he didn't ask for one. Despite the fact that I had quit, he gave me what amounted to his expulsion speech. He went to great lengths to establish that the school would in no way be diminished by my absence, that it was not me who was rejecting Bishop Feild, but vice versa.

"No one is indispensable, Smallwood," he said. "That's what I've been trying to tell you. This school will carry on just as well without you. Another boy will take your place. There are plenty waiting." He hinted that he had been right in his judgment of my character, that this was the immutable, ineluctable forty-five manifesting itself at last, just as he had known it would. He said I had squandered an opportunity that had been handed to me on a silver platter, an opportunity that boys of my background didn't often get and that I was perhaps too ill-bred to appreciate. Imagine what this would mean to my uncle, Fred Smallwood, who had taken a chance on me and sponsored me as if I were his own son. Finally, as if to say that he regretted having to give me the heave-ho and hoped that this last speech of his would in some small measure mitigate my fate, though he doubted that it would, he threw up his hands.

"All right then, Smallwood, off you go," he said briskly, as if no more could be done for me, as if he had discharged all his obligations where I was concerned, performed an unpleasant but necessary task and now it was time to move on to other things. With his hands behind his back, he faced the window and, several times in succession, rose up on his toes, rocked back on his heels, up, back, up, back. I felt like telling him, again, that I had not written that letter. But looking at him there, staring out the window, the back of his neck an outraged pink, his swagger stick beneath his arm, I realized how far short of his ambitions he had fallen, how it galled him that he had wound up where he had, and that he believed himself to have failed with me and, in his own way, was ashamed.

No fanfare attended my departure. Since the incident in the training centre, I had shunned the Townies, rebuffed the one overture Prowse made.

"Come on, Smallwood," Prowse had said. "You don't have to brood about it."

"You were quite willing to see me flogged," I said. "You thought I might be guilty."

"Well, what was I supposed to think?" said Prowse, grinning as if to say we both knew I would have done the same if I were him. "What was I supposed to do?"

I walked away from him.

"All right," Prowse said, "have it your way. Go join the Lepers, they're the only ones who'll have you now."

All the boys were in class, the windows of the school were closed and frosted over. At about the halfway point of that long walk across the frozen field, I looked at the headmaster's residence and saw Reeves at the window of one of his rooms. He raised his hand, though whether to wave goodbye or to twirl the end of his moustache I wasn't sure. When I raised my hand, he turned away. I reached the gate, by which Antle stood wearing an expression that seemed to say he had warned me it would come to this. "Goodbye, Antle," I said.

I began my walk to the Brow, my doughboy-type kitbag slung over my shoulder. Crossing the Waterford Bridge, I took off my Bishop Feild cap and threw it in the river, watching as it floated along on the current that would take it to the harbour. From the bridge, I watched the pilot boats, each of whose sails bore a giant letter *p*, darting about among the schooners and the huge, crane-bearing barges and side-wheel steamers that were piled high with coal and lumber. The schooners, with their sails down, presented a stark forest of masts along the north-side docks, bare masts and rigging and a jumble of hulls as if the whole fleet had been washed up on the apron by a storm.

I looked up at the Brow and saw our house.

Reeves had given me a note to give to my father informing him that I had dropped out. My father's hands trembled as he read the note on getting home from work that night. "Why did he stream you commercial?" he said. "Is it because of that letter?" He had heard about it from Uncle Fred. I nodded. "But you didn't write it," my father said. "Did you? I heard it was some — some doctor's daughter from Bishop Spencer trying to get you into trouble."

"It doesn't matter," I said. "Reeves streamed me commercial because he felt like it. He probably would have done it anyway. For me to keep going there would have been a waste of time."

My father stared at the note. "I don't understand," he whispered. "He knows you had nothing to do with that letter. He knows."

Later, roaring drunk, he started in. "You're ruined, boy, you're ruined," he said. "We're *both* ruined, we're *all* ruined, we're done for now." And then, as if it was somehow responsible for my dropping out, he got going about Judge Prowse's *History*, which he was now calling the Book. "That cursed Book," he said. "I wish to God I'd never seen that Book."

My father, who had never wanted me to go to Bishop Feild and, for the past three years, had been exhorting me to leave, now professed himself "heartbroken" that I had. He was soon pronouncing it to be "the best of schools."

"With a diploma from Bishop Feild, a young man could write his own ticket," he said, shaking his head. "This is it, our last hope dashed." He went on singing the praises of Bishop Feild late into the night, talking about what a great lot the masters were, how they understood the importance of tradition and refinement. "They are great men," he said, "learned men," stressing the word *learned* as if therein lay the key, as if only by fully appreciating as he did now what it meant to be learned could you understand what great men the masters were. "I know I criticized them in the past, but I am not afraid to admit when I am wrong," he said. He could see now what the future held for me, I would go to work at Smallwood's "beneath the old man's Boot." "*The boot beckons, boy,*" he roared that night from the bottom of the stairs. "*The black boot beckons, boy.*"

Fielding's Condensed
History of Newfoundland

Chapter Two:

THE GOLDEN FLEECE

In 1610, John Guy starts the first formal settlement at Cupids, and is fooled by the fluke of two successive mild winters into thinking he would like to live there. He is convinced otherwise by the less-anomalous winter of 1613, after which he returns home and for the rest of his life wakes up screaming in the middle of the night, refusing to go back to sleep until his wife assures him he no longer lives in Newfoundland.

The London and Bristol Company sells John Guy's colony to William Vaughan. Vaughan, after a long talk with Guy, which he regrets not having had before he made his purchase, does not actually visit his colony, but instead writes a book extolling its virtues called *The Golden Fleece* and sends in his place a number of Welshmen.

After not having heard from them for two years, he sends Sir Richard Whitbourne to see how they are doing. Whitbourne reports back to Vaughan that not all of them are dead and there is even talk among those still alive of building shelters of some kind. Inexplicably, the colony is abandoned in 1620.

Vaughan approaches various people and offers large portions of his colony to those who answer "No" to the question "Have you ever met John Guy?"

Among them is Sir George Calvert, Lord Baltimore, Secretary of State, who buys a huge tract of Vaughan's colony and announces his intention to establish a colony at Ferryland, which will be a haven for Roman Catholics who are being persecuted for their religious beliefs in Britain. This sales pitch does not work, however. So harried by persecution are the Roman Catholics that those he approaches with his proposal say they would rather be persecuted than end up like "William's Welshmen."

Calvert goes to Vaughan, demanding to know what they mean by this. On Vaughan's advice, he focuses his attentions on that group of men whose position in English society and lot in life are such that to move to Newfoundland seems like a good idea.

As a result, another twelve Welshmen soon accompany a Captain Edward Wynne to Newfoundland, where they establish a colony at Ferryland.

The Book

FOR WEEKS, EXCEPT when we were eating, there was nothing on the kitchen table but the Book. My father put it in the middle of the table as if it were the family centre-piece. He pointed at it, referred to it as "he" or "you" as if it were the judge himself. "'Friends as you and I would have been had we gone to school together.' Oh, yes, I'm sure we would have been great friends. You and me. Bosom buddies. Inseparable. Shoulder to shoulder through life. If only we'd met in school, we'd be spending all of our time together now, hunting caribou in Labrador. The writer and the toter. What a pair we could have been."

Sometimes, late at night, he pretended to be the judge addressing Charlie Smallwood. "I have deigned to acknowledge you, to indulge your delusions on the cover of this Book that I wrote and you did not, this Book that you could not have written, this eight-hundred-page masterpiece of mine, an accomplishment so far beyond your scope it reduces your whole life to insignificance."

"Stop talking to that book," my mother would shout from upstairs. "It's not natural, a man talking to a book."

"It talks to me," my father said. "It mocks me, it affronts me."

"You're losing your mind, Smallwood," my mother said. "It's like your dreams. It's not the book, it's the booze that's talking."

But as if he had the judge tied to a chair and was giving him a dressing-down in nightly instalments, my father walked in a circle about the kitchen, back and forth, haranguing the book. He had become fixated on things before but never for so long and never on a solid object like the book. It unnerved us all to hear him down there addressing the book as if it were some late-night visitor that none of us had ever seen, denouncing the judge, then himself as if *he* were the judge.

He missed two days of work in a row, lying on the daybed in the kitchen until nightfall, lying there while we ate, waiting for us to finish so he could have the table and start in on the book again. "You're going to be fired, Smallwood," my mother yelled at him, standing over the daybed. My father muttered insensibly and turned towards the wall. My mother sat at the table and put her face in her hands.

Long after I heard my father go to bed at the end of his third day home from work, long after I had fallen asleep myself, I awoke to the sound of someone creeping down the stairs. I heard the back door open. I looked out the window. There was my mother, in her nightgown, on the city-facing deck. She held the judge's book in both hands and stared at its cover. Then, with the book in the palm of one hand, she reared back and, as though she meant to land it on the roof of the judge's house, hurled it out into the darkness. I could dimly see it unfold in the wind, the pages flapping, and a couple of seconds later I heard it land with a dull thump far down the slope. My mother stood there silently staring after it, her chest heaving against the rail of the deck as if she were panicked to the point of breathlessness.

There was a low rumbling sound like far-off thunder that, from somewhere down the Brow, grew louder, then receded, though it continued for some time. She stood on her tiptoes, leaning out over the rail of the deck, craning her neck to see. Then, perhaps fearing the noise might have wakened the rest of us, she hurried back inside. Swiftly, almost silently, she went down the corridor and up the stairs, crossed the landing to her room and went back to bed.

The next morning, a Saturday, as we all sat at the breakfast table, my mother made an announcement. There had been an avalanche the night before, she said, an especially bad one that had started about a hundred feet below our house and had gone all the way to the bottom. A few fences had been flattened but, "thank God," she said, no houses had been hit, though the avalanche had cut a swath between two houses and now the cross-Brow road was blocked with snow.

"Right between the two houses, it went, can you imagine? Your father is going down there soon with the other men to help dig out the road."

My father, hungover, did not seem nearly so thrilled by the prospect.

"I'll go with you," I said.

Later, we went down the Brow and joined the men and boys who were going at the mound of snow from either end, working in towards the middle. Looking up at our house, I could see the path the avalanche had taken. The tops of the smaller trees had been snapped off and some larger ones had been uprooted altogether. In places, the hill had been scraped bare of even snow and ice, and the rocky yellow mud showed through. The avalanche, as my mother had said, had ploughed between two houses and left them undamaged, except that their facing sides were scraped, their clapboards splintered.

We had been at the site for about an hour when one of the men on the other side of the mound from us shouted that he had found something beneath the snow. "I think there's someone under here," he said. I stood and stared as everyone else hurried to where the man was standing and began shovelling furiously. "There," the man said, "there, that's someone's arm." An arm, elbow up, protruded from the snow. A couple of men took hold of it and tugged with all their might, without result. "He's froze solid, whoever he is," one of the men said.

Some of the fathers sent their boys away so they wouldn't see. The boys backed off reluctantly, staring at the arm. "Go home," one man roared, and two boys went racing up the hill, to break the news, I had no doubt. My father seemed to have forgotten I was there. They resumed shovelling. I kept watch from the other side of the mound. Eventually, they dug out and turned over the body of an old man, a "Mr. Mercer," who they said lived on the Brow by himself. His eyes and mouth were wide open, his mouth stuffed with snow.

"Old Mr. Mercer," my father said later that night. "Lived right at the bottom of the Brow."

"But the snow never went that far," my mother said, "and none of the houses was hit, you said so yourself this morning."

"He must have been out walking on the road," my father said. "Lived by himself. No one knew he was missing. Eighty-three years old he was. Imagine, to live to be eighty-three and then to go like that."

"He was stuffed with snow," I said, forgetting myself and the effect the words would have on my mother, so vividly did I recall how Mr. Mercer looked. "It was like he was force-fed snow right down to here." I indicated a spot between my stomach and my chest. His gullet stuffed with snow.

"Don't talk about it, Joe," my mother said. She sat down on the sofa looking frightened, stared wonder-struck into the fire. "Don't talk about it. It wasn't anybody's fault, you see. It was an accident, that's all it was."

"An act of God," my father said.

"No," my mother said. "No. It's not God's fault. What was Mr. Mercer doing out at that hour?"

"What hour?" my father said.

"Late, I mean," my mother said. "It must have been late. I — I didn't hear a thing."

For a while there was silence. Last night, a man had been buried alive a few hundred feet from where we slept. A Mr. Mercer, whom I had never heard of, a man of eighty-three, his gullet stuffed with snow, his mouth a round white O when they pulled him out.

I sat rigid on the sofa, unable to help wondering if it was possible that someone would put two and two together, waiting for some word of the book, waiting to hear that they had dug it up from under Mr. Mercer, waiting for a member of the constabulary to turn up on the doorstep, incriminating book in hand. I felt at once terrified and ridiculous. My mother sat in her chair, hunched into herself, hands clasped, and stared at the floor. My mother, the inadvertent agent of Mr. Mercer's death, the book bringing the avalanche down like a judgment on his, and her, head. It seemed almost funny, but I could not stop shaking.

After a while, my father got up and began rummaging around the front room and the kitchen, peering behind the sofa, lifting the cushions, searching the counter-top.

"Where's my Book?" my father said. "Did anybody see my Book?"

"How should I know where your book is?" my mother said.

"I left it there last night," he said, pointing at the coffee table by his chair.

"You were drunk last night," my mother said. "You might have left it anywhere."

"I left it on the coffee table," my father said, "right where I always leave it."

My mother got up, grabbed the poker by the fireplace and stabbed at the burning coals, sending sparks flying.

"There," she said, "there's your bloody book, what's left of it. I burned it last night, just like you burned the boots. I was sick of hearing about it, sick to death of it, so I burned it."

"You didn't," my father said.

"I did," my mother said. "I told you, I warned you; I was sick of hearing you go on about it. Joe goes to the trouble of taking your book to the judge to have it signed — " She struck at the embers again, sending more sparks flying.

"All right, all right," my father said, "don't burn the house down while you're at it." She threw down the poker and ran, crying, up the stairs. I was sure that my father would shout something before she reached the bedroom, but he didn't.

"She burned it," my father said, quietly. "She burned my Book. Now why would she do that?"

In the spring, when most of the snow was gone, I climbed down the Brow, following the path of the avalanche, surveying up close the damage it had done. I kept my eyes peeled for the book as well and had not edged more than a quarter of the way down the steep, rocky slope when I saw it perched bird-like among the lower branches of a large spruce tree. It lay open, face down, as if some reader had put it down like that to mark their place and had left the book behind. The front and the back cover were streaked to the point of illegibility with water stains, but the pages to which it had lain open for months were still legible, though some of the lines had run. The rest of the pages were saturated and fused together, and I dared not try to leaf through them for fear of tearing them. I gingerly began to close the two halves of the book to see if the spine would hold, and though it did, it was so deeply creased down the middle the book would not stay closed.

I took it home, smuggled it into the house, and tied it, lengthwise and crosswise, with a piece of ribbon, in the manner I had seen done with old books at Bishop Feild. Then I hid it in the shed out back. I would sneak out every day to check on it, as though I had some fugitive convalescent in the shed. It was two months before the book dried out. I tried to pry apart the pages using a straight razor, starting at the corners, where it was easiest to catch an edge, but they were still fused together.

I looked at the scrawl the judge had written and the "translation" of it that Prowse had composed, wondering how much time he had deliberated over what to write and how much his words had been based on what, if anything, he knew about my father. "Friends, as we might have been had we gone to school together."

"No harm done, I hope," Prowse had said.

And I had told him no.

Fielding's Condensed
History of Newfoundland

Chapter Three:

CROSSES AND MISERYES

Wynne sends back to Calvert over the next five years glowing reports of the success of the colony at Ferryland, saying they have "prospered to the admiration of all beholders."

In April 1623, heartened by Wynne's reports, Calvert applies for and is granted a charter to what he calls the province of Avalon, now fondly referred to as "the bog of Avalon."

After Wynne's return to England in 1627, Calvert, by this time so eager to see his colony he can contain himself no longer, sails to Ferryland, accompanied by his family, and spends much of the voyage reading and re-reading Vaughan's *The Golden Fleece*.

Shortly after his arrival, two of his ships are seized by pirates, whose long-established habit of plundering the colony Wynne had thought too insignificant to mention in his letters. After the winter of 1628–29, which his scurvy-ridden colonists assure him is not an especially bad one, but which causes Calvert to observe that "in this part of the world crosses and miseryes is my portion," he sails back to England.

Vaughan, meanwhile, known for his writerly reclusiveness, is nowhere to be found, though it is later discovered that he is writing *The Newlander's Cure*, a tract of advice for settlers about how to survive the perils of life in Newfoundland, which, though he has never experienced, he, being a writer, is able to imagine so vividly that other people who have never been to Newfoundland find the book convincing and it sells quite well.

Mundy Pond

FOR YEARS, THE ONLY religious symbol in the house had been a plain wooden cross above the stove. A token wooden cross, just in case. My parents hedging their bets.

She had never insisted we go to church, so everyone but me was quite surprised when suddenly my mother became a student of religions, "reading up" on them the way a stamp-collector might read up on stamps.

"What are you up to?" my father said, when she started bringing home catechisms, prayer books, hymn books, missals, Bibles of every denomination. They lay scattered all over the house, publications of the Church of England, the Church of England (Reformed Episcopal), the Presbyterian Church, the Congregational Church, the Salvation Army, the Baptists, the Pentecostals, the Seventh-Day Adventists, the Roman Catholic Church. She even read up on what she had formerly dismissed as "crank" religions, such as Christian Science and the Church of the Jehovah's Witnesses.

She did not just read, she went to services as well, often taking me with her because, in spite of her newly awakened curiosity, she seemed to be afraid to go alone. I believe I saw the inside of at least one church of every denomination in St. John's. My mother sat or stood, an aloofly critical observer, listening, watching not just the ministers but the congregations. She was like some dispassionately shrewd shopper who would forgo buying altogether if she had to.

She spoke most favourably of the New World evangelical religions.

"I am looking for the real thing, Joe," she said, "the genuine article, and I have yet to find it."

One Sunday afternoon, she told me she had a secret that she would tell me if I promised to keep it to myself. I thought I was about to hear about the book and Mr. Mercer. I promised and she told me she had been "convicted of sin" and would soon be "saved." She told me that she had, that past Tuesday, been converted in the Bethesda Mission of the Pentecostal faith on New Gower Street, the Ark, as it was called, and was to be, the following Sunday, one of forty baptized by immersion in a body of water on the heights of the city known as Mundy Pond.

"I don't know what came over me, Joe," she said. "I went to the mission just to see what all the fuss was about, everybody was talking about the Bethesda Mission and this woman, this Miss Garrigus, but something happened, Joe, something happened."

It must have been clear from my expression that I was frightened and did not want to hear what had happened, for she stopped speaking and turned away from me, putting her hands over her face. I wanted to keep my distance from this religious fervour for fear of coming down with it myself, losing myself to it. I was terrified of the idea that something more powerful than my own will might be moving me along, or would if I gave in to it. I could see already that she would never wholly be mine as she had been before and would never think of me as wholly hers.

The head of the Pentecostal Church in any diocese was called the overseer and had to be a man, but up to now no suitable men had been attracted to the Ark, so Miss Garrigus was unofficially the overseer, with the only sacrament she could not perform being marriage. My mother hung a large portrait photograph of Miss Garrigus above the front-room fireplace. In it, Miss Garrigus wore her hair up, piled high above her head, with a cleft down the middle so that it seemed to form the letter *M*. She wore a black dress with a perforated-lace collar, from which there hung a cross-shaped lace doily. One hand rested on a cane, the other held open on her lap a large black Bible. She stared out from the photograph disdainfully, unnervingly. She looked as though she could size you up in half a second, as though she had heard every excuse there was for loose living, moral weakness and Godlessness ten times over and could not be fooled. My father, looking at the photograph, called her Alice in Newfoundland.

Before Baptism Sunday, my mother took me to hear her preach. I wondered if she was hoping that I, too, might be converted.

Miss Garrigus was an "unrivalled revivalist" — her own assessment — from New England, who that night, in a sermon of which, for fervour and soul-stirring eloquence, my mother said she had never heard the equal, told her congregation that her own conversion had occurred in a dilapidated barn in Maine.

"Barn born I was," she said. "I have spent the last twenty years revivalling, travelling the world, preaching, baptizing and saving souls. But recently, at the age of fifty-two, I felt the call to Newfoundland; I felt compelled by the Lord to come to Newfoundland and establish here a mission called the Ark. The shape of Newfoundland began appearing in my dreams, first a vague shape that each night grew more distinct and began to look like some sort of island, though which one I could not tell. Eventually, it was Newfoundland I saw, though I did not know it, I did not know what Newfoundland looked like. I drew the shape I saw in my dreams and showed it to a friend, who told me I had drawn a map of Newfoundland, a map that was accurate in every way." Miss Garrigus then unscrolled the map she had drawn and showed it to the congregation and told how, upon consulting an

atlas, she had her "call to Newfoundland" confirmed beyond all
doubt when she saw that the capital of what was soon to be her
diocese was called St. John's, after St. John the Baptist and St.
John of the Gospels, who ended the Book of Revelations and
indeed the Bible as a whole with the watchword of the Pentecostal
Church, "Jesus is coming soon."

"Newfoundlanders, you are all New Found," she said,
"foundlings on the doorstep of salvation. You are here in my mission today because you have no church, because no other church
would take you in. Or should I say, because you would not be
taken in by other churches.

"There is a woman in this congregation," she said, "who has
been keeping to herself an awful secret, something she thinks no
one else knows, though someone does; something she believes
she will never be forgiven for, though she will. Hear me, my dear
woman; hear me, sister — I will not name you, for you know who
you are, and God knows, for God knows everything — God, if
only you will ask Him, will forgive you."

This "woman" could have been almost anybody, but I could
see why my mother had been so affected.

My mother was baptized in early June, in water from which the
last ice had melted but a month before. She arrived back home
on Sunday morning in a cart driven by a Pentecostal couple from
the Brow. She was wrapped in a blanket, her hair was matted to
her head and face and her clothes clung, still dripping water, to
her body.

"I'm saved, Joe," she said weakly, lips quivering. "I'm saved."

"Take care of your mother, boy," the man said gruffly. "Bless
you, Mrs. Smallwood," the woman said as they drove off. Their
ragged old horse clopped slowly down the hill.

I took my mother into the kitchen, where she sat shivering,
arms folded, looking like someone who had been saved, not from
damnation, but from drowning and had been hustled home before

she caught pneumonia. My sisters urged her to go upstairs with
them and change into something dry, but she looked as if she
hadn't heard them. Her eyes seemed focused inward, as though on
some vision she had had and was forbidden to reveal.

I don't know what happened to my mother that day on the
shore of Mundy Pond, but something did, something that altered
her forever. I vowed that if God Himself appeared to me, I would
assure Him that I would rather save myself than have Him do it.

Fielding's Condensed
History of Newfoundland

Chapter Four:

QUODLIBETS

Robert Hayman, who flees Cupids and helps start up and govern a colony called Bristol's Hope, from which he soon returns to England, writes a book called *Quodlibets*, a miscellany of odds and ends, a corrective to the nonsense that Vaughan is churning out, which unfortunately never appears in its original form but is amended, bowdlerized by Vaughan before publication. (Prowse, in his *History*, mistaking Vaughan's edition as authoritative, dismisses *Quodlibets* as "a curious medley." Prowse was completely taken in by Vaughan, to the point of believing that Vaughan travelled to Newfoundland and began a colony at Trepassey, when in fact he never in his life sailed far enough from England to lose sight of shore.)

We are in possession of one of the rare copies of the original *Quodlibets*. In the Vaughan edition, the following poem appears:

> The aire in Newfoundland is wholesome, good,
> The fire as sweet as any made of wood,
> The waters very rich, both salt and fresh,

The earth more rich, you know it is no lesse.
Where all are good, fire, water, earth and air,
What man made of these would not live there?

Here is the poem as it appears in Hayman's notebooks:

The aire in Newfoundland unwholesome is, not goode,
One cannot goe outside without a hoode.
The Waters, salt and fresh, they are like ice.
All who fall in perish in a trice.
Fire is rare there is so little woode,
For growing ought the earth it is no goode.
Against life do all the elements conspire.
Man made of water, earth, aire and fire,
Hearken not to William Vaughan, he is a liar.

Harold Dexter

THOUGH I LEFT Bishop Feild voluntarily, I would forever feel that I had failed there, and it would be the presiding failure of my life, the first in a list that, for a long time, seemed as if it would never end. When, in the last quarter of the century, I came to oversee the writing of my encyclopedia of Newfoundland, I would see to it that under the entry for Bishop Feild, no mention was made of me. The explanation I would give for this was that I did not deserve mention among those who, after graduating from Bishop Feild, went on to be Rhodes Scholars or otherwise distinguished themselves. The real reason was that I did not want Bishop Feild getting any credit for what I went on to do.

In 1915, I had what today would amount to a grade nine education. I would one day have a legion of learned men answering to me, deferring to me, terrified of me; Oxford-educated lawyers, Harvard-educated doctors, university professors, civil servants, all afraid to lift a pencil, and with good reason, without first clearing it with me. I would one day, in the House of Assembly, make the Sorbonne-educated leader of the opposition look like a fool. But I never stopped believing, deep down, that these men were my betters, my true superiors; nor, I now realize, did they.

My father was right. The Boot beckoned, but not just the Boot. Life back home beckoned, back in the old house among my ever-proliferating siblings. Since I had left for Bishop Feild, my mother had had two more children, bringing the total to ten, and another one was on the way. If there was any way I could avoid being one of twelve people in a three-bedroom house, I was going to take it, even if it meant the Boot. That every word that came out of my mother's mouth these days had to do with her new-found faith didn't help matters either.

My mother spoke to Fred Smallwood, and it was all but decided that I would work in the factory in some capacity. I was no more inclined than my father to spend my life making or selling boots and shoes, but for a while it seemed like the only way I could afford to move out.

Other young men were going off to war, but I was — inasmuch as a fifteen-year-old can *be* anything — a pacifist and had vowed that even if conscripted, I would not go.

I thought about leaving for the mainland. I knew that to get into the States I would need a certificate of health and TB-exonerating X-ray plates, so I went to see a doctor.

For all his sympathy, he could not restrain a smile at the sight of me when I took off my clothes in his examining room. I doubt that he had ever seen a less promising, more self-deluded applicant for emigration. I was myopic, already all but blind without my glasses. I weighed — he checked the scale a second time to make sure that he had read it right — a whopping eighty-seven pounds. I was malnourished, he said, even by Newfoundland standards. I half-expected him to tell me that at forty-five, my character was dangerously low. He determined, from listening to my lungs, that I was "pre-tubercular" and would almost certainly come down with tuberculosis unless I changed my eating habits. He prescribed fresh fruit, vegetables and meat as if these things were lacking from my diet only because of an oversight on my part, not because I could not afford them. I left his office wishing I had never been to see him.

I could not stop thinking of myself as "pre-tubercular." My mother had always been warning me against tuberculosis, telling me I had better watch out or I would wind up dead or "on my back" in the sanatorium, the San, we called it. The phrase was just vague enough to give the disease an extra-sinister dimension. I did not know that lying on your back was part of the cure for tuberculosis; I thought it was one of the symptoms, and so lived in dread of being overcome by the urge to lie supine. When I went to bed, I lay down prostrate or on my side and if, when I woke up, I was lying on my back, I feared the worst.

I walked aimlessly along Water Street, head down, brooding on my doom and was thus engaged when I all but bumped into someone.

"Excuse me," I muttered.

"The poet ponders," said a voice. Fielding's. She looked different than she had before, was dressed differently for one thing. She wore a black blazer over a white, high-necked blouse, a long pleated cotton skirt and black shoes with narrowly spaced buttons that started from the toes. It seemed to me that it suited her more than the dresses she used to wear at school, which I had always thought were fifty years out of date. (She still carried her cane. For the moment it was tucked, knob facing me, beneath her arm.) But something in her face had changed, too; its flesh seemed to have sagged slightly, as if something basic, something fundamental, had been extracted from her.

It did not matter to me who it was. I would have poured out my troubles to the first person who would listen and it never occurred to me that, all things considered, she might be disinclined to. I told her about the doctor's prognosis and about the looming of the Boot. When I was finished, she said she thought she had a solution to both my problems.

She told me that her father, the doctor, had those patients of his who needed to gain weight drink one bottle of Pabst Blue Ribbon Yeast Beer per day for 120 days. I thought she was joking, but she assured me that she was not and said we could go see her father about it if I liked. I demurred.

"Some of his patients already have tuberculosis and it works for them," Fielding said. I reminded her that I was not old enough to drink.

"Nor am I," she said, raising from the pocket of her jacket, just far enough so I could see it, a gleaming silver flask. I was taken aback.

"Don't let anyone see that," I said. She pursed her lips with scorn and regarded me as if she had not seen my like before. I began to make objections, but she dismissed them with a wave of her hand. She told me she knew how we could get the beer.

"You've got to start right away," she said, "or you won't get to 120 before Prohibition starts." A prohibition bill had already been passed in the House of Assembly and was to come into effect 127 days from now, she said, which meant I had to get started within the week.

I told her there was no way I could do this while I lived at home, and no way I could afford to move away from home until I got a job.

"Follow me," Fielding said. We walked wordlessly, side by side, up the hill to Duckworth Street, where Fielding pointed at the window of the *Evening Telegram* and an ad that said Court Reporter Wanted.

"Meet me here a week from now at nine p.m. and we'll get you that body-weight-augmenting beer," Fielding said. "Thus is Smallwood saved by Fielding from tuberculosis and the Boot."

She walked off before I could — well, not thank her, for I was not sure yet that thanks were in order, that anything would come of either the beer or the job that I was about to apply for. I went inside and I assumed I must have been the first to inquire about the job, for I had no sooner done so than I was told that it was mine and that I would start in two weeks.

When I told my mother that night that I was moving out and had found a little room in a boarding-house on Duckworth Street, she jumped up and started walking around the room, shaking her head as if she could already see me, alone, sitting, shoulders slumped, on some bed, heartbroken by journalism in my little room on Duckworth Street.

"I'll be able to get more work done if I'm on my own," I said. "And I'll be closer to where I'll be working. I'll have more money to give to you to help out with the children." My mother, though she was not so naive as to be swayed by my arguments (if I had to pay room and board, how much money could I give her?), saw that my mind was made up and gave me her blessing.

The first thing I did on moving into the boarding-house was tack up an oilcloth map of Newfoundland, not including Labrador, since it was not clear at that time, and would not be until 1927, where Labrador left off and Quebec began. I had bought it from a man who assured me that unlike paper maps, it would last forever and would never get dirty, for all you had to do was wipe it clean with a wet cloth. He cited as evidence of its durability and stain-resistantness the fact that its previous owners had used it as a table-cloth. "Ate off it for years," he said. "You'd never say it to look at it, would you?" It was quite large and I suspected that in the days before it became a tablecloth, it had been used in a schoolroom somewhere where a knowledge of Newfoundland geography was more highly prized than it was at Bishop Feild.

Every morning, before work, using the oilcloth as my model, I drew the map of Newfoundland. My goal was to be able to draw it as well from memory as I could draw the map of England. For the longest while, after I began drawing Newfoundland, it was the map of England I saw when I closed my eyes at night, as though my mind were sending forth this primary shape by way of protest — which it needn't have bothered doing, since England had been so early imprinted on my brain that no amount of drawing other maps could supplant it. Newfoundland was far more difficult to draw than England, what with its half-dozen major peninsulas, themselves endlessly peninsulated, and its infinity of bays and inlets. Perhaps this was the point my mind was trying to make; I had mastered a perfectly good map already, why was I bothering with another, more complicated one? I must have drawn the map of Newfoundland from memory a thousand times before I stopped, admitting to myself that I would get no better at it. My last maps, drawn when I was twenty, are nowhere near as good as the maps of England I drew when I was twelve.

A week after our first meeting, Fielding and I met again in front of the *Telegram* at nine at night. I could not afford to buy the beer all at once, so I decided to buy it in five batches of twenty-four. I was surprised that Fielding would have any dealings with the sort of man we got it from, an all-but-toothless fellow in a ragged overcoat whom we met at the back of a warehouse on the waterfront. He kept looking nervously around while we completed our transaction. I gave him twenty-five cents, he handed me a wooden case that he said contained the beer, though it was labelled Ginger Ale. When he took his hands away and left me holding it, it dragged me to the ground. Even with Fielding holding one end, it took all the strength I had to straighten up, and even then my arms were shaking. "Hope you don't have to go too far," the toothless fellow said. I shook my head. "If the 'Stab stops ya," he said, "don't say where ya got it, if ya knows what's good for ya." We lugged it, stopping to rest now and then, up the hill to my boarding-house.

With the door and the curtains closed, we opened the wooden case, which did, indeed, contain Pabst Blue Ribbon Yeast Beer. "There you are," Fielding said. She took her silver flask out of her pocket.

"We can't have you drinking alone," she said, unscrewing the stopper and taking a pull on the flask.

"What's in that, anyway?" I said.

"Scotch," she said. We sat at my little table. She drank from her flask and I drank my first, tuberculosis-proofing bottle of beer, all but gagging on the taste. It was all I could do to drink the whole bottle and I was as drunk afterwards as I ever would be in my life, not to mention queasy. The only thing that kept me from throwing up was Fielding telling me that if I did, I would have to drink another bottle. I thought about drinking a beer a day for 120 days and wondered if, at the end of it, regardless of what my weight might be, I would have acquired, or awakened, since it might be in my blood, my father's taste for alcohol. It seems ridiculous when I think about it now, but to a boy not quite sixteen, it was a real dilemma: which form of doom should I risk, alcoholism or tuberculosis? To my relief, the taste of beer did not grow on me. I never, after finishing one, had the slightest inclination to start another.

I hung a little slate on my wall and wrote on it in chalk the number 119. Thus began the countdown. Every night, after I choked down another beer, I erased the old number and wrote in the new one, and every tenth beer I weighed myself, only to find that I had not gained an ounce. Still, I kept at it, thinking that perhaps I would gain weight only after drinking all the beer, that after the consumption of beer number 120, presumably a scientifically arrived at number, some sort of weight-gaining mechanism in my body would kick in. It did not. At the end of Fielding's prescription, I had not gained an ounce.

"Smallwood," she said, when I confronted her with the news, "I believe you would not gain weight if you consumed a cow a day while lolling in a hammock."

That first night at my boarding-house, drunk on half a beer and wondering how in God's name I was going to choke down the other half, I brought up the matter of the letter to the *Morning Post* and Fielding's aborted attempt to frame me for writing it.

"That was a silly thing to do, Fielding," I said. She agreed that it was.

"Wanted to get back at you," she said. "And I believe I may have been a little drunk when I conceived my plan."

"Drunk?" I said. "You were drunk? You were only fifteen."

"Actually," she said, "I was seventeen. I'm eighteen now. Didn't start school until I was seven, nearly eight."

"So what have you been up to since?" I said.

"Oh, not much," she said. "My father wants me to go to school abroad, then go to college at some place like Mount Allison in Nova Scotia. But I think I've had all the schooling I can stand."

"Me, too," I said, pushing the beer away from me as if she had said it was beer she'd had enough of. She pushed it back to me.

"Drink up," she said. "Someday you'll thank me for it."

Court stories were among the most widely read in any St. John's newspaper, but for reasons that I would soon discover, the court beat did not enjoy a corresponding popularity among reporters.

The courthouse was a massive Gothic stone structure built into the side of a hill, with its front entrance on Water Street and its rear entrance a hundred feet up the slope on Duckworth Street. Consequently, about half of it was underground, and most of it was off-limits to reporters. Each of its four levels was an endless maze of courtrooms, cloakrooms, judge's chambers, registries, jury rooms, clerk's offices and, in the catacomb-like basements, the holding cells from which, by way of a series of tunnel-like stairways, prisoners in loudly clanking chains were brought up to appear before the bar. In the courtroom, you could hear them ascending long before the admitting door opened.

There were six dailies in St. John's at the time, and all of them had regular court reporters. Among the other five reporters was one from the *Daily News* who used the pseudonymous byline of Harold Dexter.

Harold Dexter turned out to be Fielding. I met her in the little room, not much bigger than a closet, that was set aside for the press.

"Hello, Smallwood," she said, not looking up from the copy of the *News* that she was reading. She pulled from the inner pocket of her jacket her silver flask and extended it to me.

"For God's sake," I said, looking around to see if anyone had noticed. No one had. She shrugged, took a long drink from the flask, then put it back in her pocket. She then took out of another pocket, unwrapped and popped into her mouth, a peppermint candy.

"You might have told me," I said.

She shrugged.

Fielding was regarded with a kind of irony-laden fondness by the lawyers. I could tell they knew her history, though they never mentioned it. One of them by lineage, if not by gender or profession, she was to them a kind of mascot. They loved indulging her apparent belief that wit could compensate for her gender and for her failure at school and put her on a par with them, make up for the fact that she, the daughter of a doctor, had had to settle for making her own living and doing it by, of all things, writing for a newspaper.

"What do you make of us lawyers, Fielding?" a beefy, prosperous-looking lawyer named Sharpe asked her one day.

"If you were paid by the acquittal, Sharpe, you'd be skinnier than Smallwood here," Fielding said, and there was a great burst of guffaws from outside the press room, Sharpe laughing loudest of all, as if the impotence of Fielding's wit was the real joke.

"Tell your father I said hello," said Sharpe.

"I'll run right out and tell him now," said Fielding, to another burst of laughter. She was facing me, back to them, and her expression belied her tone of voice, which was that of banter between rival professionals. She looked at me and smiled.

Fielding's Condensed
History of Newfoundland

Chapter Five:

KIRKE

Calvert is succeeded at Ferryland by David Kirke.

Kirke spends most of the year 1627 expelling the French from Canada. Having captured all their possessions in that country, he returns victorious to England, where Charles I congratulates him on a job well done, then tells him that under the terms of a treaty he has just signed, every inch of Canada that Kirke took from the French has been returned to them.

Enraged, livid, Kirke wonders if the king has given any thought to how the widows of the men who died liberating Canada will take this news. He even considers saying so out loud someday.

Kirke is humiliated at court and Charles feels sorry for him, so much so that he waits only six years before knighting him for his services, which unfortunately has the effect of bringing upon Kirke even more humiliation. Eventually, the presence of Kirke at court makes Charles feel foolish, so he grants him a charter to the entire island of Newfoundland.

In 1638, Kirke moves with his family to Newfoundland and settles at Ferryland. Within a year, he alienates the planters by forbidding them, on the king's orders, to erect any structure within six miles of the shore, then placates them and solves the problem of piracy by declaring that a fort is not a structure. Soon, everyone is building forts.

Civil war breaks out in England, diverting attention away from Newfoundland for about a decade, during which Kirke, anticipating that a return to government by monarchy is imminent in England, allies with Prince Rupert, cousin of the king, and transforms Ferryland into a royalist stronghold, at the same time amassing great sums of money by forcing the Cromwell-supporting migratory fishermen to pay him taxes and by seizing all the best fishing grounds for himself.

He has taverns built and spends his nights in them, mocking Cromwell. Once again, however, the king disappoints him by getting himself executed and Kirke is soon recalled to England, where he is such a figure of fun that Cromwell spares his life.

The Docks

I BEGGED MY WAY off the court beat after a few months. I convinced the publisher of the *Telegram*, who each year purchased several berths on the S.S. *Newfoundland* and sold them to sealers in exchange for a percentage of their share, to let me have a berth so that I could write about what life was like on board a sealing ship. My publisher worked out an arrangement with the *Newfoundland*'s captain, Westbury Kean, whereby I would file stories every day using the ship's telegrapher. Kean, saying he had no intention of being held responsible for anything that might happen to a boy who had never been off dry land in his life, said that I would not be allowed to go out on the ice but could watch the hunt from on board through binoculars. And he would read each day's story and convey it in person to the telegrapher to make sure nothing was published that reflected badly on him or his crew.

My family came out to see me off and to witness the annual blessing of the sealing fleet by clergy of all denominations. Miss Garrigus was the only woman among them. As the clergy, their voices magnified by megaphones, prayed God to safeguard the officers and crew of the fleet and to reward them for their labour with a bountiful harvest, I stood, imitating the crew, in the rigging of the S.S. *Newfoundland*, though not as high up as most of them were. There must have been ten thousand people gathered down below, jammed to the water's edge to see the fleet, which filled the harbour. Even with the vessels moored nose in, there was not enough room at dockside for all of them, so the rest had to anchor in mid-harbour, facing every which way. The pilot boats scooted about trying to organize the fleet's departure.

When the blessing concluded, the crowd cheered, and from where we stood we waved our hats. The first of the sealing fleet followed the pilot boats. I watched from the rigging of the *Newfoundland* as the crowd ran *en masse* along the apron to join another crowd already gathered on the heights of Signal Hill, where they would watch the fleet make its way towards the ice floes of the northeast coast. As each sealing vessel cleared the Narrows, the noon-day gun on Signal Hill was fired, a blast that echoed back and forth between the north and south side of the city. And also, each of the ships, as it cleared the Narrows, unfurled its expansive sails and was suddenly transformed to white. There came up to me from below, mixed with the old smell of the bilge-water harbour, the new smell of diesel oil from the engines of the biggest steamships. Oil and coal and sail together could barely move these boats now when they were empty of everything but men and boys. They would come back weighted down to the gunnels, inching along with their cargoes of seal pelts and whitecoats.

At an order from Captain Kean to hoist the sails, I climbed down from the rigging. The men of the *Newfoundland* pitched in, straining on the ropes, in some cases jumping and hanging in mid-air to make a sail unfurl. A light cold rain was falling but there was not much wind. Still, as the sails caught the breeze, the massive boom came swinging round and the men ducked expertly beneath it as a sealer who shouted "Low on deck" pulled me down beside him just in time. I looked up. The great soot-begrimed expanse of canvas flapped loudly overhead, black smoke billowed backwards from the stack below midship and the *Newfoundland* picked up speed as it bore down on the ice outside the Narrows.

The crew was divided into four groups, watches they were called. I was assigned, at my request, to the fourth watch, which I was told rose at four in the morning. I fancied that the daily routine of this watch would most nearly resemble my own. Each watch was assigned a master, who supervised the men on and off the ship.

There were fathers and sons, brothers, in-laws, friends, little factions with distinctive accents, in some cases distinctively incomprehensible ones, who talked exclusively among themselves. There were a few "youngsters," young men my age on their first voyage to the ice, eager to prove they could keep up with the older men and incredulous with scorn when they heard of my confinement to the ship.

I had been worried how I would be received among the sealers. Most of them did not begrudge me having it "easy," as it seemed to them I did. On the contrary, one of the older men said quite sincerely that it was a credit to me that I had made something of myself. Most regarded me with a kind of shy awe when they heard what I was doing. They could not read or write and had never met someone whom they perceived to be the epitome of reading and writing, a newspaper man.

"What did ya write about us today, now?" they asked me the first few days, as we made our way through the ice to the whelping grounds. I would read them what I wrote.

"Sher if yer not goin' over de side of 'er," a young fellow from Catalina said, "'ow 're ya gonna know what goes on out on dee ice?" They all laughed when I took out from beneath my pillow my binoculars and scanned the sleeping quarters as I planned to scan the ice each day.

The sealers wore thick-soled leather boots, many of which bore the name of Smallwood. These boots were studded with sharp spikes called sparables. They dressed in thick woollen underwear and trousers and put on as many tattered shirts and guernseys as they could, but no overcoats, for they would have been too much of an encumbrance. Each of them had a set of oil clothes but never wore them or even took them when they left the ship unless it looked like it might rain or snow. They tracked out to the whelping grounds with their gaffs held horizontally like staffs in case the ice gave way beneath their feet.

From as high up in the rigging as I dared to go, I watched them work, swinging their sharp-pointed gaffs like pickaxes, killing the seals and swiftly pelting them with knives that gleamed like razors in the sun. Beginning a few hundred feet from the ship and extending as far as I could see, the ice was red with blood. They dragged piles of pelts back along the same route each time, so that a single trail of gore led like a road from the blood field to the ship. Most of the carcasses were left behind and only the pelts, the fat-lined fur, brought back to the ship. An ice-field after a day's cull was littered for miles with carcasses, which the next day were set upon by a flock of seagulls and other birds that followed us throughout the voyage.

Everywhere there were patches of open water, massive pools of green slush that the sealers crossed, "copied," by jumping without hesitation from one floating ice pan to the next, often having to snag a pan with a gaff to pull it closer to them. The few that fell in and were hauled out hurried back to the ship, their clothing frozen stiff by the time they arrived.

My watch, which hit the ice at five in the morning, did not come back to the ship until eight at night. I was not used to a workday near that long, and so I was incredulous when I found out that they had several more hours of work to do on board before they were through.

They gathered fresh ice for drinking water, covered the pelts, shifted coal from the hold to the bunkers near the engine room, disposed of the ash from the coal already burnt, tipped great cauldrons of it over the side.

At about eleven, they were at last allowed to eat, which they did as swiftly as possible, for there was by this time barely four hours before their watch began again. They cooked seal meat over a barrel that, with its top cut off, formed a kind of spit. The only part of their meal I could not bring myself to eat was "lop scouse," half oatmeal gruel, half seal stew, which they dipped into with rock-hard cakes of "tack" bread, washing the whole vile mixture down with tea.

The last thing before bed, they filled the ship's lanterns with seal oil, the smoke from which smelled faintly fish-like and burned my eyes so badly that I lay face down in my pillow, coming up to breathe only when I had to.

They crawled into their makeshift wooden bunks and most of them were instantly asleep, which was a blessing, for unlike me they seemed not to notice that our sleeping quarters hung so heavy with coal dust it was barely possible to breathe. The floors, their bunks, their clothing, which they did not waste sleeping time by changing out of, were smeared with blood, fat, soot, ashes, coal dust.

While the fourth watch slept, the other watches worked. There was never a time when the ship was idle. The hatch by which the coal was raised up from the hold passed within a few feet of the bunks, which were therefore exposed to the open sky and whatever might be falling from it. By way of another hatch, which also went straight past our bunks but on the other side, seal pelts were dropped down to the second hold, some falling off the chute and straight into the bunks of the sealers, who were so deep in sleep they did not stir and often woke up in the morning covered with the bloody pelts.

All night long as I lay in my bunk, coal went up and pelts came down, the coal winch grinding loudly, the seal pelts spattering gore everywhere as they went sliding down the chute.

I went three full nights without a wink of sleep and finally decided that I would sleep during the afternoon, when all the watches overlapped, when the fourth watch was most likely to be out of range of my binoculars and when the sleeping quarters were empty and the coal crank and the pelt chute in least use.

At night, I lay awake on my bunk, as did some of the sealers who, in spite of their exhaustion or perhaps because of it, could not get to sleep. I think some of them resisted sleep just to experience the luxury of idleness, of doing nothing but lying on their bunks while others worked. They lay with their hands behind their heads as, in the darkness, they puffed reflectively on cigarettes or pipes. They cocked their heads in acknowledgment when they saw me looking at them, but that was all. Despite all the noise, talking was forbidden after midnight.

Sometimes the men were on the ice until well into the night, as long as there were enough seals to keep all the watches busy at once. I remember the eerie sight of the sealers setting out across the ice bearing lanterns and torches. On each spotlit patch of ice, one sealer, crouching, held a torch that illuminated a seal over which another sealer stood with gaff upraised.

When enough seals had been killed to sustain them, bonfires were built with carcasses doused with seal oil until the air was filled with the smell of roasting seal meat, on which the men covertly feasted while they worked. It was an elemental, soul-disturbing sight, yet I longed to somehow be a part of it, to feel something other than the planks of the S.S. *Newfoundland* beneath my feet. But Captain Kean was adamant that if I set foot on the ice, I would no longer have the use of his telegrapher.

It was just as well, I decided. Even if I were to forsake my purpose for coming and go over the side, I would have no idea what to do and would either soon look foolish or be dead, never having copied in my life. I might wind up on some strand of ice and have to be rescued, or have a gaff thrust in my hand and be unable to kill a seal, to raise the gaff and bring it down with the kind of resolve necessary to the task. Captain Kean was right. Better I confine myself to some pursuit where words alone would do and leave to others, like these men, the deeds that I would write about.

I sat on the gunnels, one hand on a rope lest I fall over, a puny, bespectacled spectator. And out of the lantern-lit darkness came the sound of the seals, a sound as if a hundred yelping hounds had flushed a fox.

I wrote stories that made sealing sound like hard but wholesome work. It was the only kind of story I could get by Captain Kean. But the men didn't seem to mind. They listened intently when I read aloud and afterwards said, "That was very good, sir, very good," as if I had described their life exactly as it was. Or, as I eventually realized, as if they believed the point of writing was to render the world in a manner so benign that to read about it would be a pleasant way to pass the time. Because I was the one writing the stories, and because I was not sure how they would take it, I did not try to set them straight.

They were too tired to pay much attention to me anyway, too caught up in the delirium of sealing, the endless hours of work, the noise and confinement of the ship, which provided only the illusion of comfort and asylum, the stark white icescape that, if not for their wooden goggles, would have blinded them. At bedtime, bottles of patent medicine were passed around, but that was all the drinking that was done. You could not drink much and hope to keep up the pace, let alone survive. They appeared to be caught up in some profound reflection as they ate and as they drank their tea, though I doubt they had the energy to sustain a line of thought.

I got to know barely a dozen of them by name before the time for learning names was over. But they all knew my name, and they still smiled when their eyes met mine. They liked to have in their midst a kind of mascot layabout from whose life of ease they could derive some vicarious relief.

I think they were whelmed into self-absorption in part from being the agents of a slaughter of such magnitude, killing constantly from sun-up past sundown. This was not like fishing, which is what most of them did the rest of the working year, not a mass capture of insensible creatures from another element. The death of each seal was individual, the result of a single act committed by a single person at close quarters, an act in which I was certain they took no joy and which they would happily have forsaken if to do so would not also have meant forsaking the few pennies that stood between their families and starvation. "Over the side," Captain Kean roared when a patch of seals was spotted, and over the gunnels with their gaffs the sealers went. I had the feeling it was an order they would no more have refused than they would an order to attack in time of war.

The storm came up about noon, seven hours after the men of the fourth watch hit the ice. I saw it coming, a slow encroachment of white so gradual that it blended with the sky and looked like fog. The captain saw it, too, and sent out a party of six men to find the fourth watch. At first there was not much wind, just heavy snow and sleet, ice pellets clicking and gathering like rock-salt on the deck. I watched the six men as they followed the gore-trail out of sight. The storm worsened quickly, as the wind, having changed direction several times, blew with great conviction from the east. An hour later, the search party returned, without the watch. The storm was in so close, I did not see them or hear them until they were a few feet from the rail.

The first mate took me below, telling me I could stay with his watch until it was time to bunk down, when I would have to go to my own watch as there were no spare berths in any of the others. I didn't complain that this would mean sleeping alone in quarters that could hold a hundred men, or ask him why he could not send half the men from his watch down to mine. I knew he did not want me to be with the men unless he, or one of the mates in front of whom they would not dare speak their minds, was there as well.

We were too far from open water for the wind to cause enough turbulence beneath the ice to rock the ship, but the entire ice-field drifted west until, its far edge having hit the land that was sixty miles away, it could go no farther and it began to press together and to close about the ship, whose wooden hull groaned and creaked and at times snapped loudly as if it were giving way, though as none of the sealers looked too concerned, I pretended not to be. For the first time on the voyage, the hatch was closed and it was warm enough in the ship to wear what you would around the house. The sealers stripped down to their coveralls, drank tea, smoked cigarettes. For the first time, too, the din of the coal crank and the sound of seal pelts chuting down into the hold stopped. There was not much talking done. Everyone knew the fourth watch was not on board. There was speculation, stifled by the first mate, that they might have made it to the *Stephano*, a ship skippered by Captain Westbury's father, Abe Kean. But this ship had no telegraph, so there was no way to be sure.

The first mate declared lights out at nine o'clock. If the storm let up, he said, a search might start as soon as three.

I went back to the sleeping quarters of the fourth watch, the door of which the first mate closed emphatically behind me as if to say, "Stay put."

I sat on my bunk. At first, all I could hear was the droning of the wind, which at times rose to a shrieking whistle and stayed that way for minutes, a gust so long you forgot it was a gust until it passed. Then I was able to make out the strange noise the rigging ropes made at full vibration, a whirring that would have made it impossible to sleep even had I not been wondering where the men and boys might be.

―――――――

FIELDING'S JOURNAL, MARCH 30, 1916

Dear Smallwood:

You may be safer in that ship than I am in this house. You must be warmer, for a ship as drafty as this house would sink in seconds.

The electric lights are out. And it's freezing. Because it's not safe to light the fires, all the chimney flues are closed. With each upsurge of the wind, the lantern flickers and the papers on my desk, though weighted down, turn up at the corners.

I asked my father if he thought the sealing fleet was safe. He said that as far as he knew, the ice-field extended for a hundred miles from shore, so it was doubtful that any of the ships were riding out the storm in open water.

But so many ships have sunk because their hulls were crushed by ice. What if you were forced to abandon ship? You might as well be sheltering from fire.

There seems to be no limit to how hard the wind can blow. It's hard to imagine a wind like this with nothing to impede it, no hills, buildings, houses, trees; hard to imagine it screaming along unresisted for a hundred miles or more before it hits your ship.

Sealing ships often batten down and wait out storms like this, my father told me. "Why are you suddenly so concerned about the sealing fleet, anyway?" he said.

He doesn't know. I hardly know myself. I snapped at him, asked him how any decent person could be so unconcerned. "There's nothing I can do for them," he said.

There's nothing I can do either. I will not be bullied into praying. Why would any God raise such a storm? Can it be that you will perish in a storm at sea before the age of twenty? Why should the wind blow so hard if all it wants to do is sink a ship?

I can't believe you are out there.

I can't believe anyone is out there on the ice tonight.

I spent three days like this, with the first mate's watch from morning until nine at night and alone from nine until morning. During the day, there was a whiteness as absolute, as obliterative, as pitch-black darkness. No one was allowed on deck for even there it was possible to lose your way. The obliterations alternated, white and dark and white and dark again.

On the third day, when we looked through the porthole at mid-morning, we saw something other than the single shade of white we had become accustomed to — the many subtle shades of white that comprised the ice-field.

It was several hours more before the master watch came down and told me to go to my sleeping quarters.

I did as he said. I heard the boiler being fired up and felt the ship begin to move through the ice pack, which had loosened because the wind had changed.

About three o'clock in the afternoon, they found what they were looking for. Far off on the ice, I saw a couple of dozen men trudging about in a circle. The shout no sooner went up that the men of the *Newfoundland* were found than the ship's whistle shrieked in celebration. I looked out through the porthole, but that side of the ship was at too oblique an angle to the rescue site. As the ship ploughed on through the ice, however, the stem slowly drifted starboard and I was able to see round the curvature of the hull. The men were not a hundred feet away, still tramping in a circle as if even the ship's whistle had not roused them, each man with his hand on the shoulder of the man in front. They were so coated in snow I could not tell what they were wearing or make out their faces, which were rimed with frost. Most of them were limping badly; outside the circle was a man walking an even slower circle of his own and at the same time holding beneath the armpits another man whose feet made a feeble step now and then but otherwise dragged behind him on the ice.

As we drew closer to them, some of them at last noticed the ship and stopped walking. Some dropped to their knees or toppled over onto their backs, others stared as if they doubted that what they saw was real. The crew poured over the side and led the seal-ers or carried them on stretchers to the ship.

We moved on. I had counted twenty-three men. That left eighty unaccounted for. I stayed at the porthole. The ship came hard about, and for half an hour we crashed on through the ice, then stopped again.

My heart rose when I saw what looked to be the balance of the crew standing on a mile-wide ice pan in the near distance. From on deck, there were shouts of "Hurray" and footsteps thumped on the ceiling overhead as once again the ship's whistle sounded.

Gradually we drew up close to the ice pan. Mooring lines with grapnels on the end were cast onto the ice, and the pan was slowly pulled towards the ship until it thumped against it.

For several minutes after the ship stopped, no one disembarked. I saw what I had not been able to through my binoculars: that these were not survivors but a strange statuary of the dead. I was not repulsed by what I saw. I could not take my eyes away.

Two men knelt side by side, one man with his arm around the other, whose head was resting on his shoulder in a pose of tenderness between two men that I had never seen in life.

Three men stood huddled in a circle, arms about each other's shoulders, heads together like schoolboys conferring on a football field.

A man stood hugging himself, his hands on his arms, shoulders hunched, in the manner of someone who has momentarily stepped out of his house into the cold in shirtsleeves to bid a guest goodbye.

One man knelt, sitting back on his heels, while another stood behind him, his hands on his shoulders, as if they were posing for a photograph.

Two sealers stood in a fierce embrace, the taller man with both arms wrapped round the other, holding him against his chest, while the arms of the shorter man hung rigid at his sides.

Four men lay on their stomachs side by side, all facing the same way as if they had lain down for some purpose or agreed together that they would.

Only a few men knelt or lay alone, perhaps those who had lasted longer than the others.

One man sat by himself, his elbows resting on his drawn-up knees, his bare hands frozen to his face.

The storm had started out as freezing rain. A man who must have been among the first to fall lay encased within a mould of silver thaw.

I later learned that some who, in their delirium, thought they saw a light ran off in pursuit of it and were never found.

Joined in some manner of embrace were men who before this journey to the ice had never met, men who had outlasted those they knew best and for warmth or fellowship in death embraced some stranger.

They were all there, the boys too young and the men too old, who to get a berth had lied about their ages or agreed to half a share; boys younger than me and men older than my father.

Perhaps, too tired to walk but still standing, they had been buried in snow that had blown away when the storm let up, by which time they were rooted in the ice that lay like pedestals about their feet.

Some men lay in the lee of a low shelter they had managed to erect, a wall of ice and snow that was barely three feet high.

I recognized a few of them, but only because of some distinctive article of clothing, like the orange watch cap of the man who every morning made the tea. He lay on his side, his knees drawn up almost to his chest, his head resting on his hands, which were clasped in a prayer-like pillow, palm to palm.

They had been transformed by their passion on the ice. Each had assumed in death some posture emblematic of his life. Or else they were refined to men that no one knew, as if in each face and posture was inscrutably depicted the essence of the person they had been.

Everywhere lay evidence of futile acts of courage and self-sacrifice. A man stripped down to his undershirt and coveralls lay prone beside a boy bulked out in two sets of clothes.

In various places the snow was scorched where small fires had been lit. From each a smudge of soot trailed out, a stain left from the smoke that had been flattened by the wind.

I did not want to see them moved or see the scene disturbed. I closed the porthole and sat down on my bunk.

I heard above the wind and the droning of the ropes the sound of ice being hacked and chopped. I heard the coal crank of the hatch at the far end of the ship lurch into motion. The chopping and shouting and winching of the crank went on for hours. When it stopped, I considered opening the porthole but could not bring myself to do it.

I looked around the sleeping quarters at all the empty bunks. Not all the men had been lost. Not every bunk represented a man who would not be going home. It was impossible to tell which ones did. Three-quarters of them did, but I didn't know which ones. Except for the bunk of the man who made the tea.

Something deep within me, which I hadn't known was there, gave way. My body grieved but not my mind. I felt as though someone who was sitting right beside me was crying, and though I wanted to console him, I could not.

I felt the ship reach open water. The grinding of the ice against the hull ceased suddenly, the keel rocked from side to side until it balanced and we moved smoothly on. I got up and pounded on the door to be let out. As if, in all the commotion, I had been forgotten, I heard the sound of footsteps running. The hatch slid open and I saw the sky.

The wind was northerly, offshore, so we could smell the land despite the fresh fall of snow. I had never sailed beyond the smell of the land before and so had never sailed back into it like this. Six weeks we had been at sea. A week longer than it took Cabot to sail from Bristol to Cape Bonavista. I could not only smell the land but also taste it in the air, the coppery metallic taste of rock borne by the wind across the ice. And soon I could smell the city and see the blue haze of woodsmoke in the sky. The Basilica of St. John the Baptist loomed up from the cluster of the buildings on the hill. I could not believe that the city and the ice were of one world. The city looked so reasonable, so plausible, a site in which atrocities not only did not take place, but which also somehow prevented them from taking place elsewhere.

I looked up and saw the signalman waving his flags from his bunker on the hill above the Narrows, waving to the keeper of the lighthouse at Fort Amherst and to the captains of the pilot boats. The foghorn blew from then until we docked, and minutes after the foghorn started the bells of both basilicas began to ring.

Word that we had picked up the men of the S.S. *Newfoundland* reached St. John's just hours before we arrived early in the afternoon. No one knew at that point how many had died. It was known only that some had survived and some had not. There were rumours, too: one that the *Newfoundland* alone had ridden out the storm, and that on board her were men who were saved from other ships. Women who did not know their husbands had died consoled women whose husbands had survived.

Our sails were down, our flags at half-mast as we steamed slowly through the ice, leaving behind us a wake of open water that stretched for miles. I stood by myself on deck. Above me, in the massive scaffolding of masts and spars and rigging ropes, were the small figures of men motionless and stark against the sky, a uniformly grey, after-storm sky that would persist for days. They stood on the horizontal spars as we had after the blessing of the fleet, a hundred feet at least above the ice, hands gripping the rope ladders in which other men sat as though on children's swings. Black smoke billowed from the towering smokestack halfway between mid-ship and the stern. The ship was under full throttle but barely moving, so thick and compressed was the ice. But at last we broke through the raft ice near the Narrows. The men in the rigging, who at this point would normally have clambered down, remained aloft.

Twice as many people as had turned out for the blessing of the fleet were on the waterfront. It looked as if the entire population of the island, ordered to evacuate, were awaiting the arrival of some massive ship. They had come ill-dressed from their row houses on the heights, down hills so steep that even when the ground was bare you could hardly keep from running. On this day it was so slippery that it was better to walk up to your knees in snow than risk the streets. They had come well-dressed from the valley sides and from the homes along the city streams, and in leather aprons and overalls from the factories of Water Street and the cod-crammed stores of Harbour Drive. There were so many people that some could get no closer to the harbour than the "coves," the little streets that from Water Street led down to the apron. They stood on rooftops, on ledges, hung out of windows in threes and fours.

We docked at the berth the pilot-boat captains had cleared when they heard the ship was coming. Even the sheltered harbour was partly clogged with ice because of the storm, but a passage had been cleared from the Narrows to the apron.

The crowd was eerily silent at first, but all at once there was an anxious babble of queries, pleas for reassurances and a murmuring of rumours and conjecture. I saw no one I recognized, though I found out later that many people who had come out to meet me were there, my family, my publisher, Fielding. All that had sustained my mother through the storm was the knowledge that I was not allowed to leave the ship.

When the gangplank was lowered, the 'Stab made room for a handful of thick-moustached men in bowler hats and heavy overcoats, officials of the company that owned the *Newfoundland*. First, the injured were removed. Two sealers carried a man with heavily bandaged hands and a face blistered with frostbite down the gangplank on a stretcher. He held his hands gingerly above his chest and stared at them, seemingly oblivious to the crowd through which the sealers bore him to a covered Red Cross cart. Men all but mummified in bandages were carried off on stretchers. A few were greeted by relatives weeping with relief, but most, not being from St. John's, were merely gawked at. Only when a pair of sealers rashly took it upon themselves to roll back the tarpaulin that covered the hold did those at the front of the crowd see what the company that owned the S.S. *Newfoundland* had ordered that no one be allowed to see.

"Put that tarp back on, for God's sake," Captain Wes Kean roared. The two men hastily rolled the tarp back into place. "What is it?" people said. A man blessed himself, and along the edge of the apron men and women dropped to their knees and leaned their arms on the wooden beams along the dock.

Word of what had been seen spread through the crowd. People related to crew members of the S.S. *Newfoundland* fought to get closer while the constabulary at last linked arms and would not let them through. "Did Andrew Hodder make it?" an old man shouted up to the men who still stood on the cross-spars of the ship. Everyone stared up at them. I did. I expected them to know the answer to the question. They were like birds perched among the leafless branches of a tree. "Does anybody know if Andrew Hodder made it?" the old man said again, as if he could not fathom their silence.

Soon such questions were being shouted from throughout the crowd, hopefully, despairingly. The men in the rigging seemed to look beyond the crowd at the city that stretched out behind it. A member of the 'Stab climbed the first few rungs of the rigging rope on the mainmast and asked that the immediate families of the crew of the S.S. *Newfoundland* proceed to the Harvey and Company warehouse. "Immediate families only," he shouted.

The rest of us stood still and watched as, wide-eyed with bewilderment and dread, the suddenly conspicuous relatives slowly made their way eastward down the apron, the onlookers parting to let them through and to see them better. The man who had blessed himself wandered off with his hand on the near shoulder of a woman who walked, head down, beside him.

I rushed off the ship, ran down the gangplank into the crowd, who clutched at me, begging me for news. The earth was so suddenly solid and motionless beneath my feet that my legs buckled. I would have fallen had I not been so hemmed in. When I was deep enough into the crowd that none of the people I was passing had seen me leave the ship, I slowed down, tried to catch my breath and, when I couldn't, began to run again. My ability to suspend belief in my own mortality was for the moment gone. Death, who I had thought would stay on board, who I had thought was on the ship only because the sealers were, was right behind me.

Once I was out of the crowd, a spell of dizziness hit me like a gust of wind. I stumbled backwards and almost fell, lurched against the side of a warehouse, hands on the wall, head hung, shoulders heaving. I turned my back to the sea and the ship and looked up at the stunted, wind-levelled spruce trees of the Brow.

In the days to come, I and all the newspaper reporters of St. John's pieced together the story of the men of the S.S. *Newfoundland*. They were caught out on the ice because they had had been sent away from the *Stephano*, the ship that was nearest to them when the storm began, sent back to their own vessel by Captain Abram Kean, father of the *Newfoundland*'s skipper, Westbury. They had no hope of finding their ship and must have known it, but they had uncomplainingly set off in search of it anyway, with snow and darkness coming on. They had left the *Newfoundland* lightly dressed, for the plan was that they would be back on board before the sun went down. They were fifty-eight hours on the ice without fuel, food or shelter.

I thought often of the men of the S.S. *Newfoundland*. I was haunted by the image of them turning compliantly about when Kean told them to, preferring to risk the blizzard than defy him, setting out on their doomed walk across the ice.

I thought of the second mate, George Tuff, the leader of the ice party who, though he knew the storm would soon be at full force, did not dare to even ask Kean to let them come aboard, let alone demand it. But I thought mostly of old man Kean, who was too miserly to offer those men the safety of his ship and sent them off to find his son's ship rather than have them sit on his, eating his provisions and using up his oil and coal.

Aside from the above story, which we pieced together from the survivors, I wrote two stories, one about the living and working conditions of the sealers and the other about the last days of the few men whose names I knew. I could not write about the men I had seen on the ice. I tried to but could not.

Neither of the stories was published. The incident was officially investigated and petitions were circulated calling for the arrest of Abram Kean, but little came of it. The seal hunt continued and Kean went on to become the first sealing captain to cull a million seals.

Many people asked me about the S.S. *Newfoundland*, but the only person I spoke to about it was Fielding, who did not ask. My brothers and sisters asked. I knew my mother would have listened, but I could see she was praying that I would keep to myself whatever I had seen.

So I told Fielding, one night in my boarding-house. Told her as much as I could bear to tell her or find words for.

When I was finished, I shook my head, my mind reeling. "I don't know," I said.

"I don't know either," Fielding said. "Things happen to you, or you see things, and you change. And soon you can't remember how things were before you changed. That's the strangest part, I think. You know things used to be different, but you can't remember how. I don't think it happens to everyone. Some people stay the same no matter what. Or maybe they just seem to. I don't know."

For months after my return from the seal hunt, I had the feeling of having awoken from some unremembered dream. At night I lay awake as I had on the *Newfoundland* while the sealers slept through the ceaseless racket of the coal crank and the pelt chute. One night I had got up and removed from beside a sealer a pelt that had landed in his bunk. I had never touched a pelt before. The fat beneath the fur was inches thick, thicker and more unwieldy than the sod we ripped up from the field behind the house to plant a few potatoes. It was so heavy and so slippery I could barely move it. I had intended to throw it back in the chute but had to leave it on the floor. I remembered the feel of the pelt in my hands, my thumb on the fur, my fingers slick on the blubber underneath. My hands were bloodsoaked when I dropped the pelt; I wiped the palms flat on my thighs and on my shirt as I had seen the sealers do.

The dead of the *Newfoundland* were not even in the ground when the seal skinners, standing shoulder to shoulder along the waterfront, were skinning pelts on sloping tables at the foot of which lay tubs into which tumbled the hunks of blubber they hacked off with their knives. Once the sealskins were scraped clean, they would be sent to hide houses the world over, including a few in St. John's. Someone somewhere would wear a sealskin hat made from a seal killed by a man from the S.S. *Newfoundland*.

It was while I was watching the skinners that Grimes approached me. He was so well-dressed that I took him for a merchant until I saw the little wooden wheelbarrow beside him. It was piled with blue pocket-sized books. He raised his bowler hat in greeting. "George Grimes," he said. "Member of the House of Assembly." He reached into the wheelbarrow and handed me a book.

"I am giving you this book," he said, his tone formal, the words sounding rehearsed. "It is specially designed so that you can carry it with you anywhere you go. I want you to read it, and if, after doing so, you want to be a socialist, I want you to come see me at this address." He handed me his card. Then he moved on and repeated his spiel to the person next in line.

"Who corrupted the Senate? The capitalists. Who fixes congress-men? The capitalists. Who purchased the Illinois state legislature? The capitalists. Who bought the St. Louis aldermen? The capital-ists."

So the Illinois state legislature and the St. Louis aldermen had been bought. I was outraged, though I could not have found either Illinois or St. Louis on a map. For years afterwards, whenever I heard the word *capitalist*, what came to mind was the St. Louis al-dermen as I had pictured them when I was sixteen, a couple of dozen burgomasters sitting around in a circle, rubbing their hands together with glee at the prospect of being bought.

Then there were the counter-questions: "Who can stop corrup-tion? The socialist. Who believes that all men really are created equal? The socialist. Who cares about the working man? The so-cialist." After I read the closing paragraph of *What's So and What Isn't*, I believed that I had found my calling, a way to ensure that the deaths of the men of the S.S. *Newfoundland* might be redeemed: "A socialist is a man of destiny. He is the only man who has read the signs of the time. He is therefore invulnerable. He draws his shining lance and challenges the champions of every other economic thought to meet him in the arena of debate. And they slink away like whipped curs."

That seemed like something worth being, a man someone like Abe Kean would slink away from like a whipped cur, an invulnera-ble, lance-wielding master of debate. It was all very well to want to be a journalist, but whose life could you save or even improve by writing for a newspaper?

I put this question to Fielding the next time she came to my boarding-house.

"To the best of my knowledge," Fielding said, "I have never saved anyone's life by writing for the *Telegram*, though I might save my own if I stopped."

I showed her *What's So and What Isn't*, and she browsed through it, every so often drinking from her silver flask. "Well?" I said. "What do you think?" She drew breath as if to say something, looked at me, looked down at the book, shrugged.

"I suppose there might be something to it," she said.

We went straight to Grimes's house, and on his doorstep I earnestly declared to him our desire to become socialists. Fielding stood wordlessly beside me. "I want to be a socialist," I said — "like you," I would have added, except I didn't want to sound presumptuous. I don't know what I expected; I suppose to be welcomed into the fold with equal ardour.

"Step into the porch," said Grimes. "I'll be right back." He closed the front door, opened the door to the hallway, stepped hastily inside, then closed the door.

Judging from its façade and what I had glimpsed of it when he opened the door, his house was as large and as well-appointed as my uncle Fred's, which surprised me. As Fielding and I stood waiting in the porch, we heard voices inside, Grimes's and that of a woman, his wife we presumed, with whom he seemed to be arguing, though the only word I could make out was the one with which she began every reply in a kind of "I will brook no dispute" tone, which was *George*.

Soon, the door to the hallway opened again and Grimes backed out, holding in his arms a box of books, fifty copies, he said, of *What's So and What Isn't*. As he was handing me the box, his wife poked her head out of the nearest room. I tipped my hat to her and Fielding said hello. She gave a grudging nod. She looked at me, as Fielding later put it, "as if she hoped you were not a measure of her husband's standing in the world." It would be a long time before I cut the kind of figure that would reassure the wives of my associates.

We never did get past the porch of Grimes's house, though we spent a lot of time with him over the next few months. I started pressing copies of *What's So and What Isn't* on everyone I knew or met, and one week we joined Grimes in what he called his Sunday walkabout. It was his habit on Sundays to go from door to door, pitching socialism to the citizens of St. John's. Fielding and I stood mute at his side like the socialist trainees that we were. At each house, he introduced us before reciting his speech, which mostly consisted of phrases pulled straight from John M. Work. Grimes stood on doorsteps and calmly and reasonably explained how the current economic system would be overthrown and another put in its place. And how would this come about? "Preferably by the ballot box," Grimes said. "If necessary, by revolution. Do you have any questions? Very well, then. Good day to you, now."

His manner and his message were so completely at odds that I don't think people understood what he was advocating. It was hard to square Grimes with the picture of the socialist put forward by Work. "Any revolution," Fielding said, "that depends upon Grimes drawing his shining lance will be a long time coming."

It was true. He was the least ardent, most phlegmatic, deferential socialist I have ever met. No one would be put out or inconvenienced by Grimes's revolution, let alone disenfranchised. I wondered if the Cause knew what its man in Newfoundland was like. In his arena of debate, the House of Assembly, where he ought to have been challenging the champions of other economic thought, he made speeches about the need for more jobs and better roads.

Mind you, I didn't come off too well in comparison with John M. Work's man of destiny either, in my tattered overcoat and hat and horn-rimmed glasses. We made quite a sight for a while, George Grimes and his post-adolescent aides-de-camp, Joe Smallwood and Sheilagh Fielding. There is a photograph of us from that time, standing on the waterfront with a group of grinning dockworkers we were trying to unionize behind us: the stolid Grimes in his bowler hat and tweed overcoat striking a statesman-like pose with both hands behind his back; me on one side of him like some bespectacled scarecrow, hawk-nosed, owl-eyed, Fielding incongruous on the other, smiling, one eye half-closed as though she is winking at the camera.

We succeeded in starting up a few locals of the international unions that Grimes was affiliated with, but inevitably, there was a falling out between us. I told him one day I was not content, as he was, to lay the groundwork for a revolution that I would never live to see. "Our day will come," Grimes said, sounding like some preacher consoling his congregation with the promise that in some nebulous next life, things would be better. If I had known my Marx, I would have warned him against making a religion of socialism.

"But don't you want to be there when it happens?" I said. "Don't you want to be part of it?"

"I'm part of it now," Grimes said.

"We'll never get anywhere the way you're going about it," I said. Grimes looked at me with a kind of wistful fondness, as if I was just the latest in a long line of protégés who had become impatient with him and moved on; as if he had known all along that this would happen. "We'll have to agree to disagree," he said, holding out his hand to me and smiling. I fancied there was some principle at stake that was more important than friendship or politeness and refused to shake his hand, keeping both of mine in my pockets. On the verge of tears, blinking rapidly, I half turned away from him. Grimes, as if he assumed I had spoken for her, too, extended his hand to Fielding, who took it.

"We'll meet and talk again," he said, as if he was telling me that I should not let this refusal to shake his hand keep me from contacting him once I realized how foolish I had been.

"I'm sure we will," said Fielding.

The docks, I decided, were where a true socialist should be, not canvassing from door to door.

All along the waterfront were the fish-merchant warehouses, where the salt cod was brought ashore, dried and stored and later stacked in the holds of ships bound for England, where it was consumed at ten times the rate per person that it was in Newfoundland. Barge cranes moved back and forth all day, loading, unloading stacks of salt cod the size of houses. The technology of preserving fish had not changed in five hundred years. Soak it in brine until its every fibre was so salt-saturated it would be safe from rot for years, then dry it in the open air.

Salt cod lay drying everywhere within several hundred feet of the harbour. The Battery, the fishing village within the city at the base of Signal Hill, where the rock was so solid that not even holes for outhouses could be dug, was paved with yellow cod. It lay on the rocks in backyards and on elevated fish-flakes near the water, raised up as though in some primitive funeral rite, cod split and cured in brine and set out to dry in arrowhead-like Vs. When it rained, everyone rushed out to turn the cod over so that the side with the rain-impervious, leather-like skin faced upward. Otherwise, the cod was spread out to the sky and whatever flew there, including gulls and crows who, as if to spite the fishermen for salting the cod past what even their palates could endure, shat on it from great heights. Not that it mattered, for you could not eat the cod anyway without soaking it for days in water and then boiling it for hours, after which it was still so salty that the least of the complaints that were brought against it was that once it had been smeared with birdshit. Still, though he brought it home for the others to eat, my father would not stoop to eating food treated so disdainfully by birds and dogs and everything that flew above or walked upon the earth.

All along the harbour, outside the white warehouses of the fish merchants, cod was spread out on the ground to dry. It was on every spare square inch of ground of what the merchants liked to call their premises. It was even spread on steps, with just enough room between the cod for men to walk toe to heel as though on two-by-fours. It was leaned slantwise against the buildings, spread on roofs that themselves were spread with tarp or old sails.

The cod lay airing on the ground through days of overcast and fog. On the rare sunny days, it was covered with flies that would rise up and settle down as you walked along, a single wave passing through this pool of flies, keeping perfect time with you. Inside the warehouses, the salt cod was stacked storeys high. To walk into a warehouse was to walk into a city of salt fish, columns of cod rising up like buildings between which there was barely room for a man to walk.

The docks reeked of the hybrid smell of fish and brine. The wind off the cod was so salty that it made me sneeze and my eyes run with water. Sometimes when I breathed the air, my throat turned to fire, and when I tried to speak, I had no voice, could get out only a rasping, rattling cough as if I had inhaled a chestful of smoke. I never did acquire the ability to tolerate the omnipresent smell of cod. Walking among it always made me long for the clean-aired elevation of the Brow.

Backing onto Water Street were the massive, all-white warehouses of the merchant families, warehouses that bore the names of their owners in huge block letters that you could read from the Brow. Also named after the merchants were the little side-streets that led from Water Street to Harbour Drive, the "coves," inlets between the palisade of buildings. Gower's Cove, Job's Cove, Baird's Cove, Harvey's Cove, Crosby's Cove. When you emerged from one of these coves, a gust of wind would hit you in the face as if you had just stepped outside from the cabin of a ship at sea.

The sealers, the fishermen, the barge-boat crews: it was workers such as these that could most benefit from socialism. I began making speeches on the waterfront. Fielding rounded up my audiences for me while I stood atop a crate, strode up and down the waterfront and gestured with her cane at sailors and stevedores who lined the rails of ships that were moored with hawser ropes thicker than my legs.

"Joseph Smallwood," Fielding said, barker-fashion, reciting a pitch I had composed for her, "registered member of the International Socialist Party, will give a speech at three o'clock in Baird's

Cove, the likes of which you have never heard before and will never hear again and which none of you will soon forget." Curious, bored, incredulous, they came down from the ships to hear me speak. Even at the age of sixteen, I could hold an audience, for a while at least.

"I am here," I said, to the men two and three times my age who gathered round me while I stood atop an empty crate, "to tell you how to start a union and to explain to you the principles of socialism. I am here to tell you why your children never have enough to eat; why the men you work for pay you next to nothing; why some of you are risking your lives to keep rich men like the owners of the S.S. *Newfoundland* in smoking-jackets...." I had never seen a smoking-jacket in my life, but the heroes of Horatio Alger's novels, which I read avidly, were always getting their first big break from men who wore them and afterwards aspired to wear one themselves, so I figured I was on safe ground. (I took to heart a curiously amended version of the Algeresque myth; I wanted to rise not from rags to riches, but from obscurity to world renown, and had chosen socialism as my best means of accomplishing this, thereby establishing as my mortal enemies the very characters who had inspired me to self-betterment in the first place.)

I always told the men that they were working to keep the rich in something; if Alger did not provide me with some item of frivolous affluence, then Fielding did. If it was not smoking-jackets, it was silver spittoons, gold cigarette cases, snifters of brandy, snuffboxes, satin slippers, Persian rugs. I got a roar of indignation from a crowd of stevedores by referring to some man's "heirloom-laden house," having no more idea than my listeners apparently had of what an heirloom was.

I once, at Fielding's urging, denounced men whose "lives were spent in the acquisition of gewgaws and gimcracks." This did not elicit any sort of response. "It was a good speech," Fielding told me afterwards. "The rich of St. John's will not be so quick to gather gewgaws and gimcracks in the future."

One day, a man who was standing at the rail of a ship shouted down to Fielding as she made her way along the waterfront, drumming up an audience for me. "What are you doing down here, now, my dear?" He was a burly, balding redhead whose stomach stuck out between the rails as if his shirt and pants concealed a boulder. "Prohibitionist, are ya?" he said.

"Imbibitionist," said Fielding.

He raised his eyebrows. "What's that?" he said.

"I have come to release you from the shackles of ignorance," said Fielding, "of which you seem to be burdened with more than your share."

"Oh, I've got more than my share all right," he said, rubbing his crotch to a chorus of guffaws from the other men along the rail. Fielding looked quickly away so they would not see her smile, which I was shocked to see her do. I ran along the dock towards her.

"That's quite a cane," I heard the man saying. "Big knob on it like that. Ya like big knobs, now, do ya?"

"Your wife must miss you terribly while you're away," Fielding shouted. "Still, I'm sure some kind soul helps her fill the void you leave behind." The men laughed.

"That's enough of that," I said, shaking my fist at the redhead. He threw back his head and laughed.

"Fielding," I said, "you shouldn't carry on with them like that. Perhaps you shouldn't be down here on the waterfront at all."

"Is *that* your fella?" the redhead said. "That explains the cane — "

"I'll explain something to you," I shouted. Fielding put her hand on my shoulder and turned me away from the ship.

"Thank God you showed up when you did, Smallwood," she said. "I think that man was on the verge of turning coarse. I don't know what I would have done."

"Very funny," I said and, as if in retaliation, turned and shook my fist at the redhead. "Come down here and you'll get your explanation."

"No offence," she said, turning me about with one hand, "but I think he's had more experience with giving explanations than you have. Let's just get out of here and let him think he scared us off."

I was twenty when I told Fielding I was going to New York. I had got nowhere promoting socialism and, after reading John Reed's *Ten Days That Shook the World* and finding out that he had once worked for the *Call, the* New World socialist newspaper that was located in New York, I received what Fielding described as "my call to the *Call.*"

"It would mean a great deal to me if you came along," I said. It was the closest to declaring affection for her I had ever come.

"New York?" she said.

"Yes," I said. "New York."

"I'm not sure — I'm not sure that I'm ready for New York," said Fielding.

"Do you mean because your mother lives there?" I said. Almost imperceptibly, she shook her head.

"Then there's only one way to find out if you're ready for it," I said. She looked more troubled by my invitation than it seemed to me she should have been, even if she meant to decline it.

"Are you worried about leaving your father alone?" I said.

"My father has been alone all his life," said Fielding.

"Don't tell me you're afraid to quit your job," I said. "It's not like we're making any money. That's why there'll always be newspaper jobs. No one else wants them."

Fielding nodded distractedly. "You're going for certain?" she said. "You didn't tell me you were thinking about it." I shrugged. So that was it, I thought, flattered. She was sad that I was leaving. I felt a pleasant hurt of fondness for her in my throat. It surprised me. That fleeting look of tenderness was in her eyes, that wistfulness I had seen the day we met at Bishop Feild. It was as if, for an instant, she had stepped outside her life and was seeing everyone in it from a perspective that in a few moments, she would be unable to recall. I wondered how, in those few moments, she regarded me. And I wondered if this feeling that I had for her, this curious affection, might be love.

She blinked rapidly, and for an awkward few moments I thought she was going to cry. Now she looked panicked, as she had at the Feild when I alluded to her estranged parents and when Slogger Anderson taunted Prowse into proving he was not afraid to flog her.

"When are you leaving?" she said at last. I told her in two weeks; I had given notice at the *Telegram* that day.

She shook her head. "I couldn't — you see, I couldn't make it by then," she said. "Maybe sometime after that, I'm not sure. I'd have to be sure before I — "

"Is there something you need help with here?" I said. "I could stay — "

"No, no," Fielding said, "there's nothing. Really. I'd have to be sure in my mind, that's all, you see. In my mind. I'd have to think about it for a while."

"All right, then," I said. "But I bet you'll decide in time to go with me."

She extended her hand to me, awkwardly, formally. I was gratified to see that there were tears in her eyes.

"I don't expect I'll see you before you go."

I forced a laugh. "I'm not going for another two weeks," I said.

"No," she said. "I know. But from now until then New York is all you'll talk about, you'll keep trying to convince me, and I don't want to feel pressured."

"Well —" I said, trying to laugh again, "if that's the way you want it. I'll see you in New York."

"You really want me to go?" she said. I nodded. "What are we, Smallwood?" she said. "You and I. What are we?"

"What do you mean?" I said, though I knew what she meant.

"Never mind," she said.

I was about to tell her I would write her from New York as soon as I got there when she turned around and walked quickly away from me, her cane thudding in the gravel.

Fielding's Condensed

History of Newfoundland

Chapter Six:

THE RUEFUL SETTLER

We here present another selection from the authoritative edition of *Quodlibets*, called "The Rueful Settler," in which a settler, now a resident of the renegade colony of Bristol's Hope, addresses his former master on the subject of the colony at Cuper's Cove, now known as Cupids:

> John Guy, 'twas you enticed me to this place.
> If ever I set eyes upon your face,
> I shall tell you what I think of Cuper's Cove,
> Then sit your puny arse upon my stove.
> I'll tell you why I moved to Bristol's Hope,
> Then hang you with a sturdy piece of rope,
> And when your little legs have ceased to kick,
> I'll beat your lifeless body with a stick.
> Never Wales shall I set eyes upon again.
> My sole blessings be this paper and this pen.
> In Newfoundland I live, in Newfoundland will die,
> Unknown, unmourned, because of you, John Guy.

Old Lost Land

Dear Smallwood:

*"The man who wrote 'The Ode to Newfoundland' lived there,"
my father used to tell me, pointing at Government House. The
grounds of Government House, where all the governors of Newfoundland since 1824 have lived, back onto Circular Road, so I
can see them from my bedroom window. For most of the year,
no one sets foot on the grounds but gardeners and in winter no
one at all. It always seems a strange sight, that vast, treeless,
steppe-like field in the middle of the city, without so much as a
dog's footprints in the snow.*

*When I was a child, I was always asking my father, "How big
is Newfoundland?" Using the map on the wall of his study, he
would try to make me understand how big it was, try to give me
some sense of how much more of it there was than I had seen so
far in our horse-cab drives around the bay. "We're here," my
father said, pointing at the tiny encircled star that stood for St.
John's. "Now, last Sunday, when we went out for our drive, we*

*went this far." He moved his finger in a circle about an inch across.
Then he moved his hand slowly over the rest of the map, the paper
crackling expansively beneath his fingers. "Newfoundland is this
much bigger than that," he said, making the motion with his hand
again. "All this is Newfoundland, but it's not all like St. John's. Almost all of it is empty. No one lives there. No one's ever seen most
of it." I could not imagine it. All I could imagine were the grounds
of Government House going on forever. I have yet to see it.*

*The ode was written by Sir Cavendish Boyle, governor of
Newfoundland from 1901–1904. When I was a child, I thought
his first name was Surcavendish. It conjured up a man who lived
alone, a man who was given, like me, to watching the grounds
from his bedroom window, some brooding, gloom-savouring soul
like myself in whose huge house there was never more than one
light burning. I could not imagine him ever having done anything
else, could not imagine any existence for him except sitting at that
window, looking out, brooding over Newfoundland, endlessly
writing the ode.*

*At night, with my face pressed to the window, I used to recite
to myself my favourite verse. "When spreads thy cloak of
shimm'ring white, at winter's stern command, thro' shortened day
and star-lit night, we love thee, frozen land. We love thee, we love
thee, we love thee, frozen land." It was as if this had been written,
not for all Newfoundlanders, but specifically for my father and
me, the Fielding family anthem, as if this was our windswept,
frozen land.*

*Though they are anthem-like, there is something indefinably
sad about the words, resigned, regretful, as if Boyle imagined himself looking back from a time when Newfoundland had ceased to
be. It is the sort of song you might write about a place as you were
leaving it by boat, watching it slowly fade from view, a place you
believed you would never see again. He was governor of
Newfoundland for only a few years, so he must have written it in
the knowledge that he was soon to leave.*

Fall, Smallwood, another fall, and you leave tomorrow. And me? Soon to be at sea again? I feel as though I am at sea. Nova Scotia. New Scotland. New England. New York. New York again. Where the streets are so hemmed in by buildings they never see the sun. The old New World. Where my mother and my stepfather live, which you knew when you invited me along. Perhaps you do not really expect me to accept your invitation. What will you think or do if I turn up? Sometimes I have the feeling that I am appealing to qualities in you that you do not have, that the you I love is just someone I invented. I feel that, though you are younger than me by just one year, we are lifetimes apart. Ill at ease in your own world and in other worlds unwelcome. Mocked at in both. But you will not stop demanding to be let in, or looking for an overlooked, unlocked door. You are willing to risk or forsake everything to get what you want. Including me? How it spited me that it was you, you who embarrassed me in front of all the Townies, and especially in front of Prowse. There is always this awkwardness between us because of what happened at the Feild. Because of what you think happened. That day in the training centre. We never mention it, perhaps for my sake, perhaps for yours. I'm not sure if you've forgiven me, if you think my expulsion from Spencer and my getting you a job on the paper makes us even. When the others left, you stayed, and for the first time since we met you said my name. "Fielding." More tenderly than you have said it since. I should have let you speak instead of asking you to leave. Whatever you had planned to say remains unsaid. I wonder, sometimes, if I should tell you everything. So much to risk. I don't think I trust anyone that much.

———————

I WAS TO LEAVE the next day. I walked up Signal Hill, from which you could see the whole city, though it was not St. John's I looked at but the sea, crashing on the rocks at the base of the red sandstone cliffs. The hill was carpeted with unripe, red-and-yellow partridge berries. They needed almost no soil, grew on sod that was draped like a ragged carpet over rocks. The remains of gun batteries, crumbling fortifications and forgotten barracks lay everywhere. Down below were the charred ruins of a cholera hospital so hard to reach that it was never used except for small-pox patients, who never saw St. John's, only the grotto of rock around them and the open sea.

It occurred to me, for the first time, that I might not come back. The sea brought out such thoughts in me. My virtual non-existence in comparison with the eternal sea-scheme of things. I never felt so forlorn, so desolate as I did looking out across the trackless, forever-changing surface of the sea, which, though it registered the passage of time, was suggestive of no beginning and no end, as purposeless, as pointless as eternity.

I had never liked to think of myself as living on an island. I pre-ferred to think of Newfoundland as landlocked in the middle of some otherwise empty continent, for though I had an islander's scorn of the mainland, I could not stand the sea. I was morbidly drawn to read and re-read, as a child, an abridged version of Melville's *Moby Dick*, a book that, though I kept going back to it, gave me nightmares. Ishmael's notion that the sea had some sort of melancholy-dispelling power mystified me. Whenever it was a damp, drizzly November in my soul, the last thing I wanted to look at was the sea. It was not just drowning in it I was afraid of, but the sight of that vast, endless, life-excluding stretch of water. It re-minded me of God, not the God of Miss Garrigus and the Bible, whose threats of eternal damnation I did not believe in, but Melville's God, inscrutable, featureless, indifferent, as unimaginable as an eternity of time or an infinity of space, in comparison with which I was nothing. The sight of some little fishing boat heading out to sea like some void-bound soul made me, literally, seasick.

On the other hand, I was an islander. I thought of my father's stint in Boston, where he had discovered the limits of a leash that up to that point he hadn't even known he was wearing. I wondered if, like him, I would be so bewildered by the sheer unknowable, unencompassable size of the world that I would have to come back home. How could you say for certain where you were, where home left off and away began, if the earth that you were standing on went on forever, as it must have seemed to him, in all directions? For an islander, there had to be natural limits, gaps, demarcations, not just artificial ones on a map. Between us and them and here and there, there had to be a gulf.

I walked down the sea side of Signal Hill, following the steep and winding path that led to the Narrows. When I reached the pudding-stone, the wave-worn conglomerate of rock that marked the high water-line, I saw the Boot, the old wooden boot attached to the iron rod bored into the cliff with the name of Smallwood written on it, eerily glowing, swaying slightly back and forth in the wind. The Boot was like some flag, Smallwood the name of some long-reigning monarch or a family that had laid claim to the place two hundred years ago. The republic of Smallwood. "My God, Smallwood," Reeves had said, "what are your parents trying to do, start their own country?"

But the Boot would not be the last thing I saw on leaving, for I planned to sail from Port aux Basques after, for the first time in my life, crossing Newfoundland by train. I relished the thought of a journey that would carry me farther and farther inland from the sea. I had no conception of what Newfoundland looked like outside a forty-mile radius of St. John's.

As though I had contracted from my father an irrational fear of it, I dreamed about the old man's Boot the night before I left. I was sailing out through the Narrows, alone on a boat of some kind, and there was the Boot, with my name on both sides of it,

Smallwood, glowing in the dark. When I passed it, I turned to look back at it and only as it began to grow dim did I realize that I had cleared the Narrows and was drifting out to sea. I stood in the boat and called for help, but by then I had rounded the point and the Boot, my name and the harbour lights had vanished. It was so dark I could not make out the headlands. There was no wind and I could not even smell the sea. I could not feel the boat beneath me, or hear the slightest sound. I turned around and faced what I believed was seaward, but there was nothing there but darkness. I made to touch my arms to reassure myself of my existence, but it seemed that even my own body had disappeared. I tried to shout again for help, but could make no sound. I woke from this insensate darkness to the darkness of my room and felt my arms and legs and face, and said my name out loud.

I thought of Fielding, whom I had not heard from since that day when she had acted so strangely on the waterfront. I wondered if she had insisted on not seeing me the past two weeks because she knew she would not be going to New York. It seemed to me it might be her and not my imminent departure that had given rise to the dream.

As I lay there in the darkness in my boarding-house room, I imagined kissing her and taking off her clothes. I could not picture what she looked like, I knew only that she was naked and I was not. I could not imagine myself unclothed in front of anyone. I felt the buttons of my longjohns. My fantasy was having no physical effect. Up to that point, my sex life had been confined to racy postcards. Some woman, divan-reclined, legs crossed, a feather boa wound about herself. For her, an erection like a chisel and a feverish half-hour of self-administration. For Fielding, nothing.

I had once, when I was eleven, happened on a man and a woman in the woods above the Brow. They were in a place we called the Spruces, where little light came through and the forest floor was thick with moss. It was a summer Sunday afternoon, overcast but warm, humid. There was hag hair hanging from the trees above the couple, strands and whiskers of it everywhere. The woman was faced full length away from me, unclothed, lying on her side on a blanket. All my mind would recall of her later, and recalled of her now, was her wide bare back, though I watched for so long I saw much more. All I could see of him were his hands, on her, though I could hear his voice and her laughing in a kind of teasing way each time he finished speaking. For a while, a shameful while, unable to resist, I watched, crouching down so they wouldn't see me, watched and — even more, I think — listened, for I had been told of such things and seen pictures, but I had never heard such sounds. The strange commotion they made; the ever-intensifying sounds from the woman after the man climbed on top of her, so that she sank into the moss, almost out of sight. There was the sense of something secret, something awful, letting loose. It frightened me; it was hard to believe, listening to them, that they knew where this was going, that it wasn't as new to them as it was to me; hard to believe that they hadn't just discovered it by accident, setting into motion something that they were powerless to stop and that, for all they knew, would be the end of them, so panicked, so helpless did they sound. I had heard a boy at school say his parents did "it" every night, but I was sure he didn't mean this.

I watched until they finished and then left. In memory, I was both drawn to it and repulsed by it, and ashamed of myself on both counts. I wondered what the implications of my ambivalence might be; if there might be something wrong with me.

I knew that my mother and father must have performed the act itself. My father had once said that if he merely threw his pants on her bed, my mother would get pregnant. But that they had never done *that*, that it had never been like *that* between them I was certain.

I had been awakened once or twice by the furtive and short-lived squeaking of their bedsprings in the middle of the night. And once, while returning from the outhouse, I had heard, above the barely squeaking springs, my mother sucking air through her clenched teeth as if my father were sticking her with pins. I had stood outside their door, transfixed. I heard my father shudder to a finish and my mother almost instantly afterwards saying, as if she was terrified he would fall asleep on top of her, "Get off me, Smallwood." The bed squeaked momentarily as my father obliged her, and soon after there was snoring, not my mother's, I was sure. I heard her murmur something in a plaintive, almost self-ironic tone, then all was silent.

That sound my mother made — I had been unable to rid myself of it. I could not look at a woman and not hear it, or imagine my mother in the darkness drawing air in through her teeth. The sound of air passing through my mother's teeth, and the screams of the woman whose body by the weight of the man's was pressed into the moss until all I could see was him, him obliterating her so that all that was left of her was sound, screams as if she was giving birth or being murdered.

I stopped rubbing my longjohns, then considered getting a postcard from my collection in my dresser drawer. The woman in the woods. It could not be that way for me. Somehow I knew it. Some "over me" was always watching, and not for an instant could I forget it. Perhaps it could not be that way for any man, I wasn't sure, and I had no intention of asking anyone. Nothing I had ever read in books enlightened me. On the one hand I envied her, that woman on the moss, wished I could be capable of such abandonment. But it was, I told myself, a carrot dangled by biology, the animal impulse to chase after which I must not give in to or it would mean my doom. I well understood my father's horror of domesticity, of entrapment and confinement. The thought of nights in some fetid breeding bed while the products of other such nights lay listening in the next room or outside the door I found so revolting that I vowed I would never marry. My parents' marriage was the only marriage I knew from the inside out. To me, their marriage *was* marriage. To live thus would be to forsake all destinies but the anxiety-ridden drudgery of caring for a horde of children. A pedestiny. I would never drag myself out of poverty if

I got married, let alone achieve more than the limited success considered proper for the best of my kind by men like Reeves.

Trapped in a marriage, I would be driven mad by the casual assumption of privilege and preferment and innate superiority of "the quality," if its effect on my father was anything to judge by. But unlike my father, I told myself, I was outraged by the "quality," not only on my own behalf, but also on behalf of others. I saw no contradiction in wanting to achieve greatness through altruism. How else but through altruism could one be both virtuous and great?

Before I could make up my mind about the postcard, I fell back to sleep.

Besides what little clothing I had, I didn't bring much with me except my oilcloth map of Newfoundland, a fishermen's union pullover with its codfish-emblazoned badge, which I planned to wear while working at the *Call*, and my father's *History of Newfoundland*.

My parents and brothers and sisters went with me to the railway station to say goodbye, and though they made quite a fuss, especially my mother and the girls (my father and the boys manfully shook hands with me and clapped me on the back), they were upstaged by the entire Jewish community of St. John's, about whom I had written a laudatory feature in the *Telegram* two months before and who were surreally on hand to see me off, waving their black hats and weeping as if one of their number was leaving them for good.

Because of them and because of my oversized nose, many of my fellow passengers took me to be Jewish, a misconception I did nothing to discourage, since it made them less likely to sit with me, not because they had anything against the Jews, but simply because they doubted they could sustain a conversation for long with so exotic an individual. Normally, there is nothing I would rather do than talk, and I knew if I got started I might well talk all the way from St. John's to Port aux Basques, oblivious to the landscape we were passing through. I would, many times in the future, spend cross-country train trips in just that manner, staying awake twenty-eight hours at a stretch, hardly noticing when one exhausted listener made way for the next, but on this trip I wanted to keep to myself and that, for the most part, is what I did.

The building of the railway had been one of the few great ventures in Newfoundland not connected with the fishery. Its primary purpose was not to link the scattered settlements around the coast, but to convey passengers and freight back and forth between the eastern and western seaports, St. John's and Port aux Basques, to give Newfoundlanders access to both the ships that crossed the ocean to England and those that crossed the gulf to the mainland. Its route was not determined by the sea, nor was the sea visible at more than a few points along the way.

We started out from St. John's just after sunrise. In two hours, we had crossed the Bog of Avalon, a sixty-mile stretch of barrens and rock scraped bare and strewn with boulders since the ice age. This gave way to a lonely, undifferentiated tract of bog and rolling hills devoid of trees because of forest fires that had burned away even the topsoil so that nothing would ever grow there again that was more than three feet high. It was September, but not so far into the month that the browning of the barrens had begun. An overcast day with a west wind that would keep the fog at bay. There was beauty everywhere, but it was the bleak beauty of sparsity, scarcity and stuntedness, with nothing left but what a thousand years ago had been the forest floor, a landscape clear-cut by nature that never would recover on its own. It was a beauty so elusive, so tantalizingly suggestive of something you could not quite put into words that it could drive you mad and, however much you loved it, make you want to get away from it and recall it from some city and content yourself with knowing it was there.

No one, not even aboriginals, had ever lived on this part of the island. It was impossible to speak of its history except in geological terms.

On one treeless, wind-levelled stretch of barrens, there were crater-like sink-holes of mud where the surface had collapsed. I saw an eastward-leaning stand of junipers, all bent at the same angle to the earth as though half-levelled by a single gust of wind.

Crossing the narrow isthmus of Avalon, I could for a time see ocean from both sides of the train. Fifty years later, after the train had ceased to run, travellers on the highway would be able to see from there the ruins of my refinery at Come by Chance; after it was mothballed, small amounts of crude oil would still be sent there for refining, so that, at night, you would be able to see the flame from the highest of the stacks from forty miles away.

Next came the Bog of Bonavista, and I began to think that Newfoundland would be nothing but a succession of bogs with clumps of storm-stunted spruce trees in between. We stopped at Gambo, the town where I was born and that I was really seeing for the first time, having been too young when I left to remember anything about it. Gambo was the one place in the 253 miles between Port Blandford on the east coast and Humbermouth on the west coast where the railway touched the shoreline, but it was not a fishing village, for the cod did not come that far up Bonavista Bay. It was a logging town and a coastal supply depot, boats sailing up Bonavista Bay to unload their cargo there, where it was then reloaded onto the train and transported inland to towns whose only link with the rest of the island was one of the world's most primitive railways, a narrow-gauge track with spindle-thin rails on which the cars swayed about like sleds on ice.

Gambo was not much to look at, just a cluster of crude, garishly painted one-storey houses, log cabins and unbelievably primitive tar-paper shacks whose front yards were littered with a lifetime of debris: bottles, wooden crates, discarded clothing, broken barrels. I self-ashamedly thanked God we had forsaken the place and our lumber business there in favour of St. John's. I saw the house where I was born — my mother had described its location and appearance to me. I will admit that it was one of the better houses within view, a white, blue-trimmed two-storeyed salt-and-pepper house with a gabled attic window that I could all too easily imagine myself looking out to sea from on a Sunday afternoon. I had fancied, before the trip began, that when we stopped in Gambo, I would proudly announce it to my fellow passengers as the place where I was born. But having seen it, I kept this information to myself and turned sideways in my seat, staring crimson-faced out the window and trying not to imagine the Smallwood that might have been, standing out there, staring in wonderment and longing at the train.

I saw from the windows of the train old men who I fancied had never travelled more than fifty miles from home, sitting side on to their windows, looking out. At the same time as I found the very sight of them oppressive and lived in horror of ending up that way myself — which I was for some reason well able to imagine, me in there looking out, ambitionless, untravelled and uneducated, watching the water break on the rocks in a pattern of foam I had so often seen it was imprinted on my brain — I envied them their apparent self-contentment and dilemma-less existence. For though their afflictions may have been many, irresolution and ambivalence were not among them.

I did not begin to feel better until mid-afternoon, when we crossed the Exploits River into central Newfoundland and the sudden change in the landscape revived my spirits. We travelled through a leafless forest of blazing-white birch trees, tall, schooner-mast-sized trees that went on and on until I could stand to look at them no longer.

I took out my map to see if I could fix exactly where we were. It struck me more forcefully than it ever had before that virtually the whole population lived on the coast, as if ready to abandon ship at a moment's notice. The shore was nothing but a place to fish from, a place to moor a boat and sleep between days spent on the sea. Of the land, the great tract of possibility that lay behind them, beyond their own backyards, over the farthest hill that they could see from the windows of their houses, most Newfoundlanders knew next to nothing. Just as I, who knew nothing about it, feared the sea, though I believed my ignorance and fear to be more justified than theirs. I knew of grown men who hurried home from trouting or berry-picking in a panic as the sun was going down, for fear of being caught out after dark and led astray by fairies. My mother had often told me stories of people from Gambo who, fairy-led, were found weeks later at the end of a trail of clothing that in their trance, they had discarded. They had been led in a dance by fairies until they flopped down dead from sheer exhaustion, my mother believed, and no appeal to common sense or any amount of scorn could change her mind. Yet these same fairy-feeble men would go out on the sea at night in the worst weather to rescue a neighbour whose boat was going down. Here was all this land and they had not claimed an inch of it as theirs, preferring instead to daily risk their lives, hauling fish up from a sea that never would be theirs, and to kill seals walking on ice that could not, like land, be controlled or tamed.

I watched a group of loggers driving a large boom down the river, walking about with their pike-poles like the navigators of some massive raft. Even they preferred the water; they would rather ride the river than the train, though they acknowledged our whistle with a wave as we went by.

The aboriginals were gone. There was no one on the river now, besides the loggers, except guide-led sport fishermen from places like New York and Boston, and not even any of them past a certain point, just the river, which someone had once followed far enough to guess where it was headed and put that guess like gospel on a map. But no one knew where the river went. They knew where it began and where it flowed into the sea; what happened to it in between no one still alive could say.

We reached the town of Badger, where, in the one major departure from the route the highway would take years later, we kept on heading west through what, for the men who built the railway, must have been the most difficult stretch. There were so many hills the engineers had had no choice but to go straight through them. The train wound its way through cuts of rock so sheer and high you could not see the tops of them. Down the face of the rock ran little, spring-fed streams that sparkled in the sun, unseen except for the few minutes when the train was passing by.

There were rickety, gorge-spanning trestles, the gorges only thirty or forty feet wide but hundreds of feet deep. And there were ponds, lakes. When the train curved round some pond, I could see its whole length from my window. It began to rain, a sun-shower, and soon the stretch of rails ahead was gleaming, as was the rain-washed locomotive. I saw the conductor, the seamed, soot-blackened faces of the engineer and fireman and the smoke blown back mane-like above the cars. I saw other passengers in other cars unaware that I was watching them, and I felt as the people we passed along the tracks must have felt and saw myself as they must have, as impossibly remote from them as I was to the lives I had left behind and was headed towards, caught up in the dream of travel, the travel-trance that overtakes you when there are no familiar landmarks to remind you you are making progress, when it seems you have no destination and the landscape you are moving through goes on forever.

All along the line, every mile or so, were little shacks in which the section-men and their families lived what must have been strange and solitary lives. I saw the wives of section-men standing in their doorways watching as the train, the reason they lived where they did, fifty miles from the nearest town, moved past. I saw them standing with their children in their arms while their older children abandoned the tracks they played on to let the apparition of the train go by.

This is not an island, I told myself, but a landlocked country in the middle of an otherwise empty continent, a country hemmed in and cored by wilderness, and it is through this core that we are passing now, the unfoundland that will make us great someday.

It seemed strange to think that some of my fellow passengers were heading home, but some were; they had a different look about them, that half-resigned, half-expectant look of people soon to see familiar sights, familiar faces, the circumscribed geography of home. I did not want to think that anyone was heading home, or that the train was moving for any purpose but to take me, and only me, where I was going.

Sometime in the afternoon, I dozed off and did not wake up until we were approaching the Gaff Topsails, a steep-sloped tract of wilderness, the highest point on the line and the place where delays were most likely in the winter when the tracks were blocked by snow. The train went slowly upgrade for a hundred suspenseful miles, the passengers urging it on, knowing that if we stalled, we might be stranded there for days. We laughed and rocked forward and backward in our seats as if to coax the locomotive one more inch until, when we felt it make the crest, a great cheer went up and it seemed we were leaving home in earnest now, though one-third of our journey still remained.

Though I had vowed not to, I fell asleep again and awoke at dusk to see what appeared to be some kind of snow-plain, flatter even than the barrens, with only the occasional train-borne and bleary-eyed observer to confirm that it was real. It was not until I saw that the stumps of trees, dead two hundred years and petrified by age, formed a kind of barricade around it that I realized it was a frozen lake that we were passing, Deer Lake, the first I had ever set eyes on that was so wide you could not see the other side.

When it was very late and the car was dark and almost empty and most of those still in it were asleep, I looked out the window at what, at that hour, I could see of Newfoundland: dark shapes of hills and trees; a glimpse, when the moon was out, of distant placid ponds; small, unaccountably located towns a hundred miles apart, nothing more than clumps of houses really, all with their porch lights on but otherwise unlit, occupied by people who, though it passed by every night, rarely saw or even heard the train.

From Corner Brook, we followed the Long Range Mountains southwest to Stephenville Crossing, going downstream along the black, cliff-channelled Humber River. Sometime early in the morning, I fell asleep again and did not awake until the sun was up. Someone said we were thirty miles from Port aux Basques. I had stayed in the smoking car all night and not even made it to my complimentary berth, though in my *Telegram* article, I extolled its comfort and convenience as if I had not budged from it from St. John's to Port aux Basques.

We were to cross the gulf by night and reach Cape Breton early in the morning.

I had intended to stand at the railing of the ship until I could no longer see the island. It seemed like the appropriately romantic thing to do.

I wished Fielding had come with me, though I knew she would have made some deflating remark that would have dispelled my mood.

I was pleased to discover, after about fifteen minutes, that all the other passengers had fled the cold and gone inside. I pulled up the hood of my raincoat and imagined what I must look like from in there, a lone hooded figure at the railing. But though I stood staring at it for what seemed like hours, the island got no smaller.

After a while, all but blue with cold, I went inside. And each time I went back out to see how much progress we had made, we seemed to have made none at all. The dark shape of the island was always there, as big as ever, as if we were towing it behind us.

I settled for standing at the window, looking out. When I saw the lights along the southwest coast, I thought of the fishermen's broadcast that I used to listen to on the radio when I lived at home. It always concluded with an island-wide temperature round-up.

Every evening, there was the same cold-shiver-inducing litany of place-names: Burgeo, Fortune, Funk Island, Hermitage.

I imagined myself looking out to sea at night from the window of a house in Hermitage. Hermitage. I wondered what lonely fog-bound soul had named it. It occurred to me that as Hermitage seemed to me now, so might Newfoundland seem from New York six months from now, an inconceivably backward and isolated place, my attraction to which I could neither account for nor resist. The whole island was a hermitage.

To leave or not to leave, and having left, to stay away or to go back home. I knew of Newfoundlanders who had gone to their graves without having settled the question, some who never left but were forever planning to and some who went away for good but were forever on the verge of going home. My father had left and come back, physically at least.

In the lounges, people sat listening to the radio until, about twenty miles out, the sound began to fade. There were groans of protest, but people kept listening as long as they could hear the faintest hint of sound through the static. Finally, when the signal vanished altogether, there was a change in mood among the passengers, as if we were truly under way, as if our severance from land was now complete. The radio was left on, though, eerily blaring static as though it were some sort of sea sound.

II

◆

A CONTINENT
OF STRANGERS

The voyage of Columbus is one of the grandest events
in history.... The life of the Genoese sailor is, and
always will be, the grandest romance of history.... Alas!
for the glory of our island, for the praise of our discov-
erer, there are no portraits.... No golden haze of
romance surrounds our earliest annals. The story of the
discovery of Newfoundland and North America, as
told by the Cabots, is as dull as the log of a dredge-boat.

— D. W. PROWSE, *A History of Newfoundland*

Fielding's Condensed
History of Newfoundland

Chapter Seven:

TREWORGIE'S REIGN OF TERROR

The Commonwealth Government sends John Treworgie, who has no stake, financial or otherwise, in the fishery, to govern Newfoundland. Thus begins what becomes known among the merchants as Treworgie's Reign of Terror, which lasts from 1653–1660, throughout which time the settlers are allotted better fishing grounds and are exempted from "unfair" punishment by the admirals. Thankfully, with the restoration of the monarchy also comes the restoration of law and order.

Some historians have suggested that Treworgie may have been more gullible than tyrannical, that he may have been taken in by the glibness of the settlers, with whom the rough-spoken merchants could not compete.

If so, with what welcome must the honest eloquence of the merchant Sir Josiah Child have been received at court. So eloquent is Child that the king's ministers swear they would pay just to hear him speak. Child, however, insists that so much do they honour him by listening it is he who should pay them, which he does, one at a time, eschewing ostentation by doing it behind a curtain or in some antechamber.

Child addresses several charges that have been made by the settlers against the merchants and their fishing admirals. (The fishing admirals were those captains who arrived first in each harbour, over which they afterwards, under order of the king, ruled as judge and jury when disputes arose.)

1. The fishing admirals, on the instructions of the merchants, discourage settlement in Newfoundland so as to keep the fishery all to themselves. To this end, they abuse their judicial powers, showing bias against the settlers, whom they are ten times more likely to punish than their own fishermen. As no court records are kept, the only proof of this so-called bias is the number of letters of complaint that are sent by the settlers back to England. But what does this "prove," Child says, except that unlike the settlers, the merchants are taking their punishment like men.

2. It is unfair that the settlers are forbidden to fish until the merchant fleet arrives from England, even then being allowed to fish only those grounds the merchants could not be bothered with. But is it not true, Child counters, that the king himself, eager that everyone have an equal chance of making money from the fishery, has long since decreed that the question of who fished where will be settled by a race across the Atlantic every spring. If anyone is being unfair, therefore, it is the settlers, who instead of taking part in the race, simply wait all winter at the finish line — hence their disqualification.

Not that the settlers, Child argues, are above cheating. Despite their disqualification, many of them, claiming that to endure a winter in Newfoundland is a greater feat than to sail a ship across the ocean, go ahead and fish anyway. True, they always pull their nets up before the merchant fleet arrives, but whenever it is found that a fewer than usual number of settlers have died throughout the winter, the admirals deduce what they have been up to and punish them accordingly.

Equally transparent, Child says, is their ploy of fasting the last few weeks before the fleet arrives, to shed what he calls fish fat from their bodies. Settlers are punished according to how long they have fasted, which is calculated from their degree of emaciation. The closer to death a settler appears to be, the more severely he is flogged.

"Yet," Child says, "try to imagine the admiral as he carries out the sentence, weeping tears of frustration, knowing that no matter how hard he applies the lash, he cannot replace the fish the settler has consumed."

"Enough," King Charles says. "Enough, honest Josiah. I cannot stand to hear any more about what people once possessed of English virtues have been reduced to by life in Newfoundland." The king is convinced that the only way to stop the exploitation of the merchants by the settlers is to depopulate the island.

The Newfoundland Hotel

Dear Smallwood:

I am below decks in the supposedly "dry" lounge, which contains a large number of people who are very obviously drunk. I am drunk, too, though not obviously so. A band you can hear all over the boat is playing Newfoundland music. I am familiar with most of the songs they're playing, songs about fishermen, sealers, loggers, but I know little more about the lives of such people than I know about the lives of Eskimos. It seems a pity there are no songs for people like me. You would probably think it very unsocialist of me, but to pass the time I have been making up titles of white-collar folk-songs: "Journalist's Jig," "Lawyer's Lament," "Concerning an Architect Named Joe," "The Chartered Accountant from Harbour Le Cou," "The Banker's Song," "The Real Estate Reel," "Come All Ye Civil Servants."

I remember my uncle Patrick singing, upon request at Christmas time, "The Ryans and the Pittmans," sitting in his chair with his head thrown back, his face flushed from drinking, his eyes closed as though he could smell the salt spray, as though he were revelling in voyages past, despite the fact that, so terrified was he of the water, he could not be coaxed into going once around the pond in his row-boat at the cottage.

"The Ryans and the Pittmans" is sung to the tune of "Farewell and Adieu to You, Spanish Ladies," and everyone joins in the chorus: "We'll rant and we'll roar like true Newfoundlanders, / We'll rant and we'll roar on deck and below."

I remember a photograph from our family album. Once, on a moderately rough crossing of the gulf from St. John's in 1898, almost everyone on the ship had been seasick, including my father and mother, who were heading to Boston for the funeral of some relative of my mother's. The only thing Newfoundlanders did on deck and below that day was throw up. The stewards went around wearing and distributing little paper masks designed to keep the contagion of mal de mer from spreading. Even in the throes of seasickness, my father, realizing how funny it would seem in retrospect, had the photographer on board take their picture: my parents, masked, queasy-eyed, sitting side by side, staring abjectly at the camera. On the back of the photograph, my father had written: "Summer, 1898. Here we are on the plague-ship Robert Bond."

Summer, 1898. My mother may have been pregnant with me at the time, though if she was it doesn't show. It would depend on when in the summer the photograph was taken. You can see, though she wears that little paper mask, that she is smiling. You can see it in her eyes. Smiling through seasickness and possibly the queasiness of pregnancy.

When I told my father where I was going, he said nothing. He knows I am not going there because of her. He does not know I am going there because of you. He will miss me, though he did not say so. Now that I am gone, the house will have him to itself. I told him he should sell it, but he shook his head and

smiled. "Goodbye," he said. "Goodbye, my D. D." His little
nickname for me. It means "my darling daughter."

A T MY FIRST SIGHT ever of land that was not Newfoundland, I felt a sudden surge of loneliness. On the entire continent that had just come into view, I did not know a single soul,
and it was not much consolation that I carried in my trunk letters
of reference from dozens of people in St. John's. A continent of
strangers. For the longest time, we seemed to be getting no nearer
to land, and I had the feeling that if I were to go to the other end
of the boat, Newfoundland would still be visible.

When we docked at North Sydney, I walked off the ship, trying not to look too obviously like what I was: someone for the first
time setting foot on foreign soil. I moved with a kind of purpose-
ful nonchalance, as if I had disembarked thus many times. All
around me, passengers were being met by friends and relatives.

I stood on the dock until the noise and clamour of arrival had
died down. It was six o'clock in the morning, three hours before
my train for Halifax was due to leave; the sun was barely up. I was
in a place I had never been before, there was no one there I knew.
I put down my trunk and, cupping my mouth with my hands,
shouted "Hello" as loud as I could. Up on the road, someone who
sounded as though he thought I must be off my head, shouted
back, in a kind of mock echo, "Helloooo."

I noticed after the train began to make its way across Cape
Breton that every little thing looked different. I had expected differences, of course, but it had never occurred to me that absolutely
nothing would be the same, that to some degree, the landscape
would differ in every detail from the one back home. I had seen
other places in movies, in photographs, but it was not the same.

I exhausted myself trying to take it all in, noting every little variation and departure from how things were supposed to be. My notion of home and everything in it as ideal, archetypal, was being overthrown. It was as though the definitions of all the words in my vocabulary were expanding at once.

Cape Breton was much like Newfoundland, yet everything seemed slightly off. Light, colours, surface textures, dimensions — objects like telegraph poles, fence posts, mail boxes, which you would think would be the same everywhere, were bigger or smaller or wider by a hair than they were back home. That I was able to detect such subtle differences made me realize how circumscribed my life had been, how little of the world I had seen.

Suffering a temporary loss of nerve, I lingered for a while in Halifax. I got a job at the *Halifax Herald*, but it was not much of a step up from the *Telegram*, if any at all, nor was Halifax much bigger than St. John's, so I did not think I could learn much there that would prepare me for Boston or New York. I wrote to Fielding, who did not write back. Restless, I began smoking more than I ever had before, even drinking a little more, risking arrest in Halifax, sneaking back to my room with a couple of bottles of beer in my jacket pockets.

I left Halifax after several months, taking the train to Yarmouth and then the overnight ferry to Boston, once again crossing a great divide by boat at night. Boston, like Halifax, was something of a disappointment, and after two months there, living in a boarding-house on Allston Street off Scollay Square with almost no furnishings except my map and working for the *Herald-Traveler*, I made up my mind that I was as ready for New York as I would ever be.

As the train went south along the Hudson River, I realized that I was travelling through the setting of many of the books I had read. I was not just city-bound, but world-bound, it seemed, where the books I read were published, where the papers I read were written. A relative of my father's had once written him from New York: "Dear Charlie: There are more people in my apartment building than there are in my home town!" That optimistic exclamation point. The marvels of New York.

Doubts that would never be wholly laid to rest started up in me on that journey south through the Boston states. I passed a land border for the first time in my life, the one between Massachusetts and Connecticut, an arbitrary border on either side of which the landscape was identical, as I had no doubt it was on either side of the border between New Brunswick and Maine, Canada and America. Perhaps we Newfoundlanders had been fooled by our geography into thinking we could be a country, perhaps we believed that by nothing short of achieving nationhood could we live up to the land itself, the sheer size of it. It seemed so nation-like in its discreteness, an island set apart from the main like the island-nations our ancestors left behind. Perhaps it was not patriotism that drove us on, so much as a kind of guilt-ridden sense of obligation. Yet no sooner had these thoughts occurred to me than I felt guilty for thinking them and chased them from my mind, telling myself I was only looking for an excuse to justify my leaving home, about which I was also feeling guilty.

I remember the evening sunlight on the eastern ramparts of the Hudson, as the train outraced the river and the boats. I calculated that the water we were passing now would reach New York sometime early in the morning and be parted by the island of Manhattan in the dark, hours after we arrived there. It was as though an alternate time stream was moving parallel with ours, plied at sluggish speeds by ancient modes of transportation as we in the train, city-bound, got older faster, though in space our destinations were the same.

I must confess that at Grand Central Station, my first impulse was to take the next train back to Boston while I could still afford it. I have never understood why the concourses of train stations have to be the great, vaulting chambers that they are. If the point was to impress upon the newcomer that he had arrived at a city to be reckoned with, I was suitably affected. The place was like some secular cathedral and it seemed strange, looking up at the brass-domed ceiling, not to see depicted on it some religious scene that could match the place for sheer momentousness. People were all but running in every direction, sending up an echoing murmur in the station, which despite the teeming floor seemed almost empty, so much enclosed space was there above the multitude. They were striding purposefully, skilfully dodging one another, and for all I knew, every one of them had just arrived and, like me when I got off the ferry at North Sydney, were trying only to look like they knew where they were going.

I did not know that I had happened to arrive in New York at rush hour and that the place was not always quite so hectic. It was early evening and around the edges of the concourse, on ledges, on the floor, vagrants were already bedding down to catch a few hours' sleep in that din before the cops cleared the place at twelve o'clock. Others of their number, likewise on the edges, looked all too alert, and I fancied that more than one of them had his eye on me and my pulley-drawn steamer trunk. I had no idea just how unpromising-looking a mark I was, and that though the place, as I suspected, was crawling with pickpockets and thieves, they were on the lookout for better game than me.

I was wearing the only suit I owned, the smallest adult-style suit I'd been able to find, a threadbare dark brown Harris tweed with a Norfolk jacket and trousers so oversized they bunched in folds around my feet. There survives a photograph from that time, in which I am standing with one foot up on a crate half as high as me and one arm resting on my knee, the only pose I could assume in which my clothing could be drawn tight enough to make it appear to fit me. The pose also highlights, unfortunately, my spin-dle-thin, emaciated arms and legs. I am holding in my hands what looks like some sort of scroll (a rolled-up newspaper?) and am staring resolutely at the camera, apparently confident of cutting a fine, impressive figure, a not-to-be-trifled-with ninety-five-pound twenty-one-year-old.

I crossed the concourse as fast as I could and went outside. I saw cars, taxis, streetcars, buses, newspaper vendors, a stream of pedestrians, across the street a hotel doorman waving a white-gloved hand to someone. I did not really believe that any of it had been going on before I got there. If asked, I would have said of course it had been, but I did not really believe it. I hailed a cab. I must have made on the cabbie the same impression I had on the concourse thieves, for he asked to see my money first and, when I told him where I was headed, demanded that I pay him in advance.

I went to a large boarding-house on West Fifteenth Street that had been recommended to me by a friend back home. It was known to its occupants as the Newfoundland Hotel because so many Newfoundlanders lived there, and because it fell so far short of its opulent namesake back home in St. John's. The Newfoundland Hotel was a red-brick building, comprising two adjoining blocks of seven storeys.

It was convenient, aside from the fact that I could afford it, because it was about a block from Fifth Avenue and five minutes' walk from Union Square, the speaker's corner of New York social-ism, where such giants of "the cause" as Eugene Debs and Thorstein Veblen spoke, and which would someday, I fancied, be thought of as the place where Smallwood spoke.

It was situated among a dingy maze of narrow streets that, because they were lined by warehouses and run-down office build-ings, almost never saw the sunlight. On one side of the neigh-bourhood was Greenwich Village and on the other the affluent edge of upper Fifth Avenue, which it would soon become my habit to stroll through disdainfully on Sunday afternoons.

But I could not work up the nerve to visit the *Call*. I dreamed of being the next John Reed, writing the next *Ten Days That Shook the World*, but balked at the thought of going to the very paper he had worked for and asking for a job. I began having nightmares about going back to Newfoundland after an absurdly brief period of time, a stint abroad that would make my father's notoriously short one seem like a grand success. I woke up every morning feeling anxious and depressed.

The hotel was like some sort of vertically arranged indoor community, as if the entire population of some outport had been relocated to New York and was now being housed in this one building. Each floor was like a neighbourhood, each hallway on each floor like a street. There were always people lounging about in groups in the hallways, on the stairs, in the lobby. From about eight to midnight, most people left the doors of their rooms open to indicate their willingness to receive visitors. Even when they went visiting themselves, they left their doors open, as if the thought that something might be stolen never crossed their minds. "Look who's here," I often heard my neighbour say when he came back from visiting to find his room occupied by someone who, in his absence, had made himself at home.

People seemed to take as a personal affront the fact that during visiting hours I kept my door closed. Having no money, I did not often venture out into the city. I spent my nights reading, but even had they known this, my fellow roomers would not have considered it sufficient cause to be unsociable. Sometimes, in protest, they drummed lightly on my door as they were going by. People who for some reason did not know that the former tenant, a man named Clar, no longer lived there, came looking for him at all hours of the night, knocking on the door, shouting his name. "C'mon, Clar," a man said, "open up, ya silly bastard, open up," laughing when I told him he had the wrong apartment, as if to put someone up to this had been a favourite trick of Clar's.

Once, arriving home at night in the middle of my fourth week in New York, I found myself jammed in the elevator with a group of men and women on their way to a party on one of the upper floors. Because they were gingerly holding aloft, above head height, lit cigarettes and brim-full glasses of prohibited liquor, they could not use their hands for balance and so lurched all over the place every time the primitive elevator stopped or started.

"Sorry, my love," one girl apologized as she flattened me against the wall and spilled part of the contents of her glass down the front of my coat. While alternating between genuine remorse and weak-kneed hilarity at having just spilled her prohibited drink on some total stranger in an elevator, she kept apologizing, telling me she would wipe my coat clean for me if her arms were not stuck up in the air the way they were.

"That's all right," I said. Some of them had their hands so full they had to leave their cigarettes in their mouths and were making the trip with their heads tilted back, puffing smoke upward as best they could, eyes squinting.

Every time the elevator stopped and the doors opened to reveal another group of revellers, a roar of greeting and mutual recognition went up.

"Here's de byes, here dey are. What floor are we on? Four are we? I didn't think anyone on the fourth floor stayed up after eight o'clock."

They piled off in a mad rush, announcing their arrival to the inhabitants of the host floor by letting out a roar like that of some invasion force or mock stampede, which was met with an even louder roar from somewhere down the hallway. I was all but carried off with them. Then the doors closed again and I was left in the smoky elevator, alone I thought, until I heard a voice behind me.

"Have you ever seen so many island-pining, mother-missing, sweetheart-I-left-behind-bemoaning, green-arsed Newfoundlanders in your life?"

"Fielding!" I said. I turned around and there she was, obviously drunk, both eyes squinting, a cigarette shoved to the high corner of her mouth so that she seemed to be smoking out of her cheekbone, slumped against the wall, two hands on her cane, which was customarily planted on the floor in front of her, though at a treacherous angle.

"Smallwood!" she said, in mimicry of me. I was so glad to see her I threw my arms around her and broke her cigarette in half, the lit tip falling to the floor, sparks showering between us, though she did not seem to notice. When I broke the embrace, she stood exactly as she had been, as if she dared not trust herself to stay upright without the help of the cane.

"I thought you weren't coming," I said. "I'd given up on you. Where are you staying?"

"Here," she said. "In fact, it looks like we're on the same floor, unless you're sleeping on the roof."

"When did you get here?" I said.

"Yesterday," she said. "Been drinking ever since."

We *were* on the same floor, five rooms apart. I walked with her to her room. Even in her state, she noticed me looking nervously about.

"Whose reputation are you more concerned with protecting, Smallwood," Fielding said, "yours or mine? Don't worry, I can take it from here." She fumbled to fit her key in the lock, the severed cigarette in her mouth, strands of tobacco hanging from it.

"I'll come see you when you're — when you're not so tired," I said.

"No point waiting until Christmas," she said. At last she managed to open the door.

"Sorry, Smallwood," she said, gesturing goodnight with her cane, raising it slightly and nearly falling down. "You're right. I'll see you when I'm not so tired." She went in and sprawled face up across her bed, fully clothed, cane in hand, shoes on, arms outspread. She was almost instantly asleep. I backed out and closed the door.

Fielding's Condensed
History of Newfoundland

Chapter Eight:

A PROPER CENSUS

Charles II has been unjustly blamed for what happened in Newfoundland in 1675. Historians who bother to look closely into the
matter will uncover the following sequence of events.

The king orders the fishing admirals to inform the settlers that
they have the choice of being relocated to other colonies or transported back to England. The convoy commander, Sir John Berry,
will follow afterwards to conduct a census to determine how many
settlers are still left in Newfoundland, how many houses, how many
boats, etc.

The written order, however, is lost, and the admirals are left to
remember it as best they can. Confusion reigns among the convoy
that sails for Newfoundland that spring. From bunk to bunk, from
ship to ship, men argue over which of the following two statements
is the right one: (*a*) Those who wish to live in England or other
colonies may do so; or (*b*) Those who wish to live may do so in England or other colonies. By the time the fleet nears Newfoundland,

the captains are so addled by this syntactical conundrum that the only way they can think to solve it is to flip a coin.

Luckily, advance word that a census is to be conducted reaches the settlers, who, cryptically declaring that "no goode will come of being counted," abandon their settlements and take to the woods.

The fishing admirals have been favouring statement b for weeks, burning and pillaging everything in sight, by the time Sir John arrives. Sir John is outraged by what they have have done, which is no less than to have made it almost impossible to conduct a proper census.

Sir John does the best he can, enumerates as many settlers as can be coaxed out of the woods. He writes back to a friend in England: "The harbours look like cemeteries, with crucifix-like masts everywhere protruding from the water." By counting the masts, he is able to estimate how many boats there were, and is likewise able to estimate the number of houses by toting up the chimneys that remain.

The *Call*

THE COMPANY OF FIELDING revived my spirits. I suddenly noticed how many women there were about, flappers and would-be flappers. They were everywhere with their rouged knees, bobbed hair and short skirts. Some even went so far as to bind their feet so they could walk flat-footed. Fielding, in token acknowledgement of the new trend, wore a floppy hat fringed with bright rosettes.

At her urging, I went to the *Call* at West Fourth Street. I was led to a man named Charlie Ervin, the managing editor, whom I tried to convince to hire me by addressing him as though I wanted him to join a union. He smiled with a sort of world-weary kindness while I spoke, as if he could already foresee how far short of my expectations being a socialist reporter would fall. "We are the greatest socialist newspaper in the world, Mr. Smallwood," he said. "Which puts us at the top of a very tiny ladder." I stared in mute wonder at him.

"Explain your terms," he said. I thanked God I had met Grimes. I told him what I understood socialism to be, what its aims were and how they could be achieved.

"Comrade Smallwood," he said, "there is, in what you say, more bullshit than Bolshevism." I thought I had failed the interview until I saw him holding out his hand. "There are two things we never have enough of at the *Call*. One is money and and the other is reporters willing to work for next to nothing. You don't look as though you have the former, so I guess you'll have to be the latter." I blinked at him in confusion. "You're hired," he said.

Fielding did not apply for a job there, but she was soon doing some freelance pieces for *The New York Times*. She frankly admitted she would not need regular work for a while, having been given a substantial "going-away bribe" by her father. But she spent time with the *Call* crowd and helped me fit in with them, for though they professed the same world-view as I did, they had, I discovered, more in common with her than they did with me.

There were dozens of reporters at the *Call*, some of them my age. We all but lived in the ramshackle loft warehouse that had been the paper's home for years despite having been swarmed by rioters and fire-bombed several times. There were still scorch marks on the ceiling of the newsroom.

We sought out the cheapest eating places we could find, the Three Steps Down Cafeteria in Greenwich Village, the Russian Bear Tearoom, the Fourteenth Street Automat. On Friday, payday, we swarmed Child's Restaurant on Twelfth Street and, while arguing socialism, fed ourselves to bursting on sixty-five-cent four-course meals.

The others knew about Hotel Newfoundland and were already inclined towards seeing Newfoundlanders as predisposed to oddness by the time Fielding and I came along, and it must be said that nothing about us made them less so. I was taken up by the others as something of a mascot. Some of them were Jewish and got a lot of mileage out of my story about how all the Jews of St. John's had turned out to see me off. Then there was the fact that I was Jewish-looking, a Jewfoundlander, they called me, or sometimes just Jew-fie, or Joey the Jewfie, always affectionately, though my attempts to get them to take me more seriously only made them less inclined to do so.

They would mispronounce Newfoundland on purpose just to get me to pronounce it properly, which they for some reason found hilarious and would repeat to one another, mimicking my hyper-earnest expression as they put the stress on *land*. "New-foundLAND," Pincus Hockstein would say to Eddie Levinson. "Not *NewFOUNDland*, not *NEWfoundland*, but *Newfound-LAND*, like *understand*, understand?"

The women were like none that I had ever met before. Compared with them, Fielding was withdrawn and reticent. Dorothy Day took one look at me when we met at Child's and, right in front of the others, declared that I was a virgin, "a virgin if I ever saw one," she said, as though she were unmasking me as some sort of fraud. I was too dumbstruck to deny it and, in any event, the change in my complexion confirmed her diagnosis. The table erupted in laughter, as though they had just discovered that, sitting in their midst, was the oldest, or possibly the last, virgin on the planet.

"Now tell us, Joey," Dorothy said. "Are you saving yourself for some young thing back home who, in exchange for a kiss, extracted from you the night before you left a promise of engagement, or is it just that you haven't yet worked up the nerve to ask some girl to bed?"

I prayed for a touch of the wit by which I had undone Fielding years ago, but none was forthcoming. Instead, I was saved by Fielding herself, to whom they had taken as if she was playing well some role they were familiar with but liked, Fielding with her silver-knobbed cane, her — to me — suddenly acquired political scepticism, her affected aloofness, her eloquence, her irony.

"He may not in matters carnal be an adept," Fielding said, putting one hand on my shoulder, "but Smallwood is a true socialist. He has a horde of influential enemies and" — she took them all in with a gesture of her cane — "a handful of inconsequential friends. Besides, Dorothy, how do you know that I am not the tutor in matters carnal of the alluringly emaciated man you see before you?"

They were quoting her in no time. "Well, if it isn't Smallwood's tutor in matters carnal," they said when they saw her. They were bemused by her professed lack of commitment, political or otherwise, and teased her about working for such an "establishment" publication as *The New York Times.*

They seemed too Grimes-like to me right from the start, their interest in socialism too theoretical, and I told them so. They saw themselves as advancing the cause of some worldwide movement to whose real-life effects they had not given much thought, while I was mainly interested in how socialism could be of benefit to Newfoundland, a view they dismissed as too parochial.

We argued for hours, Fielding drinking more than any of us but rarely speaking.

"Newfoundland," I told them one night, "will be one of the great small nations of the earth, a self-governing, self-supporting, self-defending, self-reliant nation, and I will be prime minister of Newfoundland."

"And I will be president of the United States," Pincus said, laughing, raising his glass to me.

"I will," I said, standing up, which I was just barely able to do, swaying, though I was only on my second drink.

"This woman here can hold her liquor better than you can," Dorothy said.

"There is more of me to hold it in," said Fielding, though whether in defense or further mockery of me I wasn't sure.

"You are looking at the future prime minister of Newfoundland," I said. They looked me up and down, and as if the disproportion between what I was and what I claimed I would become was just too much for them, burst out laughing all at once.

"What about you, Fielding?" Dorothy said. "Is it your mission in life to further the ambitions of Smallwood here?"

"It is my mission in life," Fielding said, "to further no one's ambitions but my own. Once I have decided what they are, I shall pursue them relentlessly."

"How would you describe your world-view?" said Dorothy.

"I am a phlegmatist," said Fielding.

I was presumed to be from the working class because of my appearance, my accent, my lack of formal education, my social clumsiness, my eagerness to please and be accepted. I did nothing to disabuse them of this notion, said nothing about my middle-class grandfather or uncles or my time at Bishop Feild. I was in their eyes something of a catch, a legitimizing presence in the newsroom. The more shabbily and unfashionably I dressed, the more out of place I looked among them, the better, as far as they were concerned.

Most of them lived better than was warranted by what they were paid for working at the *Call*, so I suspected that, like Fielding, they were being kept in money by their parents. Many of them were from quite well-to-do families, on sabbatical from lives of privilege to which they openly admitted they planned to return someday.

I did not describe life in my father's house. When they told stories of their own self-imposed, recently endured privation, flashing their socialist credentials, I said nothing. But I let slip that my mother was a Pentecostal.

"Pentecostals," Dorothy said. "Aren't they the ones who speak in tongues and thrash about on the floor like epileptic auctioneers?" I felt I had given myself away. Pentecostalism. The religion of the poor.

I told them they, or rather we, were not really poor, because we could stop being poor anytime we wanted to, whereas the poor thought their poverty would last forever. What I really meant, but did not say because I feared it would make me seem like too much of an authority on the subject, was that the worst part of poverty is that you believe you can no more shed it than you can your personality or character, that you see your condition as a self-defining trait that, no matter how much money you come into, you can never divest yourself of or, worst of all, hide from other people.

"Here's to a world in which no one feels they have anything to hide," said Dorothy, sincerely. We all drank to such a world, and we all knew it was me that we were toasting.

Fielding's Condensed
History of Newfoundland

Chapter Nine:

THE PROBLEME OF THIS NEW FOUNDE LANDE

Sir John Berry submits his census of the island to the king, who, in his famous Proclamatione Regardynge the Colonye of New Founde Lande, declares: "… it be certaine from the informatione contained in the census that the probleme of this New Founde Lande in tyme will solve itselfe. It is cleare that human life in this wilde place cannot be sustained and that the planters will either leave or by attrition perishe. I do hereby decree that they be not molested but lefte to encounter whatever fate or variety of fates as may please Almightye God."

It is because of its belief in the settlers' right to self-determination that England is slow to respond to the invasion of Newfoundland by France in 1696.

After every English settlement except Bonavista and Carbonear is destroyed, England decides to fortify her colony. The two countries struggle for ownership of Newfoundland until 1713, when, under the Treaty of Utrecht, England recognizes France's historical right to part-ownership of Newfoundland by giving to France what it believes to be a worthless stretch of coastline, the northeast one-third of the Newfoundland shore. England can be excused for this so-called blunder, for the only people who advise against it are the settlers who have lived on the shore for years and are to be supplanted by the French, and so can hardly be expected to give an honest estimation of its worth.

A Modest Proposal

THOUGH I HAD COME to New York as early in life as I could, I had come too late to be part of the heyday of the *Call* or the socialist movement in America. It was not long before I realized that like the Socialist Party itself, the *Call* was on its last legs. Just as I was arriving on the scene, hyper-earnest, idealistic, the others were starting to reconcile themselves to the idea that to be an American socialist was to adhere to an ideology that, though righteous, would soon be out of favour for all time, a lost, just cause.

I had been two years in New York when the paper folded and, though it soon after resurfaced as a weekly, I was not rehired. One of the results of the decline in the fortunes and membership of the party was that socialist newspapers all over started shutting down and what few reporters were left found themselves unemployed. I had had the company of like-minded people for the kind of rare, short time that in your youth you think will never end.

I managed to make some money freelancing for what few socialist publications there still were and, with Fielding's help, for

The New York Times and other mainstream papers, but because I had no full-time job, I had time for doing what I had really come to New York to do anyway, to make speeches, the result being that while my standing in the decimated party rose steadily, I grew progressively more destitute.

I was soon spending more time at the non-paying avocation of stump-speaker than I was reporting. I was much valued by the party as a speaker because I could pass for a lot of things that I was not. I was not Jewish, but because of my nose and dark features I could pass for Jewish, a Jew of inscrutable heritage once my accent was factored in, but a Jew nonetheless and one preferable to the real thing, the Jewish intellectuals who in the East Side ghettos could not hold an audience because they were so clearly not ghetto-born themselves.

I was not really working class but, luckily for the party, I was starving (I would not accept money from Fielding, no matter how much she insisted) and every day wore the same suit of clothes, so I could pass for working class. The other socialists, who dressed down for their speaking engagements, always looked enviously at me as if they wondered how I managed to look so uncultivatedly shabby and so authentically emaciated. The party would have lost a valuable asset if I had succeeded in becoming as well-fed, well-clothed and well-rested as those on whose behalf I campaigned day after day, but fortunately the one thing that poverty did not diminish was my ability to elude good fortune.

Because of my Newfoundland accent, I could pass for an Irishman, a Welshman, a Scot. The Chameleon, Fielding called me, but it was really the audiences that changed, each one mistaking me for something different.

One thing I could not be mistaken for was black, but that did not stop Charlie Ervin from choosing me from among the thinned ranks of his "stumpers," proclaiming me a "specialist in race relations" and sending me to Harlem. Fielding went with me and, as she had done along the waterfront in St. John's, went about rounding up an audience for me, standing on street corners with her cane held aloft and proclaiming: "Joseph Smallwood will give a speech in five minutes on the subject of socialism, a speech that none of you will soon forget, the likes of which you have not heard before and may not hear again...."

I stood on a soapbox and looked out over a sea of black faces, blacks at first mute with incredulity at the sight of these two whites among them — Fielding in her "finery," me exhorting them to self-betterment by voting for a party that, though it claimed to be colour-blind, had almost no black members. I was, at first at least, so ingenuously unaware of the danger I was in and so earnest in describing the racism-free society that I believed would come about through socialism that they let me speak, their expressions seeming to say that they might as well let me entertain them.

I told them I was from Newfoundland, and when they said they had never heard of it, I said, as though by way of proving it existed, that I would be its prime minister one day.

"You're the puniest politician I ever seen," one man said. I told him I was not a politician yet, but was speaking on behalf of a party candidate who was running in the state elections and who could not be everywhere at once.

"Never mind once," the man said, "he ain't *never* been here. He's afraid to come in here, das why he sent you." The crowd laughed.

"Under socialism, you will all have better lives," I said.

"You got socialism," a woman said. "It don't look like it done you much good." She turned to Fielding. "Why don't you let him have some of the food? You look like you eatin' it all and then some."

"You don't get socialism like you get religion," I said. "We can't do anybody any good, ourselves included, until we get elected."

"But den I bet you gonna do yourself a lotta good," the woman said. I felt foolish; I saw myself as they did, a strange-looking little guy of such low standing among his fellow socialists that they had sent him into Harlem, knowing he might not come back, and whose ambition was to become prime minister of some obscure, possibly non-existent country — and who was unaccountably accompanied by Fielding.

More men and women got up from where they were sitting on their tenement steps and gathered round to hear what else this prodigy of gullibility would admit to having swallowed.

"Under socialism," I said, "the black man and the white man will be equal. A black man and a white man will have an equal chance of becoming president."

"Sure," a man near the front of the crowd who was dressed in what I recognized to be the uniform of a Pullman porter said, "there'll be a black president soon. It's just a coincidence that the first thirty-six were white." The crowd roared with laughter. It was like the St. John's waterfront all over again, me being laughed at and Fielding standing mute beside me, the two of us like a pair of buskers whose routine was not yet ready for the streets.

I was supposed to speak in Union Square at seven-thirty, but the engagement had been cancelled. At about six I went to Fielding's room to tell her. The door was open, but there was no sign of her. On the little table that doubled as her desk, exactly in the middle of it, almost prop-like, was what looked like a shopkeeper's ledger, a large green book with black triangles on the corners of the covers.

I opened it. The first line of page one read "Dear Prowse." In the top right-hand corner of the page, the entry was dated March 11, 1912. I turned to the middle of the book. Again, the first line of the page read "Dear Prowse," the entry dated September 23, 1918. Years after leaving Bishop Feild, years after the near-caning, she was still — still what? I turned to another part of the book, near the middle. The first line of the page read "Dear Small-wood." It was dated two months ago, November 4, 1923.

"See anything you like?"

Startled, I snapped the book shut, put it on the table and turned around. Fielding was only a couple of feet away.

"How far did you get?" she said.

"I didn't read anything," I said. "Just the salutations."

I looked at her, expecting to see a grin of mischief on her face.

"September 23, 1918?" I said. "Dear Prowse?"

"Yes," Fielding said. "You see, Prowse is the Gaelic word for diary — " She stopped. "Look, I don't — "

"Dear Smallwood?" I said. "What are you up to, Fielding?" I said. "Is this a diary, a journal, what?"

"Both," she said. "Neither. I don't know. More like unsent letters, I suppose."

"To Prowse? And then to me? Why?"

She swallowed and put one hand to her face, rubbing her forehead with her fingers. "It's something writers do; they, they address their thoughts to their friends, you see — "

"You still considered Prowse your friend after Bishop Feild?" I said. "After what happened?"

"I still wrote to him in my journal, that's all. We never met after I left school. He never knew. Just like you never knew until now."

"What exactly is it that I don't know?" I said.

"Oh, for God's sake, Smallwood, for God's sake," she said. "I I don't really expect anything. I know you don't — I mean, I thought — I've never seen you with anyone. I mean, I know now that you don't, I know you're not — It doesn't have to mean we can't be friends." I knew what she was trying to say, but suddenly all I could think about was her and Prowse.

"You and Prowse — you dated?" I said.

"Yes," she said exasperatedly. "We were, what? sweethearts, you might say. Everyone at the Feild and Spencer knew."

"Everyone except me, apparently," I said.

"That's not the point, now," she said.

"Even after what he did, you were still — infatuated with him?"

"Yes," she said. "Even after that. But that's not the point. The point is — The point is I'm not now."

"Some of those letters say 'Dear Smallwood,'" I said. "Do you think about me the way you did about him?"

"No. I — You mean more to me than he ever did — "

This was the first such declaration that anyone had ever made to me. I couldn't find the voice to tell her that I felt the same, and had for some time now.

"Will you marry me?" I blurted out. I who had vowed I would never marry.

She winced as if I had misunderstood her. But what, other than that she loved me, could she have meant by saying what she had? Almost imperceptibly she shook her head, looked away from me.

I felt that I had been tricked into making a proposal she had no intention of accepting. I had proposed without saying her name. When I had been thinking of how I would ask her, in the instant before I did, it had seemed ridiculous to call her by her last name while proposing marriage. On the other hand, I could not, after all this time of acting as if I did not know what it was, call her by her first name, Sheilagh. "Sheilagh, will you marry me?" It would have seemed ridiculous to have transformed her into someone I did not know, someone who did not exist.

She was not Sheilagh, not to anyone except her relatives, I suppose; she was Fielding, which suddenly made me realize what a blunder I had made. She was Fielding. She was the sort of woman people called by her last name. Her expression confirmed my panic. She was at a loss as to how to turn me down. She clutched her cane in both hands, tap-dancer fashion, clutched it until her hands went white.

"Smallwood ..." she said. She paused for a very long time, more than long enough to convince me that a "yes" would not be forthcoming. It was the same for her, not able to call me by anything but my last name. She had been right on the waterfront to ask me what we were. We were not lovers. What were we? What did she want us to be? Sexual associates? How could you seem other than absurd declining a proposal of marriage from someone you only ever called by his surname? She could not say my first name for the same reason that I could not say hers.

I did not want to be let down easily, or even awkwardly, by Fielding, who after all was only Fielding and had been all along, nothing more. How could I have been so stupid, so guileless? I was not heartbroken, I assured myself, just humiliated, and Fielding was as much to blame for my humiliation as I was, if not more.

"I'm sorry — " she said. "I don't know how — "

I could think of no way to extricate myself except to pretend that I had been joking, in the hope that as she had so many times about other matters, she would pretend to believe me.

"You didn't think that I was serious, did you?" I said. For an instant, the other, unselfconscious Fielding showed her face, momentarily forgetting I was there. Fielding unlooked at, unobserved; Fielding out of time, seeing the world for what it was, for how it would have been without her in it. Then the real one was back and time began again.

"You don't really think I'd ask *you* to marry *me*, do you?" I said. "I mean, there's nothing wrong with you or anything. You're just not the type of woman a man like me would want to marry, and I'm sure I'm not the type of man you'd want."

"I don't think we should do this any more," she said ambiguously. "This" meaning "talk like this" or go on spending time together?

"I think you're right," I said. "It's really no way for two people who feel nothing for each other to conduct themselves."

"Quite right," she said, her voice quavering but clipped. "Not for two people who feel nothing for each other. Two people should feel something. Though it was, after all, you who asked me to marry you."

"If that's how you choose to remember it," I said, "it's fine with me."

"If I could choose my memories," she said, "I would choose to forget that we had ever met. I would forget a lot of other things as well." She turned her back to me, body ramrod straight, head high. It reminded me of the way she had stood after the boys of Bishop Feild released her that day in the training centre.

I doubted that anything I said could have changed her mind about me, and believed that if she knew how completely I had fallen for her, she would forever have me at a disadvantage. The thought of declaring my love and being laughed at or even tenderly rejected was more than I could bear. I had vowed never to marry, never to be ruled by mere biology or relinquish my self-sufficiency, my very self — how could I make resolutions with myself only to forget them on the impulse of the moment? My instincts had been right.

"You can go now," she said.

A few days later, I heard that Fielding had moved out of Hotel Newfoundland, to where no one knew.

FIELDING'S JOURNAL, FEBRUARY 12, 1923

Dear Smallwood:

The first half of my name was for a second on your lips. Or did I just imagine it? "Fiel — " The barest whisper.

What do you feel, Smallwood? Do you feel anything? I was not expecting a proposal, not like that, not then. Still, I should have known that one was coming, that even you would get around to it sometime. I should have been prepared.

Was ever a proposal so hastily withdrawn? At least you didn't leave me at the altar. Might there have been a way of telling you what, before you married me, you had a right to know; a way of telling you that would not have made you change your mind or scared you off? Why am I even asking? The expression on my face, the look in my eyes, was enough to scare you off.

At home I was always so careful with my journal, but in New York it seemed there was no one I had to hide it from but you. What were you doing there, hours early?

You must have been telling the truth when you said that all you had read were the salutations. You would not have proposed otherwise.

Or would you have? What do I wish you had said?

"Fielding, I am a man whose heart is ruled by foolish vanity and pride. But, Fielding, I have loved you since I was twelve years old. Fielding, when I'm with you I feel like the boy I used to be and remember, as if she were standing beside me, the girl you were when we first met that day on the field beside the school. It was sunny, but the first sad chill of fall was in the air. I remember things, too, Fielding. You on the heights of Bishop Feild and behind you the roofs of the city descending to the harbour, to the water and the Narrows and Signal Hill five hundred feet above the sea. Fielding ..."

Do men speak like that to women except in books or in the journal fantasies of jilted girls? Why, if the you I love is just someone I invented, do I care? You with your mawkish ambitiousness, your delusionary confidence. And under all that bluster, you are barely resisting disillusionment and bitterness at the age of twenty-three.

How can I have been so stupid? My heart, if I had let it, might have mended. But not now.

Fielding's Condensed
History of Newfoundland

Chapter Ten:

THE PLANTER'S 'PLAINT

It is easy enough to dismiss Hayman as a rhyming simpleton, as Prowse does, yet how poignantly in *Quodlibets* does he capture the boredom of day-to-day routine in this supposedly "new" world in his poem "The Planter's 'Plaint":

> Fish for breakfast, fish for lunch,
> Of fish I cannot stand the sight.
> And worst of all this savage bunch
> Who bugger me night after night.
> I wish we had some women here,
> I wish some womenfolk would come.
> The men then might not be so queer,
> Nor, I think, so sore my bum.

Hines

FOR WEEKS, TOO overwrought to do much work, I walked about the streets of New York, occasionally basking in the fact that none of the thousands of people passing by knew my secret, my humiliation. Fleetingly, among strangers, it seemed to me I had nothing to be ashamed of, no reason to feel humiliated or sick at heart. I told myself that whatever I had felt for her, I would feel for other women, more, in fact. There were women in the world who could inspire in me more love than Fielding had; it was foolish to fret and moon about the way I was. Not that I would marry any of these women, or even have affairs with them, or ... Gradually, in this manner, I came to miss her more and more as the weeks went by.

Things got no better in New York for reporters. In midwinter, when I could no longer afford my boarding-house, where the rent was six dollars a week, I moved out, temporarily, I hoped. I allotted myself forty cents a day for food: a ten-cent breakfast and a thirty-cent plate of pork and beans and bread, and apple pie and coffee for dessert. That was my dinner menu every day for the next two months.

I moved into a flop-house near the Forty-Second Street public library on Sixth Avenue. The room was fifty cents a night and its main drawback was that every so often, the el train would roar by, so I did not get much sleep. I stayed there for a few days, then realized I had to find an even cheaper place or I would soon be out of money. I moved into a twenty-five-cent-a-night flop-house farther downtown, a disconcertingly short distance from the Bowery, which for people down on their luck was looked upon as the point of no return.

For me, it would be the point of return, the return to Newfoundland, that is, but the thought of going home a failure, as my father had done from Boston thirty years before, made me determined that I would somehow stick it out.

I moved to a dorm-like flop-house called the Floor, where all you got for your fifteen cents was floor space. I was never more aware of not looking like I could put up much resistance. I had heard of what happened at the Floor to people too drunk or too enfeebled to protect themselves.

There was no one there to keep order, no one to appeal to for help. Behind the desk downstairs, there was a huge fellow whose one concern was that no one make off with one of the three-cents-a-night blankets and who discouraged the practice by hanging on the wall behind him a conspicuously dented baseball bat.

I spent three nights at the Floor but never slept. For fear of having them stolen out from under my head, I did not use my boots for a pillow as some were doing, but left them on my feet. I wish everyone had followed my example, for the place reeked of stinking socks and boots. Sitting up with nothing to lean against, even with my hands on the floor behind me, proved to be exhausting, and when I could no longer do it, I rested on one forearm and signalled my degree of wakefulness by smoking cigarettes at measured intervals to make them last.

It was now early spring, the middle of a milder than usual April in New York. Determined not to stay at any more fifteen-centers, and so that I could use what little money I still had left for food, I joined the ranks of men who slept behind the library on the marble benches in Bryant Park. For blankets I used newspapers that I fished from garbage cans. I woke up many mornings with my hair and whiskers rimed with frost after a night of feverish, shivering dreams in which the cold and Fielding always played a part. In one dream, I met her on the street walking arm in arm with Reeves, and when I tried to explain away the tremors and the palsied shaking of my hands, she smiled at Reeves as if she had warned me I would come to this unless I changed my ways. Other nights, it seemed the bench beneath me was a wooden bunk, and I could hear the coal crank and the pelt chute of the S.S. *Newfoundland*. To keep warm, I smoked cigarettes beneath a canopy of newspapers. I slept on the same bench every night, making sure I got back to the park in time to claim it. I somehow managed to fit my body to its distinctive shape, found a little hollow in the marble for my hip, but in the mornings awoke so stiff-limbed that I could barely move.

It was the duty of a cop named Barnes, who patrolled the park, to keep the benches vagrant-free throughout the day. Early in the morning, he walked along the bench-lined path, whacking each sleeper on the soles of his feet with his nightstick. "Rise and shine," Barnes would say. Soon, all over the park, like statues coming to life, men were sitting up, yawning, rubbing their eyes.

I wondered what my father would say if he could see me, reduced to bedding down on my marble bench at night. Yet the only thing that made this existence tolerable was knowing that anytime I wished, I could escape it and resume my other life in Newfoundland. At the same time, I hated the thought of being forced to go back home against my will, penniless and looking it. I would have to telegraph to my first cousin, Walter, who now, after Uncle Fred's death, owned the boot-and-shoe factory, for my fare home for one thing. I knew that he would send it, but I also knew that even if I paid him back, he would treat me forever after as his father had treated mine.

Bryant Park was full of men like me, trying to hold out as long as they could, hoping their luck would change, dreading the day they would have to admit that the big city was too much for them and go back home. It was the knowledge that there were so many others just like me that was most dispiriting; all of us who had come to the city convinced that we were exceptional, unique, were now beset by the same hackneyed fate, living out the last days of our stint in the big city in this rube-ville of a holding park before we went back home to take up our roles as local object-lessons for those who imagined they were different.

One morning I was awakened on the marble bench, not by Barnes, but by someone who, because I was not wearing my glasses, I could not make out and whose voice I did not recognize.

"Oh my, oh my, oh my," boomed the voice. For a while, I thought that I was dreaming. "Another starry-eyed Newfoundlander reduced to nothing in New York."

The speaker had a deep, quavering voice that projected clear across the park, prompting the men on the benches to sit up and stare, not only at him, but also at me, as if they were wondering what was wrong with me that I had to be addressed at such a volume.

I took out my glasses and put them on and saw, standing over me, a man who appeared to be well over six feet tall. He had curly, black, wildly unkempt hair that came down almost to his eyes, thick black eyebrows and burnsides that joined like a strap beneath his chin. He wore a black peaked sea-captain's hat and glasses with thick lenses that made his dark eyes look even larger than they were, which in turn, along with a knowing half-smile, made it seem that he was staring at you as if he thought you were trying to hide something and, under close scrutiny, would give yourself away.

He wore a kind of tail-coat that at one time might have been the jacket of a footman or a butler. It hung down almost to his knees and was frayed at the edges, smudged all over with what might have been dust or chalk as if he had begun the day by rolling in the street.

"How did you know I was a Newfoundlander?" I said.

"It's written all over you," he said. "Literally. You have the name of Smallwood on your shoes." He smiled and shook his head. "I walk through all the parks in the city from time to time," he said, "on the lookout for Newfoundlanders. They aren't usually as easy to spot as you. I've had my eye on you for quite some time."

I wondered how close to me he must have got to be able to read the name of Smallwood on the soles of my shoes.

"What do you mean?" I said. "Who are you?"

"First," he said, "let us settle the question of who you are. You are, judging by your accent, from St. John's. You have been in New York for three, at the most four, years. You have been shunning your own kind since you arrived, for they remind you of things you came here to forget or at least to get away from for a while. After achieving some small success at home, you came here to prove that you could be successful anywhere. You either believe, or did when you set out, that you will never go back home, or else that you will go back someday in triumph, a made man who will never have to prove himself again."

"You could be describing any Newfoundlander in New York," I said.

"If you had been spending time with Newfoundlanders in New York, you would not think so. Most Newfoundlanders come here with other Newfoundlanders and, while here, associate with Newfoundlanders. But it could have been myself I was describing, myself some years ago."

The whole thing had the self-consciously momentous tone of some biblical encounter, the first meeting of Christ with one of his apostles. It was unnerving.

"Another reason I know you haven't been associating with Newfoundlanders is that you don't know who I am," he said. "I am Tom Hines, and I am the owner and publisher of a newspaper called the *Backhomer*. Subscribers in forty different countries. More foreign correspondents than *The New York Times*."

"I've never heard of it," I said.

He smiled. "What's your name?" he said.

"Joe Smallwood," I said. "And yes, I am related to the man who makes the boots. My grandfather started the store and my cousin runs it now."

"What about your father?" he said, looking at me with those enlarged eyes of his. One of them was badly bloodshot.

"He's not involved with the store," I said.

"And therein lies a tale, I'm sure," said Hines. "What do you do? Or should I say, what did you come here in the hopes of doing?"

"I *am* a newspaper reporter," I said. "I worked for nearly two years at the *Call* before it folded."

He smiled as if he knew everything about me now that he would ever need to know.

"The *Call*," he said. "Written and read by One Worlders. It's just as well it went under. I'm told it was published on paper so thin it never made much of a blanket."

Angrily throwing off the newspapers I was covered with, I stood up with the intention of replying in kind when a wave of dizziness hit me and sent me backwards onto the bench. When I opened my eyes, Hines was still there, smiling down at me as if my dizziness was his doing.

"When did you last eat?" he said.

I shrugged.

He reached into his blazer and took out a card. "This is the address of a place where you can stay until you are better able to support yourself." He took a pencil out of the same pocket and began to write something on the back of the card. "And this," he said, "is the address of the *Backhomer*. Come see me. I don't exactly have a job for you, but if you come to work for me, I'll give you a place to stay and pay you when I can."

He extended the card to me and, when I declined to take it, tucked it into the pocket of my jacket. I was too dizzy and too weary to resist.

"Remember, man," I thought I heard him saying as he left, "thou art a Newfoundlander and unto Newfoundland thou shalt return."

I lasted two more nights on my bench in Bryant Park, sleeping in the library throughout the day with a book on my lap that I pretended I was reading.

The third morning after meeting Hines, I awoke before the sun was up, gingerly eased myself into a sitting position. I saw on the ground a cigarette butt, reached down to pick it up and toppled off the bench, hitting the ground harder, or sooner, than it seemed I should have. I lay on my back. Then, remembering my childhood misconception that lying on your back was a symptom of the onset of TB, I rolled over onto my side and went back to sleep.

When I awoke again, another man, covered in newspapers, was sleeping on my bench. I somehow managed, using the bench as a support, to get to my feet and considered waking him and telling him the bench was mine, but he looked as though I would be no match for him.

I wandered through the park, looking for an empty bench, but did not find one. I figured I was a day, two at the most, from complete prostration. I fished in my pocket for the card Hines had given me. The address was in Brooklyn. I set out for it on foot.

Twelve hours later, I arrived at my destination, just able to stand. All I noticed of the address was the number 1693 and an illuminated red crucifix above the door. I went inside and handed my card to a woman who sat behind a hotel desk. She took the card from me and scrutinized it.

"We'll be right with ya, my love," she said. Then she yelled, "George, there's one here for the Coop. He'll be one for the ward if you don't hurry up."

———————

You rode to the Coop on what must at one time have been a service elevator. On the sixth floor, all the walls had been torn down and the space had been partitioned into cage-like rooms with chicken-wire that extended to the ceiling, each room having a wire door that locked from the inside. The point of the cages, since they provided neither privacy nor quiet, was solely to protect the residents and their meagre possessions from each other. You could see from one end of the floor to the other, some men standing, smoking, talking to each other through the chicken-wire, but most, even before lights out, just lying supine and open-eyed on their bunks with their hands behind their heads as though deep in contemplation of better times or the series of events that had brought them to their present state. Most people moved their bunks and belongings to the middle of the cages, equidistant from each "wall" and as far as possible from thieves who with strung-together coat hangers would fish for loot, as my first-night neighbour told me.

He said that Hines was the landlord, "the Newfoundland-lord, so to speak." He told me that the Coop was free for two weeks, after which time, if I was able to find a job of some sort, I could, if I wanted, stay on indefinitely. Hines, he said, rented out the "rooms" — there were others like them in New York — at less than the going rate to anyone who could prove himself to be a Newfoundlander.

"Hines is a Pentecostal minister," he said. I assumed this explained his eerily accurate appraisal of me. No doubt he knew Miss Garrigus. "Born and bred in St. John's he was. But now he got this little church, the Pentecostal Church of Newfoundland in Brooklyn, he calls it. I been there. If you go regular, you can earn yourself a few extra days at the Coop."

"It looks like some kind of jail," I said, looking around.

"Oh, no, you can come and go when you wants," he said. "Except you have to be back in by nine o'clock at night, and anyone caught with booze is gone for good. And the same with anyone who gets on with any funny business."

"He must make money," I said, "or he couldn't afford to let people stay at the Coop for free for two weeks."

"He makes his money on the paper, I suppose," he said. "He never made no money off of me. I never been in the Coop for more than two weeks at a time. As soon as my time at the Coop runs out, I'm back on the street again. I can't find no job. You're not allowed back in the Coop again for three months once they boot ya out."

I stood that night with my fingers clutching the lozenges of wire, looking out across the floor at the cots on which the men were sleeping, and saw that one cubicle contained a man, a woman and two children — a boy and a girl — the children small enough to share the bunk, the man and woman sleeping on the floor, with the woman between the man and the bed. There were not often women or children at such places; most flop-houses had a policy against admitting them. The sight of the children doubled up in the bunk reminded me of my brothers and sisters back home, still sleeping three to a bed, I had no doubt. I remembered what a luxury it had been at Bishop Feild to have a whole bed to myself for the first time in my life. I looked at the couple on the floor, the man on his back, the woman on her side and turned away from him, her knees drawn up, her hands beneath her head, her posture faintly recriminatory, as if she blamed him for reducing them to this. I thought of my parents.

At first my plan was to wait out my two weeks at the Coop and then move on. But I could find no freelance work, none that paid anyway, though I went out looking every day. I thought of the nights I had spent at the Floor. I would not go back to that. It was either take Hines up on his offer or go back home, which I vowed I would never do except by means of my own money.

So I went to see Hines at the *Backhomer*, which was like the *Call* in only one respect, that of having the narrowest of mandates. The *Call*'s purpose was to promote socialism, the *Backhomer*'s to promote Newfoundland.

The *Backhomer*'s offices, if that is not too grand a term for eight hundred square feet of space, were located above a hardware store on West Fifteenth Street, half a dozen blocks from Hotel Newfoundland. They consisted of two sweltering rooms, one for Hines and one for the rest of us, Hines's little "office" and the "newsroom." (Everything at the *Backhomer* merely aspired to be what it was called, including us "reporters.")

"Well, if it isn't Mr. Smallwood," Hines said, stepping out of his office and intercepting me as I headed for the newsroom, having heard me, I presumed, as I was walking down the hall. "Mr. Joseph Smallwood. One-time reporter at the *Call* and erstwhile resident of Bryant Park. I'd all but given up hoping that you would come to the *Backhomer* and favour us with your journalistic expertise. I thought you must have returned to your life among the One Worlders." He looked at me through those eye-enlarging glasses, his left eye now almost completely bloodshot.

"Every night since our meeting, I have prayed for you in the hope that it would make you more receptive to salvation. If ever you need spiritual guidance or feel the urge to be baptized, come see me at my little church in Brooklyn."

"I've come about the job you offered me," I said.

"Did I offer you a job?"

"Yes. You just said you'd given up hoping — Look, two weeks ago you said that if I worked for you, you could provide me with a place to stay and pay me when you could."

"You say it, so it must be so," said Hines. "Step into my office."

In the office there was a desk and a single chair in which Hines sat, facing me. On the wall behind him was a large wooden carving of the Newfoundland coat of arms: an elk above a crossed shield emblazoned with lions and unicorns and flanked by two Beothuk Indians, with below it the motto *Quaerite Prime Regnum Dei* (Seek Ye First the Kingdom of God).

"We'll have to work out the terms of your employment," Hines said.

"If you'll let me stay in the Coop and let me have two meals a day, I'll come to work for you," I said. "I can't say for how long."

"As for how long," Hines said, "we know not the day, nor the hour."

Three days later, I began working for him. He ran an item in the paper announcing that the grandson of David Smallwood, the very David Smallwood who, to advertise his store, had erected one of Newfoundland's more familiar landmarks, the Narrows Boot, was now working at the *Backhomer*.

The rest of the staff of the *Backhomer* consisted of a man named Duggan and his wife, Maxine. What the terms of their employment were I never did find out.

Most of what little news-gathering went on was done from the newsroom by phone. Only rarely did anyone besides the freelance photographer have to venture out to cover something. Once a month, more to alleviate my homesickness than in hope of finding stories, I went to Green Point in Brooklyn to meet the Red Cross boat from St. John's. There I met Newfoundlanders from whom I got the latest news and newspapers from home. But like Duggan and Maxine, I spent most of every day in the newsroom, smoking, morosely, disconsolately smoking. We shared huge, bowl-like glass ashtrays that went unemptied for days, filling up with butts and ashes so that after a while, instead of stubbing out our cigarettes, we simply stuck them in the pile pincushion fashion. By late afternoon, there was a pall of smoke about head height in the little newsroom.

We were always homesick; we could not help it, since all we ever wrote or read about at work was Newfoundland. We had never had this much to do with Newfoundland when we lived there. We were even more homesick than our readers and that, judging by the letters to the editor, was saying something. We were at once homesick and sick of home, sick to death of hearing about it, writing about it, sick of keeping tabs on and interviewing other homesick Newfoundlanders.

"Newfoundland this, Newfoundland that, Newfoundland morning, noon and night; it's enough to drive you mad," Duggan said. "I swear to God, if I hear the word *Newfoundland* one more time, I'll blow my brains out."

Hines pointed what might have been the finger of fate at him and said, "Remember, man, thou art a Newfoundlander and unto Newfoundland thou shalt return." Duggan, when Hines's back was turned, revolved his index finger at his temple to indicate that Hines was crazy.

The *Backhomer* was largely about Newfoundlanders abroad and was read by Newfoundlanders at home and abroad. Hines every so often published the abroad subscription list so readers could see how Newfoundlanders were distributed throughout the world, putting asterisks and exclamation points after the names of the farthest-flung subscribers. "Millie Dinn, Ankara, Turkey.**!!!! Calvin Hodder, Hong Kong.**!!!"

Hines, in his sermon/column, forever likened Newfoundlanders to the Jews, pointing out parallels between them. There was a "diaspora" of Newfoundlanders, he said, scattered like the Jews throughout the world. He saw himself as their minister, preaching to his flock from his columns, most of which began with epigraphs from the Book of Exodus. So often did Hines liken Newfoundlanders to the Jews, we likened him to Moses, asking each other in the morning if Moses had come down from the mountain yet, meaning had he shown up yet for work.

One of my main tasks was to edit the two pages in the *Backhomer* devoted to "Lost Newfoundlanders," Newfoundlanders missing in action, so to speak. Any Newfoundlander trying to track down a long-lost relative could write the *Backhomer* and have their letters and a photograph of their "lost" loved one printed in this section. "Anyone knowing the whereabouts" was how most of them began. Often, the most recent photographs were taken fifty years ago, daguerrotypes in which the men — it was usually men who were missing — all looked alike.

There was a woman looking for her brother, whom she had not heard from since 1898. Along with a letter written by her daughter was a portrait photograph of one Joe Marsh sitting in a high-backed wicker chair, looking done up for some special occasion, wearing a suit, arms folded, head thrown slightly back, his expression that of someone who had no intention of living out his life in Hickman's Harbour. I imagined him now at forty-six coming across this picture of himself at twenty-one. I chose as the caption a sentence from the letter written by his sister: "WHERE ARE YOU, JOE? Last reported sighting twenty-five years ago. In 1898, left Hickman's Harbour with Captain Ed Vardy on a boat bound for St. John's. Went from there to Montreal. Dropped out of sight ten years later. Not seen since. What happened to him torments me to this day."

"Where are you, Joe?" There was something morbidly attractive about the idea of dropping out of sight and coming across thirty years from now, in a paper like the *Backhomer*, a picture of me as I was when I was twenty-four, accompanied by a letter from Fielding or my mother begging anyone who knew my whereabouts to get in touch. For a clean getaway, I would have to do little more than change my name.

Fielding's Condensed
History of Newfoundland

Chapter Eleven:

OSBORNE AND BEAUCLERK

In 1729, the West Country merchants convince King George II that because of the state of lawlessness among its permanent residents, Newfoundland needs a governor. They suggest the appointment to the post of the present commodore of the Newfoundland fishery, Lord Vere Beauclerk.

In response to requests from resident Newfoundlanders for the appointment of a civilian governor, the king compromises and chooses Lord Vere Beauclerk, acknowledging that while he is not a civilian, any Newfoundlander who wishes to think of him as one is free to do so. (Thus begins a tradition, which will last almost one hundred years, of filling the civilian post of governor with non-civilians.)

When it is found that if Beauclerk accepts the position, he will be constitutionally required to resign his seat in the British Parliament — which, out of loyalty to the king, he is loath to do — Beauclerk declines the appointment. Once again the king steps in and saves the day, announcing that navy commander Henry Osborne will be the governor, but that Beauclerk will go with him and tell him what to do.

Neither Osborne nor Beauclerk winter in Newfoundland. Osborne's first priority is to build a courthouse. No courthouse is built, but two jailhouses are, and stocks proliferate throughout the city of St. John's.

Osborne appoints justices of the peace, choosing them from among resident Newfoundlanders. They come into conflict with the fishing admirals, who do not recognize their authority, deeming them to be illiterate and uneducated.

Luckily, there are soon a sufficient number of West Country merchants living in Newfoundland that a pool of men whose degree of literacy is such as to satisfy the admirals is established, and from this pool justices are chosen.

In spite of this and many other such advances, the judicial system still has its flaws. But slowly it evolves. The expensive and time-consuming process of transporting suspects to England to be tried is discontinued. No longer do ships packed with suspects and witnesses set sail for England in the fall. No longer do ships packed with witnesses set sail from England in the spring.

The *Backhomer*

H INES PRINTED VERBATIM in the *Backhomer* his Sunday sermons and the keynote addresses he gave at meetings of associations like the Brooklyn Newfoundlanders Club, where Newfoundlanders met once a month to socialize. While composing his sermons, he walked around the newsroom, reading aloud from them.

"Mrs. Duggan," Hines said to Maxine, "the text for this week's sermon is 'I have been a sojourner in a foreign land.' Are you familiar with it?"

"I was just talking about it when you came in," Maxine said.

"Oh my, oh my, oh my," said Hines, shaking his head and smiling ironically. He invited her and Duggan to attend his Sunday service. He told them it would be well worth their time; it would be more fun than any party they could go to; they would not be hungover afterwards; and it would not cost them anything. But he seemed to be going through the motions, not really expecting any takers. He smiled with a kind of ironic sympathy when they declined, as if he had expected them to do so, as if he were looking down at them from heaven, one of the saved regarding two of the damned whose paths in life had crossed with his, who might now be where he was if only they had listened.

"Oh my, oh my, oh my," he said cheerfully, as if it was necessary that there be a preponderance of sinners against whom the saved could measure their good fortune.

Me, on the other hand, he saw as a convert-in-the-making. "Your conversion, Mr. Smallwood, is inevitable," he said, standing by my desk, staring seer-like into space. "I see it as clearly as if it has already happened. You shall be immersed in the waters of the Hudson seven months from now and thus shall your eternal soul be saved. I will write your mother" — he had found out from Miss Garrigus that my mother was a member of the Ark — "and tell her that her oldest child will soon be saved. God be praised."

I asked him not to write her and get her hopes up for no reason, since I had no intention of converting, but he went ahead and did it anyway. I had to write a disclaimer to my mother, who nevertheless took more heed of Hines's letter than she took of mine and wrote back to me saying she had known all along, when she heard who I was working for, that I would be baptized in the Hudson, and she predicted it would happen at the very mission she had told me of before I left, the mission where Miss Garrigus was baptized.

When, for the umpteenth time — I had been working for him for nearly a year — he invited me to attend his Sunday service, I decided I would go, though I did not tell him so. Maxine had told me that I had to go just once. She had, just out of curiosity, and had witnessed a spectacle worth seeing.

I got up early one summer Sunday morning and walked the dozen or so blocks from the Coop to Hines's church, which looked like a house to which a steeple had been attached. Out front, people were walking about the church, standing back from it to get a better look as if they had never seen it before, which reassured me.

When the service was about to start, I went inside. I was startled to see in the lobby a copy of the very portrait of Miss Garrigus that hung back home in the front room.

There was seating in the church for fifty or sixty and standing room for twenty more. Though there were a few seats still empty, most of them were near the front, so I decided I would stand. In fact, I stood behind the tallest man I could find so that Hines would not see me. Other than a large plain cross on the wall at the centre of the altar and a large wooden carving of Newfoundland on the front of the pulpit, the church was bare, the windows uniformly amber-coloured.

Hines came out onto the altar from a side door, with a Bible tucked under one arm. He was dressed no differently than he dressed for work, except that he wore around his neck, hanging halfway to his waist, a wooden cross. Hines climbed up into the pulpit and began to speak in his deep, quavering voice.

"One of my eyes," he said, "is permanently bloodshot, the legacy of a stroke that, for a time, struck me blind and occasioned my conversion. God so marked me so that I would not forget.

"This happened many years ago in Newfoundland. I was struck stone blind, stone blind, can you imagine that? I was barely twenty-nine, younger than most of you, a bibulous fornicating gambler. I was crawling home one night on my knees after some debauch and everything went dark and I heard the voice of God cry out to me, saying, 'Hines, if you wish to see the light of day again, if you wish to spare yourself the torment of eternity in hell, you must repent.' I shouted out, 'Lord, what must I do?'

"He told me I had to go where no one knew me, get away from my partners in debauchery and the places of temptation to which I knew I would be drawn, which I knew I could not pass without frequenting, so established were my habits, so puny and cowardly was my resolve, so bent was my will to Satan's ways. I had to leave that island, which once had been my paradise and which I and no one else had made my hell.

"'Hines,' God told me, 'you must go, you must venture out across the gulf and, in some strange city where no one knows you, make amends, and with good deeds and unflagging worship of the

Lord, renew your soul.' And so that is what I did. I did what you and yours have done. I came to this Sodom of a city because God told me it was here in this New York on this new island that I should build my church.

"Some of you who left that new found land were drawn here by prideful ambition. Some, like me, were driven here by shame. But most of you came here because you had to, and you believe yourselves to be as undeserving of your exile as Jonah was of being swallowed by the whale. But you are wrong, for because you are sinners, you deserve much worse than this.

"Homesickness. What is that compared with hell-fire and damnation? You were homesick before you left home. You were in exile when you lived in Newfoundland. Homesickness is but the yearning for salvation. Newfoundland is but the place your body came from. Your true home is the birthplace of your soul, the place where it began and to which, when you have breathed your last, it will return. Remember, man, thou art a Newfoundlander and unto Newfoundland thou shalt return."

"Amen," said the congregation all at once.

There was not the usual coughing and shifting about that greets the ending of a sermon, nor had Hines stepped down from the pulpit. If anything, the congregation seemed more attendant than before and some people even leaned forward in their seats while others gripped their prayer books tightly and bowed their heads as though in shame.

He looked around the little church as though enumerating his congregation, taking note of who was there and who was not.

"Gentlemen," said Hines, "will you bar and block the door?"

I looked over my shoulder and saw two men wearing blue armbands heft a large wooden bar into place across the doors, then stand, one in front of each door, clasping their hands in front of them.

"I will speak this morning to someone who is here for the first time," said Hines. There was a sagging of shoulders, a collective sigh of relief. Most of them were off the hook.

I told myself that there were, there must be, other first-timers in attendance. No one, I was somewhat relieved to see, was looking at me, though surely most of them must have known that I was new.

I stood more fully behind the large man who was shielding me from Hines and bowed my head. What was I doing there? Why, given how Hines had been talking about me these past few weeks, had I come and willingly put myself in peril? I cursed Maxine for recommending it to me.

"The name of the person I am addressing," Hines said, "cannot be spoken in this church, as he has yet to be baptized in the Pentecostal faith."

"Pray for him, oh Lord," said the congregation. I felt faint, yet clung still to the hope that Hines's target wasn't me but someone else.

"Pride is your sin," said Hines. "Pride, the sin for which Lucifer, once a chosen one of God, was hurled headlong from heaven and for which to this day he lies writhing in the lake of fire with his fellows-in-damnation, will not release you until you ask the Lord to strike him down. Not until you admit to your absolute worthlessness in comparison with God will you be free of pride. You must be convicted of the sin of pride, admit to it, abject yourself or be forever damned. The sins of the father are visited upon the son, and though your father's sins are many, all of them proceed from pride as surely as you proceeded from his seed and from your mother's womb. Your mother cannot sleep, such is her anguish that alone of all her brood, her first born will be damned."

I felt the blood surge to my head. My forehead hit the back of the man in front of me, but he did not turn around.

"Look at yourself. Your clothing is shabby and filthy. There is barely room inside you for your soul, you are so puny, so pathetic. If a mere man were to clap you on the back with any force, the breath of life would leave you and you would fall down dead. Think how easy it would be for God to strike you down. Surely He is coming soon. You know not the day, nor the hour.

"As a child, you wrote your name at the bottom of lists of men you imagined to be great. Lists of Newfoundland's prime ministers. Lists of Newfoundland historians. Lists of writers, thinking that to become one of these would somehow console you for the poverty you endured, the way the masters treated you at school and laughed at your ambition. You will never live down the mark they gave you for character. And how it galls you that the boys who at school were your inferiors have gone on to be successful. What a fool you are. God sets no store by how the masses of men regard you. What good will it do you in the next life that in this one you were held in high esteem by those God deemed unworthy of redemption? It will be no comfort to you, while you burn in hell, that a likeness of you commemorating your accomplishments stands forgotten here on earth except by pigeons. Vanity, all is vanity, saith the preacher, and a striving-after wind. I ask you to come forward now, to show yourself and for your soul's sake stand beside me or be forever damned. If you do not come forward, you will burn like the little bits of kindling that you are. Your body will burn the way your boots burned the night he threw them in the fire. After death, your body cannot be consumed by fire but will burn forever and your pain will not decrease. Your insides will burn the way his are burned by the rum he drinks and by the guilt he harbours in his soul. God is extending to you an invitation that he will not extend again. He will not beg to any man, let alone the likes of you. He does not need you, but you need Him. God has instructed me to tell you that He will wait one minute more. We will wait and pray for you in silence."

Hines made a show of taking out his pocket watch and placing it on the pulpit in front of him. He bowed his head. The congregation did likewise and many blessed themselves. One man in the nearest row of pews even took out his pocket watch, as though he were in the habit of timing this interval of contemplation with Hines when someone's soul hung in the balance.

After a time, Hines closed his pocket watch, and in a lower tone of voice, as though no one could hear him but me, he said, "There is a dreadul secret that involves a book and a man you never knew." My heart hammered inside my chest, a wave of dizziness washed over me. "Only through another book and another stranger will you find peace. These are the words of Almighty God Himself. Will you heed them now or be forever damned?"

I turned and ran towards the porch, shouldering my way through the men standing at the rear.

"Unbolt the doors," Hines roared. The two men guarding them unbolted the doors and stepped aside as if terrified that I might touch them.

I ran from the church. I took the steps in two strides, ran across the churchyard and out into the street, looked over my shoulder, for I felt as though I were being pursued and my very life depended on not being caught. I kept running until, exhausted, I collapsed on a park bench.

"There is a dreadful secret that involves a book and a man you never knew." Mr. Mercer. A man I never knew. A stranger. "Only through another book and another stranger will you find peace." Through the Bible and through God, a stranger to me. "I've had my eye on you for quite some time," he said that morning we first met in Bryant Park. For how long before we met, I wondered, and at whose request? My mother's? Miss Garrigus's? It wouldn't have been difficult for him to keep track of me, knowing the newspapers and Newfoundlanders of New York the way he did. Obviously he had found out a lot about me from Miss Garrigus or my mother. But how did he know that my mother threw the book? Even if my mother had confessed to Miss Garrigus, which I very much doubted, it seemed inconceivable that Miss Garrigus would have broken her trust by repeating her confession to Hines. And even if she had, how did Hines know *I* knew about the book and Mr. Mercer, since even my mother did not know I knew? Such was my state, I thought Hines might be capable of second sight.

I went back to the Coop and told them I would be checking out in the morning. I was determined never to set eyes on Hines again. But I could not stop thinking about his strange sermon. It seemed hard to believe that my mother had told Miss Garrigus about Mr. Mercer. The rest, about me and my father was one thing, but — And yet, she must have. That night, I lay awake for hours, then slept fitfully, and in the morning felt worse than if I had not slept at all.

I decided I would confront Hines. Immediately upon arriving at the *Backhomer*, I went to his office and closed the door. He was sitting behind his desk, the plaque bearing the coat of arms of Newfoundland behind him. He saw me glance at it. "*Quaerite Prime Regnum Dei*. 'Seek Ye First the Kingdom of God,'" he said. "Do you remember the motto of Bishop Feild?"

"What does that have to do with anything?" I said.

"The motto is 'He is not dead whose good name lives.'"

"You had no right to do what you did yesterday," I said. "Is that how you get your converts?"

"You went there of your own accord," said Hines. "I wonder what Headmaster Reeves thought of the way you left?"

"How would Reeves know anything about it?"

"He knows everything now."

"What do you mean?" I said.

"Passed on," said Hines, in a faintly ironic tone, as if to say that Reeves's passing was just another example of God having the last laugh. "Two years ago in England. We did an item on him in the paper. A lot of boys, men now, who had gone to Bishop Feild under him wrote to say how sorry they were to hear that he was dead."

"Why are you telling me this?" I said.

"I have my reasons."

"How did you find out all those things about me?"

"God makes me privy to knowledge that he withholds from others." I knew there would be no point pursuing the matter further.

"I'm beginning to think it's quite possible that you're insane," I said.

"God had us meet so I could tell you these things," Hines said.

Exasperated, I got up and left his office. My head was in such a spin that I sat motionless at my desk until Maxine asked me what was wrong. I told her and Duggan about my visit to Hines's church and his sermon, leaving out the part about the book.

"I wouldn't pay much attention to anything Hines says," Maxine said. "That stroke he had screwed up more than just his eyesight."

I looked up the issue of the *Backhomer* in which Reeves's obituary appeared. It was the standard stuff: a photograph of him, a laudatory account of his life, especially that part of it he had spent in Newfoundland. I looked up the next couple of issues in which letters from Feildians lamenting his death were printed. I was startled to see a letter from Prowse and letters from several other of the Townies who had always been offering to get up petitions protesting Reeves's treatment of me and some of the other boys.

"I have often," wrote Prowse, "since leaving Bishop Feild, had occasion to feel grateful for the lessons that I learned there from Headmaster Reeves, who, though strict, was one of the most scrupulously fair-minded men it has been my privilege to know." The letter was signed David Prowse, Q.C. A lawyer now. And Porter a doctor. I wondered if Prowse had intended those of us who had known Reeves to read the letter ironically. Even so. I thought bitterly of Prowse. His treatment of Fielding. I read the other letters. There were some from the 'Tories, including one from "Slogger" Anderson, now a member of the House of Assembly. Fondly recalling days that never were. This was how men of the sort they aspired to be were supposed to remember and pay tribute to their teachers.

There was one thing I was certain I could not do and that was go on working for Hines. I was afraid of being pulled further into that weird world of his in which there was no telling what was and was not true. And I had no doubt, despite his theatrics with the watch and his assertion that God would not extend his invitation twice, that he would go on trying to convert me. I decided to leave the *Backhomer* and vowed I would never set eyes on him again if I could help it. I decided that the next time I saw my mother, I would say nothing about my visit to the Pentecostal Church of Newfoundland in Brooklyn unless she brought it up, which I doubted, for it would horrify her to think of, let alone talk about, me running from the church with Hines's sentence of damnation ringing in my ears. And she might not hear about it at all. Miss Garrigus, knowing how it would affect her, might not tell her. Or Hines, not wanting to come off looking like a failure, might not tell either one of them.

I said goodbye to Duggan and Maxine and asked them to tell Hines that I was not coming back and that I would no longer be staying at the Coop.

I spent only three more days in New York, three days and two nights sitting and sleeping on park benches, contemplating my next move. I decided to go back to Newfoundland, though I had no idea how I would go about it.

Socialism. Better to find a cause that, though perhaps less just, had some hope of succeeding, the nearest thing to socialism that people would accept, than to revel all your life in the righteousness of your defeat.

Fielding. Thoughts of her, now that I had made up my mind to go back home, were nagging at me constantly.

In my five years in New York, I had come to know quite well the captain of the Red Cross boat that each month docked in Brooklyn at Green Point. After our third or fourth meeting, long before I was conscious of missing Newfoundland, Captain Prowdy had pronounced mine the worst case of homesickess he had ever seen.

On the third day after my visit to the Pentecostal Church of Newfoundland, I went to Green Point, keeping an eye out for Hines, who I knew sometimes turned out to bless the boat. I hung round, after the other Newfoundlanders who had come to meet the boat had left, to talk to Captain Prowdy. It was a cool, windy day, despite the time of year. The thought of another winter spent in the flop-houses of New York had become unbearable. I held my coat together at my throat, my other hand clamped on my sod cap to keep it from blowing away.

"You look like you're about done in, Joe," Captain Prowdy said. His kind, sympathetic tone made me go weak in the knees. I described to him my situation and, before I could ask, he offered me a ride back to Newfoundland in the Red Cross boat. It would take a while, he said. We would go via Boston, Halifax and North Sydney to Port aux Basques. In all, the trip would take three days, and this was no passenger ship, so he hoped I had something like a bed waiting for me back in Newfoundland, for I would need it.

I felt so relieved, I fainted.

III

—◆—

Field Day

And we believe a greater pack of knaves does not exist
than that which composes the House of Assembly for
the Colony. Take them for all in all, from the Speaker
downwards, we do not suppose that a greater set of
low-life and lawless scoundrels as Public men can be
found under the canopy of heaven.

— from "The Newfoundland Royal Gazette," 1834, as
quoted in D. W. Prowse, *A History of Newfoundland*

Fielding's Condensed
History of Newfoundland

Chapter Twelve:

HERODOTUS

The evolution of the Newfoundland justice system culminates in 1792 with the establishment of the Supreme Court of Newfoundland. John Reeves (deemed by Prowse "a most admirable selection" — judge not the judge, judge, lest ye be judged) becomes its first chief justice. Unfortunately, his objectivity is called into question in 1793, when he publishes the first history of the oldest colony and in it sets forth the thesis that England has for three hundred years been exploiting Newfoundland.

While we could hardly expect Chief Justice Reeves to write a history as authoritative as this one, since he did not have access to the enormous volume of documents, the perusal of which has been our happy task this twenty years, or to the succession of other Newfoundland histories from whose blunders we have learned so much; and while we do not wish to cast aspersions on the man whom some have called Newfoundland's Herodotus, our *History* would fall short of being definitive in one respect did we not point out that John Reeves was a peevish crank who wrote an entire history of

Newfoundland just to get back at some West Country merchants who, he said, "are so miserly that, were I to allow it, they would be constantly contesting in my court some Newfoundlander's right to breathe their air."

What do we find upon reading Reeve's successors, Anspach, Harvey, Pedley, Prowse, et al., but that they repeat in their histories this heinous lie of his as though it were the gospel truth. While we trust that our history refutes his thesis to the satisfaction of educated people everywhere, the fact that we cannot undo the harm he has done has on many occasions kept us from a good night's sleep and given rise in our nature to an irritability that many have named as the reason they will never speak to us again.

Such are the travails of the historian who, because his predecessors are dead, must content himself with lying awake at night concocting fantasies in which he so humiliates them in debate that they pledge to burn all existing copies of their books. To such lengths are we driven by reading Reeves, as well as to tapping our foot on the floor, which we must refrain from doing, for there have been complaints and we cannot afford to be evicted from yet another boarding-house, there being so few left that we can afford, having had to forgo an income these past twenty years to make possible the writing of this book. That our history will sell in such volume as to compensate ten times over for the income lost while writing it seems little comfort now.

The Walk

I TRIED TO CONVINCE MYSELF that I was ready to return, that only by leaving had I learned to live here. But I wondered if I, too, had reached the limits of a leash I had not until now even known I was wearing and was, like my father, coming home not because I wanted to, but because I was being pulled back, yanked back by the past. For a panicked while, I wondered if I had made a fatal, irreversible mistake in departing from New York the way I had. I could not go back there now, no matter what.

Something strange happened when we drew near to Port aux Basques. There had been a storm the night before, and though the sky was breaking, the easterly wind had not gone round. The clouds were still racing westward and the rock-face on the headlands was wet with rain.

It was as if I saw, for a fleeting second, the place as it had been while I was away, and as it would be after I was gone, separate from me, not coloured by my past or my perceptions, but strange and real as towns seem when you pass through them on your way to somewhere else, towns that you have never seen before but that seem remindful of some not-quite-remembered other life. A kind of hurt surged up in my throat, a sorrow that seemed to have no object and no cause, which I tried to swallow down but couldn't. It was the old lost land that I was seeing, as if, like fog, the new found one had lifted. How long I stood there staring at it, I'm not sure, seconds or minutes. When I came out of whatever "it" was, the new found land was back and tears were streaming down my face. I looked around to see if anyone had noticed, but there was no one else on deck.

I had never seen the place that way when I lived there, not even when I was very young, and I somehow knew that I never would again, not if I went away for fifty years and came back for one last look before I died.

I lingered for a while at a boarding-house in Corner Brook, got a job freelancing for the local paper and helped start up a union at the paper mill, still feeling the pull of the mainland, knowing I was back for good but for some reason unable to undertake the last leg of my journey home, the train ride that would take me to St. John's. Each night I resolved that the next day I would leave, and each morning I found some excuse to put off my departure. I did not know what I was looking for until it found me.

The sectionmen who maintained the cross-island railway had just got word of a coming pay cut and wanted to form a union in the hopes of having the cut rescinded. When they heard of my work with the union at the paper mill, they approached me and I agreed to help them.

I spent the next three days trying to figure out how I was going to organize seven hundred men who lived in section shacks strung out along the railway at one-mile intervals from St. John's to Port aux Basques and all the branch lines in between. A meeting was impossible, as was getting their signatures on union cards by writing to them, since most of them could not read or write.

The only way I could think to do it was to walk the entire length of the railway, branch lines included, gathering signatures as I went. At first, it seemed out of the question. I doubted that I was physically up to walking more than twenty miles a day for three months. Some anti-unionists at the boarding-house had nicknamed me Skab, a shortened version of Skin-and-Bones (and, of course, the last thing any union organizer would want to be nicknamed), and what would be left of me after I walked seven hundred miles I tried not to imagine.

But the idea grew on me — the idea of a grand, momentous homecoming that would hint that my five years abroad had been full of just such adventures, walking in service of a noble cause from one side of the island to the other. I pictured the last few hundred feet of rails thronged by cheering crowds who, for weeks, had been tracking my progress in the papers and had come out to witness my long-heralded arrival at Riverhead station in St. John's. My family and friends would be there, all except my doom-prognosticating, now-chastened father, whose absence would confirm that I had proved him wrong; that, having shown that unlike him I could make it on the mainland, I had come back home, my demons of self-doubt laid to rest for good, not because I had to, but because I wanted to, wanted selflessly to put my talents, which elsewhere could have made me rich and famous, to use in helping Newfoundland.

I took the train back to Port aux Basques and there began my walk, signing up sectionmen along the way, collecting from each of them fifty cents in membership fees. I set out in mid-August and had to make it to St. John's by November 1, when the pay cut was to take effect.

I fancied I was walking the lone street in a company town called Sectionville, along which houses were laid out at one-mile intervals. The residents of Sectionville travelled their single, endless street using hand-pumped trolley cars by which I was frequently almost run over, so silently did they glide along the tracks and so oblivious was I, in my near-exhaustion, to what little sound they made.

It became an almost surreal sight after a while: married couples, pairs of men, pairs of boys and girls, sitting on their trolley cars, facing each other, see-sawing, pumping the handle up and down. I tried travelling by trolley-car myself but found that even with a partner, it was more tiring than walking. A few well-muscled sectionmen who could operate a trolley by themselves assured me I could be their passenger, but I declined, knowing what a puny, foolish-looking figure I would make sitting there looking at them while they did all the work. I told them that at any rate, it was better that I walked, for the longer my odyssey took, the more hardship and privation I endured, the more likely to sign up the sectionmen would be and the more embarrassed the railway would be.

I carried my suitcase on a stick slung over my shoulder. It bumped on my back with every stride until, about a week into the walk, one of the sectionmen fashioned me a shoulder harness like cigarette girls wore and I walked with my suitcase flat in front of me, and with a book laid open on it, which allowed me to read while I was walking.

My suitcase held seven weighty books, six of them readable, one of them not — my father's copy of the judge's *History*. I had purchased another *History* in New York, and this was the book I read most often.

I plodded wearily along, after a while no longer noticing the spectacular scenery, often near-delirious from hunger and exhaustion, reading, reading, retracing centuries of history until it seemed to me the judge's whole book was written in the cryptic scrawl of his inscription to my father. I probably read the judge's *History* twenty times. It began to seem that this, and not the walk, was the epic task that I had set myself, to read the history of my country non-stop, over and over until I had committed it, word for word, to memory, as Hines had done with the Bible, the one book that remained unopened in my suitcase.

I had bought a Bible in Corner Brook because I hoped my supposed religiosity would impress the sectionmen who fed me and let me spend the night in their shacks. It did, but, more important, it impressed their wives. When their wives went to my suitcase to get any clothes that needed washing, there was the Bible. That Bible, not one page of which I read along the way, kept many a section-man who was otherwise inclined to do so from dismissing me as a Godless socialist and convinced them to sign up with the union. I told them and their wives that when I thought I could not take an-other step, I took out the Bible and was inspired by reading it to carry on.

"I could not have come this far without it," I shamelessly said, at the same time recalling the many times I had been tempted to lighten my load by throwing it away.

I had often enough heard my mother quote passages from the Bible to be able to do so myself without ever having read them. I was often asked to say the grace over dinner as if I were some itin-erant preacher who was only secondarily a union organizer.

How strange it was, that meandering town of Sectionville, the narrow stream of civilization that wound its way through the wilderness from one side of the island to the other, marked off in miles, each mile-post with its corresponding shack occupied by families driven to eccentricity by isolation.

They really were no more than shacks, clapboard shacks raised from the ground on posts, since it was either too rocky or too boggy to sink a proper foundation. Their flat roofs were waterproofed with black felt and gleaming tar, their one adornment a metal chim-ney pot, the cap of which could be closed or opened by pulling on a piece of rope beside the stove. No other kind of roof but a flat one would have stayed on for long, what with the wind. When a storm was coming, the sectionmen battened down their shacks like boats at sea, pulled to the solid shutters on the windows and the aptly named storm-doors, then lit the lamps, it being otherwise pitch dark inside even at midday. Many of the shacks were shored up on the sides by a palisade of saplings sunk obliquely into the ground, so the bottom halves of the shacks looked like the shells of teepees. If not for these "longers," the shacks would have been blown off their posts the way boxcars often were from the tracks.

The method of gauging when it was safe to send a train was not a very scientific one. The sectionmen measured the force of a gale by how difficult it was to open their front doors against it. I saw this "test" performed more than once, a man bracing his shoulder against his half-open storm-door while wearing a calm, almost diagnostic expression. There was no scale of wind velocity *per se*. It was merely deemed to be either safe or unsafe to send a train.

Each shack had a little porch attached that led directly to the kitchen/sitting room, the centrepiece of which was the pot-bellied stove in which wood and coal brought in by the train were burned and on the floor around which, on paper spread out to catch it, lay a pool of soot. The section people made do with teapots with their spouts cracked off, cups without handles, cups made from tin cans and a loop of wire, chipped plates and saucers with spider webs of fault lines, chairs cobbled together from whatever could be scavenged, tables made of doors laid across two sawhorses, doorknobs still attached. For beds, there were makeshift bunks and hammocks fashioned from old fishing nets and sails, and armchairs and sofas made from crates and burlap sacks.

Between house and outhouse, washing lines were strung and on them, almost always horizontal in the gale, flapped underwear made from flour sacks, threadbare coveralls and shirts and bedsheets so stitched and restitched they looked like ragged flags.

Some shacks were surrounded by a flock of squawking chickens that were kept for eggs until winter. There might be a horse, a single cow, a beagle for retrieving birds and rabbits.

Each night, I displaced children from their beds, and sometimes even couples, who would not hear of me sleeping on the floor. Word spread up the line that I was coming, as did word of my emaciation, so that it became the mission of the wives to shore me up with food. They seemed as eager to see if I was as wasted away as rumour had it as anything else, sizing me up as if to say my state of bedragglement was scandalous, as if my every ailment could be attributed to the neglect and ineptitude of all the wives to whose ministrations I had so far been subjected. "There's not enough of you to bait a hook with, sir," one woman told me outside of Springdale Junction. "We're having trout, sir," she said, as if she couldn't imagine why her counterparts hadn't thought of trout, as if this were a novel dish available nowhere in Newfoundland but at her house. She hinted that if I had been as well fed by all the others as I would be by her, I wouldn't be the size I was.

"You've got to keep your strength up, sir," she said when I protested that delicious as the dinner was, I could not eat another bite. Another bite of trout, I meant, for trout it had been almost every night since Port aux Basques. At her urging, I ate more and more.

That night I lay awake, stuffed to the point of insomnia with trout. In the morning, her husband took me under the armpits and, lifting me up, authoritatively declared that I weighed ninety-seven pounds, ten pounds less than his twelve-year-old boy. I was sent off, after a trout-and-eggs breakfast, with a trout and dole-bread sandwich lunch that hungry though I was by noon, I could not bear to eat, and threw away in favour of blueberries that I picked along the tracks. I felt guilty doing so, knowing how dearly come by the bread had been. It would not have mattered to them who I was; if I was walking the railroad to help them or just to pass the time, they would have treated me with the same unstinting kindness.

By the time I reached central Newfoundland, I was having a great deal of trouble with my feet, which were blistered and swollen, and it was now to healing my feet and mending my shoes that the wives devoted themselves. From the minute I entered a shack to the time I went to bed, I sat with my feet immersed in a washtub filled with some bizarre concoction, the occupants of one shack swearing by blueberry wine and partridge-berry jam as a cure for blisters, the occupants of the next night's by something else.

My feet were buttered, smeared with turpentine and rubbed with diesel oil. I slept with my feet wrapped in poultices of every description, wrapped in bark: spruce bark, juniper bark, birchbark, pine bark.

One woman tied soapbar-like blocks of fat-back to the soles of my feet. Forgetting I was wearing them, I got up in the middle of the night to use the outhouse and lost my footing, landing with a crash on my backside to the delight of the two boys, who, because of me, were sleeping on the floor.

"Oh, my God, Mr. Smallwood is crippled," the wife said, as if there lay before her a life of notoriety as the woman in whose house Mr. Smallwood had been crippled. "I'm all right," I said, "I'm all right," removing the fat-back from my feet as the two boys howled with laughter.

As I walked along the tracks, I thought of my cousin Walter's boot-and-shoe shop, the rows and rows of gleaming boots and shoes. I thought about phoning Walter and asking him to send me several pairs, but as the only way of getting them to me would have been by train, I decided not to.

Near Gander, I was heartened when a sectionman showed me a copy of the *Daily News*, in which there was a small item about what I was doing and why. There was nothing in the *Telegram*, which did not surprise me. I had left Newfoundland five years before as a *Telegram* reporter and a non-paying guest of the Reid Railway, who wanted only that I sing the praises of train travel in return for my fare, and here I was now, walking the same tracks to organize a strike against the railway.

"So they know I'm coming," I said.

"Oh, yes, sir," he said. "They know you're coming. It's a great thing you're doing, sir."

Once a day, from then on, when I was passed by an eastward-bound or westward-bound passenger train, passengers who had heard of my cross-island walk waved to me, shouting encouragement or cheering ironically as if they thought I must be mad.

Walking the branch lines was the hardest part, having to detour from my eastward march to go down the length of some peninsula, and at the end, having to turn around and retrace my steps. It was all I could do to force myself to turn due east onto the Bonavista branch line, which began so tantalizingly close to what would be the last leg of my journey.

The country here looked as if it had been put through a strainer, sifted until all the soil was gone and there was nothing left but boulders, which were then strewn haphazardly in what had been a single, massive, shallow lake, creating ponds and intervening steppes of stone that at intervals were thinly coated with bog and here and there garnished with clumps of juniper and stunted spruce.

So undifferentiated was the landscape that if not for the section shacks, I would have lost all sense of movement. As it was, I had to make a conscious effort not to wander from the tracks, not to stay the course where the track turned and walk off aimlessly across the barrens straight into some pond.

And there was always the wind, a gale in my face making a sail of my shirt and pants, or a gale at my back against which I had to dig in my heels to keep from falling forward. I thought scornfully of the moors and heaths I had read about in books. They were nothing next to this. Any wind in which you could stand upright and not be lifted off your feet was nothing next to this.

The eastern side of the island was four hundred miles from the mainland and the wind blew here as it did anywhere in the North Atlantic four hundred miles from shore. The wind blew northwesterly across the island as if its effect on it were incidental to some larger, grander mission of destruction; as if it were on its way to a place where people were not so easily impressed; or as if it were blowing just to please itself, a land-oblivious, sea-generated wind that made it hard to believe sometimes that the whole island was not adrift.

At the Southern Bay stop, I came closest to the sea. Outside the moderately choppy inlet, the wind blew unimpeded and massive black waves went by at right angles to the shore, a perpetual storm of seaspray blowing from their crests. The water a hundred feet from shore looked as deep and rough as it would have had the island not been there at all. It was strange and spellbinding, that tandem of wind and water. Where the water stopped, the wind went overland until it met up again with water on the other side, each one, it seemed, driven on by the other. Everything was headed one way — clouds, wind, water, the waves so high the horizon was near and jagged, bobbing as if I was jumping up and down. I was sure the motion of the waves must extend right to the bottom, the whole ocean running like a river infinitely wide.

It was impossible not to personify the wind. The only pathetic fallacy involved was thinking you had any business being where you were. There was a section shack called Blow Me Down House, which made me realize just how wind-obsessed its occupants must be, trying to convince themselves that they were wryly resigned to the worst the wind could do, that it was just some benign rival of theirs that would appreciate their joke.

This wind was not part of a storm that, however powerful, would come and go. Storm winds blew from the east or from either side of east. It was an abiding, prevailing, self-sustaining wind; a side-effect of nothing. The purpose, the end of this wind, was simply to blow and go on blowing.

I looked up at the sky sometimes to watch the large low clouds that always accompanied the wind. They moved so fast it was hard not to do likewise, hard to plod reasonably along while overhead there was a stampede of cloud, hard not to wonder what the implications might be for me of all that volatility.

I was, I realized, inching ever closer to some sort of breakdown. I began to feel that hallucinations were imminent; I developed a kind of hallucination phobia, which I presumed was a prelude to the real thing. I was suddenly seized by the conviction that around the next bend, I would see my grandfather walking down the track towards me, my grandfather with his long, flowing, pocket-watch-obscuring beard come to meet me, to escort me somewhere I was certain I did not want to go.

I felt the urge to turn around and run, then told myself that whichever way I turned, I could not see behind me. I hurried along, looking over my shoulder, peering up the track, stumbling. I was certain that Hines was about to appear, Hines in his strange outfit, his three-quarter-length black coat, his red, brass-buttoned vest. I wondered for the first time if, in his former life, he had been a train conductor. Hines coming down the track towards me with his Bible, in chastisement, held aloft. "Remember, man," I thought I heard a voice say, "thou art a Newfoundlander and unto Newfoundland thou hast returned." I ran, not on the track, but beside it on the crushed stone, my feet going out from under me. I heard myself sobbing, then laughing, or so I thought, for it was not me laughing but a child.

I saw her standing right in front of me, a little girl in a ragged burlap dress with her tattered shoes untied. She stopped laughing when she saw the expression on my face and stared sullenly at me. A forerunner of Hines perhaps. I heard another voice, distinctly unlike that of Hines, behind me.

"Where are you going in such a rush, sir? You look like you is runnin' from an 'ive of bees."

I turned around and there was a middle-aged man, not Hines, wearing only coveralls, his arms and shoulders bare, staring uncertainly at me and at times at the little girl as if he was still not sure if I posed a threat.

"I'm Joe Smallwood," I said.

I was back in the world, theirs, mine, suddenly aware of how I must look to them.

Fielding's Condensed
History of Newfoundland

Chapter Thirteen:

THE IRISH ARE COMING

By the early 1800s, there are a sufficient number of English merchants permanently settled on the island to support an unskilled labour force.

Thus begins the Irish immigration to Newfoundland.

The Irish pour in by the thousands. Five times as many as are needed are recruited, which creates a healthy atmosphere of competition among the workers and discourages the Irish from demanding higher wages than the honest English can afford to pay.

I Once Was Lost

Early October, mid-afternoon. Hours before, when the wind had changed to the northeast, I had felt it, but I had assumed it was too early in the season for snow and had kept walking. Now, only a few minutes since the storm had broken, the barrens were whited out.

Because the branch lines were used less than the main line, they needed less maintainance, so there were fewer section shacks and they were farther apart, three or four miles apart in some cases. The last shack I had passed was two miles back, so I guessed that I was about midway between two shacks. The chimney of the last shack had been smoking, but no one had answered the door when I knocked and I had gone on, deciding to stop there again on the way back. This meant that the closest sectionman who knew roughly where I was on the track was five miles back, where I had spent the night, and he probably thought that the man in the shack where I had got no answer would be out looking for me.

There was little I could do but hope for someone to find me, for I knew that if I kept walking, I would wander from the tracks, which were already drifting in with snow. On the other hand, I knew that if I did not keep moving, I would freeze to death. I scrambled down the railway bed and walked as far as I dared back and forth, feeling for the slope with one hand, then turning and feeling for it with the other. I wondered if I should try to feel my way in this manner back to the shack, but such was my state that I was not sure which way I had been facing when the storm had broken or what side of the tracks I was on.

I shouted for help, but I could barely hear my own voice. I was not dressed for winter (I was barely dressed for fall), no gloves or hat or overcoat, my suitcase still hung around my neck. I was dressed about as well for a blizzard as the men of the *Newfoundland* had been dressed. And without the reserves of strength that even the weakest of them had had. I cursed myself for not having had the sense to turn back when the wind had changed.

It was late in the sixty-first day of my walk, and even before the storm had set in, I had been near delirious with malnutrition and fatigue. There were almost no trees on the Bonavista branch, nothing but bog and barrens on either side, nowhere to shelter, the railway bed being of no use since the wind was blowing straight down the tracks. Soon, with my back to the wind, I could not see anything but white, and I could hardly breathe, for it seemed that all the air had been displaced by snow.

I thought of Mr. Mercer out walking on the Brow that night when the avalanche came down. I pictured my mother throwing from the deck the book that even now was in my suitcase, peering out over the rail until she heard the rumble from below. I took off the suitcase, clutched it against my chest, lay on my back against the railway bed, at an angle to the ground and closed my eyes.

To keep myself from getting drowsy, I sang, "When Joey comes marching home again, hurrah, hurrah. When Joey comes marching home again, hurrah, hurrah.... We'll all feel gay when Joey comes marching home."

They would find me, perished here, I thought. Around the remains of that pathetic wretch, the lone and level snows stretched

far away. Lost in an October blizzard while walking across Newfoundland after five years in New York, which, as predicted by his
father, left him destitute. Found frozen to death on the Bonavista
branch line, clutching to his chest a suitcase containing two hundred dollars' worth of coins, membership fees for a union, which
in the attempt to organize he perished, the punctuating failure of
his life; also containing seven books, including a Bible and two
histories of Newfoundland, one readable, one not, in revised edi-
tions of which he would not be mentioned, and several articles of
ragged clothing. As predicted by the headmaster of Bishop Feild,
from which he failed to graduate, he had, by the time of his death
at the age of twenty-five, accomplished nothing. An autopsy revealed that his character at death was forty-five. Actual cause of
death, chronic character deficiency.

I sang, without ironic intent, "The Ode to Newfoundland,"
even the winter stanza, which had always been my favourite:
"When spreads thy cloak of shimm'ring white, at winter's stern
command, through shortened day and star-lit night, we love thee
frozen land. We love thee, we love thee, we love thee frozen land."

There was a thump beside my head, and when I opened my
eyes I saw a large black boot, a boot with my name on it, Smallwood spelled out in stitching on the side. My father had been right
about the Boot, the old man's boot. Now my head was bracketed
by boots, a boot on either side. The Narrows Boots. The name
Smallwood like some luminous siren, confusing navigators, luring
them towards the rocks. Abandon hope all ye who enter here. Or
exit. Death in his big black boots had come to claim me.

I grabbed one of the boots with both hands and heard what
sounded like someone waking from a nightmare, and I wondered
if it might be me who had roared with terror. I felt myself lifted by
my collar and the seat of my pants, then laid across something on
my stomach like some bit of game someone had bagged, my arms
and head hanging down over one side, my legs over the other.
Then something, it must have been my suitcase, was placed on my

back, lashed onto me with ropes, as I was lashed to whatever I was lying on.

It was not until I felt the sensation of movement that I realized I was on a trolley that was travelling against the wind, straight into it, in fact. Once, when there was a slight lull in the wind, I caught a glimpse of the driver, going slowly up and down, straining to do what, under ideal conditions, would have been hard work for two. The hood of his canvas coat was up; he was wearing snow goggles and across his mouth a scarf, so that little more than his nose was showing. Then the wind picked up again and he disappeared from view.

I could not hear the cranking of the trolley or the rumble of the wheels along the track, or see anything to confirm that we were moving, though I could still vaguely feel that we were. Then even that sensation vanished and I thought I had just awoken from a dream of being rescued. But then I saw him, there, not there, there, not there, like some snow mirage that meant the end was near.

At some point on our journey down the tracks, I was lulled to sleep by a warm, peaceful drowsiness that I knew I should resist but couldn't. I dreamed, though it seemed more vivid and more tactile than a dream, that I was wading out to sea, a sea unlike the one I knew, a calm, warm, hospitable, inviting sea.

I awoke momentarily to find myself slumped in a washtub filled, or being filled, with hot water. Through the steam rising from the water, I could make out a figure standing over me, in his hand some kind of pot, which he emptied into the tub.

"Awake?" he said. "I heard you were coming. Don't worry, I'm not a cannibal. And if I was, I'd be eating light tonight. Pay no attention to those carrots and potatoes bobbing around in there with you. Let's see, I wonder if it might be easier just to put this washtub on the stove. Smallwood stew, Smallwood stew, tonight we're having Smallwood stew. Smallwood stew for lads and lasses; Smallwood stew, it suits all classes; Smallwood stew, it is so grand, it is the best in Newfoundland."

"He is not dead whose good name lives," I think I said. "Quite right" was the answer.

When next I awoke, I was in a bed and someone was tucking me in. At first, I thought it was my grandfather.

"Poppy," I said and tried to put my arms around his neck, but then he took on the look of one of the vultures from the Floor and I weakly tried to fend him off, striking at him with my hands, which he grabbed and held still as if they were a child's.

"Sleep," he said. It was a command, but his tone was such that I could obey him or not, pull through or not; it was all the same to him.

I fell in and out of sleep, fought it, lest while I slept the men from the Floor would have their way with me. Once, I thought I heard ice pellets hitting the other side of the wall beside my bed. Not since I had lived in the saddle of the Brow had I heard such wind. I was sure the shack would be ripped from its foundation and sent tumbling like a cardboard box across the barrens.

I awoke after what felt like a long time, lucid now, much better but famished. From my bed, through the open door of the room, I could see someone sitting at a table near a cast-iron stove, reading a newspaper.

After staring at the person for a long time, I wondered if my lucidity was just a dream. This was about the last place on earth I would have expected to encounter her. She was greatly changed, her large-boned frame no longer rounded, but bare, angular. She looked about twenty years older than she should have, was improbably dressed in a red-and-black checkered shirt, dungarees and work boots, but there was no mistaking who it was.

"Fielding," I said.

She looked up, stared at me as if she was unconvinced that I was not still feverish, then thinly smiled. Yes, it was Fielding. But there was in that ever-changing face of hers the shade of something new.

"Smallwood," she said, in the faintly ironic way one might greet the return to consciousness of some stranger you have written off for dead and whose death would not have bothered you a bit.

"What are you doing out here?" I said.

"Hermiting," she said. "Reduced to hermiting because you broke my heart."

I momentarily forgot about New York. I thought that she was talking about Bishop Feild. I felt guilty and must have looked it, for she burst out laughing, eyeing me as if it was a measure of my ego that I could believe something I had done had affected her for life. Then I remembered the last night we had seen each other.

"What happened to you?" I said. "What are you doing out here?"

She told me her story over dinner that night, while I was wolfing down a plate of fried potatoes.

"The summer I went back home, I found out I had TB. My father diagnosed it, though for a while he couldn't believe his own diagnosis. People like us weren't supposed to get it; it was supposed to be the malnourished, unhygienic, filth-ridden poor. People like you. His sister, my aunt Dot, has never forgiven me for disgracing the family by coming down with an unrespectable disease. Nor him for diagnosing it, for that matter. Or perhaps it's for not dying that they can't forgive me, for coming out of the sanatorium and reappearing at gatherings where I was supposed to pretend people didn't know what I'd been sick with. My aunt Dot still swears that my father was wrong and that I caught TB *after* going to the San, caught it from the other patients. My father has been a model of light-heartedness ever since she raised the possibility.

"Tuberculosis is not nearly as class-conscious as my relatives. It doesn't arbitrarily exclude the rich. It's really very democratic. It didn't hold my having my own room at the San against me, like the other patients did. A better-dressed tubercular they'd never seen. 'A

doctor's daughter in the San,' they said. 'It just goes to show.' TB
didn't worry about being ostracized for consorting with the likes of
me. It tried to kill me just as hard as it tried to kill the others.

"At any rate, within a year I looked like you. Well, maybe not
that bad, more like an X-ray. But I'm better now. I'm still in quarantine, mind you. That's why I live out here all by myself. To keep
from infecting people."

I fell for that one, too, there flashing across my mind an image
of the inside of the place I had heard so much about but never
seen. The San. Rows of beds. Wheelchairs. Crutches. It's a wonder
I did not ask her if, before her father's diagnosis, she had found
herself lying on her back a lot.

Fielding laughed at my distress and assured me that she was
not contagious. The only lasting effect of her illness, she said, was
that as the result of surgery, her left leg was and always would be
perceptibly thinner and shorter than her right, causing her to walk
with a limp and necessitating that she wear on her left foot a
thick-soled orthopedic boot.

I looked at her. It was hard to believe she was only twenty-six
years old. There were deep shadows beneath her eyes. She, too, was
little more than skin and bone, and the frame on which the skin
was stretched was not as large as I once fancied it must be. I could
not reconcile this body with the one I associated with her name.

The man's clothes she wore must have belonged to someone
the size of the old Fielding, for they hung as loosely on her as mine
did on me, though she still seemed she would be twice my size if
only she would stand erect. She had acquired, in addition to her
limp, a slight stoop that began from the waist. There was something, not only in the way she spoke and gestured and moved
about the shack, but also in her very posture, as if she were mocking the disease that had tried so earnestly to kill her, embellishing
its effects.

She was drinking more than ever before, making up, she said,
for the two years she had spent in the San, where drinking was

strictly prohibited and where consequently she had consumed only half as much per day as she was used to. She drank from the same silver flask. I never saw her refill it, nor did I see any bottles, empty or otherwise, about. Her silver-knobbed cane stood in a corner by the door. She saw me looking at it.

"I take it with me when I go walking on the barrens," she said. I tried without success to picture that.

"So what do you do here?" I said.

"I work for the railway," she said. "I started out just living here. I heard there was this abandoned section shack, and I asked if I could rent it. It's not the sort of place the doctors, my father included, wanted me to go, but I thought if I lived in a place like this I could get some writing done. I'm writing a history of Newfoundland.

"Anyway, the spring before last, I was hired with some other women to tar the railway ties. It grew from there. I had more free time than the other women, not having a family to look after. The men, most of whom are very sweet and treat me like a widow who's been forced by her husband's death to eke out some sort of living on her own, asked the railway to hire me to do what they consider to be nuisance work. I tar the ties, not just along my section, but for miles on either side of it. I'm also a spotter; I patrol the tracks, looking for blockages, and clear them if I can. I shore up the railway bed with gravel now and then.

"The men — I'm a half-foot taller than some of them — they do the major work, the things they pretend to think I'm not strong enough to do, or wouldn't know how to do properly. They won't let me help them lift the rails when they need replacing. They know I'm a townie and a doctor's daughter. They call me Miss Fielding."

I wondered how she was regarded by the wives of the sectionmen, the daughter of a St. John's doctor out here on the Bonavista branch line, alone. It was hard to picture her, as she was presently constituted, fending for herself, chopping the wood I had seen stacked up behind the shack, pumping the trolley, tarring the ties, shoring up the railway bed.

"What are you doing out here, Fielding?" I said. "What are you playing at, being poor or being a man?"

"I have no desire to be the latter," she said. "And as for the former, I don't have to play at it. I accept no money from my father. And I'm not paid very much, even by railway standards. Far less than the men."

"You've changed," I said and heard in my voice a tenderness I had wanted to suppress. She shook her head, as if she did not want, would not permit me, to talk about New York.

"As you can see," she said, "I am not at all embittered by the events of the past few years; on the contrary, the experience has so renewed my faith in humankind that I have forsworn the use of irony until the day I die."

"Whatever brought you here," I said, "you've been here far too long."

"I think my chances of a relapse here are actually less than they would be in St. John's, where I couldn't afford to live very well. I made up for catching TB when I told my relatives I was going to be a writer. They were overjoyed, for as you know, no family that can't count among its progeny at least one unpublished writer is taken seriously in St. John's. And then when they found out I was supporting my writing by working on the railway as a sort of sectionman, well, you can imagine how thrilled my father was, his daughter pursuing not just one but two of the most preferred professions. I'm all my aunts and uncles and cousins talk about these days."

I had never in my life heard such a steady stream of irony. I don't think she spoke more than half a dozen straightforward sentences during the three days I spent convalescing in her shack.

She told me that it was her bed I had been sleeping in and that I could go on doing so until I left, while she would sleep on the cot in the room she called her study, not because she wanted me to have the better bed, but because she did not want me in her study, her *sanctum sanctorum*, as she called it, "the San" for short; a sign bearing that name was nailed to the door, as if to ward people off.

I did not catch so much as a glimpse of the inside of her tiny study, for she kept the door closed and padlocked while I was on my feet and did not go in there to work until after I had gone to bed. What I had thought in my delirium was the sound of ice pellets was the tapping of her typewriter.

———

FIELDING'S JOURNAL, OCTOBER 21, 1925

Dear Smallwood:

How smug you'd be if you knew that I've been writing in my journal to you ever since. Not every night, but many. More nights than not.

Now, with you in the next room, it feels as though I'm talking to you through a knothole in the wall. Pyramus and Thisbe. Pyramus sleeps while Thisbe speaks words that Pyramus will never hear.

I have known for weeks that you were coming. I heard it first from the woman in the mile house next to mine. "There's a man named Smallwood walking clear across the tracks," she said. "Branches and all. To unionize the sectionmen." You couldn't just walk the main line. No. You had to walk the branches, too. I've been getting unasked-for updates on your progress ever since. "He's twenty miles outside Deer Lake. Not a lick of meat left on his bones." What do you mean left? I felt like saying. "Nor a lick of leather on his boots." Phonse at Six Mile House has been charting your progress on the map on his kitchen wall. Smallwood is coming.

My *homecoming was momentous, too. The island appeared, then vanished, then appeared again as stars do when you look at them too long. I thought it was an optical illusion. I didn't know that my eyes were opening and closing. I must already have been sick when I left New York. The woman beside me at the rail sent her husband down below to get some water. "You're burning up, my dear," she said, holding the back of her hand against my cheek. How cool it felt. I told her I was fine. The sea gale was blowing full in my face. All around me passengers were wearing scarves and hoods. How could I be burning up? But neither she nor her husband left my side until we docked in St. John's, where they led me down the gangplank, at the bottom of which my father was waiting.*

He *was so startled by how much I had changed that the first thing he did, before he even said hello, was take my pulse. People gave us a wide berth while he was doing it. I didn't even know I had changed until I saw it in his face. It had been months since I had seen anyone who knew how I used to look. "Aren't you glad to see me?" I said. "I should never have let you leave," he said.*

He *took me straight from the boat to his consulting room. And from there straight to the San. I hadn't seen St. John's in two years. Nor would I see it again for another two.*

The first few months were not so bad. At Christmas, I lined up with the others and read a message to my father that was broadcast on the radio. He was a chest doctor, but he did not work at the San — it's a wonder anybody did — and not even for him could they relax the rules of quarantine. We wrote each other letters. Mine I dictated to a nurse so that no paper I had touched would leave the place. My stenographer, my father called her. She always wrote postscripts to my letters, asking him to admonish me for bad behaviour. "Where she gets her licker no one knows."

But after Christmas it got worse. In July, they told him that if he wanted to see me one last time, he should do it soon. But he did not come. He said later he thought that if he came to see me, I would know that I was dying and might not fight as hard to live. Was this really why he stayed away? He could see I had my doubts. I still do. But he might have been telling the truth. Maybe if he had come to visit me I would have died.

I saw you, Smallwood, from my study window when you knocked before the storm. I was sure the snow would hold off long enough for you to make it to the next mile house. And even after it started, I sat here hoping it would turn to rain. I was told by men who are not often wrong about the weather that it would. What if I had waited too long and been unable to find you? Another secret I would have to keep. It reminded me of the nights I sat up writing while you were stranded in the ice on the S.S. Newfoundland. The very absurdity of you surviving that storm just to perish in one on dry land made me sure the snow would change to rain. On the other hand, a one-man catastrophe might be more your style.

You must have thought of the Newfoundland yourself. No one's shoulder to place your hand upon. Nor anyone to place his hand on your shoulder. If I hadn't found you, I'd have gone to the next mile house and asked for help. Assuming I could have found it.

I found mine because of something Phonse told me when I first came here. There would be days and nights, he said, when the fog or snow would be so bad that I would miss my signal lantern. I hadn't thought it was possible and took his advice only when he insisted. I fastened a ship's bell above the door and on the nail that held it hung a coil of rope. When I set out to find you, I tied the rope to the rail on the far side of the track.

Coming back, it seemed I had gone twice as far as I should have and still not tripped the bell. I wondered if I had tripped it and not heard it. I thought about going back, then decided that as I was pumping into the wind with half a passenger aboard, I would give it ten more minutes. A few minutes later I heard it. A muffled clanging above the roar of the wind. A beckoning bell. I groped around until the rope I could not see was in my hands.

I put you in the tub — yes, I saw, of course I saw, just how apt your name is. (Just kidding. But you see, I could have punned more cruelly on your name at Bishop Feild than to call you Splits.)

And then, for the first time in my life, and I dare say for the last, I watched you sleep. You without your glasses. (Another first for me. You were still wearing your glasses when I found you, though the lenses were coated with ice and snow. I put them in my pocket, and later, afraid they might shatter if I put them on the stove, left them to thaw out on the table where they lie now in a pool of water.) How strange you looked. As if you were missing your most distinctive facial feature, lying there minus something as uniquely Smallwood as your nose. Your head above the blankets was like a skull with nothing left but skin.

I tried to tuck you in, but you fought me off, I presumed because you knew that it was me. Finally you slept, though you breathed too rapidly at first. You reminded me of me when I was at the San. Then something in your face relaxed or was erased, and your mouth fell slightly open. I thought you might be dying. But you had just fallen deeply asleep. Vulnerably, unguardedly asleep. You as you would look if for one moment you could forget that the world was watching.

I'm glad you're still alive.

After that first day and night, when she did not think it was safe to leave me unattended, Fielding went back to work. Once, on the morning of the second day, I looked out the window and saw her, goggled and scarved like some early aviator, pumping her trolley along the tracks, going up and down, her arms out in front of her, as if she were doing knee-bends. She seemed quite adept at it, and far stronger than her appearance had led me to believe.

When she passed the shack and disappeared around a bend, I put on my coat and went outside. Though it was warmer, there was still snow on the ground and I had to wade through it up to my knees to reach the back of the shack, where I hoped there would be a window through which I could see her study. There was one, but it was boarded up. So that my tracks would not lead too obviously to the study window, I walked about in the snow on all sides of the shack and the outhouse and, satisfied that she would not guess my reason for venturing out, headed back inside, noticing, as I did, another little sign above the door that read Twelve Mile House.

I slept most of the day, read a little from each of my books except the Bible, unable to concentrate on one for long.

"I see you gave yourself the grand tour," Fielding said when, late in the afternoon, she came back to the shack. "Too bad about those shutters on the window."

I felt myself redden. I could think of nothing to say until my eyes fell on the book I had left on the kitchen table.

"Have you read Prowse?" I said, feigning innocence, picking up the book and extending it to her. "But I suppose you must have, if you're writing a history of Newfoundland." How it must have irked her to hear me say that name, though she did not show it.

"I've read him," she said, smiling as if to acknowledge a lame attempt at wit. She did not take the book.

She went about preparing a supper of salt fish and potato cakes, which we ate in silence. I told her that like so many of the people I had met in New York, she was just playing at being poor and being an artist, and like them she was sustained by the knowledge that she could go back to her life of affluence any time she liked. I *felt* like telling her this shack of hers was a palace compared with the Coop or the Floor or the marble bench in Bryant Park that for three weeks had been my bed. But looking at her while she ate, I felt that nothing I could say would faze her, that as far as she was concerned, her two years in the San had changed her in some way I could never understand.

"That letter to the *Morning Post*," I said, "was a masterpiece."

"Yes, it was, wasn't it?" she said, smiling. "Anyway, those scores were settled long ago, Smallwood. You shouldn't dwell so much on the past."

On the third night, when we were again sitting at the table after dinner, I told her that I was feeling up to continuing my walk and would be leaving in the morning. I went to my suitcase, took out a union-membership card and slid it across the table to her.

"There you go," I said. "Just sign that, give me fifty cents and you're a member of the union." She pushed the card back to me and drank from her flask, wiping her mouth with the back of her hand. "Every sectionman from here to Port aux Basques has joined," I said.

"That's their business," she said.

"The others won't mind that you're a woman," I said, "or that you do less work."

Fielding sniffed derisively.

"Why won't you join?" I said.

"That's my business."

"You know the issues — "

"I know what you think the issues are. Two and a half cents an hour — "

"That's a lot of money to some people."

"It's a lot of money to me."

"Then why won't you join?"

"I never join anything if I can help it."

"Did someone from the railway — "

She laughed.

"I know what this is about," I said, "and you said *I* shouldn't dwell so much on the past."

"It's not about the past," she said.

"Then what is it? There'll be a union with or without you. You'll get your raise whether you sign up or not. Unless there's a closed shop. In which case, you might lose your job."

"I'll get by," she said. "I'm on the lighthouse-keeper waiting-list and the waiting-lists of various other hermit professions. You aren't planning to swim the coast to unionize lighthouse-keepers next, are you?"

"I mean it, Fielding. You could lose your job."

She slammed down the flask, stood up and looked at me.

"The day of the snowstorm," she said, suddenly out of breath, "before the snow started, you knocked on that door." She pointed at it as if to corroborate what she was saying. "I looked out, and when I saw that it was you, I didn't answer. Not because I didn't want to join the union, but because I knew the storm was coming and I was hoping you would perish in it. I sat in here for two hours after the storm set in before I changed my mind, before I went out to see if I could find you."

It seemed to me that she had lost something by this admission, that the balance had tilted in my favour. She must have seen by my expression that I thought so, for she shook her head as if I had said something she felt it was beneath her to answer. She went into "the San" and closed the door.

I lay awake for hours after I went to bed, listening to the tap-tap-tap of her typewriter on the other side of the wall, measured, unconcerned, unceasing, as if to emphasize that nothing momentous had occurred, that nothing I said or did could register on her scale of significance.

She was gone when I woke up in the morning. On the table was a note, instructing me to lock the door behind me when I left. And there was a postscript: "Don't mention it. You would have done the same for me, if I were a forty-five-pound dwarf." I did not until then realize that I had not thanked her for saving my life. She would not have had to save it if she had opened the door in the first place, I told myself, which of course I had not known about until last night. I wondered if that "forty-five" was just an accident, or if an allusion to my lack of character was intended. She was so inscrutably ironic, it was hard to know what to think about anything she said.

The note infuriated me and I tore it to pieces, then picked them all up and put them in my pocket so she would not know how much she had got to me. I wrote several notes of my own, but every one seemed lame compared with hers and I crammed those in my pockets as well.

I looked at the door of her padlocked study. I had a sudden urge to break it down, to take the axe from behind the stove and hack the door to pieces. I wanted to read that history of hers to see if I was in it, for I was sure I was. And her journal. Fielding's books, her revenge upon the world, in which, I had no doubt, she portrayed herself as hard done by and stacked the deck against tokenly disguised versions of everyone she had ever known. I went so far as to take the axe into my hands. But in the end, all I did was leave and lock the door behind me.

Fielding was the sole hold-out among the sectionmen. Six hundred and ninety-nine joined the union, one did not. Sleep-tormenting numbers, numbers to obsess about, 699 and the one that got away. I remembered my mother quoting from the New Testament about their being more joy in heaven over finding the one that went astray than over the ninety-nine who were never lost. And presumably more grief if the one that was lost was never found.

Fielding had found me when I was lost. It was irksome to have your life saved by someone who seemed to value it so little, especially when she had once valued it so much. She had saved me only because she had known she could not live with the guilt she would have felt had she left me out there on the tracks to die. That was all it was, I told myself: guilt, not love. She had more than atoned for what she had done to me at Bishop Feild. I was now so far in her debt I could never pay her back.

Fielding's Condensed
History of Newfoundland

Chapter Fourteen:

NIGHTS IN THE SHIP

An Irish planter in Newfoundland describes the manner of his recruitment in County Cork, by what means he was transported to the New World and reports thereof his first impressions:

> I walked bent over from the waist,
> My head erect, my hands upraised.
> Three days had I been in the stocks,
> And now for rum did roam the docks.
> My shape betrayed my circumstance,
> As did the split seam in my pants.
> "There be one not long released,"
> Some man did say — then all sound ceased.
> I woke, the world was all a motion,
> Asail were we upon the ocean.
> 'Twas dark, I heard the sound of retching.
> "Fret not," said he, "it be not catching.
> Of what I have you need not fear.

It's nothing more than *mal de mer*."
And yet I soon did have it too,
And like this man my guts did spew,
Though he for puke did have me beat —
A week it was since I had eat.
"Where bound are we?" said I, 'twixt heaves.
"For Newfoundland, I do believe."
"For Newfoundland" said I, in shock.
"My God, there's nothing there but rock."
"Not so," said he, "'tis paradise.
The man who sold me said so, twice.
I used to him indentured be,
But soon, thank God, I will be free."
Whate'er became of this poor soul?
When they took us from the hole,
They sent him one way, me another.
We neither one did see the other.

Clara

I DID NOT ACTUALLY make it to St. John's. I made it to Avondale station, within thirty-six miles of the city, where I was met by a train at the end of which was a private car occupied by the director of the railway, who told me the pay cut would be rescinded and he would be honoured if I would agree to be the railway's guest for the last leg of my trip.

I knew what he was up to, knew he did not want me, in my state, looking the way I did, to stagger down the tracks and walk into the station in St. John's, where the press might — I liked to think so anyway — be waiting for me, a walking martyr for the sectionmen, a barely breathing symbol of the railway's miserly intransigence. But I was too exhausted to resist his offer. I rode the train the thirty-six remaining miles into St. John's.

Fielding, the renegade of Sectionville. I often imagined her out there on the bog of Bonavista, in her hermitage beside the railway tracks, imagined what her shack must have looked like late at night when she was writing, the shutters of her study creased with light, the shack otherwise unlit. I pictured her in her paper cell, composing what she fancied was a masterpiece, her history, and her self-justifying journals. What nagged me most was the expression that had crossed her face when I had shown her Prowse's book, which I now regretted doing, not because it had hurt her, but because it hadn't. Glee, scorn, contempt, recognition, it was hard to say exactly what it was.

The last of my siblings was born less than a month after I returned to St. John's, on my birthday, Christmas Eve. That was the last of the children, my mother predicted; the coincidence of our birthdays on the eve of Christ's birthday was a sign, the circle had closed, she had come back to where she had started. I stayed at the old house on the Brow for a while before I found a place of my own.

Because of how I had fared there, none of the other boys had gone to Bishop Feild. So as far as my father was concerned, there was no reason to think any of them would amount to more than I had or was ever likely to, which did not appear to be much, for a more unpromising-looking twenty-five-year-old could not have been imagined. My father strode, guilt-ridden, about the house from deck to deck and launched into an entertaining monologue of self-mockery and theatrical despair. I was surprised at how much I had missed his drunken eloquence.

"Maybe if you hadn't burned that Book," he obscurely shouted up the stairs to my mother.

"What's that book got to do with anything?" my mother shouted back, her voice quavering. He seemed to have discovered that any mention of the book was a torment to her.

"I don't know," my father said, "nothing, I suppose. But you never should have burned that Book. Nothing good will come from burning books."

"That's all I hear about when anything goes wrong," my mother said, "that book, that book, that book. I told you never to mention it again; I'm sick to death of it, that's why I burned it in the first place."

Clearly, she had not heard about Hines's attempt to convert me. There was not that flicker in her eyes that in the past had signalled she was holding something back and would eventually get round to telling me in private what it was. How had Hines known that I knew about the book? I could tell just from looking at her that my mother did not know.

Newspaper publishing and politics. These were not exactly watchwords for security and stability in the late twenties in St. John's, where papers and parties were popping up and folding all the time, the fortunes of papers often tied to those of the parties for which they were propaganda sheets, papers folding when parties did or vice versa.

Over the next couple of years, I published, which is to say I single-handedly wrote and printed, papers that were so short-lived that copies of them are now collector's items. Newspaper publishing to me was little more than a branch of politics, and I had not completely given up on socialism. Each time I started up a new paper, I included in it a new manifesto, slightly amended from the one before, trying to find some version of socialism that Newfoundlanders might accept.

I gathered around me a group of young men and women who fancied themselves socialists and were greatly impressed with my socialist credentials. They were not like the socialists I had known in New York. They were uneducated even by comparison with me, and they were poor, though they had seen so little of the world they did not know how poor they were, and though they believed in the existence of the exploited and the destitute, they would not have numbered themselves among them.

I changed my mind about marriage. I saw that men of the sort I aspired to be had wives, were expected to have them, and children, too. I took my group on picnic rallies in Bannerman Park, and during one of these I saw standing alone against the iron fence a woman I knew would agree to be my wife if I asked her. It was presumptuousness at first sight. She was twenty-three, the daughter of a fisherman from Carbonear. Her hair was pinned up in Dutch-style buns on either side of her head.

When the rally was over, she strolled across the park with the rest of us, arms folded, head down, looking as though she wished she had not come. She was wearing a raincoat that, like all her clothes, was pulled up slightly at the back because of the way she hunched her shoulders. There was a physical awkwardness about her that appealed to me, that hinted at a lack of self-confidence, which, after Fielding, was exactly what I was looking for. I left the group I was with and caught up with her.

"Hello," I said, falling into stride beside her and holding out my hand. "I'm Joe Smallwood." She cast a furtive look down at me — she was several inches taller — then looked away in a manner that discouraged me until I saw that she was blushing, nervous to the point of speechlessness. She swallowed as if to make sure her voice would not break when she spoke.

"I'm Clara Oates," she said, flashing a sheepish smile at me. She seemed not to notice my hand, so I dropped it to my side, whereupon she rolled her eyes and shook her head self-ironically as if to assure me that she at least knew she was gauche, even if she could not help being that way. With her emphatic strides, she covered so much ground I could barely keep up with her and I thought perhaps she was trying to lose me. She did not look at me throughout our conversation, though I kept looking up at her to see what impression I was making.

As was my wont, I did not so much talk to her as at her, addressing her as I would a public meeting, though she didn't seem to mind. I argued in favour of socialism as though she were opposed to it; she smiled and nodded and, thus encouraged, I went on and on. It seemed I had at last met a woman who found it charming that I spoke to her as if all I wanted from her was her vote.

She was blue-eyed, pale, with a faintly pouting mouth that opened wide and roundly when she spoke. She sometimes lapsed into a kind of English, bay-girl accent.

We were married a few months after we met. On our wedding night, in our rented row house on New Gower Street, the walls of which were paper thin, I pretended to be experienced in what Fielding had called "matters carnal," and she pretended to believe me. When the light was out, we stood up and started taking off our clothes, each of us taking off our own as if we were about to go swimming. She left on a nightshirt of some sort that came down to her knees and I, putting it down to the coldness of the room, left on my body-length, button-flyed longjohns. I started kissing her and at the same time unbuttoned my longjohns with one hand, using my free hand to support myself. Neither of us said a word. I had a great deal of trouble getting through the door, or even finding it, for that matter.

"You're so tall," I selfishly said, by way of explanation. I could feel her tensing up after that, and though I'm sure she knew it was my first time, too, she may still have thought her height was making it more difficult for me than it would otherwise have been.

We were both greatly relieved when it was over, though by tacit agreement we kept up the charade that it was no big deal for me. I was surprised that it was not nearly as enjoyable as masturbation and I wondered if it would always be like that.

"I didn't do anything wrong, did I?" she said. I shook my head, not trusting my voice at that moment, for my legs and arms were trembling. I sat up, swung my feet onto the floor. Clara put her arms around me, rested her chin on my head, the closest thing in that position she could come to putting her head on my shoulder. In addition to being so much taller than me, she weighed more than half as much again as I did and I felt foolishly childlike in her arms.

"It was wonderful, Joey," she said and, at last managing to find my voice, I said I thought so, too. She didn't smoke, but I lit up a cigarette as suavely as it was possible to do while wearing longjohns. For the first time, I realized how much she looked like Fielding had before the San.

I did not get the hang of sex. I knew the goal I was pursuing for myself, but what her goal might be and what, if anything, I could do to help her reach it and how I would know when she had, I had no idea. I assumed that it was something corresponding to mine and might even be triggered by it, the woman's satisfaction following automatically on the man's, except that hers didn't and I couldn't figure out why.

At first, she seemed not to mind, and even when she began to mind, she put the blame on herself, worrying that her not "peaking," as she put it, would make her less attractive to me, and talked as if, like all her supposed shortcomings, it was somehow connected to her awkwardness, typical of a woman who had no better sense than to be taller than her husband.

She did "peak" from time to time, but it seemed to have nothing, physically at least, to do with me. I had the sensation that I was watching something I was not a part of, as I had when my body cried for the men of the *Newfoundland* while my mind looked on. She held me still and ground herself against me. She did not scream like the woman on the moss in the spruces had, only breathed ever more shrilly as if she were giving way to panic. I watched her and listened with such amazement, such detachment, that for the first time, I failed to "peak."

Even amidst all that thrashing about, she noticed. "What about you?" she said, stroking my hair. I managed a kind of shrug, as if to say one miss for me was nothing. I kept my face buried in her shoulder. I wondered if it would have been different with Fielding. Would she have had to grind herself against me and hold me still to make sure I did nothing wrong? I also wondered if my mother had ever dared do that or if my father would have let her.

Fielding's Condensed
History of Newfoundland

Chapter Fifteen:

THE WINTER OF THE ROWDIES

In 1817, the practice of having governors spend their winters in England is discontinued when Admiral Francis Pickmore is ordered by the king to winter in Newfoundland.

Pickmore returns to England in April, but is unable to give a satisfactory account of what winter in Newfoundland is like, being by that time six weeks dead.

The winter of 1817–1818, known variously as Pickmore's Winter, the Winter of the Rals and the Winter of the Rowdies, is an especially severe one. The entire east and northeast coasts are blocked by ice from late fall until late spring. The merchants are further inconvenienced when eight thousand people left homeless by a series of fires begin looting their already depleted stocks.

Pickmore is succeeded by Sir Charles Hamilton, the first governor to survive a Newfoundland winter. He survives seven, in fact, but writes constantly to England predicting that he will "soon perish like poor Pickmore, so drafty is our tumbledown old house."

Hamilton demands that a new Government House be built, and England meets his demands not long after he leaves Newfoundland for good.

His successor, Sir Thomas Cochrane, announces his intention to build himself a house in which there will be no possibility whatsoever of catching one's death from drafts. The death-by-drafts-proof house costs a quarter of a million dollars, but would, as Cochrane points out, have cost a good deal less had not the planner confused it with another house he was building in the West Indies and built a moat around it to ward off deadly snakes.

Fielding

W<small>E LIVED</small> "on the side of the hill." It brought back to me memories of the years we spent on the hill when I was young, the years before the Brow. The poor neighbourhoods were still predominantly Catholic; their flag, the pink, white and green, still hung from makeshift poles above the doors of the houses that lined the unpaved, pothole-ridden, muddy streets. Lines of row houses that looked like motels, with each unit painted differently, faced each other down the undulating length of Gower Street.

A year after we were married, we had the first of three children, a son, Ramsay Coaker Smallwood. I was for a short time infatuated with him, the sheer fact of him, the sight of him in Clara's arms or in his crib. I had taken the birth of children for granted all my life. My childhood had been full of bawling babies, the sound they made as much a part of the climate as the wind. But I had never regarded myself or one of my brothers or sisters as a hybrid of my parents, a commingling of two natures. I had considered the Smallwood children, physically at least, to be my mother's. Their natures came from her by a process that, though set into motion by my father, was otherwise uninfluenced by him. But here was little

Ramsay, every part of him undeniably shot through with Clara and me. It seemed both miraculous and off-putting to think of myself not as my self but as being jointly derived from Minnie May and Charlie Smallwood.

I admonished myself not to be so taken with Ramsay that I would lose sight of my purpose, about which all I could have said with any certainty was that it was one no doting father or uxorious husband could achieve.

I was soon well on the way to pursuing an almost completely autonomous life, leaving Clara alone in the house for days and nights and weeks on end while I worked and travelled. I was no better a father or husband than my father was, not even when it came to providing for my family, for most of what I earned went into underwriting the cost of publishing newspapers whose purpose was to advance my ever-evolving cause.

FIELDING'S JOURNAL, MAY 27, 1928

Dear Smallwood:

He loves her, he loves me not. He loves me, but he marries her. *I have seen her, Smallwood. Met her, really. I turned a corner onto Water Street one day and bumped into the pram that she was pushing. I knew who she was, for I had seen your wedding pictures in the paper. I knew her name was Clara. I almost said it.*

The pram was a surprise. At first I thought that you were with her and that you would see me see you three together — the Joseph Smallwoods, as you must be called. Or that you might even introduce me to her. The street was crowded. It was a few moments before I realized that she was unaccompanied.

She must have wondered why I looked so startled. When she saw my cane and noticed I was limping, she apologized, as if

*even a woman with a pram must give way to a woman with
a limp. But that is not fair, for there was not a trace of condescension in her voice or in her face. I don't believe I have
encountered someone more obviously sweet-tempered in all
my life.*

*She was flustered, embarrassed. "I should have looked
where I was going," she said. "No," I said. "It was my fault."
Which it was, for it was Sunday, my day off, and I had got up
and started drinking earlier than usual. "I hope I didn't wake
the baby," I said. She said she wished I had, but that nothing
could wake him in the daytime or make him sleep at night.*

*"A baby after my own heart," I could not help saying. She
took it as an invitation to go on talking. I wondered how I
would get out of it. I could just see her describing me to you
and you recognizing me in her description. She mentioned you.
That is, she said the words* my husband *as if she was cheerfully
resigned to something for which she had heard all husbands are
notorious. A woman unaccustomed to loneliness, especially the
loneliness of marriage. The peculiar loneliness that I have seen
in so many women. As if nothing in her childhood, nothing that
had happened between her parents or that she had even sensed
between them, had prepared her for it. What had she expected?
Née Oates. Still feeling new to St. John's after three years, still
missing Harbour Grace.*

*I think if I had gone round and looked at the baby in the
pram, we would have wound up having tea or going for a walk.
Instead, I interrupted her, told her that I had somewhere to be
and that I hoped the baby would soon sleep through the night.
I was too abrupt, perhaps. I was nearly crying, and not just for
the reasons that would be obvious to you.*

*I have seen her since, pushing the baby, sometimes walking
with a man who must be her brother, they look so much alike.
Though I'm sure she wouldn't mind if strangers passing by
took them to be husband and wife. A young family out walking*

on a Sunday afternoon. Marriage as she imagined it would be.
I can see her writing letters home that make her sound lonesome
and at the same time absolve you of any blame. Letters that are
clearly fishing for invitations or for visitors.

I make sure she doesn't see me. I know the route she takes
and I avoid it. I know she would remember me, the limping
woman she collided with. A familiar face.

You are never with her, for which I should feel grateful, I
suppose, though I can't help feeling sorry for her. I can see that
she minds, but not as much as my mother must have. Or else
she minds as much but loves you more than my mother loved
my father. Or differently. She will never leave you, Smallwood.
I saw it in her eyes. I wonder what she sees in yours.

One winter day, walking along Duckworth Street, preoccupied
with trying to figure out where I would get the money to support
my new family, I realized after I had been looking at her for quite
some time that Fielding was in front of me, limping along at a clip,
a pile of books under her arm, unmistakably Fielding, though she
was even more stooped than when I had last seen her and her limp
seemed more pronounced. I shouted her name several times, but
she didn't turn around, so I had to run to catch her.

"Fielding," I said, "didn't you hear me calling to you?"

"Yes, I did," she said, "but this is as fast as I can go."

"Are you still at Twelve Mile House?" I asked.

"No," she said, "I am now at three-cent house, a marvellous
establishment on Cochrane Street, which I share with an as yet un-
unionized nest of prostitutes."

"You lost your job?"

"No," she said, "I know exactly where it is. As of two months
ago, it was taken from me."

"You didn't lose your job because of the union," I said, "you lost your job because you wouldn't join the union."

"Smallwood," Fielding said, "are you some sort of agency of fate that it would be pointless of me to resist? If you are, tell me now so I can shoot myself without regret." She looked about at the shops of Duckworth Street, the cars and streetcars and horse-drawn cabs going by, surveyed it all with an air of puzzlement as though surprised to see people still caught up in pursuits she had long ago forsworn.

"Have you found another job?"

"As I told you, I'm on the waiting-lists of various hermit professions: lighthouse-keeper, weather-observer, telegraph operator ..."

"Are you still writing that history of yours?"

"I regret to say that whenever you ask me that question, the answer will be yes."

"I suppose I'm in it."

"Why would you be?"

I suppressed the urge to turn around and walk away.

"If you can write history, you can write for a newspaper again," I said. "My newspaper, for instance."

"Your newspaper? Are you telling me there are people in this world whose livelihood depends on the success of an enterprise run by you?"

"I'm offering you a job."

"From hermit to reporter — "

"You wouldn't have to be a reporter; you could just write commentary, columns, whatever you want."

She slumped against a storefront and looked down at me appraisingly.

"I wouldn't have to cover anything, establish contacts, conduct interviews ..."

"You can write at home if you want to, as long as your copy gets to me on time."

Fielding said yes, eventually, though the list of things she insisted she be exempted from doing was endless ("no hobbing, no nobbing, no chitting, no chatting ..."). And at the first mention of joining a union, she would be gone, she said.

Twelve Mile House had been for her a kind of halfway house between the San and the world, a way of easing back into life after two years spent in limbo. But it was as if, having come so close to death and seen so many people die, she could no longer manage the suspension of belief in her own mortality that is necessary to getting on from day to day.

She drank almost constantly as far as I could tell, though she generally managed to get her copy in on time. Every day, a boy about twelve would deliver it to the cubby-hole on Water Street that I referred to grandly as my "newsroom." As per her instructions, I paid him for his trouble out of Fielding's meagre wages.

I published her in the series of papers I founded over the next few years. She wrote under the pseudonym Ray Joy, and one of the terms of her employment was that I not reveal her identity to anyone. I was surprised at how willingly she churned out the kind of propaganda I wanted. She wrote earnest socialist commentaries, scathingly criticized whatever public official I deemed to be deserving of scathing criticism. The mysterious Ray Joy was quite popular among left-leaners of all kinds and I was often pressed to admit that I was in fact Ray Joy, which Fielding assured me I could do if I wanted to. I put her willingness to be a pen-for-hire down to her cynicism, her scepticism, knowing she did not even believe in the end for which the propaganda was the means, let alone the propaganda itself.

Just how right I was I did not find out until it became public knowledge that Fielding, for the previous three years or so, had also been writing for an opposing propaganda sheet, the arch-conservative *Gazette*, under the pseudonym Harold Prowdy, attacking in one paper the opinions she had expressed in the

other and getting a war of words going between her two imaginary selves, Joy and Prowdy going at it week after week, each
denouncing the other with such fervour that it was largely to see
how Joy would answer Prowdy and vice versa that people bought
our paper and the *Gazette*. She had extracted from her other publisher a promise, like the one she extracted from me, that her
identity would remain a secret. It was when this publisher confessed to someone he thought he could trust the real identity of
Harold Prowdy, and this someone passed the information on to
me, that Fielding was found out. I phoned the other publisher
and told him that Joy was Prowdy was Fielding, and both of us
fired Fielding on the same day.

"I suppose it had to happen sooner or later," Fielding said
when, in something of a rage, I went to her boarding-house on
Cochrane Street and told her she was fired. The sight of the place
almost made me change my mind.

Outside, it was painted dark green and trimmed with white —
or those at least were the colours it had once been painted with,
for there was not much paint left, mostly grey stump-coloured
clapboard and a black-felt roof. It was impossible to tell, from the
outside, what the original structure had looked like, it had been so
frequently added on to. The whole thing was now a haphazard
agglomeration of extensions, with a dozen doors and sets of stairs.

Fielding was at the top of what, from the inside, you could
tell had been the original building, at the end of a short dark hallway in a room that faced the harbour and the Brow. Hers, the living quarters of the original owner, was the choicest room of the
Cochrane, as the place was called, the only one with its own
bathtub and sink. The hallway of that boarding-house was the
same regardless of the weather or the time of day. On clear days,
the sunlight that came through the little porthole window at the
end of the hallway could do little to dispel the time-retarding
gloom.

There was a pile of papers on the floor outside her door, and at first I thought she had been letting them pile up for days, until I saw the different mastheads and realized she was subscribing to every paper in the city. Copies of that day's *Gazette* and my paper were among them. It was always a thrill for me to see in print something I had written, and how she could stand to leave her columns there all day, unread, unrevelled in, was beyond me.

I knocked on the door, on which there was a little sign that read San. San.

"Leave it on the floor," Fielding roared from inside, though it was long past delivery time for even the latest evening paper.

"It's Joe Smallwood," I shouted back. There was a theatrical, offstage-like commotion from inside, running, limp-thumping footsteps, the rustle of paper, drawers opening and closing, as if she wanted me to know or think that she was hiding something. At last the door opened.

"He comes, I live," said Fielding and, with a flourish of her arm, motioned me inside. Whatever they had been, the sounds I had heard had not been those of cleaning up. It occurred to me that when I identified myself, she might have run about messing up the room for effect. Her silver flask and a bottle of Scotch both stood unstoppered on her desk as if she was about to transfer the contents from one to the other. There was a single unmade bed against the wall, a table, a couple of chairs, a dresser with all the drawers half open and with clothing hanging out. Books were scattered everywhere in the manner of Judge Prowse, open-faced on the floor, stacked in draft-blocking piles against the walls and on the window sill. Overhead shone a lone light bulb.

I sat on one of the chairs and Fielding sat on her bed, leaned back, her arms supporting her, her legs stretched out, feet crossed. She was wearing buttoned boots, the sole of the left boot built up several inches higher than the other. Not an inch of her withered left leg was showing.

I accused her of disloyalty, of hypocrisy, of being an intellectual whore. She smiled, lips tilted, puffing on a cigarette. She was wearing a tweed skirt with a zipper at the hip that was open, broken probably, and through which the end of her white blouse protruded like a pocket turned inside out.

"You knew I never meant a word I wrote," she said, after I told her she was fired, "but as long as you thought I was furthering your cause, you didn't care. You shouldn't expect fidelity from someone you know is prostituting her talents." I was so accustomed to her irony, it was a few seconds before I realized that she had said exactly what she meant.

"Do you believe in anything, Fielding?" I said. "Why are you writing a book if you don't believe in anything?"

"I believe you still owe me three dollars," Fielding said. "And you know where to send it."

I had the money with me. It had taken some doing to scrape it together. It was in coins, in an envelope that I removed from my pocket and threw with a loud clunk on the table.

"So how is married life?" she said, sitting up straight and lighting a cigarette.

"Better than it would have been with you," I said, instantly aware of how foolish, how churlish, it sounded.

"Never know, will you?" she said. "Besides, you were only joking when you asked me, remember?"

"*I* remember," I said. "So what about you, Fielding? Any prospects?"

As if to emphasize the shabbiness of the question, she got up and limped to the table, where, standing, she poured herself a glass of Scotch.

"I'm never proposed to," she said, "but I'm often propositioned. Mostly by men whose proposals have already been accepted and whose children have already started school. Sometimes even by men whose children have children. I seem to have acquired some sort of reputation."

"I can't imagine how," I said.

"No," she said, "I'm quite certain that you can't. Most men tell me that because I've been 'left on the shelf,' the sort of thing they have in mind is the most I can hope for. So there you are. I've been left on the shelf."

I felt my face go red. I'd thought at first that she was joking. Fielding with other men.

"You can't be embarrassed," she said. "You first spoke to me about such things when we were children. I believe you said your father 'lives with his wife, who is the mother of his children.'"

"I've got to go," I said.

"Then go," she said, and looked at the window as I got up to leave.

Once outside, I hurried home, wondering along the way if she was really propositioned by married men or if she had just been trying to make me jealous or to shock me. It was news to me that she had a "reputation." But then it would be. I knew I was looked upon as being something of a prude. The sort of sexual bantering that went on between men often stopped when I appeared, as if my distaste for it was evident, though I tried not to let it show. Often, upon departing from a group of men, I would hear a raucous laugh behind me when I was just far enough away that we could all pretend it was not me they were laughing at.

Fielding's scam did not discredit her in the newspaper business. On the contrary, all the other publishers took great delight in our being hoodwinked and printed stories about it in their papers.

She was hired by the *Evening Telegram* to write a column a day, under her own name, a column called Field Day, which appeared in the first panel on page three of the *Telegram*.

She began writing satirical columns, so irony-laden you could not pin down her politics. They would eventually become quite popular, but reaction to them was not good at first. To St. John's readers, a newspaper was a platform from which to make a speech, to defend or promote one's party or one's cause, and to attack

other causes, other parties. But here was Fielding, finding fault
with everyone and everything. And she was a woman, and women
columnists were rare enough that many people believed, or professed to believe, that Fielding's style was typical of women.

She was called a fence-sitter and was challenged to defend
herself, which she did by saying the accusation might or might not
be true.

Fielding's Condensed
History of Newfoundland

Chapter Sixteen:

THE CASE OF JAMES LUNDRIGAN

The end of the reign of the naval governors is unfairly brought about, or at least hastened, by all the fuss made over the case of one James Lundrigan, a fisherman.

Here are the facts: In 1820, Mr. Lundrigan, who twice brazenly ignored a court summons to answer to a debt that he had irresponsibly incurred, was rightly found to be in contempt of court, was sentenced and, after serving barely one-third of his sentence, was released.

Here is the interpretation that was arbitrarily imposed upon these facts by the reform agitators Dr. William Carson and Patrick Morris: Mr. Lundrigan borrowed money from a merchant to buy supplies and did not pay it back in time. His fishing property was seized, but he refused to surrender his home. He did not answer the court summons, instead sending to court a note that read: "I am busy catching fish for my family, who have nothing besides to eat." Found to be in contempt of court, he was sentenced to receive thirty-six lashes of the whip. He fainted after the fourteenth.

As a result of the outrage stirred up by Carson and Morris, the power of the Newfoundland courts is strengthened and the first civilian governor, the aforementioned Sir Thomas Cochrane, is appointed.

We can say only that those who seek justice must content themselves with the promise of a better life to come.

Sir Richard

I FINALLY MADE UP my mind that socialism in any form could not prevail in Newfoundland. The next best thing, it seemed to me, or at any rate the closest thing to socialism that Newfoundlanders would accept, was Liberalism. So in 1928, I joined the Liberal Party. I wrote its newly re-elected leader, Sir Richard Squires, outlined my credentials, highlighting my time in New York and my walk across the island, and pledged him my full support, saying I would be willing to do anything he wanted to help him win the next election. The next thing I knew, Sir Richard was inviting me to dinner at his house.

Sir Richard had been prime minister from 1919 to 1923, when four of his own cabinet ministers resigned in protest over his corruption-ridden record, to which he responded by resigning the prime ministership to sit as an independent. Shortly afterwards, two years after his knighthood, he was arrested for bribery, patronage, embezzlement of public funds and a host of other charges.

"I appeared in front of a judge, but I did not spend one second in confinement," said Sir Richard. "I was instantly released on bail and the grand jury dismissed the charges for lack of evidence. I was exonerated, completely exonerated."

The next year he was again arrested, and this time convicted, for tax evasion, for which he was fined and placed on probation. He was still on probation when he won back the Liberal leadership in 1927.

I was uncharacteristically nervous as the day of my meeting with Sir Richard drew near. The prospect of meeting the quality, as my father called them, had never bothered me before. No longer armed, however, with my contempt for affluence, no longer the aloof, sceptical, ironical spectator of an elitist class-ridden society whose overthrow and replacement by socialism was inevitable, I now realized that it was important that I make a good impression with the mainstream, that it mattered what people like Sir Richard thought of me. My bedragglement, which among socialists had been a badge of honour, a kind of sartorial credential, was now an embarrassment to me. I still fancied that I would, from now on, be using Liberal means to accomplish socialist ends, but I was more than ever keenly self-conscious, aware of how ridiculous I looked to others, wearing day after day the same suit of Harris tweed, the same patched and re-patched Norfolk jacket I had worn in New York. Courtesy of cousin Walter, I was sporting an incongruously new pair of shoes, and I had recently bought, second-hand, a hat, into the lining of which I had to stuff old socks to make it fit.

There was a stone wall around Sir Richard's house on Rennie's Mill Road and, at the front, a massive iron gate that closed in the middle to form the letters *SRS*, the *R* split in half when the gates were open. The grounds, which had been hidden by the wall, were a descending tier of impeccably kept, if modestly sized, greenways flanked by statues, incongruous fawns and cherubs. The cobbled driveway went round a large fountain, in the centre of which loomed a sword-wielding marble angel with a warring, belligerent expression, its back to the house and its wings protectively outspread.

I walked awe-struck up the steps between the pillars and, after turning round on the portico several times to gawk at the angel, was about to knock on the front door when it was opened by a fellow in full livery — ruffled breeches to the knees, below that silk stockings, buckled shoes. Above the waist he wore a scarlet doublet with a row of bright brass buttons down the front. If he was taken aback at the shabbiness of my appearance, he did not let it show. He seemed aware that a generic someone was at the door, but that was all.

"I'm hear to see Sir Richard Squires," I said, uncertain if that was how I should refer to him. The fellow did not so much look at me as slightly away from me, as though the better to hear what I was saying.

"Who may I say is calling?" he said, as if this were a mere courtesy he was obliged to perform before sending me away. His English accent sounded put on, though perhaps he had merely been so long away from home that he was losing it.

"Mr. Joseph Smallwood," I said.

"Please wait here," he said. Seconds later, from somewhere inside the house, I heard him repeat my message word for word, drawing out the "all" in Smallwood as though for comic effect, as if he were telling his listener they would not want to miss seeing what the man who bore the grand-sounding title of Mr. Joseph Smallwood looked like. Then he returned and asked me to step into the front porch, which I did, whereupon he left me without a word of explanation.

Seconds later, two people I recognized from newspaper photos to be Sir Richard and Lady Squires leaned out over the banister of the winding staircase I was facing and looked down at me.

"Forgive us, Mr. Smallwood," Sir Richard said, while Lady Squires whispered something to him, "but you look like someone just escaped from, or soon to be admitted to, the San. You can't be too careful these days, you know."

"I'm in perfect health, sir," I said, shouting down the voice inside me that was urging me to reply in kind.

"Indeed," said Lady Squires. "In that case, it must be the rest of mankind that is sorely afflicted, for I have never in all my days seen anyone still drawing breath who looked like you."

"I've always been skinny, Lady Squires," I said.

"My husband is skinny, Mr. Smallwood," Lady Squires said. "There is, to the best of my knowledge, no word for what you are."

"Contagion free, are you?" Sir Richard said. "Consumption free? We have your word as a gentleman on that?" Lady Squires looked at him as if it were about as plausible to ask for my word as a gentleman as to presume me to be a member of the royal family.

"Yes, sir," I said, feeling myself turning crimson red from shame, as though my father, along with every socialist I had ever known, was listening.

"Very well then, Cantwell, show him in," Sir Richard said. Cantwell reappeared from inside the nearest room.

And so I had dinner with Sir Richard and Lady Squires. Lady Squires, who like Sir Richard was nearing fifty, was unusually dressed, in a full-length, robe-like, maroon-coloured garment, and wore around her neck a variety of charms and amulets, half a dozen of them, medallions, stones, badge-like leather ovals and circles that she fingered while she ate. The weight of them flattened her dress and brought out the rounded contours of her shoulders and her breasts. She was quite plump, with light blue darting eyes that belied her affected mannerisms, such as every few seconds putting down her knife and fork to rest her chin on her folded hands.

Sir Richard was angular-faced, hawk-nosed, somewhat like me, I fancied, and sported a modest moustache. He was, as his wife had said, somewhat skinny, and he ate as though he did not see the point of food, pushing a lamb chop about on his plate and stirring his peas and carrots and potatoes as if he were searching for something among them. It occurred to me that about now, Clara would have put Ramsay to bed and be sitting down to her customarily solitary supper of damper dogs and baked beans.

"Where did you go to school, Mr. Smallwood?" Sir Richard said.

"Bishop Feild," I said.

"Ah, a Bishop Feild graduate," Lady Squires said. "Sir Richard and I went to Methodist College. Met there, in fact."

"Ehhm — not ... not quite a graduate," I said, blushing. I was hoping she would tactfully change the subject, but she stared at me expectantly. I told her I had had to quit school and get a job to help support my family, of whom I was the oldest child.

"How far did you get?" Sir Richard said.

"I left in the middle of the fifth form," I said.

"In the middle?" Sir Richard said. "I never left in the middle of anything in my entire life. Even when they forced me to resign as prime minister, I sat as an independent. In the middle, eh? You haven't made a habit of doing that, I hope."

"Oh, no," I said.

"Where are your people from, Mr. Smallwood?" Lady Squires said. I told her: Gambo, Greenspond, Prince Edward Island.

"Hmmm," she said, as if she had made her token attempts at conversation, had got just the sort of uninteresting responses that she had expected and would speak no more.

"But you know," I said eagerly, "I am distantly related to Benjamin Franklin Smallwood, chief of the Choctaw Nation of Oklahoma." This was one of my father's far-fetched but impossible-to-disprove stories.

"Oh, how fascinating," she said and looked at me with genuine surprise and interest. "And so you, you have some Choctaw blood in you, do you?"

"Yes," I said, "I must have."

"Isn't that marvellous?" she said.

"I'm not sure everyone would think so," said Sir Richard. "Might want to keep it to yourself from now on."

Lady Squires waved her hand at him. She said she thought that we could learn a lot from Indians about "spiritualism" and that the greatest disaster in Newfoundland history had been the extinction of the Beothuk Indians.

"I am convinced," she said, "that there are people among us who are part Beothuk. There must have been some — er — intermingling between the Beothuks and the settlers, don't you think? There may be people who don't even know that they are one-thirty-second or one-sixty-fourth Beothuk, who knows? It's not impossible." I wondered how she would take the news that she was part Beothuk.

"Do you believe in spiritualism, Mr. Smallwood?"

She was not speaking of religion as I knew it.

"No, Lady Squires, I suppose I don't," I said apologetically, "at least, not in the way I think you mean."

"Good for you, Smallwood," Sir Richard said, "that makes two of us." I felt I was making progress. It was the first time he had not put Mr. in front of Smallwood.

"Hmmmm," Lady Squires said. "Still, sometimes the presence of a non-believer at a seance can be more of a help than a hindrance. It gets the spirit's back up, so to speak, and the spirit appears just to prove the non-believer wrong."

"Smallwood won't be able to join your seance, Helena," Sir Richard said. "He and I will be talking politics after dinner in the study."

"Well, don't worry, we won't disturb you," she said.

I spoke to Lady Squires after dinner while Sir Richard changed. She wanted to be a practitioner of "something spiritual," she said, but as yet had been unable to find her "*métier*." She had been tutored by masters, mentors, gurus, adepts, in person, by correspondence, in Newfoundland, while wintering in London. (Despite having grown up in Little Bay Islands, she declared Newfoundland winters to be unbearable.) She had turned to spiritualism after Sir Richard's fall from power in 1923, though she still attended her Methodist church on Sunday mornings and said there was nothing in spiritualism that flouted her religion.

"I play hostess," she said, "to a steady succession of itinerant mediums; readers of minds, palms, tarot cards, yarrow sticks and tea leaves; crystal-ball gazers; astrologers; even escape artists and magicians. People in places off the beaten track tend to be more receptive to such people, and you can't get much farther off the beaten track than Newfoundland. It seems there is always some touring spiritualist in town, Madam This and Swami That, and more often than not, I invite them to stay here. I organize advertising and publicity for them, accompany them to their performances and throw receptions for them afterwards. We're having a seance tonight. It's a pity you can't join us."

Sir Richard reappeared wearing a long, paisley-patterned, green smoking-jacket monogrammed *SRS* on one lapel. I followed him through a broad hallway, where a chandelier hung like a great cluster of tear-drops from the ceiling, into a large windowless room with mahogany wainscoting and a plush red carpet. There was a great open fireplace, facing which were two high-backed wicker chairs. He showed me to one, then took from the mantelpiece a silver cigar box, which he opened and held out to me. I chose a cigar, hoping I did not look like I was doing so for the first time in my life, which I was. As he lit it for me, I could not keep my hands from shaking. Then he chose one for himself and, lighting that, settled himself in the other chair.

"So," Sir Richard said, "you've joined the Liberal Party and put socialism behind you."

"I wouldn't say that," I began, "but — "

"I don't doubt that you believe in socialism, Smallwood," he said, "or think you do, at least. When I was your age, I was entertaining notions even more far-fetched."

It turned out he knew more about socialism than I did, more, in fact, than most of the socialists I had met. And he did not seem to have acquired this knowledge just in case socialism caught on, just so he would know what he was up against. You would think by his manner that only after agonizing over the choice had he decided that, rather than help advance the cause of socialism, he would become rich, and was still following with interest the progress of the option he had declined.

"I like making money more than I like having money," he said, "though having money is important, too."

"Because it gives you power over people?" I said.

He shrugged. "Socialism is just another way of getting power," he said, "which is what everybody really wants, isn't it?"

I disagreed, saying that I thought what everybody really wanted was freedom.

"No," he said, "it's power. Power is what *you* want, though I'll never get you to admit it. You picked socialism because you thought it was your best way of getting ahead. Also, you want to be remembered, it's written all over you, not that it's anything to be ashamed of. I want to be remembered, too. But you, Smallwood, you can't do it by making money because you don't know how. That's written all over you, too, I'm afraid. You're not an artist, you're not a scientist, you're not an intellectual. All that's left to you is politics. But even in politics, most doors are closed to you because you're poor. And so you picked socialism, the politics of poverty. Nothing terrfies you more than the thought of dying without having made your mark. Am I right?"

"I'd like to be remembered for doing something good," I said. "Most people would."

"Tell me something," he said, "and be as honest as you can. Could you die happy knowing that your one heroic act, your one great accomplishment, would never be acknowledged, or worse yet, would be attributed to someone else? Imagine it, Smallwood. You've performed some great act of heroism, but no one knows it and no one ever will. It's one thing to sacrifice yourself for the cause, it's another thing to do it anonymously. Who would you rather be, Sergeant York or the Unknown Soldier?"

I responded with a vigorous denial that I was a socialist because I was out to make a name for myself. The distinguishing characteristic of the true socialist, I said, was selflessness. I told him his mansion was an Ozymandias-like monument to human vanity that would not endure. I told him people would still be reading Shelley's poem long after the last cent of the Squires fortune had been spent. I was ready to walk out.

"Exactly my point," he said, taking no apparent offence at my remarks. "You'd rather be Shelley than me because Shelley did something that will never be forgotten."

"So did Genghis Khan," I said. "So did Herod. So did Pontius Pilate. That's not the way I want to be remembered."

He smiled and shook his head. His patronizing indulgence, his unshakeable unwillingness to take offence at anything I said, maddened me. It was as though I was simply not of sufficient importance to offend him.

"There's no such thing as selflessness," he said. "Or if there is, I've never seen it. Martyrs expect an eternal reward for the sacrifice they make. An atheist willing to sacrifice his life anonymously for the benefit of others and able not to be smug about it, that would be the closest thing to selflessness that you could come. But I've never met anyone like that, have you?

We talked for hours, with him doing most of it and me lamely interrupting him from time to time. I was out of my depth and knew it and felt that I was clinging to my beliefs by faith alone, as if he were some intellectually superior devil whose arguments, though I knew them to be sophistry, were far more compelling than mine.

He said he had all his life gone through the motions of religion, but he did not really believe any of it. His greatest fear, he said, was that he would wind up an old man, afraid of a death that he knew was not far off, and afraid that, in his panic, he would have a fit of repentance and start begging a non-existent god's forgiveness for things he did not think were wrong and was not really sorry for.

"That's what I'm afraid of most," he said, "winding up on my hands and knees, recanting, praying to God on the off chance He might exist."

I was impressed by this admission. I had great sympathy for anyone as terrified as I was of having a conversion forced upon him, under any circumstances.

We talked politics for hours that night. We talked on many other nights, though Sir Richard never had me in when there were other guests. Either he and I and (rarely) Lady Squires dined alone, or he would simply have me over for an after-dinner brandy and cigar when his other guests had left. More often than not, I had not eaten, but I would mimic his postprandial satedness, my stomach growling from hunger as Sir Richard puffed reflectively on his cigar.

He took no pains to hide the fact that he did not want his friends to know we were associates. On the contrary, he told me not to ascend his steps when the porch light was lit, this being our signal that the last guest had yet to leave, as if class were determined by nature and I would no more presume to be his equal or be offended by his behaviour towards me than I would mind his pointing out that I was five foot six. I was in no position to object, but it took a great effort to hide my resentment as I stood in the shadows of a tree across the street, hoping the 'Stab would not see me and mistake my intentions, shivering in late fall in my little jacket.

My father dismissed the Squireses as "not even St. John's born, baymen, titled baymen, but baymen all the same," who, he was delighted to hear from me, would sometimes drop or add an aitch in conversation and at whose dinner parties the subject of their birthplaces was not often raised.

One night in his study, Sir Richard said an election would be called within the year and he needed someone to do the "legwork" for the Liberal Party in the newly created Humber district on the southwest and lower-west coasts. I told him, invoking my walk across the island, that legwork was my specialty and that I would do what he asked if he would support my nomination as the Liberal candidate in Humber district when the election was called.

"Do a good job there this winter," Sir Richard said, "and the nomination's yours."

I was in awe of him from that moment on. I had never been on the receiving end of such largesse. He had given me the Humber district nomination as if it were nothing but a trifle. He affected an aristocratic manner, as though his knighthood had been self-conferred, and yet there was something appealing about him. I still believed I put no value on refinement and sophistication, but the fact that he had worked to acquire these qualities, rather than having been born to them, made, I thought, a world of difference.

I visited almost every settlement in Humber district, no matter how small. Most of the people there had never voted, had not the faintest idea what a political party was or what difference it would make to them if one party instead of another was elected. Only in Corner Brook and a few other larger towns was I able to do some real campaigning. I spoke to lodges, church groups, unions, urging them to vote for the Liberal Party and implying, but never stating outright, that in Humber district, I would be the Liberal candidate.

From Corner Brook, I wired to Sir Richard that Humber district was ripe for the taking and I was eagerly awaiting his official endorsement of my candidacy, then made my way to a boardinghouse.

On waking the next morning and going downstairs, I was handed by the proprietor a telegram from Sir Richard that read: HAVE CONSIDERED THE POSITION OF THE HUMBER CONSTITUENCY CAREFULLY AND HAVE COME TO THE CONCLUSION THAT AS THE LIBERAL PARTY HAS VIRTUALLY CREATED THIS DISTRICT IT IS MY DUTY TO OFFER MYSELF AS THE LIBERAL CANDIDATE STOP WOULD APPRECIATE IT IF YOU WOULD MANAGE MY CAMPAIGN STOP SRS.

I could not remember ever feeling so betrayed, or so foolish. I had been recruited from the ranks of the disposable months in advance for the very purpose I had served. He had known all along that he would run in Humber, the district where people were least likely to remember his first stint as prime minister, since it had not been a district then. When Sir Richard had received my letter of self-recommendation from out of the blue, it must have seemed to him a godsend. I pictured him composing the telegram back home in St. John's and reading it aloud to an amused Lady Squires.

I left the boarding-house and walked for several hours, concocting various improbable revenge schemes, fantasizing about answering his telegram with one of my own, announcing my intention to run against him as an independent, which the Tory candidate encouraged me to do, hoping I would split the Liberal vote. I almost convinced myself that over the winter I had so endeared myself to the people of Humber district that I could pull off such an upset. But even if I did, what future would there be for me in politics? There was no question of a man with my pink past ever running as a Tory, and the Liberals would never forgive me if I ran against Sir Richard, no matter how badly I lost. I wired back to St. John's: NOT FOR ANYONE ELSE WOULD I DO THIS BUT I WILL FOR YOU STOP SMALLWOOD.

Fielding's Condensed
History of Newfoundland

Chapter Seventeen:

MUDDENING THE GOVERNOR

Throughout Sir Thomas Cochrane's disastrous nine-year reign, certain changes take place in Newfoundland society that are characterized as "advances" by Reeves-reading agitators.

Roads are built. Agriculture is encouraged. Men till the soil, thereby decreasing the surplus labour pool and bringing merchants perilously close to the brink of raising wages.

Cochrane redeems himself somewhat, however, by opposing Dr. Carson's campaign for a local legislature, declaring Newfoundlanders to be too backward a people to govern themselves.

This constructive criticism is taken in the spirit in which it is intended by all but a minority of Newfoundlanders.

When the time comes for Cochrane to leave Newfoundland, a great crowd turns out to see him off and there is inaugurated what will become a local tradition performed at the departure for home of each of England's representatives, known as muddening the governor.

Later, from England, Cochrane writes: "One might rather have had fond farewells thrown one's way instead of gobs of mud, but in strange places strange rituals are practised to which one must submit or else give offence to one's constituency."

The Dirt Poor and
the Filthy Rich

M Y HUMILIATION BECAME common knowledge, though
I played it down as much as I could, saying that the fact
that I was still working for Sir Richard was proof enough that I did
not feel ill-used. I had unwisely boasted to my father that I would
soon be a member of the legislature. This utterance had so terrified
him that he tried to mollify fate by assuring me that people like us
did not wind up in the legislature. On hearing of my treatment at
Sir Richard's hands, he said betrayal was what came from associating with "the quality." He also assured me that Sir Richard would,
one way or another, pay for his success and the means he had used
to acquire it. As if to prove that this was so, my father said he had
looked up the word squire in the dictionary and "I'll be goddamned
if it doesn't mean judge. Another judge, Joe. We have been judged
again, boy. This country is plagued with judges.

"I'm to blame, Joe, I'm to blame," he obscurely added.

"Oh, yes, you're to blame," my mother said scornfully. "You're
the reason the sun comes up and you're the reason the sun goes

down. You're the reason it snows and you're the reason it rains. Nothing can happen, good or bad, that wasn't caused by you."

My mother had no doubt about who was to blame; it was Sir Richard's "witch of a wife" who, through God only knew what sort of black magic, had prevented me from seeing what Sir Richard was really like. She said it was a well-known fact that Lady Squires was always boasting that she had salvaged her husband's career, passing on to him advice her spiritualists had passed on to her from Satan.

"It was her doing. She is an evil, evil woman," my mother said bitterly, looking at me, driven to tears by the disappointment she read in my eyes. "I'm surprised that you would have anything more to do with them, Joe," she said, "after what they've done to you. After what they've done to us."

When next I saw Sir Richard after sending him the telegram, he did not seem the least bit awkward or embarrassed. He invited me to dinner and the first thing he said to me was "Did you know that I was the Newfoundland Jubilee Scholar for 1898?"

"No," I said, "I didn't."

"Well, you have to know these things, Smallwood, if you're to manage my campaign," he said. "You can't sing my praises if you don't know my accomplishments." He outlined his accomplishments while I took notes. He had graduated from Methodist College in St. John's, as had my father. It occurred to me they would have been there at about the same time, though my father had never mentioned it. 'Friends, as we might have been, had we gone to school together.' He received his degree in law from Dalhousie Law School and had been made King's Counsel in 1914 at the age of thirty-four.

"I lost my first election by five votes, *five* votes, Smallwood, think of it. November 2, 1908. In Trinity district. I was your age, twenty-eight. Five votes. If three of the people who voted for the other fellow had voted for me, I would have won. Just three. That's haunted me, I can tell you. I would lie awake nights for months afterwards and think about that house that I decided wasn't worth a visit because it was so far down the shore, or some old fellow I forgot to wave to when we passed him on the road. Remember Trinity, Smallwood, remember Trinity when you're out there on the Humber. No house is too far down the shore, no island is too small to bother with. Wave to everyone you see. Even a house with a Tory flag out front can be converted. You should think of every person who's old enough to vote as the person who holds the balance of power...."

He went on and on until I stopped taking notes.

"Now, there's the question of how to handle all that" — he waved his hand as if to shoo away a fly — "all that business back in '23. They said 'the charges were dropped for lack of evidence,' which makes it sound like I was guilty but they couldn't prove it. I don't like that phrase. Say, if someone brings it up, that I was completely exonerated — "

"They won't know what *exonerated* means," I said.

"Then tell them I was proven innocent," Sir Richard said.

The election was called for September. I went back to Humber district to campaign for Sir Richard, who said he could afford to spend only one or at most two days in his own riding, there being so many other ridings he had to visit where victory was not as certain. He knew he would win in Humber, he said, but he wanted to win by a landslide, and my reward for serving as his campaign manager would be proportionate to his margin of victory.

"Every vote for me makes your future that much brighter, Smallwood, remember that," he said, though I could not pin him down on exactly what range of rewards he had in mind. "I'll make it well worth your trouble, you may be sure of that," he said.

Lady Squires's interest in spiritualism proved to be something of a liability during the election campaign. She was frantic with anxiety, constantly seeking reassurance from her spiritualists that she and her husband, after their five years in exile, would be returned to power. Her spiritualists were only too glad to oblige, but she would accept no assurance of success as definitive. As though she was addicted to it, the more reassurance she got, the more she craved. Word got round that while Sir Richard was away campaigning, the Squires's house was all but overrun with prognosticators and soothsayers of every kind. The Squireses became known among the ruling Conservatives as Witch and Rich, and Fielding in her column dubbed the Liberals the Hocus-Pocus Party, Sir Richard's best trick, she said, being his ability to make funds from the public treasury disappear without a trace.

The first thing Sir Richard did every morning was read Fielding's column, searching, never in vain, for some mention of himself. Not a day passed when Fielding did not make some sort of "dig" at him or Lady Squires, and often her entire column was devoted to them. There was the column, for instance, in which she "described" an interview she had with the Squireses:

Field Day, February 9, 1928

I was welcomed at the door by Lady Squires, who said she had spent the morning with her soothsayer, who had been showing her how to tell the future by pawing through the entrails of a goat, hence the blood on her hands, which it seemed would never come off. You look like Lady MacBeth, I quipped, and we both laughed. She told me she was in the study entertaining a mind-reader whom Sir Richard was for some reason anxious to avoid, so the interview would take place in the dining room.

Sir Richard expressed concern that his wife's harmless hobby might affect the voters' view of him, but seemed greatly relieved when I assured him that if they didn't hold his criminal record against him, it was doubtful they would think any less of him for having a wife who spent her spare time communicating with the dead.

Lady Squires, her mind-reader having left, joined us shortly after and sat in on the rest of the interview. Asked if she missed being the wife of the country's prime minister and all the prestige and power that went with it, she said it was all the same to her what her husband did, as long as he was happy. She chuckled appreciatively when I joked that the doll-sized effigy she held on her lap and into which she was poking pins bore a remarkable resemblance to our present prime minister.

We were then joined by an old friend of mine, Joe Smallwood, and he and I fondly reminisced about our school days. Smallwood, who used to be a socialist, has thrown in his lot with Sir Richard's Liberals.

"You might say we've formed an alliance of sorts," Smallwood said. "The dirt poor and the filthy rich."

That, in fact, is Smallwood's nickname for his new employer, Filthy Rich.

"I love a pun at someone else's expense," Smallwood said, and we laughed, as did Sir Richard, eyeing Smallwood good-naturedly.

Smallwood was on a break from campaigning for Sir Richard in the Humber district, where he himself once thought of running and every frozen inch of which he walked last winter.

"You have to learn to walk before you can run," Sir Richard said, smiling tenderly at Smallwood.

"We're a pun-loving pair, aren't we, Sir Richard?" Smallwood said, and Sir Richard nodded.

When I raised the delicate matter of the charges that were brought against Sir Richard after his last tenure as prime minister, he reminded me that the charges had been dropped and he had never gone to trial.

"But where there's smoke, there's Squires," I said, laughing, and it was all the pun-loving pair could do to keep from falling on the floor.

I asked Sir Richard if he thought Smallwood had a future in politics.

"When it comes to the future, I defer to Lady Squires," Sir Richard said.

Her Ladyship said she had recently dreamed of a small wooden cabinet, which she took to mean that Smallwood would one day be prime minister of Newfoundland.

The high point of the afternoon's hilarity came when I thought Sir Richard said something about libel and bribery, when in fact what he said was "I have to read the Bible in the library."

"She has a following, this Fielding woman," Sir Richard said one night when I joined him in his study. "I'm told the *Telegram* has nearly doubled its subscription rate since she started writing for them."

"Yes," I said, "I believe she's caught on with a certain kind of reader."

"That's just it. We've got the working-class vote," Sir Richard said. "It's the people who can read I'm not so sure about."

"Fielding's gripe is with the world," I said, "not you *per se*. She gives those two Tories, Monroe and Alderdice, as good as she gives you. She calls them the kissing cousins — "

"I don't care what she calls Monroe and Alderdice," Sir Richard said. "It's what she calls me that I don't like. I'm told that you know her."

"Oh," I said. "Ehmmm, yes, I do. We're not great friends or anything. We more or less went to school together. When I was at Bishop Feild, she was at Bishop Spencer."

"Do you think you could talk to her, ask her to let up on me a bit?"

"I don't think that would be a good idea. If I were to ask Fielding to let up on you, she'd say so in her column."

I tried to placate him by playing down her column's significance, saying it was so laden with irony and puns that no one understood it anyway. Sir Richard might have been convinced had the phrase "Where there's smoke, there's Squires" not been picked up by the Tory government, Prime Minister Alderdice using it at every opportunity to invoke Sir Richard's scandal-racked administration. Signs bearing that slogan were printed up and plastered all over St. John's and in ridings throughout the country.

One night when I went to his house, Sir Richard said he had "found out" about what happened between Fielding and me at Bishop Feild, how she had tried to frame me for something she had done and had confessed only when threatened with a caning.

"That's not quite — " I began, then thought better of correcting him before I knew who the source of his misinformation was. "I mean, who told you about that?"

"He'll be here in a moment," Sir Richard said. "Together I think the two of you can do quite a job on Fielding." Five minutes later there was a knock on the door, which Cantwell answered.

"Show him in," Sir Richard said.

I did not recognize him at first, he had changed so much since I had last seen him, changed for the better, of course, as how else could Prowse have changed? He still wore that collusive, aren't-we-a-pair-of-rascals grin of his. He had filled out but was not fat. He was a broad-shouldered, robust, confidence-exuding six-footer to whom success still came, I had no doubt, as a matter of course. He was the Prowse I had imagined upon reading the letter to the *Backhomer* in which he had paid his respects to Reeves in the slightly patronizing manner of a student who now occupied a station in life far superior to that of his former headmaster. I remembered how much of Fielding's journal had been addressed to Prowse. Dear Prowse. Dear Prowse. He was wearing a wedding ring, I saw. He looked me up and down as if to say that I had turned out pretty much as he expected. We shook hands wordlessly.

"No introductions necessary, I see," Sir Richard said, as if we had hugged each other. "Prowse took his degree in law from Dalhousie just like me, Smallwood." Prowse smiled. Sir Richard was under his spell, or else he would have seen in that smile what I saw: the hint of scornful amusement that the older man put so much store by such things as two men having graduated from the same school.

Sir Richard had Prowse explain what had been done to Fielding, and why, back at Bishop Feild. Prowse related his story with relish, sitting forward on the edge of his chair and demonstrating how "we boys" had dragged Fielding into the training centre, where, under threat of flogging, she confessed. "I wasn't going to flog her, of course," Prowse said, "but she didn't know that." I wondered how Fielding would feel if she heard him lie like that. I wished she had. Prowse looked at me, apparently not worried that I would contradict this version of events, that I would remind him in front of Squires that Fielding had confessed *before* the threat was made. His complacency unnerved me and I said nothing.

Sir Richard roared with laughter. "Why didn't you tell me about this before, you two?" Sir Richard said. "This is just the kind of thing we need. Fielding, the great moralist, so pure she will not take sides, kicked out of Bishop Spencer."

Prowse sat there smiling, showing his prominent, gapped, gleaming white front teeth; Prowse whom Fielding had once loved. And perhaps still did.

"Fielding the turncoat," Sir Richard said, "bent over a sawhorse, all the boys of Bishop Feild threatening to whale away on her with her own cane. I want you two to write a letter to the editors of all the papers about this. Make it clear you never laid a finger on her and never intended to. Just so long as her humiliation comes across. And then say that she's making up lies now, writing lies now, just like she did at school; writing lies for a newspaper just like she did at school. There's a lovely irony for you. Say that nothing's changed, she's still the same old Fielding, conducting her smear campaigns against men like us, men of action whose courage and accomplishments she envies."

It was clear that Prowse had already agreed to write this letter and that if I did not help him and co-sign it, I would fall in Squires's estimation and he would conclude that I did not have the stomach for politics. When he saw my reluctance, he acted almost hurt, as if, after such a promising start, I was turning out not to be the man he had thought I was.

"Of course, if you'd rather leave it all to Prowse," Sir Richard said, smiling at Prowse, who smiled back as if he had often done this sort of thing on Sir Richard's behalf.

"It might turn the public against you," I said. "A band of boys ganging up on a girl."

"If it were any other woman, I'd agree with you," Sir Richard said. "But this is Fielding. People know Fielding. She's twice the size of most men. Are you telling me you won't do this, Smallwood?"

"No, no," I said. "I will. I will. It's just that — "

"I don't just want to win this election, Smallwood," Sir Richard said. "I want every vote, every polling station, every riding I can get. I want to pay them back for what they did to me in '23."

"Of course, but — "

"You're the one whose future this Fielding woman destroyed," Sir Richard said, apparently oblivious to the possibility that I might be embarrassed by this bleak assessment of my prospects. I could not help wondering what sort of post-election victory reward he had in mind for me if he considered my future to have been destroyed.

"Is there something between you and Fielding that could damage us?" he said. "Are you afraid that if you write this letter, this something might come out?"

I shook my head and looked at Prowse. It occurred to me, for the first time, that Fielding might have confessed to protect Prowse, that it might have been Prowse who wrote the letter to the *Morning*

Post. Fielding might have thought, when she saw him accusing me, that he had panicked, and might have confessed to prevent a controversy that could have ended badly for him. It was possible; it was the kind of thing he would let someone do for him. Whether it was the kind of thing that she would do I wasn't sure. In one way, I would rather have been wronged by him than by her. But it was unbearable that she would have been willing to sacrifice so much for him.

"Why did you hire that woman to work for your paper, anyway, after what she did to you?" Sir Richard said.

I thought about telling him that Fielding had saved my life, but I could not bring myself to do it, for it seemed to me that the more people there were who knew of Fielding's heroism, the more indebted to Fielding I would be. I not only felt indebted to her, I felt, for reasons I could not understand, that her having saved my life rendered me morally inferior to her. Perhaps it was our keeping it a secret and not even speaking of it ourselves: she, it seemed to me, so affectedly noble, humble; and me so begrudging with my gratitude. Or perhaps it was because we both doubted that I would have risked my life to save hers.

I told Sir Richard about organizing the sectionmen's union and Fielding's refusal to join and how I felt "indirectly" responsible for her losing her job.

"It served her right," Sir Richard said. "She had no business working on the railway anyway, but she should have joined the union. She's anti-labour, anti-working class." My list of champions of the working class would not have had Sir Richard at its top, but I said nothing, and in any case what he said was true, if only because Fielding was anti-everything.

"Why in God's name would the daughter of a doctor want to be a sectionman?" he said. "Maybe you could play that up in your letter. There might be an angle there. This is your chance to get even with her, Smallwood. Getting her fired from one job doesn't make you even, not after what she did to you."

In the end, I agreed to write the letter with Prowse. We wrote it on the table in the front room of my house. Clara and the children — my second son, William, had just been born — were visiting her parents in Harbour Grace. On entering my house, Prowse looked about at its cramped dinginess as if it to say that it was more suitable for skulduggery than his posh place on Winter Avenue.

"There are a lot of people out there who know that what you told Sir Richard isn't true," I said.

"Don't worry, Smallwood," Prowse said. "You just write the letter and leave the rest to me."

I wrote drafts that Prowse critiqued. He kept telling me I was leaving too much out, going too easy on Fielding. I remembered how he had been willing to flog the "truth" out of me, to cast me off as a friend as abruptly as he had Fielding, but I held my tongue about it, as I had done throughout our meeting with Sir Richard. I remembered his last words to me when I refused his attempt to patch things up after I had been exonerated by Fielding's confession: "Go join the Lepers. They're the only ones who'll have you now." Eventually I wrote a draft that he thought was good enough. We brought it to Sir Richard, who said he could guarantee publication of every word of it in every paper, the *Telegram* included.

We wrote that our letter was an answer to an anonymous letter written long ago and never published, though attributed to me by Headmaster Reeves, who was genuinely unaware that I was not its author, having been led to the conclusion that I was by the letter's postmark. Fielding, we said, when threatened with a caning, had confessed to writing this letter to the *Morning Post*. I was every bit as graphic in my description of Fielding's humiliation as Sir Richard insisted I should be. I then revealed how the letter controversy had affected me, how I had been "blackballed" by the faculty and streamed commercial, after which, my hopes of a college education dashed, I was forced to quit the school and get a job to help support my family.

The letter was printed verbatim, as Sir Richard had promised, except that it was signed not only by Prowse and me, but by all the boys, now men, who had been at the Feild that day. Prowse, at Sir Richard's behest and unknown to me, had gone round to all of them and got them to sign it.

In no time it was the talk of St. John's. Letters to the editor in defence of the ganged-up-on girl-Fielding poured in just as I had predicted and were printed in the *Telegram*, but in the other papers, both Tory and Liberal, there were gleeful editorials and letters, the gist of which was that Fielding had been revealed to be the hypocrite people had all along suspected her of being.

There was now an explanation for Fielding, a history her enemies could point to that explained the way she wrote, her irony, her sarcasm, her cynicism, her misanthropy. To the riddle of Fielding, her school days were the answer; the freakishly tall girl, the bitter loner, the doctor's daughter who, because of her unpopularity and because she could not live up to her father's expectations, had written to a newspaper a letter falsely smearing the school and had framed another student for it, a poor student for whom Bishop Feild was his one chance for advancement and whose improbable popularity Fielding envied.

I suppose if Fielding had been a writer of the sort of earnest editorials that appeared daily in all the other papers, our letter might have done even more harm than it did.

The *Telegram* ran beside her next column a picture of Fielding from her schooldays; Fielding at thirteen, looking almost like a send-up of the disdainfully embittered girl we made her out to be in our letter; Fielding layered in petticoats, standing sideways to the camera but looking straight at it, two hands clasping the knob of her cane, eyes scowling out at the camera from under some sort of bonnet, which she had never worn at school, something she must have been cajoled into wearing, by her father perhaps, just for this portrait; Fielding before her confession, before her days as a reporter at the courthouse, before New York, before the San and Bonavista.

Field Day, March 17, 1928

Excerpt from *Hooligans Seized Her*, by Sheilagh Shakespeare:

Her father begged her not to go to school that day. He had had a dream, he said, in which eight who once had called her friend did set upon her, and tore her clothing from her body strip by strip and sent her forth into the street, where horses at the sight of her did neigh, and grown men groaned and boys did shriek and squeal.

"You have misconstrued this dream," said Fielding. "This signifies my greatness, which, though I were stripped of all my earthly power, all my wealth, would still shine forth, for I am Fielding."

Her father, bowing his head, replied: "I pray you again, my dear, go not to the school today."

"What say the augurers?" said Fielding.

"Lady Squires sends this letter," her father said. "'Plucking the entrails of my husband forth, I could not find a heart within the beast.' What can this signify?" her father said.

"That Fielding would be heartless did she not venture forth," said Fielding.

"Your wisdom is consumed in confidence," her father said. "Stir not from this house today."

"What can be avoided whose end is purposed by the mighty gods?" said Fielding. "Fielding shall go forth."

"Say you are sick," her father said.

"Shall Fielding send a lie?" said Fielding. "Give me my cane, for I shall go."

And so Fielding went to school and, surrounded by her worshippers, did survey the Feild.

"Let me have men about me that are fat," said Fielding. "Yond' Smallwood has a lean and hungry look; he thinks too much: such men are dangerous."

They, on some pretext, did entice her to the Annex and she did there confess to falsely accusing the school in a letter to the *Morning Post* of feeding the boys of Bishop Feild spit-roasted rat and withholding from them toothpicks so that with rat ribs were they forced to pick their teeth.

One Porter did goad the other boys, including Prowse, who, in former days, had been her friend of friends, into caning her. The eight of them did bend Fielding over a saw-horse and, lifting up her skirts, did reveal to all what heretofore none but Fielding in a mirror had admired.

"When buggers lie," said Fielding, "there are no back-sides seen. The heavens themselves blaze forth the breadth of Fielding's."

"Speak, hands, for me," said Porter and with her own cane was Fielding flogged while Smallwood watched, once by each of them until only Prowse was left. *Et tu*, Prowse. Then bawled Fielding.

They left her there, by eight abused, by eight forsaken; friendless Fielding, fanny-flayed.

The evil that men do lives after them. The good is oft interred with their bones. The noble Feildians have told you that Fielding was malicious. If so, it was a grievous fault and grievously hath Fielding answered it. If not, the Feildians lie.

Fielding's answer mystified even those of us who knew our Shakespeare. Sir Richard was nonplussed and stared at the column and the picture of Fielding beside it as though he had been outdone by their sheer inscrutability.

"She's hiding behind that cleverness of hers again," Sir Richard said to Prowse and me. "What kind of answer is this to being called a liar and a cheat? And she says you caned her, caned her with her bloomers down around her knees. Is that true?"

"She's lying," Prowse said.

"A lie for a lie," I could not resist saying.

"What's that?" Sir Richard said.

"Nothing," I said. "Prowse is right. She was never caned."

"You shouldn't have provoked that Fielding woman," my father said, the next time I saw him. "You shouldn't have written that letter. Nothing good will come of writing letters to newspapers." All the while I was at the house, he walked about reading *Julius Caesar*, searching out the allusions to it in Fielding's column, reading the most portent-ridden, fatalistic passages aloud.

"If not, then Feildians lie," my father said, shaking his head. "She says she wrote the letter, yet she accuses you of lying. 'The evil that men do lives after them. The good is oft interred with their bones.'"

"What evil does she think you've done?" my mother said to me. "If you ask me, she's the evil one, talking in riddles and circles just like the devil does."

"Were there really eight of you?" my father said.

"No," I said. "More like forty."

"Five times eight," my father said. "I've never liked the number eight. Eight men to kill one man. All you boys and just one girl. That's the kind of thing that stays with you all your life." I wondered if he meant Fielding's life or mine.

Throughout the campaign, I received telegrams from Sir Richard from all over the island. YOU ARE MY MAN IN HUMBER STOP REMEMBER THAT STOP AM COUNTING ON YOU STOP SRS.

It was obvious that Sir Richard was going to take Humber with a massive majority, but he could not stop fretting about what his margin of victory would be. DREAMT LAST NIGHT BARRETT SHUT OUT STOP NOT A SINGLE VOTE STOP SRS.

I travelled, as I had throughout the winter, to every household in the district. Sir Richard took a swing through Humber near the end of the campaign, spent two days there, but by that time he was so exhausted that his speeches were almost incoherent. In one town hall, he five times reminded the audience that he was the man who had brought to Humber district the country's second pulp-and-paper mill. I sat on the platform behind him, leading the applause, and when I saw that the audience was growing bored, scuffed my shoe on the floor, our signal that he had talked long enough and should start summing up. He nodded his head, mumbled some closing words, then staggered off the stage. Anything more than a public lapse into unconsciousness would have seemed to them a triumph, so completely had I convinced them of his virtue.

Sir Richard was swept back into power, taking 83 per cent of the vote in Humber district, and across the island twenty-eight of thirty-six seats. I was in Humber and he was in St. John's when the votes were counted.

"We are back in power, Smallwood," Sir Richard said, when I called him by telephone. "For four years, they have been dancing on my grave, the bastards, and now my turn has come to dance on theirs. In return for everything you've done for me, I'm making you a justice of the peace. What do you think of that? Not bad for someone who never finished high school, eh?"

I was so disappointed I could barely speak, and when I did manage a few words, I was on the verge of tears.

"I was hoping for something ... political," I said. "Hoping to work with your ... administration, with ... you."

"A successful politician has many debts to pay," Sir Richard said. "My list of people whose generosity I feel I should — reciprocate — is long, Smallwood, very long."

Justices of the peace travelled in pairs throughout the island, accompanied by a bailiff/bodyguard, trying cases too insignificant for the higher courts to bother with. I had seen them conducting their proceedings on fishing wharves, using wooden crates for benches and weighting down their papers with beach rocks so they would not blow away. I could see myself in itinerant exile from St.

John's, could see before me years spent wandering the outports of Newfoundland, prosecuting people driven, out of poverty and boredom, to petty crime, sending to jail and fining and making life-long enemies of people whose vote I might be looking for someday. It would be like a life spent at the wretched courthouse, only worse, less grand, without the pomp and circumstance of courtrooms; like becoming a modern-day fishing admiral.

I knew Squires wanted me out of the way to spare himself the embarrassment of having to acknowledge my existence from time to time. I knew it, but told myself I did not resent him for it, for it was what I would have done in his situation. A politician had to do what was expedient. I somehow had to show him that I was not what he was fully justified in presuming me to be. As well, I assumed that all ambitious young men went through some such phase of exploitation by the politicians they helped to get elected.

I wrote to him, telling him, with thanks, that I was declining his offer and returning to "my first love," writing for newspapers. He wrote back, tersely wished me well and, for a long while, that was that. It was not until I learned that Prowse had been hired on as Sir Richard's executive assistant that I vowed I would never speak to either one of them again.

Fielding's Condensed
History of Newfoundland

Chapter Eighteen:

SIX CLEAR-SIGHTED PROTESTANTS

In spite of Cochrane's painstakingly-arrived-at objections, a local legislature is established on June 7, 1832.

In the first election, ten of the fifteen seats are won by Protestant Conservatives, five by Catholic Liberals. Governor Sir Henry Prescott notes the obvious inequity and suggests measures to decrease the number of Catholics.

He proposes, among other things, that only those occupying property valued at ten pounds or more per year be allowed to vote. But his suggestions are rejected by the Colonial Office, with the disastrous result that after the next election, Catholics outnumber Protestants nine to six.

Luckily for Newfoundlanders, and owing to the foresight of Governor Prescott, there is a non-elected, governor-appointed Senate-like council consisting of six clear-sighted Protestant opponents of self-rule, with absolute powers of veto. By sending back all bills sent to it by the House, this council brings the business of government to a standstill.

What a debt is owed to these six men who stood alone against the enemies of Newfoundland, and whose only support consisted of the governor, the Colonial Office, the Privy Council, the British Parliament and the king of England. If not for them, the 1830s would have seen the Poor Relief Bill passed in spite of the opposition to it of the poor themselves, on whose behalf the merchants marched in protest through the streets.

Fielding's Father

I WENT TO WORK for a paper in Corner Brook (sending money on to my family in St. John's), and as each day went by, my bitterness abated and common sense got the better of me. As I had concluded before, Liberalism was my only way of advancement in politics, so I had to swallow my pride and try to stay in Sir Richard's good graces. I began keeping track of his administration in St. John's and even wrote him letters of advice from time to time, which he did not acknowledge.

But in 1930, he wrote me from St. John's and asked me to come see him right away. I took the train across the island and went to his house, where Cantwell gave me a small amount of money and instructed me to hole up in the Brownsdale Hotel on New Gower Street until further notice.

I knew that Sir Richard was soon to call a by-election in the district of Lewisporte, and I was hoping that, guilty over not having rewarded me properly before, he was going to offer me the Liberal nomination. I languished at the Brownsdale for three weeks, thinking Sir Richard had forgotten me, until finally he phoned. Before he could speak, I did. I told him this by-election was especially important to me because the Lewisporte seat had formerly been held by George Grimes, my first mentor, who had just passed away.

"It would be a great honour for me to run in Lewisporte, Sir Richard," I said. "I can win there for you; I'd like the Liberal nomination."

"I'm sorry, Smallwood," Sir Richard said, "but I've already promised it to someone else."

"Who?" I all but shouted into the phone, certain the someone else must be Prowse.

"Lady Squires. My wife will be the first woman elected to the House of Assembly," Sir Richard said, as if he were announcing yet one more thing he would be remembered for, as if he considered it to be more of an achievement for him than for her.

"Then what do you want me to do?" I managed to choke out. He said he wanted me to start up a Liberal propaganda sheet, to be called the *Watchdog*, whose sole purpose would be to counter the Tory propaganda sheet, which was called the *Watchman*. My job would essentially be to dig up dirt on members of the Opposition and other of Sir Richard's enemies.

The *Watchman* and the *Watchdog*. To make it easier to distinguish between them in conversation, the papers were referred to simply as the *Dog* and the *Man*. "We got the worst of that abbreviation," Sir Richard said, as though it were my fault. Sir Richard got some revenge by "obtaining" the *Man*'s mailing list and having me send the *Dog* free of charge to lifetime Tories, not in the hope of converting them, but in the hope word would get round among their fellow Tories that they were subscribing to the *Dog*. We managed to stir up quite a lot of trouble before our ruse became common knowledge.

There appeared in a Tory paper a cartoon depicting me as a bespectacled, emaciated mongrel sitting in rapt attention to a phonograph from which were issuing the words "Sic him, Smallwood, sic him." The caption read "His master's voice." To me, to be depicted, however unflatteringly, as a sidekick of Sir Richard's was a breakthrough. I cut out the cartoon and pasted it on the wall above my desk.

Every so often, Prowse would come by the *Dog's* offices, which were located in a freezing, ill-partitioned warehouse on Water Street, with some press release that Sir Richard wanted translated into propaganda. There was no doubt that even at age thirty, Prowse looked prime ministerial, and that Sir Richard was the mentor to him I wanted him to be to me.

One day, after he threw a hand-scribbled note from Sir Richard on my desk, Prowse lingered, as he did not usually do, and I knew that at long last he wanted to talk, I presumed about our falling out at the Feild, to talk about it and smooth it over, since our paths had crossed yet again and would likely go on crossing.

"So," he said, "I hear that you were in New York when Fielding was there."

I reddened, wondering if he could possibly know what had happened between Fielding and me there.

"She was there when I was there would be a better way of putting it," I said. "She didn't last long. It's a big city. Not like St. John's or Halifax."

"But you came back?" Prowse said, disingenuously interrogative, mock-earnest.

"After five years," I said. "Who told you Fielding was there, anyway?"

"She did," Prowse said.

Dear Prowse, September 12, 1918. Years after the caning. Years after Prowse had carried me about in triumph for mocking Fielding's father on the pitch at Bishop Feild. When had she stopped loving him? Had she stopped? Had she ever loved him? Or me? She said she felt more for me than she ever had for him. It seemed to me now that that could mean almost anything. Even after the letter Prowse and I had co-written and the other boys had signed, she might be writing to him. Or more. Those stories she had told me about being propositioned by married men, men with children. Had she intended me to assume that it was Prowse she meant? It might have been her way of saying that she was available to me, a married man with children. Or her way of making me think she was.

Forget Fielding, I told myself. You never so much as held hands with her. Your courtship lasted about three minutes, from her declaration of affection, if that is what it was, to your blundering proposal. I felt as foolish as I had that night when I saw in her eyes what I should have seen all along. Still, here was Prowse. The thought of him having her almost made me sick.

"You're still on speaking terms? You still see each other?" I deadpanned. "In spite of everything, I mean."

"Oh, I bump into her on the street from time to time," said Prowse. "It's a small city. Not like New York."

"She never mentions you," I said. He smiled.

"You worked at the *Call*," Prowse said. It was not a question. I nodded. "I can't imagine Fielding working there — "

"She didn't," I said.

"Oh, I know," Prowse said. "Fielding a socialist, can you imagine?"

"She *was* one," I said, aware too late of how ridiculous it sounded, as if we were fighting over Fielding, whom we both claimed to despise.

"Not really," Prowse said. "She may have pretended to be one. Just for a lark. More grist for the mill, you know. One more thing to write about. Fielding would never have taken seriously anything as ridiculous as socialism."

The gauntlet had been thrown down. A challenge of one-upmanship, which I declined. I thought of Grimes, the Sunday afternoons when the three of us had gone canvassing from door to door. Fielding and I, the two of us not yet twenty, trying to start up unions on the waterfront. Fielding's decision to follow me to New York. Fielding inexplicably crying the day I told her I was leaving Newfoundland. Inexplicable then. I savoured the memory now. A woman crying at the thought of losing me. I had plenty of ammunition if I cared to use it. Still, there was nothing to be gained from provoking Prowse. I would let him imagine whatever he liked. It even occurred to me he might be trying to get me to admit to something he could someday use to buy my silence.

"No," I said. "You're probably right. Her heart was never in it. Her heart was never in anything as far as I can tell."

If Prowse was wounded, it didn't show. What did he want? He stood up and looked around the makeshift, grubby "news-room," which I manned alone day after day.

"I don't know how you stand it here, Smallwood," he said. "I know I couldn't."

I said nothing. It was a feeble parting shot, and I could tell by his expression that he knew it.

Lady Squires was elected in Lewisporte by a landslide, by a mar-gin of victory even greater than Sir Richard's had been in the last election, not that I brought this fact to his attention. "Having the prime minister's wife as your member in the House is as good as having the prime minister himself," Sir Richard said when I went to see him one night. "She will not embarrass me," he added reas-suringly, as if I had all along been saying that she would. "She has completed courses in elocution and public speaking at the Emer-son College of Oratory in Boston." Whereas I, I felt like saying, had merely completed a course in public speaking as a means of self-preservation in the slums of Harlem, where it was my daily task to convince blacks whose ancestors had been brought to America in slave ships that the election of thirty-seven white presidents in a row was no cause for them to do something cyni-cal like refuse to vote. It also occurred to me that the subject of the only speech I had ever heard Lady Squires give was "Why women should not be allowed to vote."

I was trying, unsuccessfully it seems, not to scowl. Though I need not have bothered, for Sir Richard seemed more puzzled than displeased by my dismay, as if, his happiness being uppermost in everybody's mind, he could not understand my disappointment.

I saw Fielding struggling towards her boarding-house one day in mid-winter, trying to make her cane look like an affectation, trying not to look as though she needed it to walk. I followed behind her, making sure she didn't see me. She stopped every fifty feet or so, exhausted, chest heaving, mouth open, and leaned against something, a wall, a gatepost, as if the better to examine something that had caught her eye, or as if she were pausing at the halfway point of a long walk and would soon be on her way again. To the people passing briskly by she nodded, as if to include herself in this fellowship of walkers.

She resumed her journey and eventually reached her boarding-house and, with me mere feet behind her, began to make her way up the icy steps, clutching the rail. When she got to the top, I called her name. She turned around and looked down at me.

"Oh, to be in England, now that Smallwood's here," she said. We had not met since we had written about our school days in the papers.

"It was just politics, Fielding," I said, trying to sound as if I had got the best of the exchange and so was magnanimously offering the olive branch. "You can't expect people not to fight back if you write about them like you do. Some of my best friends are people I've accused of doing worse."

"There must be something about you that inspires forgiveness, Smallwood," she said, "or else you'd have been murdered long ago. Come up and have a drink with me. I find myself in a mood that makes even your company seem preferable to none at all."

We went up to her room.

"Do you know," she said, "my intake of rum exactly matches my output of words. A column a day, a bottle a day. When I wrote two columns a week, I drank two bottles a week. One sip, one sentence; one drink, one paragraph; one bottle, one column. I don't know if the drinking helps me write, or the writing makes me drink. Both perhaps. At any rate, I have been told by a doctor that I have to cut back to one bottle a week, one column a week, if I want to witness Sir Richard's second resurrection from the dead, which by my reckoning should take place eight years from now. I'd just as soon miss it, to tell you the truth, if the alternative was anything but nothing."

"I practically write the whole *Dog* myself," I said. "I hardly ever take a drink."

"An extraordinary accomplishment, to be sure," she said. "I can't even read it while I'm sober. It's not how you foresaw yourself at thirty, is it, Smallwood? Defending Richard Squires in a paper called the *Dog*?"

"Prowse works for Sir Richard," I said. "He's his executive assistant. But of course you knew that?" When she didn't answer, I got up to leave.

"Sit down, sit down," Fielding said, putting her hands on my shoulders and all but forcing me into the chair. She poured herself a drink and stood with her back against the wall.

"My father died last week," she said. "They didn't tell me. Some kind of mix-up. My uncle thought my aunt was going to, and she thought he was going to, or something. I don't know. The desk editor at the *Telegram* assumed I knew, or else he would have called me when they phoned it in, he said. I read about it in the paper. Ever since I left the San, I've been scanning the obituaries, keeping tabs on the old crowd. Ghoulish of me, I know. And there, Tuesday last week, was my name. Fielding. I bet a lot of the San crowd thought it was me. It didn't dawn on me until I was halfway through the obituary who it was I was reading about."

"I'm sorry," I said, and I was, though I could not help sounding like I begrudged her even my condolences, as if for her to lapse from irony even to confess her father's death was not playing by the tacitly agreed-upon rules that governed our relationship.

"Was your father religious?" I said.

"He went to church," Fielding said. "Why do you ask?"

"Do you believe in God?" I said.

"I believe in God the way I believe that this is my last drink," she said. "I believe it, even though I know it's not."

"Well," I said, "I have to go."

"You won't have a drink with me," said Fielding.

"I can't," I said, certain I could not hold out much longer against the urge to feel sorry for her and lose the sense of grievance against her that I realized had become curiously sustaining. "I have to go," I said. "I have — I have to meet someone." I looked around the room, at the bed. I felt as though we had last spoken that night in New York at the Hotel Newfoundland.

"Prowse came to see me," I said. "To ask about New York." I was not sure if I was trying to make her feel better or worse.

Fielding said nothing, only raised her eyebrows in a token of mock surprise. She stared at her glass.

"It might not be a bad idea," I said. "Cutting back on the booze."

She shrugged. Tears welled up in her eyes.

"Well," I said again, "I have to go."

"You don't have to," she said. "You can stay. For as long as you like."

"No," I said, "I've got to — I know you're — I'm sorry about your father."

I hurried out and closed the door behind me. When I got outside, I had to grab the rail to keep my hands from shaking.

FIELDING'S JOURNAL, JANUARY 17, 1932

Dear Father:

You were a doctor, a "chest man," scornful of your profession because you loved your patients and pitied them for having no one better to turn to for help than, as you put it, "the likes of me." If you muttered aloud in your consulting room the way you did at home about some man who, for all you knew, your remedies were inadvertently murdering by slow degrees, your patients must have been a fretful lot.

You inherited from your father a reprint of a pamphlet that was written in the sixteenth century by a John Fielding, who was probably not an ancestor of ours, though you liked to believe or pretend that he was. The pamphlet described in great detail a medical procedure that you called mental ventilation, that is, the drilling of holes in the skulls of the sick to let the "evil spirits" out. You loved to read the pamphlet aloud. "This yeere have we the skull drille employed with great success. Three men died who woulde anywaye have perished, but three still live and showe signes of recoverye that we hope will soone make possible a seconde application of the drille."

You were my mother's husband when you were home and aware of her existence, which wasn't often, not nearly often enough. You worked long hours. We lived in a place, you said, where nothing thrived except disease. My mother was from Boston and went back there when I was five. And moved from there to New York when I was ten.

For a long time I believed, and was probably right in believing, that you wished my mother had taken me with her when she left. There was no question of her doing so, of course. Even a widow with a child would not have made a good marriage prospect, but a woman who, however justifiably, had left her husband and had in her care a constant reminder to herself and others of that fact would not have fared well in Boston. My mother had no resources and no means of getting them but marriage. She could not have had any confidence when she thought of setting out from Newfoundland that she would soon or ever be able to support a child.

I have only the faintest, possibly counterfeit, recollections of my mother. I don't remember her saying goodbye to you. There was apparently a divorce worded with sufficient vagueness as to absolve both of you with faint blame. My mother's father came from Boston to escort her home. He did not come into the house, or perhaps he did and I was kept from seeing him, I'm not sure. I think I remember my mother walking down the driveway with her father, presumably to a waiting cab. I remember her crying, squatting down to embrace me.

What I was told was happening and by whom, I don't remember, but I'm sure I wasn't told she was leaving us for good. Nor do I remember when I realized she wasn't coming back.

You did not purge the house of her after she went back to Boston. As if to prove you were neither broken-hearted nor humiliated, you left her picture on the mantelpiece. My mother as she was not long after you first met. Perhaps that was the point, to distinguish the girl you fell in love with from the woman you divorced. You did not so much show me as leave where I might find them the albums in which there were pictures of you and her together, Dr. and Mrs. Fielding and with them, sometimes, Baby Sheilagh.

The kind of silence that follows the slamming of a door persisted in that house for years. It was there even while the radio was playing and when relatives came to visit, and when we talked. We were never quiet in each other's company if we could help it; the silence made her absence so palpable. It was as though life as it would have been if she had stayed was taking place in some room in the house that, no matter how long we searched for it, we could never find.

You cursed your body's need for sleep and, in token protest of it, slept while sitting in a chair with all your clothes on. I was always in bed before you got home, always in bed but never asleep. Even the housekeeper, on your instructions, never waited

up, but left something in the stove for you to eat, which was
often still there in the morning.

After I heard you coming up the steps and opening the front
door, I waited for you to settle down, then tiptoed out to see if
you were still awake, which you sometimes were, tipped back in
your recliner, staring at the ceiling.

You rarely noticed me until I was standing right beside you,
though the sight of me never startled you. As though you were
as immobilized as one of your patients, you turned just your
head and smiled and reached out your hand for mine, squeezing
it lightly. "Hello, there," you said. You looked at me, and as if
my very age was an expression of unwarranted optimism, you
shook your head in fond disbelief that anyone could be so naive
as to be five years old. You didn't see girlhood so much as a
stage in life as a character trait. I was girlish, you were mannish;
these things would always be the case.

And so you told me everything, things five-year-olds should
not hear, I suppose. You told me of patients who had died or
were going to, and of others who were getting better, always
speaking of the latter with a tinge of irony, as if to say that however much better they got, the world they were returning to was
still the same.

Sometimes, you fell asleep while talking to me, or I came
out and found you asleep, your arms folded across your chest. If
you were wearing your hat, I took it off and put it on the floor
beside your chair, as you did when you remembered to. I didn't
have to be especially careful not to wake you, for, once asleep,
you slept soundly, deeply, as if your body was making the most
of the few hours it had you in its care.

It was a strange sight to see you sleeping. It was hard to
believe you'd trust something so unreliable and treacherous as
your body to sustain you without your supervision. I stood
beside you, marvelling that there existed in you something more
basic, more fundamental than your will, something that made

your chest move up and down, drew air into your body and forced it out again. It always made me think there must be more to your waking self than met the eye, not that you seemed to me lacking or deficient in anything exactly. Perhaps it was your sleeping in your clothes, sometimes even in your hat and coat, that did it. It seemed to me that your impressive hat and coat and vest and pants and shoes were sleeping, too.

In the way you would say of someone, "He's not himself today," I thought of you as being permanently not yourself. Lack of sleep, overwork, your wife's absence, made you what you seemed to others to be, but I believed there was another latent Dr. Fielding and was always waiting for him to show himself.

You were a good "chest man," but not an especially good one, not, as you said of other doctors in other fields, "top-notch." I was ten before I realized this, before I realized that others did not see you as I did, were not as awed by you as I was, that there were men in the world in whose company you felt inferior, deficient. I noticed you never referred to other "chest men" as "top-notch," not even those who visited St. John's from places like New York and London. There were, and still are, a good many "chest men" in St. John's. This was the specialty where you could not only do the most good but make the most money, and you would leave it to me, you said, to decide which of these two considerations mattered most to your colleagues.

I think that over the years, you made some sort of peace with your limitations. Not that admitting to yourself that you would never be top-notch made you any less inclined to push yourself or more inclined to sleep. But you were motivated now by guilt, not by ambition. You were still trying to compensate for being unexceptional, but you were doing so for your patients now.

When I was twelve, you asked me if I wanted to go to a private school in Scotland like so many other girls my age were doing. I told you I would go if that was what you wanted. You took me in your arms and hugged me. "We'll send you to

Bishop Spencer instead," you said. "How would that be?" I
nodded and you kissed me on the cheek. It was the only time in
my life that you ever hugged or kissed me. I didn't understand
then that the point of the question was not to try to get rid of
me, but to see if I wanted to be rid of you.

We drifted apart after they released me from the San. Not
that we saw each other any less frequently. I still went to the old
house on Circular Road, but I could see in your eyes that you
wanted me to stay away. I knew why, though we never talked
about it. We would sit there on Sunday afternoons and often, in
spite of yourself, you let me make you laugh.

You were so ashamed of yourself, you couldn't bear to see
me, couldn't forgive yourself. You thought I didn't understand,
or that I was pretending not to understand, how profoundly you
betrayed me by not coming to the San to say goodbye. But it
was because you stayed away that I knew how much you loved
me. I didn't feel abandoned or betrayed.

And you thought I didn't know that you had done
something else for which you thought you didn't deserve to be
forgiven. But I knew.

In the end, you found what you must have thought was the
perfect way of making restitution.

You told the other Fieldings not to send for me.

You knew that they would do as you said, that they thought
you didn't want me there because, like them, you were ashamed
of me, because you had come to your senses at last and
disowned me.

You fancied that by this, it was yourself you were denying.
You had abandoned me and so you deserved to be abandoned.
An eye for an eye. How could you not have known that this, of
all the ways you might have hurt me, was the worst?

Still, you cannot stop me from remembering.

On those rare occasions when you were able to make time
for me, you used to give me make-believe check-ups. You put

your stethoscope on the soles of my feet and listened with an air of grave concentration. You put it on my forehead and claimed that you could hear what I was thinking. You tapped me on the head with your little rubber hammer and looked at me quizzically, appraisingly, as if awaiting some result. To test my eyes, you put a tongue depressor on your own tongue, said, "Ahhhh," and asked me to tell you what I saw.

You were nominally, perfunctorily, a Methodist. We went to church regularly because, you said, "Patients like to think their doctors are in God's good books." But whether you believed in God or some promised land, some happy sight, some "Bonavista" that was waiting for you on the other side, I don't know. Asked to declare yourself on the subject, you once said, "The grave's a fine and private spot / where none I think do ought but rot."

I love you now no less than when I was just a girl. To quote the inscription on the headstone of your favourite writer, "He has gone where savage indignation can lacerate his heart no more."

Fielding's Condensed
History of Newfoundland

Chapter Nineteen:

THE COLONIAL OFFICE SEES ITS ERROR

There is dancing in the streets of St. John's on April 26, 1841, when the legislature is dissolved and the constitution is suspended.

It is recommended that in their place should be put an amalgamated assembly consisting of fifteen elected and nine appointed Protestant members.

When it is observed that all the Protestant Conservatives need to dominate the assembly is to win four of the fifteen elected seats, the Colonial Office sees its error and increases the number of appointed members to ten.

The passage of bills is found to be much easier under this system. Unfortunately, it lasts but seven years, and would not have lasted even that long had not the city of St. John's been destroyed by fire on June 9, 1846, twenty-seven years after the Reevesian Reverend Lewis Amadeus Anspach published his maddening *History of the Island of Newfoundland*.

The Nones of 1932

NEWFOUNDLAND WAS one hundred million dollars in debt, much of it owing to the cost of fighting on the side of England in the First World War. The interest charges alone equalled half our annual revenue. Over 50 per cent of the country's population was unemployed.

I devoted an entire issue of the *Dog* to explaining why the worldwide depression, and not Sir Richard, was to blame. I even went about the city, stump-speaking as I had done in New York, sermonizing those who could not read, trying to explain to them what the word *depression* meant and how the success of our economy was tied to the economies of other, larger countries where things were almost as bad now as they had been five years ago in Newfoundland.

I became known throughout St. John's as Crackie, a pun on the *Dog*, a crackie being a small, incessantly barking dog whose inconsequential tenacity strikes people as hilarious.

I stood one day in early April in Bannerman Park on a kitchen chair while hundreds of unemployed men gathered round me and demanded to know why Sir Richard was letting this "depression" go on. A hundred feet away, inside the Colonial Building, Sir Richard was having this very question disingenuously put to him by the Opposition, who knew the depression had nothing to do with Newfoundland.

I looked out across a sea of sod-tweed caps and suddenly realized that if I delivered my defence of Sir Richard in Swahili, it would have the same effect. I indignantly denied, without having any idea whether it was true or not, an allegation that had been made by Sir Richard's own finance minister, Peter Cashin, that Sir Richard had falsified cabinet minutes to conceal misuse of public funds. I told those men assembled there in the pouring rain that there was nothing hypocritical about him paying himself, over and above his salary as prime minister, a yearly stipend of five thousand dollars as Newfoundland's war reparations commissioner while at the same time reducing benefits to war veterans.

They were on the dole, being paid by the government six cents a day, which worked out to twenty-one dollars and ninety cents a year. They stood there in the slantwise driven rain, coughing, shivering, faces fiercely braced against the wind, and they listened to me, and it seems incomprehensible to me now that they did not take me and hang me from the nearest tree. All that saved me, as it had so many times in New York, was my appearance, for I was dressed no better than they were and, if anything, had less meat on my bones.

When I heard that the Tories were organizing an anti-government march on the Colonial Building, I searched the public accounts and set out in detail in a special edition of the *Dog* the large sums of public money that had gone to opposition leader Alderdice's firm over the last twenty-five years.

I joined the march minutes before it reached the Colonial Building. The merchants had declared the day of the march a holiday and ordered their employees to attend, an order they had complied with, as I could tell from how well, relatively speaking, some of the crowd were dressed.

But most of the men there were unemployed and Tory hench-
men were going about among them with boxes, handing out free
bottles of rum. By the time the march reached the Colonial Building, most of the mob of ten thousand were well on their way to
being drunk.

I worked my way through the crowd, handing out free copies
of the *Dog*, some of which were thrown back at me. But as most of
the men there could not read, they thought I was a Tory handing
out anti-Squires propaganda sheets and not only let me through but
cleared the way for me.

While Alderdice was speaking, denouncing what he called Sir
Richard's scandal-racked administration, I managed to get within
earshot of him and so often and so loudly demanded I be allowed to
address the crowd that he gave in and invited me up on-stage, literally gave me a hand up while around me men were telling me what
my fate would have been were Mr. Alderdice not such a gentleman.

I thought he was being gracious, but I was not long into my
speech before I realized that I had been had, that Alderdice had
foreseen that nothing would incite the crowd against Sir Richard
like someone getting up to speak in his defence. I told the ten
thousand I was facing to beware of Greeks bearing gifts, beware
of Water Street merchants giving advice in politics.

"Shut him up," the crowd roared. "Throw him off the steps."
But Alderdice allowed me to continue. I walked back and forth on
the steps as though I were on a stage, wagging the finger of my
upraised hand each time I enumerated one of Sir Richard's suc-
cesses as prime minister.

I had often envisaged a scene like this when I was under the
tutelage of Grimes, "the people" storming the Colonial Building
like the Bolsheviks storming the Winter Palace. I had not imagined
a revolution led by businessmen, or that I would be fighting to
preserve the status quo.

I wandered too near to the side of the steps and a pair of massive hands reached out and grabbed me by the ankles. I was still

singing Sir Richard's praises as I toppled over onto a canopy of upraised hands. Thus held aloft, on my back and still declaiming, I was passed from row to row all the way to Military Road, where I was dumped onto the pavement and where a man told me he would "stop my gob for good" if I said another word.

I hung back at the edge of the crowd, which soon turned into a mob. They no longer listened to Alderdice. They threw rocks and empty rum bottles at the front of the Colonial Building. A cheer went up each time a pane of one-hundred-year-old glass was broken.

In a last-ditch attempt to restore order, the Guards Band came out on the steps and struck up a shaky rendition of "God Save the King." Every man in the crowd stood rigidly to attention and took off their caps, some with rocks still clenched in their fists, and stayed that way until the anthem ended, at which point they put on their caps and went back to rioting. The Guards Band struck up "God Save the King" a second time, but they were pelted with rocks and forced to disperse.

Alderdice and his caucus looked about at what they must have known they would be blamed for starting. They shouted and ran about, trying to restore order, but when it became clear that the distinction between government and opposition supporters was becoming lost on the crowd, they fled in all directions.

Government members who had been inside the building also began to flee, and though they were pelted with rocks and denounced as thieves and worse, no one tried to prevent their escape. It was Sir Richard the mob wanted, him and no one else.

They moved forward, hurling rocks and bricks through already broken windows, forced their way through a line of constabulary members on horseback that had just begun to form and proceeded to loot the lobby, dragging furniture out of it, rolling armchairs, sofas, flower-pots and vases down the steps. They piled them in a heap, threw some rugs and paintings on top and set fire to it all.

The grand piano, on which, on formal occasions, "God Save the King," the "Ode to Newfoundland" and anthems of other nations were played, was sent, keys clattering, down the steps and wound up on its side with a crescendo twang. A cheer went up and soon the piano was ablaze.

I made my way, as inconspicuously as possible, along the iron fence, accepting an occasional kick in the backside rather than fight back and draw even more attention to myself.

"Where are you headed?" a voice off to my left said. Fielding was leaning on the Bannerman Park side of the fence, watching the riot through the iron bars, notebook in hand, frantically scribbling. It was like some tableau of her life: Fielding the critic, aloofly watching a riot from the safe side of the fence.

"If you're planning to make another speech, I'd choose a different theme if I were you," she said.

She was wearing a heavy woollen overcoat and a stevedore-style stocking cap, her hair hanging down from beneath it. I noticed that her hair was greying and that it had picked up a yellowish tinge from the smoke of cigarettes. But it was still the thick and full hair of a thirty-five-year-old woman. A strand of it, when the wind blew, clung between her lips. She pulled it away with exactly the same flourish of annoyance as when she was a girl. Her cheeks were pink with the cold, her nostrils raw from rubbing and over her eyes there was a glaze of wind-bidden tears, which she kept blinking back. In spite of her overcoat, her lips were quivering. It made me want to touch them with my fingers. For an instant I saw her as I had seen Newfoundland when I had returned to it the first time. It was as if we had never met and never would, Fielding as she would have been if I did not exist, a person apart from me who would remain when I was gone. The world resumed; the mob roared all around me and a gust of wind that seconds ago had come in from across the water blew hard against my face.

"I didn't think you actually covered anything," I said, gulping down a lump in my throat. "I thought you only wrote about what you read in other papers."

She wryly smiled. "I just followed the crowd," she said. "They went right below my window."

"The Squireses are still inside, both of them, Sir Richard and Lady Helena," I said. "I'm trying to get in there, but I'll never make it by myself, I'm such a runt. I don't suppose you'd help clear the way for me."

"What good will you be able to do once you get inside?" she said.

"I don't know," I said. "But for all I know, they may be in there by themselves."

Fielding looked at me, then at the Colonial Building, pursed her lips, sighed. "I'm sure there's a column in it," she said. She put her notebook and her pencil in the pocket of her overcoat, passed her cane through the fence to me, undid her overcoat, hiked her dress up above her knees, then, with surprising quickness, climbed onto the fence, hoisting herself up onto each of the rungs with her good leg, then lifting the other. I saw the bad leg, or the shape of it, at least — she was wearing longjohns — for the first time. It was not malformed, it seemed, just shrunken, withered, each part in proportion to the others, as much of it as I could see, at least. It might have looked perfectly normal on a woman half her size.

With one leg on either side, standing on top of the fence, she paused to look out over the crowd, shook her head. Then she climbed down, good leg, bad leg, good leg, bad leg, as before. She jumped the last few feet to the ground, took her cane from me and waded into the crowd. She took off her hat and stuffed it in her pocket, shook out her hair, I presumed so the men, seeing that she was a woman, might let her through.

For a while it worked. The more tractable part of the mob, the rear one-third of it, stood aside when she prodded lightly at them with her cane. I followed her, my hand clinging to the belt of her overcoat, hiding behind her lest I be recognized. She tried to make her way to the front steps, but everyone else was trying to do the same, and we were gradually pushed to one side as the mob surged forward.

"We'll never get in through the front," Fielding shouted. "We'll have to try the side." We doubled back and went along the fence, where the going was easier because the crowd was thinner. We made our way past the west corner. Fielding put her cap back on, tucked her hair up under it, buttoned up her coat. She looked like a ringleader-sized man.

There was a door without a handle on the side of the building. We pounded on it; Fielding tried to break it down. "We already tried it," said a man who mistook us for fellow rioters. "Someone's gone off to get an axe."

"I can go up the drainage pipe," I said. "It's not that high."

"I might as well go with you," Fielding said. As the two of us, Fielding second, began to scale the pipe, a clump of men still believing us to be of their faction gathered to cheer us on and a couple of them even gave Fielding's rump a hoist to get her started. I had little trouble shinnying up the pipe, but I could hear it creaking with Fielding's weight and that of the men who had started up after her.

"Smallwood," she gasped. I looked down. She was hugging the pipe, leaning her forehead against it, eyes closed, face beet red.

"Go back," I said. She shook her head.

"Resting," she said breathlessly, a lit cigarette at the corner of her mouth. I kept going. Just as I was climbing in through a broken window of the main chamber, I was set upon by a member of the constabulary, who tried to push me back out.

"I've come to help Sir Richard," I shouted, clinging to the window sill with both hands, which the constable eyed, billy club raised to strike. "I'm Joe Smallwood," I said.

"Smallwood?" I heard a voice I recognized as Sir Richard's say from inside.

"Yes," I shouted just in time to freeze the constable in mid-swing.

"Let him in, Byrne, let him in," I heard another man say. The constable pulled me inside.

"The woman behind me is with me, too," I said, "but the men below her are part of the mob." The constable looked down.

"They're all men," he said. I checked to make sure that Fielding was still there.

"That first one is Miss Fielding of the *Telegram*," I said.

A man I recognized as Chief Inspector Hutchings of the 'Stab joined the constable and me as we helped Fielding in through the window, after which she collapsed on the floor, clutching her chest, breath surging from her as if she had been immersed in ice-cold water. I knelt beside her.

"Are you all right?" I said. She nodded.

"Catch ... breath ... be all right," she wheezed.

"We've got to pry that drainage pipe loose or they'll all come in this way," Hutchings said.

As the leading edge of the mob was progressing up the pipe, we looked about for something we could use as a lever and settled on the Speaker's mace, the narrow end of which barely fit between the building and the drainage pipe. Fielding recovered, and with all four of us pulling on it, the mace dislodged the top joint of the pipe, making it impossible for anyone to climb beyond the first storey. The man farthest up the pipe shook his fist at us. "We're coming back with ladders," he said.

All this time, Sir Richard and Lady Squires must have been standing as I saw them now, arm in arm on the legislature floor. Lady Squires wore a maroon cape pinned at the throat with a brooch but was otherwise not dressed for the outdoors; neither was Sir Richard, who wore a black longcoat and a vest.

"Smallwood, Fielding," Sir Richard said, "what are you two doing here?" It sounded as if by "here" he meant "together."

"God help you," Fielding said, "but we're the reinforcements."

The men we had prevented from scaling the drainage pipe hurled a volley of rocks through the broken windows.

"We've got to take cover," Hutchings said.

"The Speaker's room," Lady Squires said, and we followed her to a large door behind the Speaker's chair. The Speaker's room adjoined the main chamber, and it was not much bigger than a kitchen, but the door, which we bolted and barred with the Speaker's desk, was made of heavy mahogany. There was a lamp, but Hutchings advised we not use it, for fear the mob would see the light beneath the door. He said there were constabulary members outside the main chamber and they had so far been successful in holding back the mob.

It was dark in the Speaker's room and we could only vaguely make each other out. We all fell silent for a while. I looked at Fielding. She was here to help the Squireses if she could, had risked injuring herself to help them, showed no sign now of wanting to let them fend for themselves despite our situation. I could not reconcile this woman with the girl who had been so eaten up with bitterness that she had written that letter to the *Morning Post* to get me into trouble. It did not seem to me that even when drunk, she would stoop so low. She seemed now more like the sort of woman who would sacrifice herself for a lover, even one as ungrateful as Prowse had proved to be. The hunch I had had at Sir Richard's house the night we hatched our own letter-writing scheme did not seem so far-fetched as it had then. She might have confessed for Prowse. I could not stand the thought that she had ever loved anyone but me that much, but perhaps she had. I had known myself what it was like to be favoured by Prowse, remembered how important he had made inclusion in his circle seem to be.

Shouts of "Hurray" from outside, as if some new hurdle that lay between Sir Richard and the mob had just been cleared, brought me out of my revery.

"What in God's name do they want?" Sir Richard said.

"You," Fielding said.

"Me?" Sir Richard said, as if this was the first he had heard that the riot had anything to do with him, as if he thought he had just been caught up in some pointless conflagration like everybody else, as if it was inconceivable to him that others might value his well-being less highly than he did.

"Well, this is quite a fix we're in," Lady Squires said.

Sir Richard turned to me. "Do you actually think they'll do me harm, Smallwood?" he said.

"As far as I can tell," Fielding said, "the only remaining subject of debate is the mode of execution. Several have been proposed and dismissed on the grounds of being too good for you."

"Miss Fielding," Lady Squires said, "I can barely hear you above the sound of your knees knocking together. Do you always talk this much or only when you're terrified?"

"My God, Smallwood," Sir Richard said, "they really do mean to murder me?"

"Nonsense," Lady Squires said, taking off her cape and fanning herself with her hand, "there'll be no one murdered here today." She draped the cape across a chair. "They're nothing but a crowd of ruffians and cowards. They wouldn't dare do anything. We should march straight out the front door, that's what we should do, and face them down."

"They're drunk, Lady Squires," Hutchings said. "They're not in their right minds; they're all worked up. There's no telling what they'll do. I don't think we should leave this room."

"This is a fine state of affairs, I must say," said Lady Squires. "The prime minister of a country forced to hide out from his own people in some cubby-hole. My God, what is the Empire coming to?" She looked at Sir Richard, but it was obvious that neither the outrage to the office of prime minister nor the unprecedented depths to which the Empire had sunk were uppermost in his mind.

"I can't believe it," Lady Squires said. "It's not like Newfoundlanders to carry on like this. It can't just be booze that has them so worked up. The Tories started this, you mark my words."

"I hope no one will stoop so low," Fielding said, "as to invoke that old cliché about how poverty, chronic unemployment, malnutrition and disease bring out the worst in people. As to what inscrutable impulse causes people to take out their frustrations on the very politicians they voted into office — " She shrugged.

"If booze was their excuse," said Lady Squires, "you, Miss Fielding, would be out there with them. You smell like a one-woman riot. I can just imagine what they'll say about us at Whitehall, Richard, when they hear of this. Squires, the man who was prime minister when the Newfoundlanders ran amok, that's how they'll remember you. There'll be no postings abroad for us after this, let me assure you."

Suddenly there was a loud pounding on the door.

"Merciful God," Sir Richard said, as Byrne and Hutchings drew their billy clubs and I picked up a poker from the fireplace.

"Are you there, Sir Richard?" said a voice from outside. "Are you there? We've come to escort you out."

"Is that you, Emerson?" said Lady Squires. Emerson was a member of the opposition.

"Oh, my God," said Emerson, "are you in there, too, Lady Squires?"

"Yes, I'm in here, too. I'm an elected member of the House of Assembly and the wife of your prime minister, where else would I be? This riot is all your fault — "

"We didn't think they would take it this far," Emerson said, his voice quavering. "It's got out of hand; we can't control it. We're afraid they may set fire to the building."

"You lot should have thought of that when you got up this parade," Lady Squires said.

"Emerson," Hutchings said, "how many of you are there?"

"Thank God, it's Hutchings," Emerson said. "There are four of us, sir."

"Well then, you take Lady Squires out and the four of us will stay here with Sir Richard until you get back."

"I'm not going anywhere without my husband," Lady Squires said. I whispered to Sir Richard that he should tell her he would be safe and urge her to leave. He nodded distractedly, but said nothing.

"If Richard and I go out together, they'll leave him alone for fear of harming me," Lady Squires said. "I'm everyone's best chance of getting out of here unharmed."

"I don't think we can count on them to act like gentlemen at this point," Emerson said.

"Don't speak to me about gentlemen. You're a disgrace, an absolute disgrace is what you are. You and your crowd put them up to this. You're no better than Guy Fawkes. You should all be shot as traitors — "

"Lady Squires, please — "

"I believe," Fielding said, "that Mr. Emerson's main reason for wanting to save your life is to avoid being blamed for your death, which is to say that he will guard you as though you were his reputation, so you need have no fear."

She was nearest the door and, before Lady Squires could protest, unbolted it, grabbed her around the waist, threw her out into Emerson's arms, then bolted the door again.

"Let go of me," we heard her say. "Let go of me, I'll not be carried from the House by a handful of Tory backbenchers, let me go...."

By the sound of it, Emerson and the others had to lift her from the main chamber by the arms and legs. "If they hurt one hair on his head, you Tories will pay for it," she shouted between grunts of exertion. "The country will know, the world will know who's to blame for this...."

"Helena, I'll be all right," Sir Richard managed to say, his voice breaking as if it was himself he was trying to convince. I suppose the thought that it might have been more appropriate to assure her that *she* would be all right did not occur to him.

"Richard, be careful," she said, though we could barely hear her now. "Don't make a move without Inspector Hutchings. Inspector Hutchings — " Before she could admonish Hutchings, the chamber doors came to with a bang.

"Miss Fielding goes next," Hutchings said. "As soon as they get back."

Fielding lit up a cigarette. "Don't worry about me," she said. "They won't want to murder me unless someone tells them who I am."

We stood about in silence for a while. Whenever the furniture-fuelled bonfires outside flared up, we could see a faint flickering of light beneath the door and were better able to see one another. Sir Richard was wide-eyed with alarm and kept looking about appealingly, almost resentfully, at the rest of us, as if it was not fair, or was even somehow our fault, that in this roomful of people, he was the only one the mob was after, as if he had been randomly singled out for persecution.

Another volley of rocks and bricks clattered against the Speaker's door and a cheer went up that I feared might signal some new development. I wondered aloud when it would occur to the mob outside to scale the building with the ladders of a fire truck.

"Thank God they're so drunk," Hutchings said.

"Speaking of which," Fielding said and took her silver flask from the inner pocket of her overcoat, drank from it, then passed it to Inspector Hutchings, who, after drinking from it, passed it to Sir Richard, who regarded it, as he was regarding everything now, as though it were a confirmation of his doom.

"Take a drink, Sir Richard, sir," Inspector Hutchings said, and Sir Richard looked around as if he was trying to read in our faces what we thought his chances were. Sir Richard took a drink, tipping the flask back too quickly, so that the Scotch went down the wrong way and he gagged and sputtered. Byrne looked away, embarrassed. Sir Richard dropped the flask and some of its contents spilled onto the floor. Fielding recovered the flask and, after offering Byrne and me a drink, which we declined, put it back in her pocket. Hutchings slapped Sir Richard on the back. After a while, Sir Richard nodded to indicate that he had recovered.

"I don't think Emerson will get back inside again," I said. "We'll have to get Sir Richard up in some disguise."

"Sir Richard and the constable here could switch clothes," Hutchings said.

"But Byrne is twice his size," I said.

"Then Byrne can give Sir Richard his helmet and his constabulary jacket," Hutchings said. "They should at least buy us some time."

Byrne had not spoken a word since we had locked ourselves in the Speaker's room. He was about my age and was awed into silence, I dare say, by his close proximity to the prime minister and Lady Squires, as well as Hutchings, at whom he kept darting nervous glances.

"It's worth a try," Hutchings said. Byrne took off his helmet and his jacket, wordlessly handed them to Hutchings, who gave Sir Richard the jacket first after Sir Richard had removed his own. The constabulary jacket was much too big, less obviously so with the sleeves tucked in, but even then the corporal's chevrons, which should have been at Sir Richard's upper arms, were almost at his elbows. The helmet was an even worse fit. It was a London bobby-type helmet and all but enclosed Sir Richard's entire head, the front of it well down past his nose.

"All you need now is a suit of armour and a horse," Fielding said.

"We need to line it with something," Hutchings said. I gave him the sweater I had been wearing inside my jacket. Hutchings stuffed the helmet, then put it on Sir Richard. It was still too big, but at least he was just able to see out from beneath the brim.

It was decided that Byrne, Fielding and I would lead the way. Fielding gave Byrne her overcoat so he would not look conspicuously underdressed for the time of year, and so there would be no doubt even in what was left of the rioters' minds what gender she was, and put on Lady Squires's cape. Hutchings and Sir Richard followed close behind us. Hutchings unbolted the door, peered out and, satisfied there was no one in the chamber, motioned the three of us ahead of him and Sir Richard.

We left the chamber by way of the cloakroom, and the building by the cloakroom door, which opened only from the inside — it was the one Fielding and I had pounded on with our fists — onto a set of steps that faced the park. To our advantage, it was dark and we were a good distance from the nearest bonfire.

The men who were jammed up against the steps begrudgingly made way for us, though we were jostled and sworn at.

"Where's Squires?" they said. "Where is the bastard? Is he still inside?" They recognized Hutchings first; several men shouted his name. They must have assumed that he and the "constable" were escorting three minor functionaries from the building. Then they recognized me as the man who had hours earlier spoken in Sir Richard's defence.

"That's Crackie Smallwood, how did he get in there?" someone said, and someone else speculated that I was short and scrawny enough to have crawled beneath the door. Byrne and Fielding stood on either side of me. I was barely able to resist the urge to look back to see how far behind Sir Richard was.

We had moved beyond the mob and were almost to the fence when Sir Richard, his vision impaired by the helmet, tripped over an iron gate that had been torn down. The gate clattered loudly on the pavement, and as Sir Richard stumbled and fell forward, the helmet toppled from his head.

"There he is, the bastard," the cry went up from the mob. "It's Squires dressed up like the 'Stab."

They came after us with a roar, wielding clubs and rocks and torches.

"Hutchings," Sir Richard said despairingly as he tried to disengage his feet from the bars of the gate. Fielding, Byrne and I went back to help them. Fielding raised her cane above her head and some of the men stopped in their tracks. But most did not, and all five of us were bowled over by the mob.

Sir Richard, now free of the gate, was first to his feet. "Run, Sir Richard, run," Hutchings said. Sir Richard, helmetless, with the now-unrolled sleeves of Byrne's jacket flapping at the ends of his arms, did as he was told. He dodged the leading edge of the mob and lit out across Bannerman Park with the mob behind him, our prime minister surreally pursued by his constituency. Had there been only five or six in pursuit of him, they would have run him down in seconds, but as every man in the mob wanted to lay hands on him, they moved as one for a while, impeding each other's progress, and the bottle-neck at the gate was such that Sir Richard got a good head start.

Field Day, April 7, 1932

We were cheered to see such a marvellous turnout this past Thursday afternoon for what may well become an annual event. The Nones, once a widespread custom in Newfoundland, has regrettably all but died out, though it persists in the more remote outports, where it is held on what I am told is still referred to in such places as "the Nones of April," April 5.

According to Judge Prowse, the earliest mention of the Nones in the literature is in a book published by one Wiliam Douglass in 1755: "The custom is called the Nones [pronounced like bones] after the day in April on which it is held. Likewise the person chosen to be pursued throughout the settlement is called the Nones. In some places the leading citizen is chosen, in others the fleetest of foot male adult, who repeats as the Nones from year to year until he is caught. One old gentleman boasted to me, whether truthfully or not I cannot say, that in his young manhood he had been the Nones six years running. (I believe the pun was not intended.)

"Everyone chases the Nones, shouting at him all manner of abuse, calling him names and even threatening to murder him. On the night of the Nones, once the chase is over, a kind of anarchy prevails throughout the settlement, with citizens wandering the road and setting one another on to acts of mischief, while consuming great quantities of liquor. It is a strange custom and a strange spectacle to witness."

Prowse refutes Harvey's theory that the Nones has its roots in the English fox-hunt. Harvey believed the Nones to be a kind of poor man's fox-hunt, saying that Newfoundlanders unable to afford horses or hounds had to settle for chasing one of their own on foot. But Prowse argues, convincingly, in our opinion, that the Nones is a form of scapegoating, "which was a ritual communal cleansing whereby the sins of the tribe were laid upon a blameless goat who was taken to the wilderness and there released, never to return. (See Leviticus, XVI.)"

The Nones fell out of practice in St. John's in the mid-nineteenth century, by which time the city had become so large that it was simply impossible, in the judgement of the authorities, to conduct a chase involving the entire population. The Nones is still practised in some of our more remote outports, however, where a ballad perhaps no longer known to those of us too long in cities pent is still sung. By way of augmenting Sir Richard's attempts to revive a custom unique to Newfoundland, and like so many such customs on the brink of extinction, we here repeat in full the nineteenth-century ballad "The Nones of 1823":

He hid himself beneath the wharf,
'Twas in April, on the Nones.
On April 6 found they his scarf,
In '33 found they his bones.

Before nor since was there a chase,
Like that which took Pierce Fudge.
He coopied down, he hid his face:
"From here," swore he, "I will not budge."

They searched the bay, they searched the shore,
No sign found they of Pierce.
Back home that night they paced the floors
Their grief 'twas something fierce.

A week went by, a month went by,
The Nones went on and on,
Till even Mary Fudge did sigh,
"'Tis sure, poor Pierce is gone."

In six months all were of one mind
'Twould be pointless more to search:
"His body we will never find,
For his soul we'll pray in church."

On the Nones in eighteen thirty-three,
In the morning at low tide,
A woman from her house did see
Poor Pierce, where he did hide.

Ten years, you say, by kelp concealed
Looked they not beneath that wharf?
His secret now can be revealed:
Pierce Fudge, he was a dwarf.

He hid himself beneath the wharf,
'Twas in April, on the Nones.
On April sixth found they his scarf
In '33 found they his bones.

All this is by way of preamble to yesterday's events, and
to an advertisement that ran a week from yesterday in all the
papers, surely one of the most unusual advertisements to
appear in this country in quite some time: "Sir R. A. Squires,
P.C., K.C.M.G., K.C., prime minister of Newfoundland, invites
the citizens of St. John's to a revival of the old Newfoundland
custom the Nones, which will begin at the Colonial Building
on the afternoon of April 5. Sir Richard Squires himself has
volunteered to be the Nones. All are welcome to take part in
what, it is hoped, will become an annual event. (Participants
will be encouraged to make a small donation to charity.)"

We must admit we were concerned upon first seeing this
ad, given that Sir Richard is fifty-two years old and surely not
capable, we assumed, of running at the speed expected of
the Nones without doing himself harm. To the extent of our
underestimation of Sir Richard, the following attests.

The enthusiasm shown by the crowd of ten thousand
that turned out was remarkable. Who would have blamed
them had they all stayed home, given how careworn they
must be in such troubled times as these.

"We want Squires," they chanted, outside the Colonial
Building. When a spokesman for Sir Richard came out onto
the steps and told them that the fee for participating in the
Nones would be one day's dole, every man present flung six
cents at him and seemed unanimous as to where Sir Richard
should keep the money before dispersing it to charities.

How tickled they were when they realized, some time
later, that Sir Richard had tricked them by sneaking past them
in disguise, slipping through the crowd dressed like a member
of the 'Stab, his hat pulled low, his glasses off, his collar
turned up to hide his face. Not until he intentionally tripped
over an iron gate did they recognize him, and then the cry
went up. "There he is, God bless him, it's Sir Richard." And
the Nones was on!

Merrily they set out in pursuit of him, shouting jestful imprecations, hurling stones. Was ever such a sight seen before in the Commonwealth, the citizens of a country chasing their elected leader through the streets? What a pleasant diversion it must have been for men who have been unemployed for years to chase Sir Richard through the city shouting, "Drown the bastard!" "Down to the harbour with him!" "Lynch him for the thief he is!" as if they meant it.

So completely did Sir Richard get into the spirit of the Nones, so determined was he to lighten the hearts of his pursuers, if only for one day, that a member of the Newfoundland Constabulary was later heard to say he could not keep up with him on horseback. If you could have seen, dear reader, the expression he wore as he went by me, his eyes fair popping with delight, on his face a smile of mischief so pronounced that a person not well acquainted with him might have mistaken it for a rictus of despair. He ran, dear reader, your prime minister ran so fast that soon the heels of his shoes were bouncing off his backside. You could see in him the boy he must have been, running flat out for the joy of it, all inhibition cast aside, his knighthood, King's Council membership and law degrees forgotten. He dashed across Military Road and onto Colonial Street, then further incited his pursuers to delight by ducking into a house uninvited and sending out the other side a decoy dressed like him, who was pursued and caught by the crowd. When they realized he was not Sir Richard, they gave him a mock thrashing, then set after the real McCoy, who by this time had left the house, jumped the fence behind it and begun a successful dash for "freedom" down Bannerman Street.

But back to the "mob," without whose spirited involvement the revival of the Nones would have been a failure. I doubt that any of them had ever run a Nones before, yet how well they played their parts. Just when it seemed his age and the "mob" were catching up with Sir Richard, some new "threat" would be announced that would set him running even faster. Among the methods of execution recommended by some, and by others rejected on the grounds of being too good for him, were hanging, drowning, shooting, stoning, crucifixion and castration. At various times throughout the Nones, Sir Richard was told he would soon be:

Swimming with the fishes
Floating arse-up in the harbour
Hanging by his ankles from a lamppost
Sorry he was ever born
Wishing he was dead
Begging for mercy and forgiveness
Drawing his last breath
Dying like a dog
Aware that all the money in the
world couldn't help him now

Such inventiveness! By nightfall, Sir Richard had still eluded capture but was too fatigued to take part in the post-Nones revelry. Upon being made aware that a large contingent of the "mob" was waiting outside his house, he decided to spend the night elsewhere, lest the sight of him so run ragged dampen their spirits.

The next day, when Sir Richard went to his office, a crowd of a couple of hundred gathered and waited for him to leave. He walked through the crowd, accepting their congratulations on a Nones well run. Just as he was about to get into his chauffeur-driven car, a man reached out his hand, grabbed the pipe from Sir Richard's mouth and put it in his own!

IV

———◆———

INTERREGNUM

The sorrows of Newfoundland have at last awakened
the sympathy of the mother country, and Englishmen
were never so ready as they now are to learn more
about its inhabitants.

—EDMUND GOSSE, FROM HIS PREFATORY NOTE
TO D. W. PROWSE'S *History of Newfoundland*

Fielding's Condensed
History of Newfoundland

Chapter Twenty:

ONE AGITATING CATHOLIC

Representative government returns. A clamour for responsible government begins. Anarchy looms.

Led by the Catholic agitator Philip Francis Little, the Liberal Party campaigns on the issue of responsible government in the 1852 election, promising to petition the British government for it if elected.

The Liberals win and their victory is seen by some as an endorsement by the electorate of responsible government. Their position can be summed up in the following syllogism: The Liberals supported responsible government. The people elected the Liberals. Therefore, the people want responsible government.

The argument put forward by the Conservatives to the Colonial Office that the syllogism fails because it depends on the assumption that there is a connection between what people vote for and what they want falls on deaf ears. Responsible government is granted in 1855 and Little becomes Newfoundland's first prime minister.

Dark days follow. Among the darkest is March 26, 1857, when the infamous Labouchere Despatch is issued, in which the colonial secretary instructs Governor Darling to tell the Newfoundland people that henceforth, if they want their territorial rights arbitrarily amended, they will have to do it themselves.

Thus is Newfoundland all but set adrift by Britain, though certain deluded individuals hail the Despatch as our "colonial *Magna Carta*."

The British

CERTAIN THAT OUR party would lose by a landslide, Sir Richard at last consented to let me run for election, in the riding of Bonavista South, site of my near death and rescue at the hands of Fielding. Only two Liberals won their seats in the election, and I was not one of them. I lost badly, as did Sir Richard and Lady Squires.

Prime Minister Alderdice asked Britain to appoint a commission of inquiry into the state of the Newfoundland society and economy. Or as Fielding said, "he has dropped the pink and green from the flag and is waving in surrender the white part that is left."

Whitehall complied, sending out Sir William Warrender Mackenzie, first Baron Amulree, who conducted hearings throughout the country and was treated to a country-wide admission of misconduct and inadequacy. The baron and his commission were received like parents in whose absence we had torn the house apart and to whom we were now relieved to unburden ourselves of our guilt, having lived with it so long.

I travelled with the commission to cover its hearings for my paper. In Spaniard's Bay, a fellow told the commission that "where

I comes from, your honour, all we does is drink, even the women is at it; half the children don't know who their fathers is. Oh my, oh my, it's something shocking is what it is, I don't know why we acts like that. We're just low-born, I suppose, we don't know no better." As I sat there, I felt myself turn crimson red and for a moment I hoped the commissioners might mistake me for an Englishman.

Every Newfoundlander in the room but me was laughing, but the baron, bankerly Scot that he was, looked gravely diagnostic, as if he had just shrewdly detected the fundamental flaw in the character of Newfoundlanders. He was the most open-minded man I had ever met. Told two contradictory versions of the same event, he believed both, as long as each reflected badly on the character of Newfoundlanders. I have never met a man so eager to have his sensibilities offended. A day was not complete until he had professed himself shocked by something.

A contagion of self-debasement swept the land, as if we had lived in denial of our innate inferiority for centuries and at last were owning up to it. There was more than a hint of boasting in it, a perverse pride in our ability to do anything, even fail, on so grand a scale. Whether our distinguishing national trait was resourcefulness or laziness, ineptitude or competence, honesty or corruptibility, did not seem to matter as long as were famous for it, as long as we were acknowledged as being unmatched in the world for something.

In the end, the baron recommended that the House of Assembly and the elected government of Newfoundland be done away with, and a Commission of Government be set up to rule the country, all the members of the commission to be appointed by Britain, three to be from Britain and three from Newfoundland. In return, Britain would underwrite Newfoundland's debts. This state of affairs would last until the country was again self-supporting and independence would be restored "upon request from the people of Newfoundland."

Newfoundland was entering a limbo, the whole country now was on the dole. We had admitted, neither for the first nor the last time, that nationhood was a luxury we could not afford.

I was choked with shame and anger, anger without object, unless it was the land itself for imposing upon us an obligation for greatness without giving us the means to meet it, a greatness commensurate with our geography.

My father at first welcomed the Commission of Government, and I could understand why. He had himself been just such a commission for decades now, endlessly taking stock of himself and the world, postponing action until all the findings were in, knowing they never would be. It was as if, at last, the rest of the country were in step with him, as if this new national development vindicated the way he had lived his life, as if he had known the country was headed down a dead end and would have to double back and for this reason had remained aloof. The failure of an individual in a country fated for failure was inevitable, excusable.

But soon it disturbed him that everyone was as unresolved and full of doubt as Charlie Smallwood, that everyone, now, not just him, was on the outside looking in, faces pressed against a black glass through which we could barely make out certain shapes and moving forms, the commissioners fussing busily about, weaving our fate.

My father dreamed one night that the Narrows boot was gone. "The Boot is gone, the Boot is gone," he claimed he woke up shouting.

"If you did, you didn't shout loud enough to wake me," my mother said.

In the dream, the Boot had been blown away in a storm and nothing but the iron bar and the chains that hung from it remained, the chains swaying back and forth, faintly rattling in the wind; the whole thing like a swing from which the seat had been removed. Then suddenly he was on the Boot as it floated raft-like out to sea, a boot-shaped vessel bearing its name in luminescent paint: Smallwood. This was not unlike the dream I had before leaving Newfoundland. I shuddered to think that through his blood my father's very dreams had been passed on to me.

When cousin Walter decided soon after to give up making boots, my mother declared it was of that his dream had been portentous. Smallwood's boots were made of leather, and fishermen's leather boots had been doomed to extinction by the invention of the rubber boot, the lighter, more flexible, less expensive, imported rubber boot, as my father gleefully described it. The day of the leather boot, that most pedestrian of all footwear, had come and gone.

"For leather no one gives two hoots / We've seen the last of Smallwood's boots," my father roared for hours one night when I slept over on the Brow.

Field Day, February 1, 1934

The British are coming, the British are coming ...

Field Day, February 21, 1934

You may wonder, commissioners Hope Simpson, Lodge and Trentham, what sort of country this is that you have been appointed to run. (That you have been appointed to run it tells us all we need to know about how highly esteemed you must be among your colleagues.)

You have arrived in February, perhaps not the best month to form a first impression of Newfoundland. By April, it may seem to you that the snow, which covers everything, will never melt. But it will, and the first soul-uplifting knobs of granite should come peeking through about mid-May. As for midsummer blizzards, they are so rare that they are hardly worth talking about.

You may have heard Newfoundland described as a sports-man's paradise and so it is, though the local saying that trout are easier to catch here than tuberculosis should be taken with a grain of salt.

I hope you will soon feel at home here. There are some, the nay-saying churls let us call them, who think you should not have made it a condition of lending us financial assistance that we relinquish to you our right of self-government. But we are in your opinion unable to properly conduct our own affairs, and you more than proved yourselves qualified to make such a judgment at the Battle of Beaumont Hamel, where one out of every four Newfoundlanders you sent against the Germans came back neither dead nor wounded. As if that was not enough, so judiciously did you employ the Newfoundland Reg-iment at the Battle of Arras ten months later that when it was over, fully half of them were still standing. In other words, in the space of ten months, you doubled your efficiency.

If I hear one more Newfoundlander whining about the "suspension of democracy," about how, now that we have given it up, we will never get our independence back — well, let me make a suggestion. All those Newfoundlanders who don't like it should take their passports and their X-ray plates and emigrate to Canada. Only British know-how can get us out of this mess, for which we have no one to blame except ourselves.

Fielding's Condensed
History of Newfoundland

Chapter Twenty-One:

THE AXE, THE FOX AND THE WOLF

Newfoundland misses its chance to right the blunder of responsible government when a referendum on Confederation with Canada is held in 1869.

One of the strongest supporters of the confederate cause is David Smallwood, prominent citizen of Greenspond, Bonavista Bay, population sixty-three.

Smallwood flies the confederate banner from his house. A crowd gathers.

Smallwood states the case for Confederation. The crowd listens, mesmerized by his eloquence and the axe that he keeps swinging back and forth.

Confederation is defeated, largely because of a demented merchant named Charles Fox Bennett, who circumnavigates the island, in every port repeating:

> Our face towards Britain, our back to the gulf,
> Come near at your peril, Canadian wolf.

Many believe it is divine retribution when Bennett is struck down seventeen years later at the age of ninety.

Consummation Comes

WITH THE COMMISSION of Government in power, I could not stand to be around St. John's. I decided I would try to start up a fishermen's union along the south and southwest coasts of Newfoundland. It would mean going to places that could not be reached except by boat, and not even by boat in the winter, when the ice-field floated south and ice and land fused together like two halves of a jigsaw puzzle. From that point on, I would have to walk, unaccompanied. Winter would be the best time of the year to go, for most of the fishermen would not be fishing, and meeting with them and organizing them would be, if not easy, at least possible.

Using money I borrowed from people sympathetic to the labour cause, I hired an old thirty-eight-foot one-masted schooner with an eight-horsepower motor and a crew of one, a retired fishing skipper named Andrews from the southwest coast, who assured me he would go only as far on this expedition of mine as his schooner could, so I had best decide before we set out if I could manage the rest of it by myself. I assured him I could and told him of my walk across the island. "That ya have yer land legs I don't doubt," he said. "But those don't look like sea legs to me."

We set out from St. John's after Christmas. Within a day, Andrews resigned himself to the fact that he had not a first mate but a passenger who would be no help to him no matter how painstakingly he explained to him what to do. Because of the motor, Andrews was able to take an occasional break from his struggles with the sails and rigging while I stayed below trying to fool my body into believing that it was not at sea.

I had seen hundreds of men like Andrews on the waterfront years ago, men who in their old age had not softened, men who by their forties had achieved their final form. He would climb the rope ladder in the roughest of weather to the top of the mast and, with one hand on it, lean out and scan the sea ahead for obstacles. He was about my height, but much stockier, and dressed in what I can only describe as a full-body butcher's apron, a begrimed white leather raincoat with a hood he never used, going bare-headed no matter what the weather.

We sailed for several days, putting in at harbours on the south coast at night, there being no unionizing to do until we were well past the halfway point of the coast.

Andrews took me to the community of Garia, abandoned since 1873 when the entire population of two hundred left *en masse* for Anticosti Island. He took in with a sweep of his arm the grey houses hunched together in the snow, their roofs saddle-backed, windows gone, doors hanging on a single hinge or like-wise gone; houses built on the site of other houses of which now there was little trace, perhaps some rotting, fallen fence posts, the sunken pilings of some old foundation that lifted the house so high off the ground that a man could crawl beneath it.

"My father came from here," said Andrews. "There used to be two hundred people here. A lively place it was one time." The day would come when, because of me, there would be hundreds of such places around Newfoundland, abandoned islands and coastal settlements, ghost ports whose populations had been forcibly transferred to employment centres.

There were many reasons why the people lived where they did on the south coast, Andrews explained. The small islands, for instance. There was another country around the coast of Newfoundland, a country of islands, a circumscribing archipelago of satellite republics, bound together only by their residents' tacit agreement not to interfere with one another. Before the invention of the engine made it possible to do so, the only way to reach the fishing grounds was to live offshore on little islands that lay within a shorter, less arduous and treacherous row or sail of the deep water. And far from civilization, there was little or no competition for the fish.

Between stops, we stood on the bow of the schooner, regarding the somehow oppressively spectacular scenery, the houses in their drearily bright and cheerful, state-of-the-universe-denying colours, the fiord-like inlets, the pink-sunset sea, the pewter-coloured water of the harbours in the dusk, the light on the hillsides fading like a fire burning down. As always, I felt obliged to say or do something commensurately profound, but could think of nothing.

Andrews told me that if we sailed straight south from where we were, we would miss South America by several hundred miles, never so much as come within sight of it but bypass it altogether and eventually come up against ice at the other end of the world. "Nothing that way but water," he said, as if our facing in a direction in which there lay no land until you reached the edge of the Antarctic ice-field summed up perfectly how he felt at that moment.

We sailed sometimes within a few hundred feet of shore, looking up at great ramparts of granite and sandstone, sheer cliff faces of islands that rose abruptly from the sea, as if large pieces of the main island had broken off like icebergs from a black glacier, never-melting bergs of rock. We passed between these islands and the larger one, facing the latter, the headlands of which were even higher and so sheer that in most places not even birds could find a spot to perch. If you were so close to the cliff that you could not see the top, you were too close, Andrews said, for there were undertows that this boat, even with its little engine at full throttle, could not escape.

It was hard to believe Newfoundland was an island and not the edge of some continent, for it extended as far as the eye could see to east and west, the headlands showing no signs of attenuation; a massive assertion of land, sea's end, the outer limit of all the water in the world, a great, looming, sky-obliterating chunk of rock.

I did not see until I was almost upon them the first fissures in the cliffs, the first real fiords, which were a mile or two miles wide at the mouth, sunless corridors of stone so well sheltered from most winds that they were calm, glacial green, like the water in streams above the timberline, a deep opaque green five hundred fathoms deep. These fiords meandered inland, gradually narrowing, the cliffs slowly sloping down on either side to where a stream or river poured into the sea.

We sailed up some of these fiords, all the way up to where, on river plains, lay communities whose wharves and fishing stages from a distance could not be distinguished as such, they looked so much like driftwood on the beach. Only when we were very close to it did the "driftwood" resolve into artificial shapes, as did the houses on the slope behind them. The only things well kept in these places were the headstones in the cemeteries, stones that, like so much else, had been brought in by boat from St. John's or some other part of the world that the people whose resting places were marked by them had never seen. Three-century-old cemeteries. How startling, how incongruously opulent the green-veined marble monuments seemed, the tablets, pillars, columns, angels, stark stone crosses and bronze crucifixes among the shabby huts and shacks. Some marked burial plots for so long left untended that only the tips of the monuments showed above the scrub and snow.

There was a point on one beach where you could see all the way down the fiord to the sea, a jagged line of light between the cliffs, a lightning-bolt's width, a bolt caught as though in a photograph. As we headed back down the fiord towards the sea, the bolt of light widened slightly each time we took a turn until it suddenly spread outward like the flash from some explosion and we were in the world again.

Churches were visible for miles offshore. They were built on the highest points of land. Their three-spired façades, two of equal height flanking a taller one that bore a cross, made them look like Pentecostal doves, giant, once white, now grey birds perched where fishermen could see them while they worked and use them for navigation aids while they rowed back home.

At last I began my "unionizing," a grand word for it as it turned out. Not even Andrews, who had spent most of his life on the southwest coast, could believe the places I insisted that we visit. On one tiny island there lived a dozen people in one house, a single extended family, only three of whom were fishermen. I could not make them understand what a union was. The population of another island had dwindled down to one, a man who might have been anywhere from fifty to eighty and who, it was clear by the state of his wharf, had not fished for years.

Often we were far enough out from shore that I could see into more than one bay at a time. I sized them up, trying to decide which of them looked most promising. The settlements in the farthest recesses of the bays looked as if they were hiding from each other. The houses were perched at staggered altitudes on steeply sloping cliffs, often shored up by stilts where no foundations could be dug.

One day I pointed to a scattering of houses on the main island and told Andrews to head there. He complied, shaking his head. To get there, we had to navigate a set of reefs, the upcrops of which he told me were called Hit or Miss Point and Nervous Rocks. By the time we had passed between them, I had decided I would just as soon spend the rest of my life in this tiny place as navigate those reefs again.

At the sight of an unfamiliar person in their harbour, people came running from their houses. They ran, it turned out, because to the first person to shake my hand would go the privilege of serving us a cup of tea or putting us up for the night. I was greeted with open-hearted bemusement, welcomed into a home where my insistence on talking unions and politics was viewed as a forgivable, though not to be encouraged, shortcoming. Of course they would join my union, they said, seeming embarrassed, as if it impugned their hospitality for me to have to ask them for anything. But it turned out they had no money for union dues, nor for anything else.

As the winter wore on, the islands of bare rock were vastly outnumbered by those of ice. Any colour but white was incongruous among the growlers, bergy bits and icebergs, as if the rock and not the ice were only passing through. Most of the coastal towns looked like base camps for expeditionaries who had long since moved on to somewhere else, box-like houses, a cluster of buildings like provisions stacked on some ice-surrounded point of land.

The cliffs became what Andrews called snot-faced, coated in places with sea-water-green ice. What the rest of the year was a trickle of water down a cliff face had by increments throughout the winter become a frozen torrent, a freshet of ice layered lava-like with a sheen of running water on the top.

When finally Andrews spotted the ice-field in the distance, he put in at the nearest port. "If I were you, sir," he said, "I'd turn back now. I wouldn't walk this coast in winter for the king himself, let alone for unions." He gave me a pouch of oatmeal and raisins, which he assured me I would be glad to have before too long.

I bade him goodbye and the next day, telling myself that as long as I knew which way land lay, I would not end up like the men of the S.S. *Newfoundland*, I set off along the shore until I reached the ice. On the map I had prepared before leaving, virtually every community was highlighted by an *x*. Most of the place names were French, though their inhabitants did not pronounce them as the French would have. It was a long time since people of French ancestry had fished here. French ships had been confined to fishing the northeast coast by the terms of the first French shore treaty in 1713. The French had never lived here, only fished here in the summer, then gone home. But the names they gave the coves and bays and islands remained, their meanings unknown now to the people who spoke them every day. Rencontre. Isle aux Morts, Deadman's Island. It was pronounced *Ilomart*. Grand Bruit. Big Bear. Cinq Cerf. Margaree. Rose Blanche. Harbour le Cou. Petites. Lapoile. Bay le Moine. Bay de Vieux.

The walking was treacherous, especially near the shore, where the ice tended to accumulate first and where there were the most pressure ridges, rafted ice layered vertically in jagged crags created when two opposing pans had met, neither yielding, so there was nowhere for the ice to go but up. I sometimes had to walk for miles just to find a way between the ridges.

There was always open water far out from shore, and the waves from without carried on beneath the ice, the surface of which exactly mimicked that of the water beneath it, rolling, swelling, cresting, troughing, for the ice was not like lake or pond ice, not a solid sheet from shore to shore, but pans of ice from elsewhere that had packed together. Walking on it was about the closest thing to walking on water that you could get. It was like riding a vessel that took on the shape of the water. I could see the water move beneath the ice like limbs beneath a blanket.

As I walked along, I felt the ice rise beneath my feet, felt myself being lifted and then lowered and then lifted again. I discovered that it was possible while walking on the ice to become seasick. One second you were walking uphill, the next downhill. The water below moved shorewards but the ice did not; you rose to a crest on the ice, then felt and saw that crest move on ahead of you while another swell began beneath your feet. It was like walking on the skin of a massive animal.

Jumping to shore, dismounting the ice, was an art in itself. It was in many places pushed up onto the rocks, so although it was easy, once you were on the rim ice, to step ashore, getting onto the rim ice was something else. There was often a fissure between the rim ice and the pack ice through which, at the arrival of a wave onshore, sea water bubbled up. It took a certain knack to time your step — and a step was all it was, not a jump, if you knew what you were doing — from the shorewards-heaving pack ice to the rim ice, a knack that I never did get, so I always waited until someone on land saw me standing there, forlornly, incongruously.

When I made my inept leap with my distinctive flourish of self-abandonment, all but resigned to being swallowed up in the fissure, falling the moment it opened its green sea-water-frothing mouth to take me in, the men on land would grab me. As the wave of ice I should have used to launch myself to safety passed beneath my feet, I would lose my nerve, jump too late, just as the water bubbled up, and would wind up all but running on the spot, the slick wet ice beneath my feet, before I was yanked ashore, toes dragging on the ice behind me. "We got ya, sir, we got ya," the men said, politely trying not to laugh.

In oil-lamp-lit houses that reminded me of living on the Brow, I was given to eat dearly come by tins of ham or generic "meat," treats reserved for visitors, to put in front of whom the salted or, even worse, fresh fish the others had to settle for would have been the height of bad manners. How I longed to have what they were having and what they thought they were sparing me the hardship of having to eat; how I longed to gorge myself on damper dogs fried in oil or fat dumplings in a boiling pot of codfish stew.

Not that they "gorged" themselves. Even of fish, salted or fresh, there was precious little. These people in whose houses I nightly increased by one the number of plates that must be filled were verging on starvation. Because the merchants could not afford to give them credit for their fish, most of the fishermen did not have the wherewithal even to catch enough to feed themselves and their families. They had no diesel oil for their engines, no tools or wood to repair their codtraps or their boats, no canvas for their sails, no twine to make new nets, their old ones having frayed to bits of string that now were used for mending socks or making mitts.

Everyone had the same breakfast, boiled duff, which was flour and water cooked in a bag then left until it hardened like a biscuit. The only way to get it down was to eat it smothered with molasses, which there seemed to be no shortage of. They sent me off in the morning with what they called a sealer's lunch, hard bread so hard you did not so much chew it as gnaw on it and thereby got the soothing illusion that you were eating something. They also gave me chunks of fried salt pork that when it froze in my pocket or rucksack became so brittle it snapped off like toffee. It was unbelievably salty and every so often I got down on my hands and knees to drink from pools of water on the ice.

One day, when there was not a breath of wind and no sign that any might be in the offing and it was therefore possible for those whose dories were still seaworthy and whose coves were not iced in to row out to the fishing grounds, I went out at the invitation of a fishermen before sunrise to handline for cod. I faced him in the boat as he took the oars and, with his eyes averted from mine, looking out across the water, rowed for hours without changing his pace or his expression. He was, he told me later, keeping his eyes fixed on some landmark, but landmark or not I'm sure he would have looked the other way. I had yet to have someone look me in the eye for long, as if to do so would have been an impertinence.

After reaching his destination and dropping anchor, he slumped over exhausted, head down so that I couldn't see his face. The sun was coming up now, the first pale light of dawn was in the east and in the sky a silent seagull rose and fell.

After a few minutes, the passing of which we both pretended not to notice, the fisherman rose wordlessly and took out from

beneath the prow a wooden spool of fishing line. There was perhaps a hundred feet of line, but only about every tenth knot was
fitted with a hook. The sea was as calm as it ever gets, with the
dory rising on tidal swells a hundred feet apart and not a crest in
sight. The water was impenetrably black and strewn with dark
green kelp, the air what he called green, meaning fresh, though to
me it was pungent with the smell of brine.

  We lowered the hooks and smoked in silence until he deemed
it was time to haul them in again. He knelt nearest to the gunnel
and I knelt beside him. The line that had slid so easily into the
water was unbelievably heavy. The two of us tugging with all our
might took in at most three feet before I had to rest. He nodded,
straining to pick up the sudden slack. "I finds it better not to
stop," he said, as if to rest or stop was just a matter of personal
preference and to do the latter nothing I should be ashamed of.
"Jus' tell me when yer gonna stop, sir, so's I won't let go the line."
His teeth clamped on his cigarette, he went on pulling. I joined
him every few minutes, taking breathers in between. Of the ten
hooks, seven of them bore codfish that he said weighed between
fifteen and twenty pounds and that we, mostly he, had dragged up
through a hundred feet of water. When the last of the line was in
the boat, he lay back against the prow, chest heaving. I looked at
him lying there, eyes closed, in his tattered watch cap and layers of
bedraggled clothing, the palms of his gloves worn through, his
hands rope-burnt and bleeding, the butt of a burnt-out cigarette
between his lips. And now he had to row us back. I had expended
the energy of a day's walk in about an hour; he, in the past few
hours and the few to come, about five times that.

The farther from the ice-free part of the coast I travelled, the more
eccentric became the people I encountered. In many places, I could
barely understand what was being said to me, and barely make myself understood. On one little island, a man hand-pumping water
into a wash-pot in his porch informed me in explanatory tones:

"For now we dips the bucket right into the well." Since he was clearly not dipping a bucket, but was using a pump, I was mystified as to what he meant, not realizing until hours later that by "for now," he meant "'fore now" — before now, in the past. He had, as far as I could tell, no other way of referring to the past except by this phrase, which to me meant the present.

On another island I was told, until I could no longer stand not knowing what it meant, that I looked like my night had been nothing but a "dwall" from start to finish. "What's a dwall?" I said to the man in whose house I was waiting out a storm, which earned me a long look. After an explanation largely consisting of other words I did not know, I was able to discover that to "dwall" was to spend a night neither asleep nor awake but somewhere in between. I at last had a single word to describe how I almost always slept.

I dwalled every night on mattresses that consisted of "brin bags," tightly meshed potato sacks filled with woodshavings or hay. I preferred the woodshavings to hay, which made the bedrooms smell like the stalls where they kept their horses.

There was, of course, no electricity in any of the houses, no running water, no heat other than what the single woodstove in the kitchen could produce. In a few houses there were fireplaces, but they went unused for lack of coal or scarcity of wood. Many of the little islands had long since been denuded of whatever trees had once grown on them, and their residents had to set out like hunting parties across the frozen bays in search of wood on horse-drawn sleds on which I often hitched a ride, shielding myself against the chips of ice thrown up by the horses' hob-nailed hooves.

Often there were no schools. There might be a small church in which the most prominent citizen each Sunday morning spoke some sort of service. Perhaps there would be a visit or two a year from some missionary minister or doctor. They had never seen an automobile, a train, a motorized vehicle of any kind except a boat. They had travelled farther from their houses by sea than by land, and even then only as far as their fishing grounds, their longest land journey being the two-hundred-foot-long horse path that wound its way among the houses and the rocks.

I had been prepared for resistance to the idea of unionizing from people who led such a solitary, atomized existence. What I had not realized was how cut off from the world in both space and time these people were. Most of them did not understand or even have a word for the concept of government. Had never heard of Sir Richard Squires. Did not know there had taken place any change in our status as a country. Had only the most rudimentary understanding of what a country was. And at the same time were destitute beyond anything I imagined when I first set out. And these were the people I had thought to unionize, organize? I was able to get across only the notion that I had come to try to help them. But as I had with me none of the forms of "help" they were familiar with — no supply boat, no medicine, no clerical collar — they regarded me as something of a crackpot, showing up from out of nowhere empty-handed but apparently convinced that my mere presence among them would somewhow improve their lot. Yet if I had told the head of any household that from now on I would live with him, he would have assured me I was welcome.

It would take more than unions, and more than anything the Commission of Government might be inclined to do, to save these people. I felt ridiculous, useless, little more than an itinerant beggar, a deluded townie who fancied he had come to help them and who without them would not have made it through one night.

In bed, on overcast nights, there was a darkness so absolute that I lit matches just to assure myself that I could still see. It was hard to believe in the existence of St. John's, let alone New York, while confined to such a place.

On moonlit nights, the glow from the ice and snow was such that you could see for miles along the coast or out to sea, everything looking as it might have after days of freezing rain. Somewhere out there, there was water; somewhere out of sight the sea began, the ice-field formed its own coastline, and along that line, when the moon was out, light and darkness met, the light ending so abruptly it was as though beyond the ice lay not water but the emptiness of space, the edge of the world, if a man were to fall off which he would fall forever.

On clear nights, when there was no moon, the sky was more star-filled than dark. The light seemed to be shining down upon us through some threadbare fabric.

Always, at night, the darkness making it more noticeable, there was the sound of the sea, each place with its distinctive sea sounds; in the rare open harbours there was the clattering of beach rocks and chunks of ice as a wave withdrew, or if there was no beach, the din of breakers crashing in a pattern that was constantly repeated on the rocks below the house.

In the iced-in harbours, during the coldest nights, when there was not enough room for the expansion of the ice between islands that might be miles apart, fault lines formed. I could hear, as I lay in bed, the ice-fields grind together and boom as fault lines two miles long were created in mere seconds. Sometimes the booms were faint at first, the sound becoming louder as the crack in the ice drew near to the house, or fading into silence, depending on which way the fault was headed. If it grew louder, I would wait for it to pass the house like a roaring train, wait for it to pass and then recede. Some of the fault lines travelled more or less straight towards the house. I lay there, imagining that bearing down on me was a horizontal lightning bolt that would strike the house to pieces. There would be a final, deafening boom when the fault ran through the rim ice that coated the first twenty yards or so of shore, then the sound of shards and chunks of ice raining down upon the house.

And there was the strange sound, too, when the tides were changing, of the water beneath the ice, a low rumbling as though from underground and vibrations that made the windows rattle.

One night I heard a rumbling that I thought must be an avalanche, for it came from behind the house. I jumped up in a panic, only to be assured by a young man dressed like me in longjohns and staring out the back window that "it's the Lapoile 'erd, that's all, sir. Nuttin' to get all worked up about." His parents obviously concurred, for they were still in bed.

He may not have been "all worked up," but he was watching them nonetheless, watching them pass by his house on their way down to the ice, the Lapoile herd of caribou that he said always came by this time of year. I did like him and stood there with my hands and face pressed against the glass. All I could see at first was a torrent of shadows, but soon I could make out some slower-moving caribou. They were smaller than I had thought they would be, three or four feet high, each with racks of antlers so large and many-pointed they seemed head-heavy, barely able to look up to see where they were going.

"Where are they headed?" I said.

"Northeast," he said. "Back 'ome to the barrens for the summer. Lookin' for food."

"Do you hunt them?" I said.

"We got all we can use out in de smokehouse," he said. "Not everybody got a gun and even less got bullets. Black bears gets more of them than we do."

Codfish, now caribou. Rather than subject me to which they had served me tinned bologna.

All night long they passed the house, between the house and other houses, a deafening stampede that made even a dwall impossible. In the morning, when I got up, they were still going by. They stretched as far as I could see along the coast, between the rim ice and the rafted ice, a stream of antlers and moulting, shaggy, white-grey rumps, winding its way along the base of the headlands, bound for the first fiord or riverbank that it could follow north.

I was told that there were ten thousand of them in the herd, and that, like me, they were using the ice as a shortcut to get where they were going. I stayed put that day, doing nothing but watch them trot by in their mass migration. The smell of them was overpowering, a musky acrid smell. They trod their droppings underfoot, churned it with the snow, so for days afterwards their road-like trail stretched out of sight in both directions.

I was not used to sleeping so close to the sea. I preferred nights when, because of a storm, the sounds of the ice were as various and deafening as thunder. Better I be kept fully awake than mesmerized into a dwall by the haunting drone of sea sounds. I thought, not of uncomplaining Clara grown accustomed to my absence or my children by whose progress through infancy I would not allow myself to be diverted more than momentarily, but of Fielding.

I could only imagine for us a union so devoid of context that it was almost featureless. To invest it with detail, to try to imagine where and how we might be together and what it would be like only made me realize how foolish of me it was to brood on something that would not only never happen but that I didn't really want.

What a nuisance her existence was to me. I was certain that if I could somehow purge her from my mind, I would be much the better for it. How much easier might it be then to cleave to Clara, to not begrudge her that modest allotment of devotion that a proper sort of wife deserved. I was obscure and destitute, but soon not to be, I hoped. Married to Fielding, I was certain, I would have stayed obscure and destitute forever.

And yet it seemed the woman had fated me to a life of furtively and shamefully attending to myself like a schoolboy in the dark. I wondered if enlisting in some rigorously prescriptive religion might constrain me from this habit, which I sometimes slipped out of bed to indulge in even with Clara sleeping there beside me. For days afterwards, I would feel guilt-ridden and depressed.

Sometimes, to keep the length of the interval between our couplings from becoming a source of embarrassment between us, I gave in to her suggestion that we have what she playfully referred to as a "bout," but I would find myself losing interest midway and,

determined to see the act through to its conclusion, inspired myself
by picturing Fielding reclining on the moss in the Spruces. Poor
Clara, at such times, thinking something she had done had caught
my fancy, would so fervently respond she would have to turn her
face in to the pillow to keep from crying out.

Lying in these houses on the southwest and west coasts, I
would hear someone in the next room toss and turn on their mattress and it would remind me of my mother the night I stood outside her room. The sound of her breath indrawn through clenched
teeth as if my father were sticking her with pins. Could she have
been doing it to muffle moans of pleasure? I wondered. It seemed
inconceivable to me. "Smallwood, get off me," she had said dis-
missively when the squeaking of the bedsprings stopped.

I visited almost every settlement on the south and southwest coasts,
no matter how small. Most of the people there had never heard of
unions, had not the faintest idea what a union was or what difference it would make to their lives if they belonged to one. Only in
Corner Brook and a few other larger towns was I able to find anyone who would listen to me. By this time it was early spring and in
some places, where there was not much sealing done, the fishery
had started. In the Bay of Islands, my old stomping grounds from
the days when I campaigned for Sir Richard, I signed up hundreds
of fishermen to my co-operative union.

Unfortunately, and unknown to me until too late, most of
them, after six months, had not paid one cent of dues and my
co-op had collected less than 6 per cent of the Bay of Islands
catch. I had thought we were getting somewhere with the 6 per
cent and had been as surprised as the fishermen to find out that all
the earnings from it had been eaten up by overhead and we were
bankrupt. Explaining to fishermen that they would have been no
poorer if they had given their fish away or never caught it in the
first place had been difficult, though not so difficult as getting out
of the Bay of Islands unharmed after doing so.

I made it unscathed to the mill town of Corner Brook, found a bed in a boarding-house and slept for thirty-six hours, not in a dwall but deeply, obliteratingly. When I awoke, I went without breakfast to the train station.

Feeling humiliated by my failure, my ineptitude, I hardly glanced out the window as the train began its eastward run across the island. Just before nightfall we came to an unscheduled stop in the Topsails, where the snow on either side of the tracks was piled so high it was dark inside the train. We started, stopped, started, stopped, stalled in that eerie tunnel of snow for hours at a time, barely inching forward when we moved, the cowcatcher groaning against the snow that blocked the tracks. I had no food, having spent all the money I had left on my train fare home. What should have been a twenty-four-hour trip took nearly three times that.

We arrived in St. John's on a Friday afternoon. I walked home to Gower Street, up the hill from the train station with my suitcase only to find there was no one in the house. I guessed that Clara and the children, whom I hadn't told that I was coming home, had gone to spend the weekend in Harbour Grace with Clara's parents. Clara had left the door unlocked, as she always did when she went out while I was away.

There was mail for me on the kitchen table, among it an invitation to a press reception at Government House. I threw it aside, sat there as the house grew dark. I was a would-be politician in a country in which politics was obsolete. A would-be unionist in a country where even the minority that understood what a union was were too poor to pay their dues. A reporter in a country in which reporters were told by a commission from abroad what they could and could not write. And if all this would ever end nobody knew.

I picked up the invitation from the floor. It had always been the case that you were no one in St. John's society if your name did not appear on the Government House invitation list, but this was especially so under the Commission of Government, when Government House was viewed as some far-flung wing of Whitehall.

The commissioners wished to meet the press. There was a dinner party to which the publishers and editors of the long-established papers were invited, after which there was a reception for the rest of us.

With my engraved invitation was included a reminder, bearing the commission's letterhead, of what constituted "proper attire."

"While we realize," it read, "that it would be unrealistic of us to expect some of those to whom invitations have been sent to attend dressed in the manner normally required at such functions, we do ask that you do everything within your means to make yourself presentable." It read almost as though they wanted me to have the good grace to decline and settle for the honour of merely having been sent the invitation. I considered declining, telling myself that to attend such a lavish event would be hypocritical even for the somewhat compromised socialist-at-heart-if-not-in-practice I had become. On the other hand, I would, by staying away, be doing only what they wanted. I would go, I decided, dressed just as I was. How else *could* I go, having no better clothes than my Harris tweed slacks and Norfolk jacket anyway?

By the time I set out for Government House, there was a northeast wind blowing in from the ice that for weeks had jammed the entrance to the Narrows. A freezing rain that I was certain would soon change to snow was falling, but as I had no money for a cab, I had no choice but to walk to Military Road from my house.

When I knocked on it, the door of Government House no sooner opened than it began to close, and all that saved me from having to march straight back home was my sodden invitation, which I fished from my pocket just in time. A liveried fellow who reminded me of Cantwell, the Squireses' butler, took it from me and, holding it by thumb and forefinger, looked doubtfully at it as if he thought I must have stolen it from someone or found it discarded on the ground.

"You are Mr. Smallwood?" he said, as if he had heard of me, which flattered me, though his tone of incredulity did not. He spoke with a heavy St. John's accent, which, given the way he was dressed, struck me as ridiculous.

"Come in, sir," he said, kindly, deferentially. "You'll catch your death of cold in what you're wearing. I might be able to find you something dry."

I didn't realize until it was too late that his concern was genuine. I assumed this was his way of hinting that Governor Anderson had made provision for fellows like me who showed up attired "unpresentably." I pictured myself walking about in some obviously borrowed, ill-fitting suit.

"I'll wear what I'm wearing," I snapped. "And I won't stand here waiting to be inspected. Either show me in or show me out."

"Of course, Mr. Smallwood, of course," the poor fellow said and took my hat from me. "You can go straight in, sir."

I smoothed back my hair with my hands, wiped my glasses dry on my lapel, put them on and strode quickly into the reception lobby, hoping to so abbreviate my entrance that I would not be noticed. It worked, except that the managing editor of the *Daily News*, who I was sure had been at the pre-reception dinner, spotted me and waved, not so much by way of greeting as to draw attention to me. Or so I thought. I felt so conspicuous I suspected everyone of trying to make me more so.

I waved back but walked with feigned purpose in the opposite direction, vaguely entertaining the notion that I would keep moving until I was sufficiently dry that when I stopped a puddle of water would not form at my feet. I was wet through to the skin; my clothes, for once, were clinging to me, my pants matted to my thighs.

I think I would have left had I not seen Prowse standing with a group of men who I knew worked for the commission, Prowse dressed just like them in a smart-fitting tuxedo with a black bow tie. I wondered what he was doing there, this being a reception for the press. They were all standing at one end of the buffet table; beside Prowse, champagne glass in hand, was a woman who I

guessed was his wife. She was dressed as impeccably as the governor's wife, in a blue evening gown, a black hat with a large white
feather, elbow-length white gloves. Prowse saw me looking in his
direction and nodded at me, half raised his glass in a token of
salute. I sloshed across the room and joined his group.

"I've often wondered what you weighed soaking wet, Smallwood," Prowse said. "I don't suppose you'd let me lift you." The
others laughed.

"What are you doing here, Prowse?" I said.

"Working. I'm an assistant of Sir John Hope Simpson's. What
are you doing here? I thought you'd retired from the press — "

"I can't believe you would have anything to do with this lot,"
I said. "Only a year ago, you were working for the Liberals, for
Squires."

"Are you implying that the commission is not politically neu-
tral," Prowse said, "and that for me to work for it makes me some
sort of turncoat? What does that make a socialist who works for
Richard Squires?" Again the group broke out in laughter.

"So what have you been up to lately, Smallwood?" Prowse
said. "I hear your latest attempt to unionize the fishermen met with
the usual success. You really are a hack of all trades."

"And what are you?" I said.

"A master of one."

"You're so full of it, Prowse," I said. "I'm surprised there's
any room left for the booze."

"If a man looked at a woman the way you're looking at that
food, Smallwood," Prowse said, "he'd be arrested. Why don't you
just go over there and eat something, for God's sake?"

I *had* been looking at the food. I suspected this reception did
not rank high on the Government House scale of lavishness, but
there was more to eat and drink than I had ever seen gathered in
one place before, all of it arrayed on tables pushed against the
back wall. I could not take my eyes from it at first. There were
heaping platters of smoked turkey, slices of cloved ham, salmon

and trout and arctic char carved into chunks and adorned with wedges of lemon and pineapple, piles of cucumber sandwiches, bowls of pâté, cakes with thick pink icing, frosted jugs of lemonade and bowls of punch. At the end of the tables opposite ours, a white-hatted chef stood beside piles of plates and trays of glasses and cutlery. When he was not carving or pouring, which was most of the time, he stood with his hands behind his back and his feet spread wide apart as though he was guarding the food.

The Newfoundlanders acted as if they knew, and wanted the British to know they knew, that such a spread was not meant to be eaten but to be admired. Some were simply too proud, in front of others, to admit to being hungry, though I doubted that more than one in ten of them had eaten properly that day. I was in this last group, though the "others" I was primarily loath to admit my hunger to were those who with money from our treasury had supplied the food, namely, the British. I knew that if I were to touch a morsel, I would put aside all thought of keeping up appearances and gorge myself. I knew because others, a few so famished or so weak-willed they could not afford the luxury of self-consciousness, were doing just that.

On the other hand, opinion seemed to be unanimous that to take a glass of champagne when offered one from a well-loaded tray was quite acceptable. A waiter bearing aloft a tray of champagne-filled glasses did not even slow down as he neared me, so I helped myself. I moved away from Prowse's group.

It was possible to look amused, aloof while sipping champagne or even while tossing it off a glass at a time, as I began to do.

I drank several glasses, and though I found it sickly sweet, I preferred it, near teetotaller that I was, to rum or whisky. Soon I began to feel better, less concerned than I would have been without the champagne to see in the oval mirror on the wall what might have been a sculpted likeness of myself, my clothes hanging in rigid folds on my body. I dispelled the illusion by toasting my image in the mirror, and felt pleased when it reciprocated. The Guards Band seemed to be playing all my favourite songs. I felt like dancing. I felt a hand on my shoulder and looked up into the eyes of a man I vaguely knew, a reporter who seemed to be swaying back and forth.

"Better sit down," he said sympathetically, and led me to a chair against the wall. "Haven't exactly got a hollow leg, have you? When did you last eat?"

Not that day or the day before; the day before that perhaps, I wasn't sure. I remembered that while recruiting in the Bay of Islands, I had walked over five miles of hills to a place called Tickle Cove, where I was invited in for a meal by a fisherman who lived alone in a makeshift shack. Everything in the place was makeshift. His table was a door laid across two sawhorses, his two chairs were lobster crates, his cups tin cans. He boiled tea in an empty biscuit tin, rendered a thin slab of fat-back pork on the damper of his woodstove, then smeared a slab of dole bread in the melted fat-back, laid it on the lid of the biscuit tin and handed it to me. It was not until I was nearly finished that I realized that what I was eating was to have been his dinner, that he was not eating, though he seemed to be getting great satisfaction out of watching me. Whether it was this poor fellow or myself I felt sorry for now, I was not sure, but I suddenly felt myself on the verge of tears.

"What do you think, Smallwood? Will you go over with me and shake their hands?" my acquaintance said. Across the floor, the reporters were queuing up to a receiving line that consisted of Governor Anderson; commissioners Hope Simpson, Lodge and Trentham and their wives; our three commissioners, Alderdice, Howley and Puddister, and their wives, one Anglican, one Catholic and one non-conformist, as if it mattered that all three factions be represented, since our commissioners had no power anyway. I looked at the wives, wearily, perfunctorily shaking hands with men they hoped they would never see again.

"We live in an occupied country," I said, "and that it has been occupied at our request only makes it that much worse. All these Newfoundlanders, putting on airs to impress the British who laugh at them behind their backs, trying to pretend it's because of other Newfoundlanders the British had to bail us out, not them, as if the British are just reinforcements who will help them do away with laziness and ignorance, then leave."

The commission had been convening now for more than a year. Though Governor Anderson was the titular head, "chairing" the commission the way he "governed" Newfoundland, it was common knowledge, and clear from the way the others, Anderson included, deferred to him, that Hope Simpson ran the show.

I walked unsteadily across the floor and joined the queue. Prowse was now standing at Hope Simpson's side, introducing him as each member of the press corps stepped forward.

Hope Simpson wore, aside from an unwavering, stern, hyper-vigilant expression, round-rimmed spectacles, a knee-length coat with turned-up cuffs and a line of large silver buttons down the right-hand side and a waistcoat buttoned tightly to his neck. He wore some sort of pantaloons, with stockings over those, and on his feet a pair of low-cut, square-buckled glistening black shoes. At his left side, he wore an ornamental sabre, the handle of which he held against his body with his arm. In his left hand he held, for no reason I could think of, a small green book and a pair of white gloves. He had spent most of his life in far-flung, exotic postings — India, China, Greece — heading commissions made necessary by the slow dismantlement of the British Empire, overseeing the abandonment of colonies no longer worth colonizing or the withdrawal from those no longer willing to put up with being colonized.

He was sixty-five years old and his stockings brought out the shape of his old man's legs up to his knees, a fact that, in my drunken state, seemed especially affronting. He had strong-looking calves and a pair of finely turned ankles, which only made it seem all the more ridiculous that an old man should be so vain as to show his legs in public.

While waiting my turn, I drank another glass of champagne. Prowse whispered something to Hope Simpson when I was next in line to shake his hand.

"Lord Hope Simpson," Prowse said, "this is Joe Smallwood."

Hope Simpson extended his hand, and giving Prowse a withering look in the face of which he did not flinch, I shook it, trying to affect mock admiration, bowing so low I almost fell over.

"It is a pleasure to at last meet the man whom I have for so long admired at a distance," I said.

"I would thank you for saying so, Mr. Smallwood," Hope Simpson said, "and would be more than willing to return the compliment if I believed it was sincere. You're the Bolshie fellow who's been trying to unionize the fishermen, are you not?"

I looked again at Prowse.

"Are you aware," I shouted, adopting my stump-speaking voice, "that some people believe you insulted the Newfoundland people when you divided their legislative chamber into offices? But then, you must be, or you would not have been overheard saying, 'What need do a people without a legislature have for a legislative chamber?'"

"Mr. Smallwood, as you seem to be the only person in the room who is unaware that you are drunk, I am willing to ignore that remark."

"You dismantled the Newfoundland Museum," I shouted, "to make way for more offices, and so scattered its exhibits that they will never be recovered. 'And so I have,' you tell people, 'but what of it? What did that museum commemorate but three hundred years of misery and failure?'"

"Good night, Mr. Smallwood."

"You have been quoted as saying, 'St. John's is a squalid town — '"

"There is a man behind you, Mr. Smallwood, who would like to shake my hand."

"There is a man in front of you, Sir John, who would like to wring your neck."

At this, Prowse and another man moved forward and took hold of me by the arms and began to drag me towards the lobby.

"Let him go," Hope Simpson said. Lodge stepped up to him and whispered something in his ear, his head bobbing emphatically.

"Let him go," Hope Simpson said again, dismissing me with a flick of his gloves and turning away. Prowse and the other man released me but watched me closely. My glasses had fallen off and as I bent to retrieve them I staggered.

A group of men, Prowse included, surrounded me and walked with me towards the door.

Outside, it was snowing. We stood in shelter on the steps of Government House. No one said a word. Prowse stared at me, but I pretended not to notice. The snow, driven by the northeast wind, was thickening and beginning to gather on the ground. Despite the lateness of the hour, it was brighter now than when I had arrived, the snow reflecting what little light there was. That in any other context the sight would have been a cheerful one made it all the more depressing.

"Here," Prowse said, thrusting some bills at me, "take a cab home." Again I ignored him. "You're ruined in this town, Smallwood," Prowse said. "You're ruined in this country."

I looked at the horse-drawn cabs and motor cabs that lined the driveway, the horses stamping and blowing. The drivers had taken the sudden appearance of a dozen men on the steps as a general exodus and were watching us expectantly.

The man who had greeted me at the door came running from inside with my overcoat. I put it under my arm and stepped out into the snow.

"Like father, like son," Prowse shouted when I was halfway to the gate. I did not stop.

The next day I longed to talk to Fielding, though I had no idea what I would say to her, nor any reason to think I would be cheered by what she said to me. I went to her boarding-house on Cochrane Street, knocked on her door but got no answer. I began to leave when the door across the hall opened a crack. I could barely make out a stubble-bearded old man in a grimy undershirt.

"Lookin' for her what writes the columns, are ya?" he said. I nodded. "She's at the Harbour Light," he said. "Went in yesterday. Says she's gonna quit the booze. When I heard ya comin' down the hall, I thought ya might be her. 'I knew ya wouldn't last,' I was gonna say." He chuckled and closed the door as if my coming to look for her somehow bore out his prediction.

The Harbour Light was operated by the Salvation Army. It was on Harbour Drive and bore the painting of a lighthouse on its exterior, a lighthouse from which a beacon blared out the words Blessed Are the Poor in Spirit.

A small set of marble steps led to the lobby and a desk, behind which sat a Salvation Army nurse, a middle-aged woman all dressed in black with the initials S.A. sewn onto her collars and lapels. I asked her if I could see Miss Fielding. She brightened immediately. "You're the first visitor she's had," she said. "It will lift her spirits a great deal to see that someone still cares about her. It's a good thing you came when you did. She won't be in any shape for visitors much longer."

She escorted me to a small empty room in which there were a table and two facing chairs, not what I thought the visitors' room would look like. I sat down and minutes later Fielding came in, wearing not a hospital gown but her own clothes; she even had her cane.

"Look at you," I said.

She sniffed and raised her eyebrows, then sat down sideways to the table, stretching her long mismatched legs, her button-booted feet crossed, the thick-soled boot on top. She tapped her cane repeatedly on the floor.

"The nurse says you're not getting many visitors," I said.

"Not true. There's been a steady stream of aunts, uncles, cousins," she said. "The Fieldings have always been famous for pulling together when one of their own winds up in the drink tank. My aunts have been baking non-stop — " She sighed, weary of her own irony, it seemed.

"Are you sure you want to do this?" I said. "You haven't gone a day without a bottle in fifteen years, let alone without a drink."

"I've had my last drink," she said. "I had it two days ago, April 16, 1936."

Her whole body was shaking already.

"What made you decide?" I said. "Why now?"

"It seems to be a time in Newfoundland when people do strange things." She smiled. She had heard about my run-in with Hope Simpson. Why shouldn't she have, since word of it was all over town?

"Did you know," she said, "that our first legislators met in an inn, a tavern from which they were evicted because they couldn't pay the rent? Their landlady sold their mace and their Speaker's chair. Put an ad for them in the papers. For Sale: One mace and one Speaker's chair. And sundry regalia, including the sergeant-at-arms' ornamental sword. It all wound up in England. We had to buy it back at an auction. 'What am I bid for these articles from the Parliament of Newfoundland?' Apparently, the bidding was quite brisk."

"I'll come to see you every day if you like," I said.

"Really, Smallwood," Fielding said, "I wish you wouldn't —"

"You'll need someone to help you pass the time," I said. "I know what drinkers get like when they're not drinking."

When I went to see her two days later, she was much worse. Her head quivered uncontrollably as if she were in the advanced stage of some sort of palsy. Every so often a jolting tremor passed through her whole body as if she had awoken suddenly from sleep.

"You looked better when you were drinking," I said.

"I'm trying to quit drinking, Smallwood," Fielding said. "And there's something about the sight of you that counteracts that impulse."

"Everything counteracts that impulse," I said.

"Why are you ... here, Smallwood?" Fielding said, trying to stifle a tremor that passed through her when she was in mid-sentence. "You must think there's something to be gained from it, is that it? I heard about your run-in with Hope Simpson. Perhaps you'd like me to write a column about it, make up a lot of witty things you wish you'd thought of at the time, and let you pass it off as yours."

"You're the most cynical woman I've ever met, Fielding," I said, standing up. "You — you helped save Sir Richard's life. I'm just returning the favour, that's all." I still could not bring myself to mention that she had saved my life, or to thank her for it.

I swore I would not go again, but the next day I changed my mind. The nurse at the desk told me that Fielding was very sick. "She really is," she said. "Sometimes visitors think the patients just don't want to see them. They had the doctor in last night. They had to put her in a straitjacket. He gave her some sedation, but we may have to send her to the hospital."

I was not able to see her until ten days later. We met in the same room as before, but I doubt that it seemed the same to her. She hobbled into the room on her cane, still tremulous but not looking quite so wild-eyed as before.

"Two weeks," she said. "The doctor said I'm passed the worst of it, the withdrawal part of it. I hope to God he's right. This is the only place I've ever been that makes me miss the San. I can't say I'm any happier to see you, though."

Before I could react, Fielding held up her hand. "Sit down,

Smallwood, sit down," she said. "I take that last one back. It must be sobriety talking."

I sat down.

"You know what I'm afraid of most?" she said. "I'm afraid that now that I've quit drinking, I'll quit writing, too. Or I'll keep writing, but it won't be any good. And I might not even know it."

"Maybe you'll be a better writer," I said. "Maybe you'll get more work done than before."

Fielding was silent for a while. Then she told me she was dreading being released because she doubted that "out there" she could resist temptation. I told her I was sure she could, but she shook her head.

"You may not believe it," she said, "but I've appreciated your coming to visit me. In fact, I've got something for you. A token of my appreciation." She took an envelope out of her coat pocket and handed it to me. Inside it were two letters, one that read:

Miss Fielding:

I'm leaving Newfoundland, for good, thank God. I was going through my files recently and found this. I thought you might like to have it.

Headmaster Reeves

The "it" referred to was the letter to the *Morning Post*. I had had only a glimpse of it before. Reeves had read it aloud while standing with his back to me. Though the glue with which the words had been pasted to the sheet had dried, the words, crumpled and shrunken, still adhered to the paper.

I sat down again. "Why would he send this to you?"

Fielding shrugged. "Perhaps he really thought I would like to have it. As a keepsake of sorts."

"I guess he was right," I said. "You've kept it for the past ten years. It must mean something to you."

"Well, I don't want it any more. You can have it if you want it," Fielding said. She put up her hand before I could protest. "I just want to get rid of it, that's all. I've had it long enough. If you don't want it, I'll throw it away or burn it or something. I just thought I'd offer in case it meant something to you. It means nothing to me any more." She spoke the last sentence so pointedly I realized that she saw herself as having made a new beginning now that she had quit drinking.

But why was she offering me the letter? Her explanation seemed unconvincing. If I were in her position, I would have destroyed it the instant I set eyes on it. It was certainly not the kind of thing I would hand over to someone else, let alone the very person it had been designed to injure. It must be that it would mean something to her for me to have it.

I had not let drop the possibility that someone other than Fielding had written it. Since I had first suspected it might be Prowse, that night when he and I met at Sir Richard's, I had thought about it a lot. And although I could come to no conclusions regarding Prowse, it had come to seem more and more unlikely to me that Fielding was the author of the letter. There was the question of why she had waited so long to get her revenge. Nearly three years. And why, having gone as far with her prank as she had, would she have been so stricken with remorse that to clear me she confessed? I was merely suspected of having written the letter; it could never have been proven that I had, and therefore the trouble she had saved me from was out of all proportion to what she caused for herself. None of this explained, of course, why she had given me the letter. If she wanted me to know the truth, why didn't she just come right out and tell me what it was?

At any rate, now that I had seen it again, I could not stand the thought of the letter being destroyed. Perhaps I believed that as long as it existed, there was some hope of finding out for certain who had written it.

"I'll take it," I said. "And the note from Reeves, unless you want it?" She shook her head. I shrugged. "Then I'll take that, too." I put both letters back in the envelope and left.

Fielding's Condensed
History of Newfoundland

Chapter Twenty-Two:

THE ISAAC MERCER MUMMER MURDER

Our history would not be complete did we not denounce the pagan practices to which people in this country have for so long clung and which some seek to preserve in the name of "culture," "folklore," "custom," or "tradition." No good can come of such things.

Mummering in Newfoundland has long been a way of getting revenge for past grievances. There are many recorded instances of people disguised as mummers setting upon their enemies or religious rivals and beating them severely. (Mummers, for the information of those fortunate enough never to have encountered them, are revellers who go about at Christmas in disguise, wreak havoc in the streets, barge their way unannounced and uninvited into people's homes and, until bribed with food and liquor and lewd dancing, will not leave.)

Take the case of one Isaac Mercer, who on December 28, 1860, is set upon and murdered by a troupe of mummers in Bay Roberts, after which mummering is outlawed in St. John's, which only serves to increase its popularity.

How often have we thought of poor Isaac Mercer at the bottom of that scrum of mummers thinking it was all in fun. A friend described him in a newspaper as "a cheerful, optimistic sort of fellow upon whom fortune always shone and who, it seems, incurred the wrath of dozens without even knowing it. He was the kind of man who never suspected that anyone thought badly of him and probably did not know until the act was well under way that he was being murdered."

We were once in our youth visited by mummers. There was a knock on the door, followed by the question "Any Christmas here?" The mummers spoke ingressively, that is while breathing in, in order to disguise their voices. My father consequently misheard the question and opened the door to assure his interlocutor that no one who was *not* a Christian ever set foot inside his house — and in they came.

They wore fearsome masks, animal-heads, or had their faces covered with veils of lace or net curtains. One had between its legs a stuffed stocking that was so long it dragged the ground.

Another of their number carried a stick to which was tied a bladder full of peas with which he went about whipping all those whom he deemed not to be in the Christmas spirit, for some reason focusing his attentions mainly on me. Never will I forget the loud rattle of the bladder as he chased me through the house from room to room.

He did thereby incite to pursuing me another member of the troupe known as the Horse-chops who rode a kind of hobby-horse, which consisted of a stick with the figure of a horse's head on top, a head that had movable jaws with nails for teeth, which I heard snapping viciously behind me. All of this took place as though set to music, the balance of the troupe having holed up in the kitchen, from whence could be heard the horrible accordion, the spoons and some sort of dreadful drum.

Even as I cringed beneath my bed, just out of range of the bladder and the chops, I heard them sing ingressively their beguiling "The Terra Novean Exile's Song": "How oft some of us here tonight / Have seen the mummers out / As thro' the fields by pale moon light / They come with merry shout / In costumes quaint with mask or paint ..."

Mercifully, the mummers departed our house only minutes later, going next door, where the inhabitants, unable to repel them, affected pleasure at the sight of them to save themselves, and thus were stuck with them for a night throughout which, my father assured me, nothing sustained them but our prayers.

The *Morning Post*

T HERE WAS NOT a night when, after work, I did not pore
over the letter to the *Morning Post*. Judging by the thickness of the paper, all the words and the individual letters the writer
had used to make words had been cut from books and not from
newspapers or magazines. One lower-case typeface was predomi-
nant, and although I did not know what it was called, I had seen
it many times before in many books. All of the whole words were
of this typeface and were in every other way identical, so I presumed they were from the same book. The words fashioned from
individual letters were of various sizes and appeared in various
typefaces, one word sometimes composed of more than one typeface, and all these individual letters were upper case, presumably
because it would have been easier to cut them out. Some were in
what I recognized to be Gothic typeface, others in Italic, others in
typefaces I had seen before but didn't know the names of.

For some reason, the Gothic letters E, C, F and R seemed
especially familiar. They were all of the same size, and so again I
felt certain they were from the same book. If I had not by chance
written them down in that order — E, C, F, R — I might never

have remembered where I had seen them. I thought of them off and on for days and had given up trying to recall their source when, as I was headed to the paper one day, my mind on something else, it came to me.

"English, Colonial and Foreign Records."

I hurried home and, consulting my legible copy of the *History*, confirmed my hunch. Those four characters and a couple of others from the *Post* letter appeared on the title page, as did the whole words *three* and *note*. Poring through the book, I found other whole words and letters that matched, in typeface and size, those from the letter to the *Morning Post*.

I was certain I knew now who had composed the letter. I was certain that my father had — or so it must have seemed to him in his drunkenness — killed two birds with one stone. He cut the words and letters from the book whose author, he believed, had patronized him: "Friends as you and I might have been had we gone to school together." He composed from them a letter that he sent to a newspaper in the hope of causing trouble for Reeves, who, by slighting his son, had slighted him.

I took my father's copy of the *History* from my dresser drawer and vowed that even if it meant destroying it, I would pry apart the pages from which, I was sure, the letter to the *Morning Post* had been excised.

I figured the easiest page to get at would be the title page, since it was only three pages in, though it was also the page I would most regret needlessly spoiling. The words I was looking for, or the gaps in those words where the letters should have been, would be about a quarter of the way down the page.

I started from the top right-hand corner, trying to cut the pages apart with a razor blade, using my intact copy of the *History* as a guide. I began, ever so slowly, to work my way towards the middle. I thought about all the things I would do once I had conclusive proof — confront my father, apologize to Fielding, write to Hines, asking him why, in the sermon in his church in Brooklyn, he had said, "There is a dreadful secret that involves a book and a man you never knew." But then, if my father really did write the letter, Hines would be right in saying that I never knew him.

I had freed from the page above it a triangle of the title page that measured about an inch across, when the surface of the title page began to come off, so completely fused together were the two pages. I had almost despaired of my task when the title page reappeared again and I uncovered the first word, *land*. I kept going and had uncovered *foundland* when the last letter, *s*, of the Gothic-typed word *Records* appeared. Next came the other lowercase letters of the word: *d-r-o-c-e*. I paused, knowing that next, if my suspicions were right, should come a little window in the page where the *R* had been.

But the upper-case Gothic *R* was there. The *F*, the *C* and the *E* were also there, as were the words *note* and *three*, farther down the page. I confirmed from my copy that there was nowhere else in the book the letters could have come from. The letters and words had not been cut from my father's copy of the *History* but from someone else's, presumably by someone not my father.

FIELDING'S JOURNAL, APRIL 19, 1936

Dear Smallwood:

It's been a long time since I faced the day, or even worse, the night, without a drink.

Often, though I'm so tired I can barely move, I cannot sleep and wonder if I ever will again.

I am mocked by thoughts of famous sleepers. The apostles who dozed off the night before the crucifixion. Rip Van Winkle. I tell myself that if I have to, I can go out and buy some sleep. I have put aside the price of one night's sleep, one bottle of

Scotch, put it in a can and taped the lid tightly shut. I don't plan to spend it, but I need to know that if I wanted to, I could.

Even at three in the morning there are places I can go. Places I used to go. Tap, tap, tap on the window with my cane. "Is that you, Miss Fielding?" A man who expects such interruptions climbs out of bed to let me in. "Writing late tonight," he says as the money changes hands.

I miss that, walking with a purpose through the streets at night when every house is dark. The elation of that long walk home.

When things were going well, I slept through the day, rose when the sun set, wrote in summer until midnight and in winter until three, then stayed up until sunrise.

It seemed that it was always night. I looked out on the rows of houses, the theatres, the shops on Water Street, cars parked in driveways — all part of some existence that for years had been on hold, that hadn't changed since darkness fell.

I still walk at night, more than I used to, though for different reasons now. I cannot sit still doing nothing the way I could when I was drinking. I walk around my room, reading, smoking, for as long as I can stand it, then go out.

I walk through the neighbourhood where I grew up, past what used to be my father's house, past Bishop Spencer, where I went to school. I pass the Newfoundland Hotel, where the Hope Simpsons occupy three suites, which they say they find "cramped."

I go past the sprawling solitude of Cochrane's house and then the hundred-year-old legislature, which from the outside looks the same as it did before the commissioners came. The old Colonial Building. How much older it seems now than it did two years ago.

I climb the steps and sit between the pillars, in this city, in this country that, at this time of night, still feels like mine. I am on the eastern edge of the island, on a peninsula joined to the rest by a strip of land so narrow it could vanish with one tidal wave.

I have never crossed the island. I have left Newfoundland but only from St. John's by boat.

I think often, while sitting on those steps, of the core where no one lives and through which no roads or railways pass and where lakes no one has canoed or even seen go on for miles, the core that William Cormack and a Micmac named Sylvester walked in 1822 just to prove it could be done.

At some point I head home. From my fire escape you can see between two trees the lantern lights of dories as they put out through the Narrows, and you can hear their engines unless the wind is up.

In the houses of the Battery, the lights come on when mine go off. People whose lives are spent in counterpoint to mine, whose days start when the sun comes up and end when it goes down. Before the sun comes up, in fact.

They are out there on the water now, hooks baited, a hundred hooks on a thousand feet of line played out/hauled in by hand, waiting for the bottom-feeding cod. Almost no one can afford to buy their fish, but they catch it anyway and with it feed themselves.

As they start their day, I draw the blinds, lie down on my bed and pray for sleep. The can that holds a great deal more than the price of one night's sleep lies out of sight, at the back of my closet.

What if this vigil I am keeping never ends?

Fielding's Condensed
History of Newfoundland

Chapter Twenty-Three:

WHITEWAY THE GOAT

Newfoundland is notorious for getting the best of absurdly one-sided deals, yet Newfoundland herself has sometimes been taken.

No name in Newfoundland history is more synonymous with "goat" than that of William Whiteway, who in 1878, when the British respond to his request for a trans-island railway by offering instead to make him a Companion of St. Michael and St. George, declares that he will hold out for the railway. Henceforward, in Newfoundland, it is said of anyone who is hoodwinked that he was "Whitewayed."

The Barrelman

FIELDING WAS RIGHT. It *was* a time in Newfoundland when people did strange things. Like a lot of Newfoundlanders, I was given to starting up enterprises that everyone but me knew were doomed to fail. There was something about abject hopelessness that inspired a delusionary optimism in me, a belief that for me, if for no one else in Newfoundland, prosperity lay just around the corner. It was like the euphoria I felt in New York after going without food for days, or the warm drowsiness that overcame me when I almost froze to death on the Bonavista.

The country was crawling with destitute inventors, entrepreneurs seeking "backing" for one thing or another, and they were, I was convinced, undermining my credibility. How could I get backing for *my* sure-fire schemes when investors took me to be just another of the crackpots who were rolling up like capelin on the beach? Among my sure-fire schemes was an encyclopedia called *The Book of Newfoundland*, which I edited and thousands of copies of which wound up stacked like cod in some warehouse on the waterfront, for no one could afford to buy it.

I approached the manager of a radio station called VONF, the Voice of Newfoundland, and pitched to him an idea for a fifteen-minute program to be called "The Barrelman," after the masthead lookout on a sailing ship, a program of local history and anecdotes, of which there were several years' worth in my unsold, unread, un-heard-of encyclopedia.

In October 1937, I began broadcasting to Newfoundlanders as the Barrelman on Monday to Friday, from 6:45 p.m. to 7:00 p.m. each night. I stated that the purpose of the program was to make Newfoundland better known to Newfoundlanders. No one was more surprised than me when it caught on.

"The Barrelman" began and ended with six chimes of a ship's bell. "BONG, BONG, BONG, BONG, BONG, BONG. F. M. O'Leary presents 'The Barrelman,' a program dedicated to making Newfoundland better known to Newfoundlanders." And there was a single chime before and after each commercial for products made or distributed by F. M. O'Leary Ltd., the company that spon-sored the show and paid me fifty dollars a week to host it. I was at last making a decent wage and was able to buy a house for Clara and the children.

At first, I merely plundered *The Book of Newfoundland* for ideas. I spoke about Newfoundlanders who had made a name for themselves abroad — Sir Cyprian Bridge, the only Newfoundlan-der to become an admiral in the Royal Navy; John Murray Ander-sen, who succeeded Flo Ziegfeld as the producer of the Ziegfeld Follies. I told tales of disasters, shipwrecks, battles, war heroes, Newfoundland inventors — like the Newfoundlander who had invented a device for diverting torpedoes and another who had made important refinements to the gas mask.

Then I lessened my workload by having my audience write a portion of the program; that is, I read on the air stories I encour-aged my listeners to send to me, stories that showed "how brave, hardy, smart, strong, proud, intelligent and successful Newfound-landers are."

"Some people," I said, "and some of them are living among us, don't think much of Newfoundlanders. I am trying to show that they always succeed every time they get a decent chance. Send me your own stories. Send me your verses, your home remedies, your recipes." I promised that all those whose items were used on the air would receive a free bar of Palmolive soap. I killed air time by announcing on each program how much air time I had so far filled as "The Barrelman."

"I have been broadcasting to you now for a total of seven thousand, three hundred and forty-three minutes," I said. "I have spoken seven hundred thousand, four hundred and ninety-seven words."

Field Day, December 3, 1940

BONG, BONG, BONG, BONG, BONG, BONG.

F. M. O'Leary presents "The Barrelman," a program dedicated to making Newfoundland better known to Newfoundlanders. And now, Joe Smallwood, the Barrelman.

"Good evening, Newfoundlanders. Here is tonight's interesting fact, sent to us by a Miss Fielding, whose fascinating letter I will read in full: 'Dear Mr. Barrelman: It has come to my attention that there are in the world a number of books — I am endeavouring to find out how many and will let you know when my research is complete — in which no mention whatsoever is made of Newfoundland.' BONG.

"Serve your pet Pet Milk. Pet Milk is made in Newfoundland and is therefore better than any other pet milk in the world. BONG.

"Miss Fielding further writes: 'I am myself in possession of several such books, including *A Guide Book to Chilean Songbirds*, the absence in which of the word *Newfoundland* is so inexplicable that I have written its publisher demanding an explanation.'

"The Barrelman says, 'Go to it, Miss Fielding.' This is the kind of pride in Newfoundland I was hoping my program would ignite. Why should we take this kind of treatment lying down? We deserve to be mentioned in books as often as anybody else. Imagine a book in which no mention whatsoever was made of Iceland.

"Newfoundlanders, send me your recipes, your sayings, your local customs. All over Newfoundland the old ways are dying out. I for one would want nothing to do with a Newfoundland in which it was no longer the tradition to shoot the Christmas pudding out of a pot with a shotgun. BONG.

"Buy Palmolive soap. It is not made in Newfoundland, but it smells better here than it does anywhere else and also cleans the skin more effectively. I myself have found this to be true. BONG.

"I am privileged to announce that among those people who listen with rapt fascination to my show each day is no less a personage than Governor Walwyn, who writes, 'Dear Barrelman: Congratulations on your marvellous program. Every day, Mrs. Walwyn and I invite people in from the street to sit with us in Government House around our little radio to listen to your show. At six-thirty, Mrs. Walwyn goes down to the end of the driveway and beckons to passers-by, hailing them with her now-familiar greeting: "Come one, come all, the Barrelman will start in fifteen minutes." Seconds before you go on the air, she comes running, skirts held aloft, back to the house with a horde of excited citizens behind her. What a merry time we have, her ladyship and I, listening to your program while our guests politely bolt down every drop of tea and every crumb of biscuits that we put before them, some so intent on not offending our hospitality that they selflessly forget to listen to you. It is all we can do to hear

your voice sometimes, what with all the munching and slurp-
ing that goes on, and no amount of urging can convince
them to put aside their concern for us and indulge themselves, which breaks our hearts, knowing as we do how
starved for information they must be.' BONG, BONG, BONG,
BONG, BONG, BONG.

"Well, ladies and gentlemen, the time has come to say
goodbye until tomorrow. This is the Barrelman, on behalf of
F. M. O'Leary, bidding you farewell from the masthead."

As I sat at my microphone in the radio studio in St. John's, I
remembered sailing the south coast with Andrews in the *Margaret
P.*, and then walking the ice-bound southwest coast; the people I
had met. Take away their radios and they lived not much differently than people in such places had a hundred, even two hundred
years ago.

Castaways making do with what they were able to salvage
from the wreck of their arrival.

And I had still not seen most of Newfoundland, the Great
Northern Peninsula, the northeast coast, the east coast beyond the
Bonavista, the coast or interior of Labrador. It was in such places
that the lost Newfoundlanders whose photographs appeared in the
Backhomer were born and from them made a clean break, never to
return. It was strange, sitting at my microphone, knowing I was
being listened to in places I had never seen and never would but
whose names I knew by heart. The people in these places knew my
voice but not my face, thought of me not as Joe Smallwood but as
the Barrelman, a mythical personage like Santa Claus.

When I first began broadcasting, I had to resist the urge to
shout to make myself heard, as if I thought I was addressing the
whole country through a loudspeaker. I sounded on my first broadcasts as though I were issuing a country-wide order to head inland
because of the imminent arrival of a tidal wave.

Nothing so enisles you like the sea. A people surrounded by wilderness can at least imagine that wilderness being cleared and occupied someday. I wanted to make it possible for my audience to suspend its disbelief in the existence of the outside world, at least for fifteen minutes a day, five days a week. The supply boats that came from some nebulous elsewhere and put into each bay once a month did not do that. Nor did the large ships that appeared, mirage-like, on the horizon, or the seagull-sized planes the people saw but could not hear.

I had inherited my father's terror of domesticity. I travelled to escape, not just the rote predictability and repetitiveness of life at home, but the loss of a sense of self that, for me at least, came with it, the feeling of being subsumed, submerged in that collective entity known as the family.

I went on many more field trips collecting material for "The Barrelman" than I need have. It was my latest excuse for spending time away from home, away from Clara and the children, to whom I must have seemed like a literal barrelman, aloft, aloof, removed. I drove to as many outports as I could reach in my second-hand Dodge, which, since no one but me drove it, was more my home than my new house was. I ate meals in it, slept in it, pulling over to the side of the road at dusk in the middle of nowhere.

I affected an interest in lustreware and drove around the bay collecting, inquiring, inspecting the contents of china cabinets — and only rarely did I wonder what in God's name I was doing or stop to think what a queer fish I had become. Anything rather than stay at home, than be at home when it got dark. Once a homesick exile, I was now a wanderlusting patriot.

Often, at dusk, a hundred miles from home, I parked on some headland, facing seaward, smoking one cigarette after another, watching the sunset. The sea either induced in you a fateful resignation or made you all the more ambitious, restless, determined to accomplish something that, even in the face of the eternal sea-scheme of things, would still endure. I had that abiding sense that something, though tantalizingly close, was out of my reach, but now it seemed to me that it would be for all time.

Even when I was not travelling, I often went out in the car at night and drove for hours through the city or parked on some hill where I could see it, better able than ever to appreciate my father's fondness for his deck.

On such nights, the whole island seemed to me a glorified outport, so hemmed in that to own a car was pointless, absurd, a mere reminder of your confinement. For the first time in my life, I understood how a man might be attracted to the sea, even prefer it to the land, especially an island. The land was secondary, a temporary elevation of the ocean floor over which the waters would close again someday.

The old men I saw in my drives around the bay, sitting side-on to their windows, looking out across the water that was often separated from them by nothing more than a stretch of beach, there and not there depending on the tide — I fancied that I understood them now. Each putting-out to sea you could imagine was the start of some journey that, though endless, was not pointless, the point being simply to go and keep on going. They sat, these men, looking out at the sea they were now too old to fish or even venture out onto. But still they were held fast, sea-spellbound.

On such nights, too, I thought of Fielding, whose life was more like that of a barrelman than mine, Fielding in her boarding-house, alone, unfettered, free. I envied her, missed her, wondered what her life was like now that she had quit the booze, and if, having quit it, she wondered why she had ever loved me, or if she ever really had.

I remembered how on edge we Smallwoods had been when my father wasn't drinking, his agitation, his craving nervousness so palpable that it spread to us, our bodies shaking in sympathy with his, so when finally he took a drink it seemed as though we all had. Surely no one could persist for years like that.

Sometimes, late at night, I drove down Cochrane Street, past her boarding-house, where Fielding's was often the only light still on. I pictured her up there, pursuing her solitary occupation while the city slept, writing through the night, sitting just out of sight, keeping vigil until between the Narrows rocks there appeared the first faint trace of blue. Then off to bed.

The Barrelman. Standing in his barrel on the masthead, keeping watch, gazing ahead into the future. Except the fog was in so close there was nothing to see, nothing now for years. To the doldrums we were in, no end in sight.

Fielding's Condensed
History of Newfoundland

Chapter Twenty-Four:

A DELEGATION OF GROVELLING INDIGENTS

It seems that by 1894, Newfoundland has learned its lesson.

It has been two years since St. John's was for the second time destroyed by fire. The colony is in the midst of a deep economic depression and unprecedented unemployment. It is bankrupt, all of its savings banks having collapsed. In other words, it will never be in a better position to negotiate the terms of union with Canada.

This statement will seem less strange in light of the following observation made by the British diplomat Alleyne Fitzherbert: "When dealing with Canadians, it is advantageous to seem to be negotiating from a position of weakness, for when faced with an abject opponent, they become concession-happy and will accede to almost anything."

Concession-happy, compassion-prone, suckers for a sob story, call them what you will, one cannot help pitying the Canadians when one imagines how they must have felt when they heard that a delegation of grovelling indigents was on its way to Ottawa from Newfoundland.

Warned by the Newfoundlanders that he better not hold it against them that they resoundingly rejected Confederation in 1869, Prime Minister Mackenzie Bowell mumbles that one thing Canada will never stoop to carry is…? On the question of what words he spoke next, historians agree it was either "a grudge" or "an economic sink-hole like Newfoundland."

After the Newfoundland delegation pours out its tale of woe, the Canadians propose such terms of union as might be expected from a people fated by an excess of compassion to be duped time and again by the unscrupulous paupers of Newfoundland.

The Canadians, so emotionally wrought up that to even think of negotiating further makes them weep, declare it to be their one and final offer. Luckily for them, they are dealing with a people whose character is just as fatally flawed. The Newfoundlanders pull a "Whiteway" and go home.

Unwilling to let history take its natural course, the head of the Newfoundland delegation, the meddlesome colonial secretary Sir Robert Bond steps in, pledges his own personal credit to underwrite a loan from England of three million dollars and "saves" the country.

Fort Pepperrell, 1943

THE COMMISSION of Government might have ended sooner if not for the war, during which it seemed that Newfoundland was triply occupied: by British civil servants and by British, Canadian and American servicemen. The reign of this hybrid occupation force was for many Newfoundlanders their first glimpse of the outside world.

"Someone ought to tell you people what century this is," an American soldier whom I was interviewing said in the fall of 1943.

I knew in theory that things were better in America than when I had been there, but I still thought of "America" as the New York of the 1920s.

It was the casual, staggering largesse of the Americans that impressed us the most. Once they entered the war, it seemed that army bases, airports, roads and drydocks popped up in Newfoundland overnight. St. John's was crawling with free-spending Americans, with their stories of how much better off their people back home were than Newfoundlanders.

The variety of uniforms worn by the men and women walking the streets of St. John's was bewildering, remindful, to me at least, not only of the war, but also of our tenuous identity, our non-status as a country, the interregnum that by now was eight years old. It seemed hard to imagine that pulled so many different ways, we could survive.

Each branch of each country's armed forces dressed differently — white, khaki, green, black, navy blue, grey — each colour marking the person wearing it as a foreigner. There was no Newfoundland Regiment in this war; we could not afford one. Our volunteers joined the British regiments or the merchant marine, dressed in British uniforms and fought with British weapons. In the city, from a distance, they were indistinguishable from the British. Only close up could you see the little coat-of-arms-bearing badges marking them as Newfoundlanders.

Though we were fighting on the same side as all these foreigners, though our national income had doubled because of their presence and twenty thousand unemployed Newfoundlanders had been put to work, I could not help resenting them. There were times when I could not stand to walk the streets, for anyone, of whatever age, who was not in uniform, was presumed to belong to another, remote, less interesting world. Or perhaps I only imagined it. I saw the Yanks smiling at my prisoner-of-war, concentration-camp physique, which I still had, having somehow managed to maintain it through twenty-seven years of peace. I was a whopping 127 pounds, balding and bespectacled.

I skulked about St. John's, my hands in the pockets of my overcoat, a cigarette in my mouth, watching all the robust servicemen walking about arm in arm with local girls. The absurd image of a whole generation of Newfoundland men stranded for life in bachelorhood because the Yanks had stolen their girls away flashed through my mind.

I had another, more personal reason to resent the presence of the Americans in particular. Radio Station VOUS (the Voice of the United States) had started broadcasting out of Fort Pepperrell in St. John's. It carried, commercial free, all the most popular American network programs, most of them not previously available in Newfoundland, as well as the armed-forces broadcasts, endless war updates that seemed to take it for granted that the American war effort was uppermost in the minds of everyone.

This station was more listened to than any local station, including mine, and I took its popularity as an affront to Newfoundland and a threat to my livelihood. I became a bigger "boomer" of Newfoundland than ever. I never spoke a word on air against the Americans, of course, but neither, except when I absolutely had to, did I mention them.

On a rainy night in mid-October, I drove to Fort Pepperrell to see a movie at the Pleasantville movie-house. While standing in line outside, I noticed that American servicemen were being allowed to walk straight in.

"Why should all the Yanks be going in?" I shouted, "What's wrong with Newfoundlanders? This is our country, isn't it?"

I was among townies who knew I was the Barrelman, knew me by sight, and I had even signed a few autographs. A big lumber-jacket-wearing fellow at the head of the line shouted, "You tell 'em, Joe." But when the next Yank, a corporal with two chevrons on his shoulder, passed in front of him, he said nothing.

"Wait your turn in line," I shouted, stepping out of the queue so the American could see me. The corporal, a tall, lanky, pimply-faced young fellow, stopped just short of the door and at first seemed dumbfounded.

"We built the place," he said, when he recovered, affecting a good-natured chuckle at my audacity. "It wouldn't even be here if not for us."

A pair of white-helmeted military policemen seemed to appear from out of nowhere.

"There are women here soaking wet," I said. "And older people, too. At least let them in." That "at least" gave me away.

"Plenty of seats for everyone," one of the military policemen said.

"Then why don't you let us in?" I said.

"We wouldn't get all the best seats then, would we?" the cor-poral said. He flashed a grin at me, then went inside.

"Never mind, Joe," said the big fellow at the head of the line.

"Never mind them, Joe," "Forget about them, Joe," men mumbled up and down the line. Someone snickered and was told to shut up.

The next few servicemen who went in were ineffectually heck-led, but after that nothing more was said. We waited there in the rain, deferring to the servicemen. The MPs, the rain spattering on their white helmets, stood in conversation at the head of the line. An easterly wind was blowing up through the Gut from Quidi Vidi Village, straight in from the sea.

I told myself I should have provoked something, got some Yank, a military policeman, to lay his hands on me, take a swing at me; that would have got the townies going, one of their own being manhandled by some Yank, the Barrelman being picked on by someone twice his size and half his age.

I stood there brooding in the rain, an old, all-too-familiar feel-ing of inconsequentiality taking hold of me. The land on which Fort Pepperrell and other bases in Newfoundland was built had been leased by the Americans for ninety-nine years. Bargained down from one hundred by the British commissioners, no doubt. Ninety-nine seemed longer anyway. An eternity. It was what crim-inals who were not meant to see the light of day again were sen-tenced to. Not even in my family, whose members were notorious for their longevity, had anyone lived that long. I would have to live to 141 to witness the Americans' departure. The Americans here for ninety-nine years. Just in case.

Who knew what the coming decades would bring? The Com-mission of Government was here for no one knew how much longer. I was forty-two years old, and if I was to speak out loud to anyone now the ambitions I had when I was twenty, they would laugh. I vowed that I would leave Newfoundland if things went on

like this much longer. But where would I go? I was glad Clara was
not with me tonight. I winced to think how I would have looked
beside her standing in the rain, watching her. I imagined with
what envy she might have looked at the local women walking into
the movie-house on the arms of their Yankee sweethearts.

Finally, the MPs started letting Newfoundlanders in. I shuffled forward and, when I was almost at the box office, considered
stepping out of line and leaving in a gesture of defiance. The Barrelman slinking away like a whipped cur with his tail between his
legs. I was suddenly keenly aware of how little my local fame
would have mattered to any American who by some chance was
made aware of my existence. The Barrelman. It was like some
ironic nickname, for I was anything but barrel-shaped.

I paid my twenty-five-cent admission at the box office. A WAC
in a khaki hat took my money and handed me my ticket. The lights
were still up when I went inside. Most of the preferred seats were,
as the corporal had hinted they would be, occupied by the Americans. A few of the ones still empty were marked "reserved." Newfoundlanders sat off to either side or in the middle section at the
back, a drab civilian horseshoe within which the Americans sat,
looking, because they were all wearing the same uniform, as if a
light were shining on them.

The Newfoundlanders did not look as though they minded
the seating arrangements in the least. The Fort Pepperrell movie-
house was by far the most popular one in the city. Just released
movies that otherwise would not have made it to St. John's until
years later, if ever, played there every Friday and Saturday night.
Tonight's movie starred Betty Grable and Clark Gable, "Grable
and Gable" as they were billed on the sparkling new marquee outside. There was a murmur of excitement and anticipation in the
air. I half expected to see Grable and Gable come strolling arm in
arm down the aisle.

I settled into one of the plush red seats, choosing one on the
left-wing aisle, and looked around. The corporal had been right.

This was their movie-house, a pavilion of Americana, a haven for the homesick, who, although they had to spend time in Newfoundland, did not have to live like Newfoundlanders. It was absurd to resent them for it, I told myself. Newfoundlanders in this situation and having the means would have done the same.

I was just beginning to feel a little cheered and reconciled to my circumstances when I heard a familiar gait on the steps behind me. First foot, second foot, stop. First foot, second foot, stop. I had no doubt it was Fielding, whom I had not seen in months.

My heart rose, and so did I, with the intention of inviting her to join me. She would be ideal company for this occasion; she would wittily dismiss the Yanks as she had for so long been doing with the British.

I turned to face her. It was Fielding, but she was not alone. She was being helped down the steps by one of *them*, the first time I had ever seen her accept such help from anyone. He held her left hand and supported her left elbow while Fielding with her right hand held her cane. Each row of the movie-house fell silent as they passed, everyone watching this display of gallantry, gawking at Fielding, who was taller than her escort and who some of the Newfoundlanders must have recognized, for there was much whispering and conferring of heads.

Fielding, I was certain, was embellishing her limp, not so much to win sympathy for herself, it seemed, as to magnify the gallantry of the young man to whose arm she clung as if, without him, she would have fallen to the floor.

Fielding, even roaring drunk, had never needed this much help to negotiate a set of stairs. And here she was, sober — I wondered if there had been some change for the worse in her physical condition.

At first I assumed that having seen her trying to navigate the stairs by herself, this man had offered his assistance, and I was still intending to invite her to join me. He did not wear the folding, inverted wallet-like cap of the enlisted man, but an officer's peaked cap. I caught a glimpse of his insignia: two horizontal black bars, a captain. Fielding wore some sort of fur wrap that I had never seen before, but otherwise no coat. And there was no coat check in the movie-house. She must have come with someone. Him. He must have sent a car for her. Or they might have had dinner somewhere on the base.

I had halfway extended my hand and, forced to do something to disguise the gesture, put it on the back of my seat and with my other hand pretended to wipe something from the cushion. Then, head bowed, affecting a kind of brisk irritability, I turned abruptly and sat down again. I prayed that Fielding hadn't seen me. I thanked God that she and her captain would not be sitting behind me.

They went on by. No question about it, Fielding was playing up her limp for all it was worth. When they reached the American section, the enlisted men jumped to their feet — clearly they had not been expecting a captain — and stood at attention, saluting — saluting Fielding, it might have been. I could well imagine how much she was enjoying herself. The captain, a trimly robust man who looked to be in his mid-thirties, perfunctorily returned their salute. The enlisted men sat down again, though a few of them and their dates vacated a clutch of seats in the middle about twelve rows from the front. Fielding and her captain, with no one directly behind them, in front of them or beside them, took their seats.

I was flushed. My ears were burning. I was certain the people behind me had noticed the change in my complexion. This — Fielding and the captain — could not be a date of any kind, I assured myself. The captain was merely escorting her so she would not have to sit alone, merely being chivalrous in the army tradition to a woman whose game leg had left her on the shelf and forced her into earning her own living.

There was still the question of how they had met. I watched them. He leaned close as if to confide in her and Fielding laughed out loud. A girlish laugh. The captain laughed, too. Fielding, I

could not help noticing, was a good deal more attractive since she
had stopped drinking. Her face was full, her eyes wide and round.
I looked closely. It hardly seemed possible, but she was wearing
make-up. Lipstick. Some sort of rouge. When the captain looked
away for a second, Fielding looked at him, darted a glance at him,
just for a moment, almost shyly, as if making a good impression
on him mattered to her. I had never seen her give anyone such a
look before, had never known anyone to make her laugh out loud
like that.

The lights went down. "The Star-Spangled Banner" began to
play. The American flag, fluttering, appeared onscreen. I saw, in
silhouette, the captain help Fielding to her feet. As if she needed
helping. I recalled her scaling the iron fence the day the Colonial
Building was mobbed. Fielding must have arranged all this, I
thought. She must be planning to write a piece on the Americans,
must have contacted someone at Fort Pepperrell and, not knowing the sort of columns she wrote and charmed by the novelty of
a woman reporter and further by her disability, which Fielding
would somehow have found a way to work into the conversation, they had invited her to be their guest at Pleasantville and
had appointed this captain to escort her to the movies. What a
surprise they were in for. What a shock it would be to the captain
to see how she portrayed him in her column.

The anthem ended. All sat down. The newsreels began. A voice
that sounded as though it had been narrating world events since
time began told of the impact the Americans were already having on
the war. There was footage of an American destroyer, all guns blaz-
ing, and of presumably enemy planes trailing smoke as they nose-
dived into the sea. Pearl Harbor was mentioned and Roosevelt was
heard describing how the Americans in their "righteous might"
were going to retaliate. The enlisted men cheered. I watched Fielding and her captain. Every time he pointed at the screen, Fielding
nodded vigorously. She was either sincerely interested in what he
was saying, or sincerely wanted him to think she was.

The movie must have been rushed into production to shore up American morale, for Grable and Gable were war-crossed lovers, she a WAC, he a pilot in the possibility of whose death at the hands of the enemy we were supposed to believe. I was not convinced, but I was hoping for it nonetheless as if it were Fielding's captain up there on the screen.

When I guessed it was only minutes until the lights went up for the intermission, I decided to go outside to the lobby. I doubted that Fielding would go to the bother of pretending she needed her captain's help to scale the steps, but she might get up to stretch her legs, might turn around and see me.

I went out to the concession area, where a line-up for popcorn had already begun to form. I lit a cigarette and stood at the glass doors of the lobby, looking out. The wind was blowing even harder now. On Quidi Vidi Lake, there was a lop whose white-caps I could make out even in the darkness. What a night. I considered leaving; I told myself it would be the sensible thing to do. But I stayed.

I thought of what Fielding had once said to me while sitting on her bed in her boarding-house. "I am not often proposed to, but I am often propositioned." I wondered again if this had been an invitation. Why could I never read what people meant, what women meant, when they said such things? An invitation to be just one of many, to join the crowd, was that what she meant? Had she been mocking me to get revenge for that night in New York? What, if I had taken her up on the offer, if an offer it was, would she have done? Not that I *would* have taken her up on the offer. Could this American captain have already got wind of her reputation? Did she really have one?

I did not often go to places of entertainment, even movie-houses. Sheer melancholic boredom had driven me out of the house tonight. Perhaps Fielding was often seen in the company of men. I had many times considered asking around about her, but I could think of no way of doing it that would not make me look ridiculous or cause someone to be suspicious of my intentions. Smallwood, married man and confirmed prude, inquiring into the private life of an unmarried woman about whom jokes of a certain kind had been going round for years.

"Excuse me, please," a voice behind me said, that of an American from somewhere in the South. I was blocking the door. In one motion, I turned and stepped aside ... for Fielding and her captain, who were leaving the movie at intermission.

"Oh — " Fielding said, sounding genuinely startled. O Captain! my Captain! What school poem did that come from? She looked flustered. So must I have. The captain looked back and forth between us. Fielding extended her black-gloved hand. I shook it lightly.

"I haven't seen you in quite some time," she said, as if it was unusual for our paths not to have crossed for so long. She was pretending to this captain to be someone or something she was not and was tacitly inviting me, even pleading with me, to play along. I looked at the name-plate on his tunic. Captain D. Hanrahan.

I would be damned if I would play along for Fielding's sake, whatever she was up to. She must have seen this in my eyes. "Captain Hanrahan," she interjected, "this is Joe Smallwood, a colleague of mine in the journalism trade." I had never heard her speak my first name before. That she had done so on the occasion of introducing me to an American soldier whose intentions where she was concerned were all too obvious from the stilted way she spoke enraged me. I thought of the knowing look in that corporal's eyes after I withdrew my horns while standing outside with all the other Newfoundlanders in the rain.

"So what have you been up to lately, Fielding?" I said. I knew it was exactly this, my calling her by her last name, that she had been trying to head off. I was not about to call her Sheilagh for the first time in my life just because she had a captain on her arm. He took a step forward.

"I don't believe that is the proper way to address a lady," he said, in his southern U.S. accent. I saw now that he was younger than I had guessed, in his late twenties perhaps. Young to be a captain. His rank and the way he carried himself had fooled me.

"No," I said, "It's — "

Fielding stepped forward, put her cane between us, pressed it, in a way that implied familiarity, against the captain's chest.

"Everyone in the newspaper business calls me Fielding," she said. "I take it as a compliment. The men all call each other by their last names. Smallwood, this is Captain David Hanrahan."

Not until he extended his hand did Fielding lower the cane. I shook his hand. He held mine so firmly while he spoke that I could feel his pulse. "You'll have to forgive me, Smallwood," he said. "We in the military only address our subordinates by their last names."

"See you again, Smallwood," Fielding said, smiling. By the time I realized that I had been slighted by this captain, they were headed out the door.

Outside, beneath the marquee, they paused while the captain opened an umbrella. Fielding took his outstretched arm and they walked off, umbrella angled into the wind, in the direction of the officers' barracks. I turned away and lit another cigarette. What did it matter to me, why should it matter to me, what Fielding did and with whom?

Fielding's Condensed
History of Newfoundland

Chapter Twenty-Five:

GOSSE *FILS*, GOSSE *PERE*, AND PROWSE

Prowse's *History* is published in 1895.

It sits on the desk in front of us as we write, goading us to refutation, disputation, sustaining us through this corrective.

"D. W. Prowse, Q.C." A pair of initials pretentiously placed on either side of his surname. A prefatory note by Edmund Gosse.

My name has no need of initials, my *History* no need of Edmund Gosse and his fond reminiscences of a place he never set eyes on in his life. He devotes more of his two-page note to capelin than he does to Prowse.

He claims an "old family tie with Newfoundland," namely, that his father spent eight years here running about with a beetle bottle, catching insects, managing to pass off as "entomology" behaviour that in others would have been sufficient proof of madness.

We are supposed to be charmed that the Gosse household in Devonshire was full of insects, pickled and preserved, from Newfoundland.

Perhaps Gosse might not have found them so charming had they attacked him in the manner their like did me when last I ventured out of doors six months ago.

Perhaps Gosse *fils* was kept from visiting Newfoundland by reading this passage in Sir Richard Whitbourne's *Discourse on the Island of Newfoundland*: "Those flies seeme to have a greate power and authourity upon all loytering people that come to the New-foundland; for they have the property that when they find any such lying lazily, or sleeping in the Woods, they will presently bee more nimble to seize on them, than any Sargeant will bee to arrest a man for debt."

But no mind. It is November now, and even the hardiest of bugs will have retreated to whatever hellish places bugs retreat to in the winter.

We are supposed to feel a kinship with Gosse, or acknowledge his with Newfoundland, because there arrived each year of his childhood at their house in Devon kegs of capelin from Carbonear. Easy enough it is to speak bravely of capelin when they are dead and if put down one's shirt do not flop about and cause one to act in a manner amusing to one's less bookish siblings.

We are supposed to commiserate with Gosse that his father did not live to see the fruit of Prowse's labours. Rest easy, Philip Henry Gosse. In what agonies might you have spent your final days had you not had the good fortune to die before you were obliged, by your son's sycophantic friendship with its author, to read the cursed book.

That BOOK! Had we departed from this world ignorant of its existence we should have been happier than we expect to be when the final curtain falls. Little comfort is it now that upon the publication of our History all memory of his will from the minds of the reading public be erased. If not from mine. No, never from mine, unless one of the balms of heaven be amnesia!

The Most Intimate of Circumstances

I READ FIELDING'S COLUMN every day for the next few weeks, still expecting to find in it some irony-laden account of her "date" or some send-up of the Yanks, who, it seemed to me, badly needed sending up. But nothing like that appeared. I even thought I detected a certain mellowing in the way she wrote, but dismissed it as being nothing more than my imagination.

I did not go so far towards acknowledging the possibility that Fielding might be "in love" as to think the words. Even had I acknowledged the possibility, it would have been only to refute it something like this: Fielding could no more fall in love than I could. The relationship we had had was the closest to falling in love that either of us would come. It was not in our natures. There were too many more important things to dedicate one's life to than romantic love. It was because we agreed on this one thing that we could not bear each other's company. I had married sensibly, and Fielding, sensibly, had remained unmarried. Still, it was important to me that I knew and sometimes crossed paths with a kindred soul of the opposite sex. It was important to me that Fielding go on being Fielding, and in the life of the real Fielding there was no place for Captain Hanrahan.

And so, what happened three months later in mid-January was, at first at least, almost comforting. I met an acquaintance of mine from the *Evening Telegram* while walking along Duckworth Street one day. We talked for a while, then parted.

"Oh, by the way," he shouted back. "Did you hear about Fielding?"

"No," I said, trying to sound offhandedly interested, "what about her?" He made a drinking motion, hand to his mouth, head tilted back. Then, shaking his head and grinning, he walked off.

Fielding drinking again after — what had it been? — nearly seven years. I had not seen her since that night at Fort Pepperrell. She had shown no signs of backsliding then.

I headed straight for her boarding-house on foot, for it was closer than my car. I dreaded the thought that this Hanrahan meant so much to her that he had something to do with her going back on the booze. Had he jilted her? Had he been killed in action? This last possibility was intolerable. A lover whom she had not known long enough to discover his flaws, whom she would idealize forever.

I climbed the stairs to her floor, walked down the dingy, cabbage-reeking hallway to her room. I could understand why she lived there when she was drinking and spending all her money on Scotch, but why she had stayed there through seven years of sobriety was beyond me.

Taped to the door was a note bearing Fielding's barely legible scrawl: "Shorthall: Gone to Press Club. Do not disturb unless absolutely necessary. Tell Harrington to run one from the file. F." Shortall was the printer's devil who collected her copy every day to spare her the walk to the *Telegram* and back. She did not own a car, did not have a driver's licence. The "file" was an assortment of all-purpose columns of hers that the *Telegram* kept on hand for days when she was too sick or otherwise indisposed to write.

I all but ran down the hill to my car, then drove to the Press Club, where reporters in St. John's gathered after work but at which, as far as I knew, Fielding was not a regular. But then, neither was I. It was three o'clock in the afternoon.

The Press Club was in the basement of an office building, accessible from a narrow alleyway that ran between Duckworth Street and Water Street. I descended the two steep flights of stairs to the landing, opened the door and went inside. Lit only by a fireplace just inside the door and by one ground-level window in the far wall, the place was so dark that at first I could make out next to nothing and simply stood there, waiting for my eyes to adjust to the lack of light.

I barely heard her call my name, though she pronounced it emphatically as if she had already said it several times to no effect. I looked in the direction of her voice and saw her in the alcove formed by the walls of the washroom and the coat check. She was sitting on a pew-like bench, side-on to a table, with her bad leg fully extended. Her left hand was heavily wrapped in a white-gauze bandage.

"What happened?" I said.

"Fell down," she said. There were two brim-full glasses of Scotch on the table.

"I'm replenishing with my own supply," she said, tapping her blazer. I heard the clunk of what I presumed must be her flask. "Don't tell him," she said, cocking her head in the direction of the bar, where a waiter from whom she was hidden and whom I knew in passing nodded at me, looking as if he was glad to have the reinforcements.

"What can I get you, Mr. Smallwood?" he said.

"Just a glass of ginger beer," I said and sat down opposite Fielding. We were the only customers. The place oppressed me. I was all too familiar with the way bars look and feel on winter afternoons when there is not much light left. I remembered it from my childhood, when on Saturdays my mother sent me to fetch my father home from one of his "establishments."

"What brings *you* here?" she said.

"You do," I said.

She put her cigarette in the ashtray, picked up her Scotch, sipped it, put it down, picked up the cigarette. "Best I can do with one hand," she said. "Who told you I was here? Harrington?"

I said nothing.

"Figures," she said. "So you're today's knight in shining armour."

"You had it licked," I said. "Why did you start again?"

"Suddenly I'm everybody's business."

"How long?" I said.

"Two weeks, I think," she said. "Haven't written a word in two weeks. More fun talking, don't you think? I was talking to myself when you arrived."

The waiter came with my beer, looked at Fielding, then meaningfully at me.

"Been giving him a hard time, have you?" I said when he went away.

"He has come to the conclusion that there is no way that he can throw a crippled woman with a broken wrist out of his bar that will not make him look ridiculous." She stretched out her leg, wagged a new orthopedic, thick-heeled shoe back and forth. "It's supposed to make me limp less. I think it's why I fell." She patted her cane, which lay on the bench beside her, as if to assure it that it would never be replaced by this new shoe.

"What happened, Fielding?" I said.

She shrugged.

"Seven years," I said. "Something must have happened. Was it Captain Hanrahan?" I prayed for a scornful reply.

"I haven't seen Captain Hanrahan," she said, "since that night you two met at the movie-house. It was by that time not quite three days since he and I first met."

"You seemed to know him fairly well," I said.

She shook her head. "I didn't," she said. "I didn't know him at all."

"So you started drinking again for no reason?" I said.

"I stopped for no particular reason," she said. "I stopped. I started. As simple as that. Things are almost always that simple, Smallwood. Almost everything is exactly what it seems to be. No surprises. No disappointments. Life so far has met my expectations."

"I think you should go home, Fielding," I said. "You've only been back on the bottle for two weeks. It wouldn't be that hard to quit again. Not as hard as it was before. Not as hard as it will be a year from now."

She picked up one of the glasses and drank it dry. "I should have stayed home," she said. "But I can't bear to be by myself these days."

"I'll go home with you," I said.

She raised her eyebrows and put her hand on the neckline of her dress.

"I mean I'll make sure you get there," I said. "I'll even listen to you for a while."

"I probably should leave before the boys from the *Telegram* show up," she said. "You never know who might take advantage of a girl with a bum leg. Lucky for me it's hollow, too. I'm widely presumed to be hard up for it, you know."

"Yes, I know," I said under my breath as I stood up. "You're not often proposed to, but you're often propositioned."

"I'm often disposed to, too," she said.

"You're drunk," I said.

"Probably," she said. "I'm out of practice after all." She downed her remaining drink, took some money from her coat pocket and put it on the table, then picked up her cane from the bench. I left some money, too.

"Where's your purse?" I said.

"Do you mean to say, Smallwood," she said, "that in all this time, you've never noticed that I don't carry a purse?"

She laughed, eased out from behind the table, then stood up. Swayed, eyes closed. I took her beneath the arm.

"Out we go," I said. "Purse or no purse."

"You haven't touched your ginger beer," she said.

"Out," I said, waving to the sheepishly grateful bartender.

Outside, we barely managed to climb the stairs together. Fielding paused every few seconds to lean back against the building, her overcoat open, her bandaged hand on her chest, her breath coming in rasping plumes of frost. She closed her eyes and looked as though she was ready to fall.

"Come on," I said. "My car is parked right at the top of the steps."

We made it to the car and Fielding, once inside, revived somewhat, catching her breath, smiling, closing her eyes in relief as if we had found shelter from a cloudburst. I drove to her boarding-house and helped her up the stairs to her room, the door of which she had left unlocked.

"Wait here," she said, "there are some things I have to put away." She closed the door. I heard her inside, moving slowly about, her cane clunking on the hardwood floor. I heard a door, a closet door it must have been, opening then closing. Likewise some dresser drawers. Fielding crossed the floor again.

There was a prolonged silence, then suddenly the sound of the cane clattering with force on the floor and something overturning with a crash. I pushed open the door and hurried inside. Fielding, still clutching her cane, lay supine on the floor, her chest heaving, beside her an upended kitchen chair. "I'm fine," she said. "I'm fine. It's just my leg. And that damn new boot. Nothing new in falling down. Done it a thousand times."

I helped her to her feet, followed her as she headed for her bed, a daybed that was pushed against the wall between her closet and the bathroom. She collapsed onto it, lifted her bad leg up with her good one, hooking one boot beneath the other. She was instantly asleep, her cane companion-like on the bed beside her.

She might be there for days like that, I thought, in her coat on top of the blankets.

"Fielding," I said, nudging her shoulder. She stirred, murmured some complaint.

"*Fielding*," I said. "You've got to take off your coat and boots and get under the blankets."

In the manner of someone irritated at having been woken from a deep sleep to perform some pointless task, she sat up in bed and swiftly began to undress. She seemed amazingly supple under the circumstances — sitting up in bed without support, with one bad leg and one bad arm, while profoundly drunk. She gave a little hop, just enough to raise her backside so she could pull her coat out from beneath her. She was wearing a white blouse and a full-length pleated black skirt.

When she drew her legs up to get at her boots, her skirt and the slip beneath it rode up almost to her knees. I caught a glimpse of garter belts and the undersides of thighs. Her bad leg was closer to the wall, but I could see it, clearly from the knee down, in shadow from there up. She wore nylons, but I saw that from just above the heel to behind her knee, her leg was serrated as if parts of her lower calf had years ago been cut away and what was left laminated pink and red and white. Above the knee, the serration continued, but it looked as if more of the flesh of her upper calf had survived.

Fielding swiftly unsnapped the buttons of her boots; as she was tugging the boots off, toe of one boot on the heel of the other, her skirt and slip slid down into her lap and I was afforded a more detailed view of the undergarments of a woman who was not my wife than I had ever seen. Finally chastened, I looked away and waited.

After I heard the squeaking of bedsprings, which I assumed meant she had climbed beneath the blankets, I turned around.

Among the articles of clothing on the floor were her blouse and skirt. She lay with the blankets pulled up to her chin, her arms outside them, eyes closed. Asleep again.

I thought of her legs. The left leg was about half as wide as the right, the leg of another, smaller woman or the leg of a child, as if, as she aged, that one limb had lagged behind. On top it was intact, unwithered, almost as shapely as the other one.

She opened her eyes, staring straight at me as if she had been watching all along.

"I should go," I said.

"Pull up that chair and stay a while," she said. I turned the chair upright, placed it even farther from the bed than it had been. From where I sat, I could see out her one window. It was getting dark. A snow flurry was encroaching slowly from the Brow, blotting out more and more of the city, the black felt roofs of flat-topped houses.

"It's not that hard to look the other way," she said. "Really it's not. Most men manage it. Even under the most intimate of circumstances."

My heart hammered. I could think of nothing to say.

"I suppose it's not fair of me to talk like that," she said. "I'm drunk. You're not. You're married. I'm not."

The snow pattered lightly against the window and the room grew darker. I thought of what her legs would have looked like pressed flat against the blankets, the bad leg sunken slightly so you could not see the scar. I pictured two flawless but mismatched legs, a disparate, inverted, lopsided V-like pair. And me between them? Had any men seen her like that? How many? It might just all be talk. Fielding starting rumours about herself. Her wanting everyone to think, to wonder. It might be that was all she had. Talk. Had any man ever touched her there, on the underside of her bad leg. Would she want him to? Would he want to? Did I? I thought of scenes from movies and books in which men gallantly pretended not to mind some scar or physical defect and thereby proved their everlasting love. But in the movies it was always some barely perceptible imperfection, a little lightning bolt above the lip.

I could not. I could not do it. No matter how flat she lay. No matter how much my weight sank her legs into the bed. I could not do it because I was married, I told myself. Because she was drunk and just back on the bottle after seven years. Otherwise—

"Hanrahan is my half-brother," she said. "His first name is David. I also have a half-sister named Sarah. The issue of my mother's second marriage to a Doctor Hanrahan of Gramercy Park."

"I don't remember you going to see them in New York," I said.

"I didn't," she said. "I would have had to see my mother, too. And my stepfather probably. Neither of which I wanted to do."

"Hanrahan didn't sound like he was from New York," I said.

"He went to Virginia when he was seventeen. To a military college. He was only at Fort Pepperrell for three days, but he looked me up. Knock, knock, I open the door and there he is."

"And something has happened to him?" I said.

She nodded. "I used the present tense to describe him. I should have used the past." I did not know that she was crying until I saw a tear emerge from beneath her eyelid and run down beside her nose.

"Are you sure you'll be all right?" I lamely said. She nodded. "What if I just sat here?" I said. "Until you fall asleep?"

She nodded again, turned her face away from me.

I sat there until the room was dark. Fielding, eyes closed and unmistakably asleep, went on leaking tears. Her face, in repose, was quite relaxed, her breathing deep and regular. What did she think of me, I wondered. Did she think I wanted to but lacked the courage? To how many others did she extend such invitations? I looked at her grey hair with its tinge of yellow, still full, still young, despite its colour. Her nicotine-stained fingers on the coverlet, the bandaged hand cradled tenderly against her side. There must have been no one there to keep her from falling when she fell.

"Fielding," I said, as if the name expressed completely what she was, who she was, this woman I was watching over and whose bed I did not dare go any closer to. Her tears kept coming. Her heart sending forth a surplus of tears while her guard was down, seeping sorrow while she slept. I stayed until the tears were coming minutes apart. I stood up.

I could kiss her now and she would never know. But she would see it, see something in my eyes when next we met that would put me at a disadvantage. I had said no. I had had my chance and made my decision.

On the way out, I removed from the door the note to the printer's devil telling him where she was. I set off to the *Telegram* and conveyed to Harrington her message that she was indisposed.

No sooner was I in my car again than it occurred to me that it was still not too late to go back, to climb into bed beside her. It could all be done in the darkness without words. There was no question of my leaving Clara, of course, nor would Fielding want me to. It was just —

Lately, during times when I had felt as if the world without me in it would in no way be diminished, I had found myself thinking of Fielding. It was not that this sustained me, not that she was some sort of antidote to despair. It was just that at such moments, an image of her came unbidden to my mind. Not the lights that in my childhood traced out the streets at night as I stood looking down upon them from the back deck on the Brow. Not the faces of my children, not Clara's as she stood in the doorway waving and I shouted to her from the car that I was leaving for a month or maybe more. Not these, but Fielding.

I pictured her waiting at the gates of Bishop Feild, outside the gates, holding the bars and watching as I walked across the field to meet her. Behind her was the sloping city, its old black rooftops gleaming after rain. And beyond the city, through the Narrows, the sea, which, after all, it seemed, was not my fate and which I no longer feared. I imagined it was summer, early evening, not yet dark. We wound our way among the streets, following the street-car route to where the car barn was and past it to where a train that should not have been leaving at that time of day sat waiting just for us. We boarded the train together and settled in our seats. In my mind, our leaving like this broke no one's heart, no one felt abandoned or betrayed. We would not be coming back, but nei-ther would our journey ever end. Could I leave my wife and chil-dren? Fielding's mother left her husband and her child....

What a fool the woman made me be. Even if she *had* agreed, for me to do what I'd imagined would have been the end of every-thing I hoped for, for no man who left his wife and child would ever be elected in St. John's or otherwise amount to anything. And would a life with Fielding have made up for that? Stupid, point-less, adolescent dreams, fantasies of escape, not from my life, but from life itself. I felt sorry for her for having lost her half-brother, but that was all.

Instead of going back to her, I went to the radio station. I had done almost no preparation, got there just in time to go on the air. The station manager was in a panic. I was supposed to give him hours of notice if I couldn't make it. I somehow managed to get through fifteen minutes, ringing the ship's bell, feeling ridiculous as I yanked once on the cord before and after each advertisement. This was what I did; this was who I was. A man who read tooth-paste and pet-milk advertisements to an audience of people clois-tered in their outports by the sea. I was not a man who made love to women on winter afternoons.

It was probably the most uninspired, perfunctory episode of "The Barrelman" I ever did. When it was over, I got out of there as quickly as I could.

By now it was fully dark. The early evening darkness of mid-winter in St. John's. It had never seemed to get dark my first win-ter in New York, and by the second winter, I had revised my notion of what darkness was. During my first winter back in New-foundland after five years in New York, I could not believe it had ever been this dark before. How had I never noticed? This darkness was like the prevailing wind. It came, self-propelled, across the ocean on some mission of obliteration not primarily concerning us. We just happened to be in the way, in the middle of the ocean, a place to erase while passing time between the Old World and the New.

She had asked me in such a way that if I turned her down, I would seem to be doing so because of her leg. "It's not that hard to look the other way. Really it's not. Most men manage it. Even under the most intimate of circumstances." Most men. So presumably there were some who tried but did not manage it. Did she say it for her own sake or for mine? It's not me you'll be rejecting, just my leg. I wouldn't blame you if you did. As if she knew that I wanted to and that her leg was all that held me back. Perhaps she hardly knew what she was saying. She was drunker than I'd ever seen her and grieving for Hanrahan.

Virginia. The continent's first colony. Jamestown. The birthplace of America. A hundred and twenty years after Cabot broadsided Newfoundland, yet so far ahead of us by now that Newfoundlanders went there to begin again. I remembered him from Pleasantville. No rough edges. Almost a parody of chivalry, gallantry. In his voice a kind of drawling grace. A captain before the age of thirty. Star graduate of some military academy renowned for teaching horsemanship, no doubt. Fielding's affluent half-brother.

I phoned Clara to tell her I had to work late. She was used to such calls. I could not go home. I drove aimlessly around the city, or not altogether aimlessly, for I often found myself approaching Fielding's boarding-house from one direction or another. Sometimes I glanced up to see if her light was on, sometimes resisted doing so just to prove that I could. Always, her room was dark. She must still be sleeping. It had been only a few hours since I had left her. She had been so exhausted that in spite of the booze, she might sleep for days.

I parked the car in empty lots throughout the city and sat in silence, thinking. Would she remember having extended her invitation when next we met? Would she pretend to have forgotten? Would we both tacitly agree it hadn't happened?

About ten o'clock, assuring myself that I would soon go home, I drove in sight of her boarding-house again and saw that this time her light was on. Far from sleeping for days, she was up already. Perhaps working, working for the first time in weeks, revived despite my rejection, reinvigorated, diverted from her sorrow by my act of kindness. I pictured her writing longhand at her desk, unable to use the typewriter, her bad hand on her lap. Better she was thus engaged than at the same desk drinking, holding a bottle of Scotch between her knees while trying to untwist the cap with her one good hand.

Her light went off. Perhaps she had merely been to the bathroom. I put the key in the ignition, ready to head home at last ... and saw Prowse emerge from Fielding's boarding-house, prosperous Prowse in a long beige overcoat, putting on his leather gloves, jauntily skipping down the steps, his arms swinging like a sprinter's. I watched him walk down Cochrane Street away from me to what I now recognized to be his car. Had it been there all along, every time I had driven by? It could not have been. For half the time since I had finished the show? For all of it? Surely I would have seen it. Surely it was only there since the last time I drove by. Twenty minutes at the most.

When Prowse reached his car, he lit a cigarette, then turned and faced the boarding-house, looked up at the window, which I was able to see quite well for I had slouched down behind the wheel to avoid detection.

Fielding's light came on, went off. Prowse kept looking up. Came on again, went off again. Prowse tossed down his cigarette, turned, got in his car and drove off, accelerating a little too quickly, so that the car fishtailed slightly on the snow-covered road, then straightened out. As if Fielding had signalled him to do exactly that.

Prowse who threatened to cane her. And would have if not for Slogger Anderson. And scorned her on the playing grounds once her star had fallen. And with me wrote that letter which appeared in all the papers. And crossed over to the British and grabbed me when I said that I would wring Hope Simpson's neck.

Prowse in Fielding's room. In Fielding's arms. In Fielding's bed. A signal of some kind that dimming of the lights had been. How familiar must they be to be using signals? Lovers using signals. Lovers' little games. Prowse standing by his car, looking up, waiting for Fielding to bid him goodnight; their private, presumably long-established, signal. Prowse had not signalled, had not waved. But then Fielding's one light switch was nowhere near the window; it was just inside the door. He knew she could not see him while she signalled. On, off. On, off. An interval of perhaps two seconds in between. A last kiss, momentarily prolonged.

And Fielding, that afternoon, only hours before, had invited me into her bed. "Even under the most intimate of circumstances." Spoken from experience, I had assumed even then, but not experience with Prowse. Prowse who, like me, was a married man with children. Had she perhaps told him of my visit, had she known I would say no and asked just to see how I would react, what excuse I would make?

My eyes burned with tears of spite. Had she called him, had he called her? So many times as I drove by, the room had been dark. Dark for hours. For hours. While I presumed she was in there as I had left her, sleeping, her wounded hand outside the blankets, her lame, little girl's leg beneath them. When all the time she had been with him.

Was Prowse some sort of replacement whom she had called because her afternoon with me had left her in the mood? I would have preferred that to this. On, off. On, off. Goodnight, sweet Prowse.

I had sat with her while she slept until the room grew dark. *I* had done that, not Prowse. What a fool I was, what a fool to think that I played as large a part in her life as she did in mine. I vowed that she would no longer play any part in my life, that with this betrayal, a curtain had come down between us, a severance of the absurdly one-sided love that had succoured me for decades. But no more. Fielding, as soon as the sting of this wound faded, would be consigned to the outer darkness of my life, a place inhabited by the likes of Prowse and Reeves and Hines.

I hoped there were a lot of men, not just Prowse. A different signal for each one. Tears streamed down my face. It might just as easily have been Prowse she had been crying about, a falling out with Prowse that had driven her to drink again. How could I ever have doubted that she had written that letter to the *Morning Post*? The wonder was not that she had written it, but that she had confessed.

Could I possibly go up there now and demand an explanation, denounce her, tell her I knew at last what everybody else had known for years? No. She must never know I saw Prowse leave or saw him look up at her window as she flashed the light. Prowse must never know. It would be a long while before I could stand to see either of them, before I could be certain I would hold my tongue and not blurt out everything I knew.

It would not be enough, however, to know that my humiliation was a secret. I would have to find some way to hide it from myself.

FIELDING'S JOURNAL, APRIL 22, 1944

Dear David:

In this journal I write to people as if I am bidding them goodbye, as if they are asleep in the next room and will read what I have written in the morning when I'm gone. I keep on writing to them, though, over and over. That's what this journal is, I think; one long goodbye.

I went for a last look at you and Sarah before I left New York for Newfoundland in 1923. I stood at the iron fence and watched you with her on the school playground, holding her hand as if my mother had warned you not to leave her side. A swarm of children and the two of you among them. How mortified you looked at having to hold your sister's hand. But you held it and she let you. She seemed frightened, overwhelmed. As if she was hoping some recent misadventure would not repeat itself. For three nights I couldn't sleep, remembering that expression on her face. There she was, in mid-existence, and there was I, merely watching. Spying. Speculating. How easily I could have — intervened. How reckless, how foolish of me just to be that close.

It seems like only yesterday that you were here. Remember? I could not stop looking at you, marvelling at the man you had become, searching your face for ways we looked alike, for signs of me in you. You caught me once and looked away, embarrassed. You must have thought me strange. You remarked that you could see our mother in my face. And so you could. And that I looked like you and Sarah, though I did not think so.

I watched you when you had a drink at dinner. You can tell a drinker by the way he holds his glass, by the way he looks at it. A million other ways, too. Had you been a drinker, I would have known it from watching just one sip. But you were not. How relieved I was that whatever else we shared, we did not share that.

You did not know about me or else you would not have had a drink. Nor, when I declined one, would you have encouraged me to change my mind, which I almost did. That was the closest I had been to booze in seven years. "C'mon, sis, have one drink with me, just one drink," you said. I knew what you meant, that this might be my only chance to have a drink with you, though I refused to consider that that was even a remote possibility. I don't know what I would have done had you insisted, but you didn't.

I was glad you didn't know, glad that my mother seemed to have told you nothing about me or my father except that we existed. When you insisted on seeing my father's grave, I could not bear to go with you, but I told you where it was.

I'm glad we met when we did and not when I was drinking. As I am now. Again. After so long. You might not have found this half-sister quite so charming, might not have taken her to the movies or to dinner or walked with her and held her arm. I would have had even more to drink than usual, knowing that in three days you were off to war. God knows what I would have said or done. Nothing that would have put you in the right frame of mind for France. Though nothing I said when I was sober did that either, did it?

When you went away, I was afraid to sleep, for it seemed to me that you were most in peril while I slept. Still, I did sleep and every day, like a dozing sentry who thinks he hears a noise, woke up with a start. At bedtime and when I awoke I would calculate what time it was in France, as if by that the gap in my vigil was accounted for. I still do that. I always know what time it is in France.

While you were overseas I had all sorts of strange thoughts. That it was up to me to see you safely through the war. That if I imagined the worst, the worst would happen. That there was something fateful about our meeting just before you joined the war. I'm sorry, sweetheart, that I couldn't see you through it.

I hugged you when you were leaving and I kissed you on the cheeks a dozen times. To think I held you in my arms just once. Half-sisterly hugs and kisses. Half-sisterly tears. But you could see that I was troubled beyond what the situation called for, though you could not guess why. "So long, sis," you said. "Everything will be all right." Meaning not that you, but that I would be all right, that this sorrow of mine, whatever it proceeded from, would pass.

There were other things and other people on your mind. My mother. Your father. Sarah. The war. You may have been in love for all I know. The man I mourn, I hardly knew. I know no one who knew you. Perhaps, one day, I will find out from Sarah who you were. It will make me miss you more. I may be wrong in thinking that my heart is broken now. It may be that I know nothing yet of heartbreak.

I could not tell you that I loved you, not the way I wanted to. I had to hold that back or else it would have all come pouring out. I can tell you now, for what it's worth. I love you, David.

The black-bordered telegram they sent me ended with their motto of condolence, a quote from Tennyson's "Ulysses," though I'm not sure if they know it is Tennyson they're quoting: "Though much is taken, much abides." What of you abides for me? A smattering of memories.

I did not know you for long, David. For me, your life begins on a sidewalk in New York and ends with the letters you wrote to me from France. And there is almost nothing in between. Still, I fancy we are linked by something more important than mere blood.

"I will drink / Life to the lees." That is also from "Ulysses."

As are these lines: "'Tis not too late to seek a newer world.... To sail beyond the sunset and ... all the western stars." As it must have seemed to Cabot he was doing; Cabot, who, the second time he set out, did not come back.

I am not at that point yet. I think that as long as I can write, I never will be. And even when I'm drinking, I can write.

David, are you reading as I write? Can you hear me say the words as I form them on the page? I wish I could make myself believe that you can. I have never wanted there to be an afterlife more than I do now.

Fielding's Condensed
History of Newfoundland

Chapter Twenty-Six:

WINTERING THE REIDS

Prime Minister James S. Winter negotiates one of the most controversial contracts in Newfoundland history, the Railway Contract of 1898, with Scots-Canadian railway magnate Robert G. Reid.

Having completed construction of a trans-island railway under the terms of what was known as the Labour of Love Contract, Reid seeks to negotiate a more favourable agreement for the operation of the railway and the construction of various branch lines.

So straitened is he by the first contract, Reid has little choice but to consent to the following new terms: he must accept five thousand acres of Crown land per mile of new railway; if he wishes to own the entire Newfoundland railway outright for all time, he must give back half of this land and some of the money he was paid to build the railway; he must assume ownership of the Newfoundland Telegraph service, the St. John's drydock, seven steamships, sundry hydro and railway stations, and finally, must agree to pave Water Street from end to end with granite cobblestones.

Thus will Newfoundlanders say of someone they get the best of in negotiations, "We Wintered them," or in the case of an especially one-sided deal, "We gave them a good Wintering." Newfoundlanders are more given to Wintering than being Whitewayed. For all their supposed hospitableness, there is something in the character of Newfoundlanders, a deviousness let us call it, that comes out in their dealings with outsiders who would do well to stay away.

As one-sided as the Reid deal is (one observer draws an inverse analogy with the purchase of Manhattan), the degree to which Reid has been bilked is not known until it comes out that finance minister Alfred B. Morine acted as Reid's solicitor during the negotiations, talking him into the deal by assuring him that "Newfoundlanders are too green to burn."

It is further revealed that, in total, the Newfoundland government has palmed off on Reid four million acres of land that it claims is "neither barren, boggy, nor otherwise unsuitable," a patently false claim since there exists in Newfoundland less than half that many acres of land of that description.

Such is the public uproar over a contract for which Winter can offer no better excuse than the need to avoid a major financial crisis and reduce the public debt that Governor Murray collects twenty-three thousand signatures on a petition in protest of the contract and forces Morine's resignation from the Cabinet.

The harm is done, however, and though Reid is given some relief in 1901 under the administration of Sir Robert Bond — 2.5 million dollars and permission to give back the railway after fifty years — he embraces a world-view into which cynicism too often creeps and in 1908 dies in Montreal, a broken man tortured by the thought that he leaves to his son a company that employs more people than the government of Newfoundland.

In 1907, he is knighted, no doubt at the request of the Newfoundland government, for Newfoundlanders think a knighthood fixes everything. They are forever petitioning the Colonial Office for knighthoods to appease some badly Wintered financier. The Colonial Office, to its discredit, is only too happy to oblige.

The worse the Wintering, the more promptly the face-saving knighthood is conferred and the sooner Sir Someone or Other is slinking off under cover of darkness for the mainland.

Only if one imagines them all on a single ship — cramming the decks, lining the rails, hunched figures in overcoats and bowler hats, clutching their scrolls of knighthood in their hands, their florid moustaches belying their despair — can one even begin to appreciate the enormity of our crime. There they go. One sees them sail out through the Narrows on the S.S. *Winter*, bilked, duped, outmanoeuvred, hopes dashed, expectations thwarted, taking their last look at Newfoundland.

V

CONFESSIONS

Both from an Imperial and Colonial point, the union of the British North American colonies is a consummation devoutly to be wished.

— D. W. PROWSE, *A History of Newfoundland*

Scuttlework

Field Day, April 17, 1945

Joe Smallwood is back in town. But where, the reader may wonder, has he been these past few years?

In 1943, Smallwood became bored with being the Barrelman. He became bored with life. The Commission of Government was still in power. There were no causes to espouse or oppose. A friend observed that "you are not yourself these days." To make you understand just how far from being himself he was, we need only point out that he started to resort to repetition. He of whom it has been said that there are not in the English language enough synonyms to get him through a single day began to repeat himself. He rewrote old programs, hoping no one would notice, then wondered what the implications were when no one did. He sat down and, using a pencil and paper, calculated that he had spoken two million, five hundred thousand words on the air in the past six years. He had had enough. It was time for a change.

Unlike most broadcasters, who switch to swineherding in their fifties, Smallwood did so at the age of forty-two. He went to Gander and started up on the Royal Canadian Air Force Base what became known as the perpetual motion piggery. Under Smallwood's scheme, swill from the mess rooms was fed to pigs to keep the mess rooms in pork to keep the pigs in swill. In other words, the airmen ate the same pigs over and over again.

He was referred to in Gander as the "Pork Barrelman." One writer asserted that, should Smallwood ever make it into politics, the nickname would become "doubly apt," a phrase to discover the meaning of which we have puzzled for hours without success.

I N GANDER IN 1945, when I heard that Whitehall had announced that self-rule was to be returned to Newfoundland, I was at first crestfallen, for I foresaw a return to the old system under which, if you were not a member of some merchant family, you had no chance to get ahead in politics. An image of Prowse as prime minister flashed through my mind and I felt sick with envy and resentment.

But instead of handing back independence immediately, as had recently been done in Malta, Whitehall ruled that Newfoundlanders should first elect forty-five delegates to a National Convention, which would debate and recommend future forms of government to be voted on by the public in a national referendum. I did not see immediately the purpose of this deviation from the 1934 promise to give us back our independence when we were once again self-supporting.

But I was elated about the National Convention, for I was certain that none of the established "names" would come out in favour of Confederation with Canada, which I intended to do. I de-

cided I would be its champion in part because it was the one cause
that, far-fetched and unlikely to succeed, had no champion.

While away from St. John's, I had thought a lot about the time
I had spent on the south and southwest coasts, and I had begun to
wonder if independence really was a luxury that Newfoundland
could not afford, a prideful dream, a vain delusion impossible to
sustain if you lived anywhere in Newfoundland except St. John's.

That fisherman in 1936 when I tried to unionize the southwest
coast, slumped over his oars, embarrassed to have me see him so
exhausted. The sealers of the S.S. *Newfoundland*, the survivors
with their bandaged frostbitten hands and feet, and the pairs and
threesomes of men who embraced, not for warmth, but for fellowship in death and were found and brought back home that way. The
trout-subsisting families in those little section shacks strung out
along the railway.

I believed in the cause I had decided to fight for. I believed any
decent person who had seen what I had seen would do the same.
But I recalled, too, Sir Richard's assessment of socialism as the
"politics of poverty" and therefore the only means of gaining
power that was open to a man like me. I fancied I had at last found
the version of socialism that Newfoundlanders might accept —
confederation with a country that some thought of as a social welfare state. I would do what no politician in Newfoundland had ever
done. I would make as my constituency, not the merchants or the
hordes who voted as the merchants told them to, but the poor who
were greater than the others in number if in nothing else.

Here was the something commensurate with the greatness of
the land itself, which I had so often felt was just beyond my understanding. The paradox of this permanent imminence was solved
at last.

All this, of course, was as much of a pipedream in 1946 as
getting rich from *The Book of Newfoundland* had been ten years
before. But it was not long after I announced my support for
Confederation with Canada that what I can only describe as the

"interventions" began. Without my lifting a finger, the obstacles that had always stood between me and doing something great began to fall.

There was, for instance, the announcement that candidates for the National Convention must run in the ridings where they normally resided. I would therefore stand as a candidate in the Bonavista riding, which included the Gander air-force base where I had spent the past two years — as unlikely as it already seemed to me — farming pigs. I had gone there to get away from Prowse and Fielding. Had I stayed in St. John's, I would have had to run there, where a confederate would not have stood a chance.

At exactly what point Governor MacDonald and the Commission of Government began to keep their eyes on me is hard to say. Some would later claim it was so I could run in Bonavista that the new residency requirement was imposed, that that was the first sign the British had singled me out as their champion of Confederation.

I very much doubt that they thought, or that it was possible for anyone to think, that far ahead during those times. But the residency requirement *was*, I think, intended to keep anti-confederate merchants in St. John's who did not want to lose to Canadians any portion of their Newfoundland monopoly from running in outport districts — and by extension, to give outporters who were more likely to be in favour of social programs, and therefore pro-confederate, a chance to win seats.

I ran and was elected by a landslide in the riding of Bonavista, the only declared pro-confederate to win a seat in the National Convention. Nothing much was made of this. Barely one-fifth of the province turned out to vote in the National Convention election. Few people believed that any result but a return to independence was possible. My victory was put down to my popularity as an entertainer, which it was presumed I would not get any real political mileage out of — I would never be anything more than a backbencher if by some fluke I should ever get myself elected to the legislature.

The National Convention opened on September 11, 1946, in the Lower Chamber of the Colonial Building. A week before that, while I was preparing a speech in the house I had rented in St. John's, I received a phone call from Prowse, who said that Governor MacDonald would like to meet me. At first I refused.

"You're not still sulking about getting thrown out of Government House are you, Smallwood?" Prowse said. "I was just doing my job."

"It's who you were doing it for that bothers me," I said.

"Look, no hard feelings, all right?"

I said nothing.

"I'll come by and pick you up in my car," Prowse said. I wondered if I could stand to be in his company and not mention Fielding. I assured him I could make my own way to Government House, which was barely half a mile from where I lived, but he insisted that we use his car.

"I'll just wait at the curb until you come out," he said. "We don't want to start any unfounded rumours."

Reluctantly, I agreed and at eight o'clock that evening a car that I knew was not Prowse's but that he was driving stopped in front of my house. I went out and got in the front seat.

"Hello, Smallwood," Prowse said, extending his hand, grinning in that same collusive, aren't-we-a-pair-of-rascals way of his. I shook his hand perfunctorily.

Prowse was still working for the Commission of Government. In spite of the fact that new commissioners from England were appointed every few years, he had survived each transition and was now deputy minister of something under Commissioner Flinn. He had run for the National Convention in one of the St. John's districts and been defeated, having campaigned as neither a confederate nor an independent. He had been one of the few candidates to declare himself in favour of the status quo, a continuation of the commission. He had won the civil-service vote in a district where a minority of people were, one way or another, employed by the

Commission of Government, for which he had argued throughout his campaign, dispassionately, regretfully — he wished he could say Newfoundland was ready to resume its independence, he hoped he would one day be able to say it, but he could not, in good conscience, do so yet. He had seemed during his campaign to be going through the motions, expecting to lose, running only so as to demonstrate his loyalty to his employers, perhaps even running at their behest, an apologist for the record of the commission since its appointment in 1934.

"Since when do you run errands for the governor?" I said. Prowse laughed, but looked as though he would have liked to reply in kind. "When you work for the commission, you see the governor a lot. He knows I am someone he can trust."

"You have somehow fooled him into thinking that," I felt like saying, but didn't.

Prowse drove up in front of Government House and parked his car off to the side, in the shadows of some overhanging fir trees. We got out, walked to the front of the house and up the steps. Prowse rang the doorbell, the door soon swung open and standing there was, I was fairly certain, the same liveried fellow whose sincere solicitousness I had mistaken for condescension the night I arrived at Government House years ago for the press reception.

"Good evening, Mr. Prowse, Mr. Smallwood," he said. There was a trace in his voice of an English accent now.

"Good evening, Rodney," Prowse said.

"If you would follow me, gentlemen," Rodney said. A butler's name, or footman's, whatever he was. We followed him through the stucco entrance, then right, off the lobby, past a curved flying staircase inlaid with marble. A navy blue runner spilled down the staircase onto the oak floor, where it branched out through the house in all directions. We proceeded through a maze of gloomy, wainscoted, portrait-hung hallways until at last I saw ahead a room in which a light was on and the fireplace was lit.

"Your excellency," Rodney said grandly, "Mr. Prowse and Mr. Smallwood have arrived," as though he were announcing some visiting heads of state.

Crimson-faced, I walked into the room and before I could see the governor I heard him rise from his chair, an emphatic but unhurried commotion, a faint grunt of exertion, an exhalation of breath that it seemed betrayed a touch of impatience or exasperation, as if he was about to perform one of the more tedious tasks he was obliged by his office to perform.

I was barely inside the room when I found myself face to face with him. Prowse introduced us and we shook hands. He was dressed businessman fashion, in a dark blue, faintly pinstriped suit, a plain red tie and a white shirt. He was quite a large man, though how large I had not until this moment appreciated, never having been this close to him before. His hairline was receding, and as if to compensate, he had let his hair grow slightly, and shaggily, at the back. His eyebrows were black and bushy, protruding almost awning-like above his eyes; resting almost on the tip of his nose were a pair of thick, black-rimmed bifocals, over the top of which he looked at me as he held out his hand for me to shake.

He motioned us to two chairs that were angled towards the one in which he had been sitting — the red plush was still faintly imprinted with his weight, and as he settled down, he emitted the same sort of spirit-weary sigh as before. Directly overhead was a three-pronged, cod-jigger-like chandelier, three bulbs burning lowly. I crossed my legs and put my hat on my knees, feeling somehow responsible for the fact that I was still holding it, though I was fairly sure that Rodney should have taken it from me.

Governor MacDonald, in the instant before he spoke, looked me up and down. I was wearing my best clothes — the best clothes of a man who had spent the last two years farming pigs, his expression seemed to me to say, for I had no doubt that Prowse had filled him in about me.

"You wouldn't like a drink, *would* you?" he said, as though he was assuring me that I would not. I wondered if this was a veiled reference to my ten-years-past encounter with Hope Simpson. But I knew MacDonald to be a teetotaller. There had been much grumbling in St. John's lately about how no tedium-relieving liquor of any kind was served at Government House parties.

"I don't drink — at all, your excellency," I said, wondering if it was proper for me to refer to him as Rodney had. It was true, I had recently sworn off liquor completely, though it would not last. He raised those conspicuous eyebrows of his, whether out of surprise at the fervour of my declaration of abstinence or because of the gaffe in protocol I had just committed and that he must, loath as he was to do it, ignore, I was not sure.

"Laudable," he said. "Very laudable." I knew him to be a Welshman, as was Commissioner James, while Commissioners Flinn and Neill were Irishmen, all appointed since Whitehall's call for a national convention in 1945. The lack of Englishmen among the foursome had been widely noted, though what if anything it portended no one was certain. Irishmen and Welshmen would find favour with the outporters and the urban poor, so many of whom were descended from Irish and Welsh settlers, whereas most of the "ruling" families of St. John's were English.

Governor MacDonald's accent was as English as Hope Simpson's had been, but that did not matter, since it was only those whose favour he did not need to curry who ever heard him speak. I knew he had once been a coal miner, and after that the leader of the Welsh Co-operative Movement and the Welsh Miner's Federation, then a Labour member of Parliament and ultimately a Labour Cabinet minister. It did not seem to me there was much of the coal miner or Labour Party member left in him.

"You may smoke if you wish," he said. Thinking his abstinence might extend to smoking; I was about to decline when he took out his pipe, at which point I took out a cigarette and accepted a light from him.

"Thank you," I said. He nodded his head and winced as if it pained him to be thanked, or as if he could not stand the thought of having to spend the evening pretending not to notice or not to mind my social clumsiness. He exuded a sense of weary exasperation that it was not as obvious to others as it was to him what was wrong with the world. He sighed continually, shifted in his chair, ran his hand over his face, leaned his head sideways on his hand as he looked at me as if he had long since despaired of making himself understood to anyone and therefore believed the only hope for the world was if people contented themselves with doing exactly what he told them to without understanding what purpose they were serving.

His origins, rather than making him feel sympathetic towards me, must have allowed him to foresee all too clearly the tiresome lengths someone of my social standing would go to not to seem gauche in front of him. Perhaps I reminded him of some younger, intolerable-to-remember version of himself.

"Let me first assure you," he said, "that by inviting you here this evening, we are not attempting to interfere with the proceedings of the National Convention or the upcoming referendum. We are bound by our office to neutrality in such matters, as I believe we should be. But like anyone else, we have our own opinions about what would be best for Newfoundland, and though it would not be proper for us to tell you what they are, we are naturally curious to hear from such people as you. Mr. Prowse tells me that you believe it would be in the best interests of its people if Newfoundland were to confederate with Canada."

"Yes," I said, "I — "

"The problem, I suppose," he said, in the tone of someone taking a polite interest in the technical aspects of a profession he was not much familiar with, "is how to get Confederation on the referendum ballot paper?"

This was close to being the very sort of impropriety he had just assured me he had no intention of committing. I resented it, yet at the same time felt euphoric at the possibility that however improper it might be, he was about to, implicitly or explicitly, pledge me his support. It must have been only the trace of resentment that he noticed, for he sighed wearily as if to say, "I'll wait while you give your high horse a token trot around the room."

It crossed my mind that I might be in over my head, that he might be planning to use me as Sir Richard had and afterwards discard me. I wondered if I ought to politely take my leave of him, but it also occurred to me that if I did, he and whoever he was taking his instructions from would find someone to replace me. (Since the convention had been elected, a handful of other delegates had come out in favour of Confederation.) I knew in that instant that no matter what happened at the National Convention, Confederation was going to be on the ballot paper, and I would accomplish nothing by walking out now besides cutting myself out of whatever the spoils of a confederate victory might be. By asking me this seemingly innocent question, MacDonald had given me the choice of playing along or ending my newly resumed career in politics. The real question he had asked was "Are you or are you not our man?"

"Yes, that is the problem," I said. "But I think I can convince a majority of delegates to agree to put it on the ballot paper."

MacDonald smiled broadly, looked at Prowse as if this meeting had been his idea. Prowse beamed back at him. No doubt about it, I had been recruited at Prowse's urging.

"Mr. Prowse tells me," MacDonald said, "that you are quite popular in Newfoundland, especially in the outports, because of a radio program you once hosted called 'The Barrelman.'"

"For that and for other reasons, I suppose," I said.

He nodded his head emphatically, as if to say he had no doubt that I was a man of many accomplishments. He seemed to have taken to me now that he knew that boorish scrupulosity was not among my faults.

I wondered when he would commit himself more explicitly. I assumed that what I was hearing was a prologue to some plan he was about to unveil and wanted me to implement. But he went on in the same vein, and I wondered if the resentment that I was sure had fleetingly crossed my face when he said the word *Confederation* had put him off, as if he saw before him someone too naive or loose-lipped to be trusted as a partner in impropriety. Then it occurred to me that he might be planning to have Prowse fill me in later in his absence.

After about half an hour of asking me small-talk-provoking questions, he said it had been a pleasure meeting me, and he had Rodney show Prowse and me to the door.

As Prowse was driving me back to my house, I kept waiting for him to say something, but all he did was grin; Prowse, now forty-six years old, grinning as he had when he confessed to not having shown his father my father's book — or so I thought at first, until I realized he was grinning as though he had caught *me* out in something, caught me down on the ground with the rest of them, my high horse nowhere to be seen. Nothing had been said at my meeting with MacDonald, but something had been agreed to. I was their man. I wondered what, in the long run, that would mean.

Were invisible hands at work in the months that followed? Almost certainly. But they were invisible even to me. It was not necessary that I know when my efforts were being facilitated. It was better that I didn't. I would often feel I was making my way along a path that was being cleared by someone who was always just out of sight.

MacDonald had needed to meet me to size me up. It seemed that I would do. I suppose he could tell just by looking at me that I was powerless to cause him any trouble, and that I was desperate to make something of what in all likelihood was my last chance for success. He himself was sixty-one years old, this his last posting before retirement. Newfoundland was all that stood between him and a peerage in the House of Lords, for which he was known to have an un-Labour-like craving.

I had read somewhere that there were once more than two hundred structures in the British Empire that went by the name of Government House. The scuttlework of empire having been under way for years, there were not that many now.

I understood, without having been told in so many words, that I had a new mandate: either to cause Confederation to be included on the ballot paper by parliamentary means, or to drum up sufficient support for putting Confederation to a vote that Britain would seem justified in flouting the National Convention if it had to.

It was not hard to reconcile this with my conscience. I told myself it did not matter how it came about that Newfoundlanders were given the opportunity to consider Confederation, since Confederation would not happen unless a majority of them voted for it. As for the interference of the British, once they were clear of us so would we be clear of them. A mutual good riddance.

I lay awake most of the night in a state of great excitement, my only nagging concern being that when and if the referendum was won, I might, having done the legwork, be pushed aside or thrown a bone as had happened when I helped Sir Richard win in 1928. Prowse's involvement was especially disconcerting. Now it was an image of Prowse as premier, the first premier of the newly created tenth province of Canada, Newfoundland, that nagged at me. Prowse, premier.

Soon afterwards, Fielding wrote in her column: "Smallwood does not really want Confederation. He has come out in favour of it only because he believes this is the best way of ensuring its defeat. He is our truest patriot."

Fielding's Condensed
History of Newfoundland

Chapter Twenty-Seven:

SIR CAVENDISH

Governor Sir Cavendish Boyle writes a quartet of quatrains that, when set to music, become the official anthem of Newfoundland, "The Ode to Newfoundland."

Six musical settings are written to "The Ode to Newfoundland," the first by German bandmaster E. R. Krippner. Boyle so dislikes the Krippner setting that he buys the rights to it to prevent it from being published.

Newfoundlander Charles Hutton writes two settings in 1906, and Newfoundlander Alfred Allen another in 1907.

What Hutton and Allen were hoping to accomplish remains a mystery, since the Newfoundland government had, on May 20, 1904, adopted as the official setting one written by Boyle's friend, the famous British composer Hubert C. Barry.

Tradition in Newfoundland has it that Allen's version was superior to all the others, Barry's included. But this is typical in a country where the animating myth is that the true king is always in exile or in rags while some pretender holds the throne.

The Night of the Analogies

ALDERDICE AND SQUIRES were dead, the more prominent members of their cabinets dead or retired. What well-
known figures there were left over from the pre-commission days
opposed the idea of a National Convention and, even when reconciled to it, assumed the convention would decide not whether
we would have independence, but merely what form of independence we would have.

They intended to use the convention as a way to advertise
their prime ministerial and ministerial qualifications. They considered Confederation a "crank" option, the latest in a long line of
hopeless causes by which I vainly hoped to rise to power. That
they did so did not bother me, for I hoped that by the time they
began to take me seriously it would be too late.

All that was left of Sir Richard's old Liberal Party was Gor-
don Bradley, one of the two Liberals who had managed to get
elected in the Conservative landslide of 1934. Bradley, a sad-faced
man with raccoon-like rings beneath his eyes, was the closest
thing to a "name" I was able to win over to my cause to give it
some respectability.

He had been elected to the National Convention and I persuaded him to "lead" the confederate movement, which, as I expected, he was loath to do.

"All you have to do is what I tell you to," I said, though I doubted that any movement even putatively led by Bradley could succeed. Bradley professed himself willing to comply if only he could find the energy, his search for which usually proved fruitless and exhausting.

Bradley ascribed his phlegmatic enervation to being swaddled for days as a child while ill with scarlet fever. "They never should have swaddled me," Bradley told me, over and over, convinced that whatever it is in the body that produces energy was stifled for good by that marathon of swaddling. I literally dragged him from place to place and wrote speeches for him which he delivered in so languorous a fashion that sometimes even I fell asleep.

The National Convention began. The Commission of Government installed microphones in the assembly and allowed the proceedings to be broadcast throughout the island, disingenuously denying the other members' accusations that its purpose was to get the voice familiar to all Newfoundlanders as that of the Barrelman back on the air again.

A motion was passed to send a delegation to London to inquire as to what sort of assistance an independent Newfoundland might expect to receive from Britain.

Governor MacDonald secretly preceded the delegation to London and spoke with dominion secretary Lord Addison about it, "just so his lordship would be properly informed," MacDonald said later, when his actions were discovered.

Lord Addison told the delegation that, exhausted by its war efforts, Britain could afford to carry Newfoundland no longer. Peter Cashin, the unofficial leader of the independents and the head of the delegation, reminded Lord Addison that Newfoundland became bankrupt in the first place by helping Britain win the *First* World War.

"God help Newfoundland," Cashin said upon departing.

"God helps those who help themselves," Lord Addison said.

It was next decided to send a delegation to Ottawa for "exploratory discussions" as to what Confederation with Canada would mean for Newfoundland. Bradley and I headed this delegation — a few non-elected officials went with us — and it, too, got off to a bad start.

It was June and there was a heat wave in Ottawa, which so reminded Bradley of the time when he was swaddled that all he could do was lie abed in the Château Laurier begging me not to make him go outside. I was frantic that unless we did *something* in Ottawa, Britain would replace Bradley and me with someone who had at least an outside chance of getting Confederation on the ballot paper.

I asked Bradley if he might consider not wearing longjohns beneath his clothes or wearing a suit less likely than one made of Harris tweed to bring on heat prostration. Bradley consented and accompanied me to Woolworth's on Sparks Street, where I bought him six pairs of boxer shorts, Bradley standing beside me at the checkout counter and telling me that our mission was futile, that Confederation would never be placed on the ballot in the upcoming referendum, and even if it was, it would be overwhelmingly rejected and we should therefore catch the next east-bound train.

Unfazed by this prognostication, I bought Bradley a linen suit. For the first time in his life, he wore short underwear and a suit not made of tweed. Though these changes afforded him some relief, he still lolled about Ottawa, constantly and profusely sweating, all the more so, for some inscrutable reason, in the air-conditioned buildings in which we at last met the Canadian delegates, who, it was clear right from the start, planned to do everything they could to help me sell Confederation to Newfoundland.

Day after day for three months, Bradley sat beside me, continuously mopping perspiration from his brow, his face, his neck, tugging on his collar, drinking water by the jugful. I wrote home to the convention that "Bradley is making a fine impression on the Canadians and I must confess that I am proud to have him as our chairman."

I briefly met with Liberal prime minister Mackenzie King, who told me he was about to retire from politics and would very much like to crown his career by bringing Newfoundland into Confederation with Canada and be remembered as the man who completed the long-ago-predicted dominion that would run from sea to sea. King's heir apparent, Louis St. Laurent, was just as openly in favour of my cause, though he kept assuring me that Confederation would happen only if asked for by the people of Newfoundland. "You're a Liberal, of course," said St. Laurent. "I mean, they tell me that you are." I assured him that I was and would be for all time.

Clearly, the question in all of their minds was to what degree my appearance and rough edges belied my shrewdness and ability, for the sight of me never failed to raise an eyebrow on the Hill. Bradley was of more importance to me than, before leaving for Ottawa, I had imagined he would be. He was tall, well-dressed, well-educated, well-schooled in the social graces. I think a hybrid of Bradley and me would have reassured the Canadians that their cause was in good hands.

Suspicions were rampant back at the convention in Newfoundland as to why our visit to Ottawa was dragging on so long. Demands were made daily that we come home and tell the other delegates what we had been up to. What we were up to was securing a detailed draft of the Terms of Union with Canada, which I had no more authority to do on behalf of Newfoundland than a randomly selected citizen of Portugal.

When we arrived home, Cashin accused us of being traitors. I replied that we had at least done better in Ottawa than he had in London. Outside the chamber, he threw a punch at me, which I dodged, then grabbed both of his wrists and fell backwards onto the floor. When Cashin attacked me, I was inhaling on a cigarette, and even as we were lying there on the floor, I blew smoke up into his face, so enraging him that it took several men to drag him off me.

Field Day, October 19, 1947

Yesterday, at the National Convention, Peter Cashin quoted from a document signed by Newfoundland and Britain in 1933 in which it is stated that "a full measure of responsible government will be restored to the colony when it is once again self-supporting." Why, in light of this, Cashin demanded to know, are we even having a National Convention? Why, now that Newfoundland is again self-supporting, has this restoration not taken place? Is this not a violation of the agreement? Is this not treachery?

To this question, Smallwood proposed the following analogy. He likened Britain's promise to Newfoundland to a father who promises to give his son House A when he turns twenty-one. The son turns twenty-one. The father says, "You can have House A. Or, if you like, you can have House B or House C. The choice is yours." Where, as Smallwood asked, is the treachery in that?

Cashin countered with what we shall call the Cashin Analogy, though it was a mere derivation of Smallwood's: The father promises to give his son House A, just down the street from his, when he turns twenty-one. The son turns twenty-one. The father says, "You can have House A, or you can have a room in a house that you have never seen five hundred miles away from here, though it's a marvellous house and I'm not just saying that to get rid of you. The choice is yours."

Thus began what members of the National Convention are already referring to as "the Night of the Analogies."

Smallwood fired back an amended analogy: Choice of shack or splendid room in splendid mansion, take your pick.

Cashin countered: House you own versus room you rent.

The amendments continued. The other delegates watched in open-mouthed silence as these two giants of debate went at it.

The house analogy exhausted, they moved on to horses.

Smallwood: Nag versus Steed.

Cashin: Newfoundland Pony versus Show Horse you have to board in someone else's barn.

The hours passed, darkness fell. Smallwood sucked on lemons to ward off laryngitis. Still they went at it.

Smallwood (briskly): Leaky dory versus berth on ocean liner.

Cashin (wearily): Self-owned dory versus berth on the Titanic.

About midnight, those delegates and radio listeners who were still awake may have noticed that while Smallwood's analogies were becoming more succinct, Cashin's were becoming more long-winded and laboured.

Smallwood (crisply): Tricycle versus train car.

Cashin (groggily): Used but independently owned and operated automobile that, though it could use some fixing up, still runs versus the last row of seats at the back of a bus whose rear shock absorbers would be lucky to survive the slightest bump and would certainly be no match for the kind of potholes that occur on roads in Newfoundland between the months of March and May.

Smallwood, alternately smoking cigarettes and sucking lemon wedges, pressed on. Finally, the Night of the Analogies ended at three-thirty in the morning.

Smallwood (peremptorily): Motel versus top floor, Château Laurier.

Cashin began to croak out an analogy involving the New-foundland Hotel, then crumpled to the floor. Smallwood informed the Newfoundland people listening that Mr. Cashin

had succumbed, then proceeded to list a further fifty unanswered analogies while Cashin lay there helplessly prostrate.

Smallwood, who as we stated in an earlier column is
endorsing Confederation only because he believes his support to be the kiss of death to any venture, may someday
regret defeating Cashin so convincingly, but now it merely
seems to him that he is putting up a good front.

I gradually won over more delegates to the idea that Confederation should be an option in the referendum. Even so, most of
them were still opposed to Confederation and were concerned
only that it be seen to be rejected democratically.

Thirty-eight days remained before the final adjournment of
the National Convention. I spread rumours that I was near collapse, in the hopes that this would provoke a reinvigorated attack
that would win me the sympathy of the public. Fearful, however,
of just that, that they would be blamed if I suffered some sort of
breakdown, the independents let me speak uninterrupted for
thirty-four of the remaining thirty-eight days. The independents
used — wasted — their four days denouncing the record of the
Commission of Government, believing the commission to be the
only real rival to independence.

It seemed they were proven right when a resolution to include
Confederation on the ballot was defeated 29-16. I denounced the
twenty-nine as dictators, to which they retorted that they were
democratically elected to cast their votes as they saw fit. The
National Convention adjourned for good. A lot of people, though
I was not among them, believed Confederation to be dead.

Britain, as I expected, ordered that Confederation be included
on the ballot, overriding the findings of the National Convention,
which had been Britain's idea in the first place.

Field Day, April 25, 1948

June 3, Referendum Day, is drawing near. Smallwood still believes himself to be the other side's best hope of winning.

His attempt to alienate supporters by wearing bow-ties and double-breasted suits in public has backfired. He is now being referred to in the papers as "the nattily dressed" Joe Smallwood.

The confederates have started up a newspaper called the *Confederate*. The independents have started up a newspaper called the *Independent*.

Smallwood is trying to keep the level of debate in the *Confederate* as low as possible. The *Confederate* recently ran a cartoon showing the Grim Reaper holding a sign saying "Vote for Responsible Government," his cloak bearing the words "Graft, Hunger, Dole, Disease." To Smallwood's dismay, the *Independent* responded with a cartoon showing a donkey with "Newfoundland" stamped on its hide straining to pull a cart loaded down with boxes marked "Taxes."

But he has calculated how he can best earn the ire of Newfoundlanders. He warns us against excess of pride, talks of Newfoundland's "backwardness" and "seaminess" in comparison with the rest of North America. It seems to be working. The message has been confused with the messenger.

At a recent rally, a large number of independents who pretended to be confederates so as to get close enough to him to lay hands on him barely missed their chance when his supporters intervened and he wound up escaping while spread-eagled on top of a car.

"What this movement needs is a martyr," Smallwood screamed as the car pulled away, only realizing too late that people would think that by "this movement" he meant Confederation.

Smallwood again painted an uncomplimentary portrait of Newfoundland while broadcasting live on radio just the other day. He had to point out he was broadcasting live and give his location five times before a mob of independents finally surrounded the station and dared him to come outside. He was just about to do so when the 'Stab arrived and the crowd dispersed.

Smallwood has begun to second-guess himself, wondering if even by *secretly* supporting a cause he predisposes it to failure.

Sitting in the Grumman Widgin, we shouted to one another above the deafening drone of the plane's propellers. Looking down I saw demarcated, as I never had before, whole peninsulas, whole bays and lakes. I wished we could fly high enough so that I could see the island whole, all of it at once in its map-drawn shape, a single entity, no longer composed of many parts, but one distinctive, discrete shape among the many that comprised the world. We drew a map of Newfoundland with the plane, drew its coastline perfectly to scale. We circumnavigated the island counter-clockwise, land always on our left.

I remembered my other trips around the island. The seal hunt. Crossing the barrens endlessly by train. Sailing the south coast with Andrews, the headlands looming over us. The nights I spent lying in bed in some cliff-perched house on the southwest coast in winter.

Travelling by plane, I was not lulled into the usual mute, inert wonder by the landscape. It was possible, at least for as long as we remained aloft, to believe that I really had found the "something" I could do that would match the land itself, which had seemed an impossible-to-meet obligation until now. I hoped I would at last be free of Fielding and the nagging tug of the past, my pointless preoccupation with things as they were not and never could have been.

And that moment in New York when I had chosen love, then lost my nerve.

Though I told myself, while flying over the island in that plane, that I had come to my senses in that room, not lost my nerve.

We landed in the harbours of as many of the little islands and settlements as we could. The north and northeast coasts were still iced in, which made landing easier. Whole populations trooped out across the ice to meet us. It was more difficult in the ice-free harbours, for there was nowhere to land except on water, and the plane, while I stood on the pontoon and clung to the strut with one hand and held a loudspeaker in the other, bobbed up and down. The people lined the shore to listen while the pilot every so often put the plane into reverse to keep us from wrecking on the rocks.

What a strange sight the landing of the plane must have been for the people in the outports. From a distance, there comes the sound of an engine, an airplane engine, that of a Grumman Widgin that flies low across the harbour. From a pair of megaphones attached to the undersides of the Widgin's wings comes Joe Smallwood's voice, loud enough to be heard above the noise the engine makes: "Citizens of Lamaline, this is the Barrelman, this is Joey Smallwood; I have come to speak to you about Confederation, I repeat, Confederation."

The Grumman Widgin landed in the harbours, and the people crowded the beaches or put out towards the plane in boats as if with the intention of sinking it. The door of the plane opened and there I was, loudspeaker in hand. By the time I left, they were always loudly cheering. It happened in outport after outport.

I wondered if it was the manner of my arrival and departure that won them over; if they believed that I had singlehandedly brought this plane, the one and only such device in all the world, into existence.

I did not speak to them about Canada. What could they know about Canada, these people who had never seen St. John's? For these people, there would be no dilemma. To them, voting for Confederation would be no great sacrifice.

Their homes were worlds unto themselves. The fishermen were not nationalists of any sort, defined themselves as neither Newfoundlanders nor colonials, but as residents of chthonic origin, sprung from the earth of whatever little island or cove they had grown up in. Confederation would not make them think of themselves as Canadians. All they knew or would ever know of Canada was that it was some nebulous place from which, somehow because of me, money trickled in to them. They would vote for Confederation to get the mother's allowance and would live after Confederation exactly as they had before, only richer by about twenty dollars per month.

That I was doing what was best for them I was able to satisfy myself just by looking at the way they lived. They had starved through a depression that had ended when the war began. Now, three years since the war had ended, they were terrified that another decade like the thirties was on its way.

A politician should believe that the welfare of his people depends on his success. Everything I do for me I do for them. And so the day may arrive when to tell the difference between selfishness and selflessness becomes impossible.

That day came for me. It may have come before Confederation. It may not have come until decades later. I don't know. It is like noticing that the colour of the sea has changed and trying to remember when it happened.

It seemed to me that unless I did something that historians thought was worth recording, it would be as if I had never lived, that all the histories in the world together formed one book, not to warrant inclusion in which was to have wasted one's life. It terrified me that if it were possible to extrapolate the judge's book past 1895 to the present, I would not be in it. And I was forty-eight years old.

On referendum night, we crowded round a radio at Confederation headquarters, listening as the returns came in. Responsible government took an early lead, but we had expected that, as we knew the St. John's polls would be the first to report. Throughout the night, the gap between independence and Confederation gradually narrowed. But not quite enough.

No option had received a majority of votes, so there would have to be another referendum. Commission of Government, which had finished a distant last, was dropped from the ballot. The second referendum was set for July 22. Six weeks.

Fielding's Condensed
History of Newfoundland

Chapter Twenty-Eight:

BOND ON BOYLE

Sir Cavendish is governor of Newfoundland from 1901–1904, throughout which time and for years afterwards he labours to perfect his ode — it must be said, to the neglect of his duties as governor.

He is often absent from official functions, which forces his wife to say that he is sick, though no one believes her, for it is common knowledge that he is upstairs in his writing room, the window of which looks out upon the rear grounds of Government House.

People walking on Circular Road on their way to Government House receptions often see him sitting side-on to the window, looking out, lost in brooding contemplation.

To a colleague who tells him in a letter "I fear we have another Pickmore on our hands," Prime Minister Sir Robert Bond warns him not to be taken in by "the apparently inexhaustible inventiveness of Lady Boyle when it comes to devising ailments for that versifying derelict Sir Cavendish. Rest easy, my friend; the man is not sick, or no more so, shall I say, than any man who spends his days and nights composing poetry, which if that be illness he is for embalming long past due."

In such a way are poets talked about behind their backs; in the knowledge that such things are being said of them must they persist, as I have done, my ears burning.

A Man You Never
Knew

I COULD NOT, THEY would not let me, go outside without
them. They were my bodyguards, a former paratrooper and
an ex-wrestler who were hired by others over my objections to
protect me. I carried with me at all times a fully loaded, unregis-
tered revolver. I was getting anonymous death threats every day,
by phone, by mail, at the *Confederate*, at my home, the windows
of which were boarded up. On going outside in the morning, I
often found the house plastered with posters that said Traitor,
Judas. Finally, my supporters convinced me that my wife and children and I should move from one safe house to another each
night. We were bundled off in the van of a confederate dry-cleaner,
which appeared promptly at six each evening to take us to yet
another house.

When I was campaigning in St. John's, I went every Sunday
night to my parents' house on the Brow for dinner. My bodyguards remained outside on the deck that faced the road, conspicuous to any anti-confederates who might recognize my car. My
parents' house was not a target in my absence because my mother

was known to be Pentecostal, and the Pentecostal and Catholic churches had come out against Confederation, ostensibly because they feared it would mean the end of the separate school system. My father was known to be an anti-confederate, as well, though no one, him and me included, could have said on what grounds, except that it was by now a matter of principle to him to be against anything that I was for. It was the same with the confederates, who did not harass my parents either.

One Sunday halfway through the second referendum campaign, my mother seemed agitated when she met me at the door. She had not said when I called that anyone would be joining us for dinner, she had said only that my father would not be, but there was a car I did not recognize outside.

"Hello, Joe," she said, her voice unnaturally loud, as if to alert me to the presence in the house of strangers, or to alert them to my presence. "There's someone here," she said, looking at me meaningfully, as if to say I should prepare myself, "who would very much like to see you."

She led me into the front room, where a man was sitting in the armchair that faced the door, his legs crossed, his hat on his knees. I would not have recognized him so quickly if not for his still bloodshot left eye. Now only the lower half was bloodshot, as though his eye were floating half-submerged in blood. The lenses of the glasses he was wearing were so thick I guessed he must be nearly blind.

"Mr. Hines says he knows you from New York," my mother said nervously. Hines did not get up, nor did I step forward to shake his hand.

"It's been a long time, Mr. Hines," I said.

"No time at all in the eternal scheme of things," said Hines.

"Mr. Hines is — " My mother paused. "Mr. Hines is here for the referendum, Joe."

"I am a Newfoundlander," Hines said, looking at me, "and unto Newfoundland I have returned." I sat down in the chair across from his. My mother sat on the edge of the sofa between us, inclined slightly towards Hines but looking at me.

"I'll pour you some tea, Joe," she said. There was a tea service and a plate of biscuits on the table.

"Are you still publishing the *Backhomer?*" I said. He smiled as if to say he was sure I knew he was, which I did.

"I'm here to see what this Confederation fuss is all about," said Hines. "I hadn't realized until the first referendum that so many of our flock had gone astray. I must say, when I knew you in New York, you didn't strike me as having much leadership potential. But you were young then. Not the man you are today, I'm sure."

I guessed he was in his late sixties. The whole left side of his face was downturned from the stroke, as if, despite the partial clearing of his eye, its effects were worsening with age. Or perhaps he had had another stroke.

"None of us is what we used to be," I said.

"My name has not always been Hines," he said. "Did I tell you that?"

I shook my head.

"I changed it when *I* changed, though I have never tried to hide my past. I depict myself in my sermons as an object-lesson to my flock. I once was lost but now am found. You can be too, Joe Smallwood."

"I've been warning Newfoundlanders against excess of pride," I said.

Hines nodded. "The devil will often use God's words against Him."

"I'm sure Joe is only doing what he thinks is right," my mother said.

"And you, my good woman," Hines said, "you are saying only what you think is true. I wish I could say the same thing for your son. Faith before all, Mrs. Smallwood. Faith before family, if need be."

My mother hung her head.

"I would not trust this man," Hines continued, "as far as I could throw him. But then, even at my age, I believe that I could throw him quite a distance."

Before my mother could respond, Hines uncrossed his legs and struggled to his feet. My mother got up, too, crimson-faced, her hands clasped in front of her. She was on the verge of tears. The recent death of Miss Garrigus had left her shaken.

"It's not enough that you and Miss Garrigus betrayed my mother's confidence," I said. "Now you have to stand here pretending you're the Pentecostal Church — "

"What do you mean, Joe, betrayed my confidence?" my mother said.

"Miss Garrigus told him about the book and Mr. Mercer" — Hines looked startled, discomposed, which I took as confirmation that I was right — "and when I went to his church in New York — "

"But no one knows about it, Joe," my mother said. "How could Mr. Hines — How did you — Oh, my God. What, what's happened?" She looked horror-struck at me as if she suspected the devil to be involved. "I never told anyone about the book and poor Mr. Mercer, Joe," she said, her eyes wide with fright. "Not a single soul." I looked at her, was about to accuse her of lying when I saw by her anguished perplexity that she could not be.

Then Hines did not know about the book and Mr. Mercer. Unless he had somehow found out about it from some other member of the family. I wondered if, during his "days of debauchery" in St. John's, he had known my father. But my father had been passed out drunk, in bed asleep, the night my mother threw the book. And I was the only one who had looked out the window above the city-facing deck.

I looked at Hines. He was flustered, eager to leave, regretting he had come. I stepped towards him.

"You said — You said in your sermon that a book and a man I never met had played a large part in my life. What book and what man did you mean?"

"I meant — I meant this Mr. Mercer whom you just mentioned," Hines said. "As I once told you, God makes me privy to knowledge that he withholds from others."

"Then tell us what happened to Mr. Mercer," I said. "Go on," I said, when he looked away from me. "Tell us. Tell us what book I'm talking about." Hines said nothing, edged his way towards the door, but I moved with him.

"You have a secret of your own, don't you?" I said. Hines blanched. "You know about the *Morning Post* letter and about the judge's book."

Hines smiled weakly. He stepped around me, walked across the room, headed for the door, then stopped to look back at me. "You had your chance years ago," he said, his voice quavering. "God offered you salvation, Joe Smallwood, and you refused it." He put on his hat, his hands shaking, opened the door and walked out.

"You've known all along about the book and Mr. Mercer?" my mother said, her hands over her mouth, tears streaming down her cheeks.

"I saw you," I said, determined not to break down with her, though a gust of grief rose in my throat. "That night. I heard you going down the stairs. I looked out the window and I saw you throw the book. I heard the avalanche." I decided not to tell her that I had retrieved the book.

"You've kept it a secret all these years?" she said. "Just like me?" I nodded. Sobbing, she ran to me and she took me in her arms. "Oh, my boy, my poor boy," she said. "I'm sorry. What you must have gone through since then. You were only, what, fifteen? There's not a day goes by when I don't think of Mr. Mercer. Every month, since he died, I've been going by myself and putting flowers on his grave. To think that someone else knows, that someone else has always known. You can't imagine, Joe, what a relief that is to me. I'm glad it's you, Joe. God made sure that it was you."

It was not the reaction I had expected. I hugged her hard but broke our embrace and told her I could not stay for dinner after all, there was something urgent I had to do.

"I'll pray for you," she shouted as, my vision blurred with tears, I ran from the house. "I'll pray for you and your side in the referendum. I won't vote for you, Joe, but I'll pray for you. Don't tell a soul."

I had my bodyguards take me to Fielding's boarding-house. I was certain now that Hines knew who had sent the letter, and that probably it was Hines himself. For what reason he had done it, I had no idea, but I was sure he had. I felt elated. Whatever else Fielding had done, however much she preferred Prowse to me, she at least had not done *that*. I had been right all along about that if nothing else.

"There is a dreadful secret that involves a book and a man you never knew." The "book," the only book that had played a large part in my life, had to be the copy of Judge Prowse's *History* from which the words comprising the letter to the *Morning Post* had been cut. And the man I never knew had to be Hines.

Of course I planned to use my discovery to discredit Hines, who I believed could do our cause quite a bit of harm, especially since the *Backhomer* was so widely read around the bay where our support was strongest. But then, too, there was Fielding, who had yet, in her columns, to declare herself either for or against Confederation, but had been attacking independents and confederates alike. She was read almost exclusively by townies, and it was in St. John's that our support was weakest. I doubted that she would go on writing as she had been once I told her what I knew.

"Smallwood," Fielding said when she opened her door. "With Cashin here just last week, I wondered how long it would be before you showed up."

"Cashin was here?" I said. I knew he had been. She knew I knew.

"To ask me to support him," Fielding said. "I regretfully declined. Come in, come in. Sit down and stay a while."

I went inside. The room looked just as it had when I had last come to visit, the afternoon I sat beside her bed. Now we sat at her writing desk, which was swept bare of everything except a bottle and a glass.

"Hard at work?" I said.

"You seem fated to come begging favours from me, Smallwood," Fielding said. I decided that for a while, I would let her think it was that simple.

"You know," she said, "I would have come out in support of the Commission of Government, I offered to before the first referendum, but Commissioner Flinn told me that, in light of what I had written about the commission over the years, yet another encomium would be superfluous."

"Still at it," I said, pointing at the bottle on the table.

She smiled. "Compared with the old days, I'm a prohibitionist," she said.

"You think Confederation is just another hare-brained scheme of mine, don't you?" I said. "Like the piggery. Like the *Book of Newfoundland*."

"Actually," she said, "I had a somewhat longer list in mind."

"We'll win this time," I said.

"Smallwood," Fielding said, "much as I look forward to these once-every-five-years visits of yours — "

"Aren't you going to take a side in this thing, Fielding?" I said. "Don't you care which way it goes?" I was going through the motions, waiting for my chance. "What did Cashin have to say?" I said.

"Oh, you know the major," Fielding said. "'Aren't you going to take a side in this thing, Fielding? Don't you care which way it goes?' That sort of thing. I helped him drink the bottle of Scotch he brought with him, but more than that, I said, I cannot do."

"What did Cashin say about me?" I said.

"He said that you were worse than Judas Iscariot, who at least had the decency to hang himself. But that's as close as he came to insulting you, I swear."

"I have nothing against the major," I said. "He's fighting for what he thinks is right. He's not afraid to take a stand — "

"Don't go getting all homiletic on me, now," said Fielding.

"It's hard for a certain class of Newfoundlander to get ahead in Newfoundland, Fielding. Under the Commission of Government or responsible government, it always will be. Under Confederation, we can make a new start. We can make them pay for what they've done to us."

"Who's we? Who's us? Who's them?"

"Oh, for God's sake, Fielding. Look around you. You live in a hovel. You drink yourself unconscious every night. You write yet another column every day. And you think *I* repeat myself. Where do you think all this is leading? Journalism is a poorly paid, losing game. You're not the daughter of a doctor any more, don't kid yourself."

"I know whose daughter I am," she said.

"I wonder if you know the man who was in my mother's house this afternoon? I think he knows you."

"What in God's name are you talking about, Smallwood?" Fielding said, a touch too loudly to sound convincing.

"He calls himself Tom Hines now," I said. "I don't know what he used to call himself. I worked for him in New York at a paper called the *Backhomer*, which he still publishes. I didn't know then that he had changed his name. Apparently, he left Newfoundland, it would have been while you were in the San, I think, went to Boston and, over the next five years, nearly drank himself to death. Then, or so he said, he had a stroke, and because of it some sort of vision or conversion. He was baptized in the Pentecostal Church and left Boston for New York, where he became a minister. The paper was his ministry and his readers were his congregation. His flock, he called them. The *Backhomer*. You must have heard of it."

"I know it," Fielding said. "I glance at it from time to time, looking for ideas. There's always a picture of this Hines fellow in it standing in front of this tiny church in Brooklyn — "

"The Pentecostal Church of Newfoundland in Brooklyn," I said. "As you know, the Pentecostals and the Catholics are against us. Hines is here just for the referendum, a few weeks to help defeat Confederation, then he's going back. I think he could be quite — influential — if he isn't stopped."

"But what does all this have to do with me?" Fielding said.

"I think you know who Hines used to be." I said. I took out from inside my jacket a keepsake copy of the *Backhomer* from the twenties. I opened it to the page that bore Hines's picture and handed it to Fielding. She stared at it.

"By the time that picture was taken," I said, "it would have been ten years since you'd seen him. Ten hard years. I dare say he had changed a lot, even aside from the stroke that paralysed one side of his face. Do you recognize him?"

"It's ... it's not a very good picture," Fielding said, keeping her eyes averted from mine. "It's so old."

"It's the picture in which he looks most like he did when you saw him last," I said. "You know him, don't you?"

Fielding nodded. "He never had a beard back then. Never wore glasses. He never dressed like that. His face ... his face is not — "

"He told me you didn't write that letter or send it to the *Morning Post*."

Fielding stared at me, then hung her head. "I don't know how you wormed it out of him," she said. "But you've got all you need to stop him now. What do you need me for?"

I sighed. For this at least I did not have her to blame. I was not cursed with loving for life a woman who had once hated me enough for that. And I did still love her, for all that I had sworn otherwise when I saw Prowse jauntily emerge from her boarding-house that night. I had thought of her many times since then and had come to the realization that it was not the sum of her words and deeds but some essential Fielding I was drawn to, who for me could never change and from loving whom I would never be reprieved.

I tried to look poker-faced, but when she glanced up she saw that I had tricked her. She smiled ruefully and shook her head. "Well, you must know something," she said. "What is it?"

"When you were in the Harbour Light, you gave me the letter that Reeves gave you, remember? The *Morning Post* letter."

I took out of my pocket an envelope and gingerly removed the letter, which was itself like an envelope now, for most of the words had fallen from the paper. I poured them out on the table, where, curled up and yellowed, they looked like pared fingernails.

"These words," I said, "that were pasted on this paper came from the judge's book. The *History*. I recognized one or two of the words and then I looked through my copy of the book and found the others. I've written out the text of the letter." I handed her a folded piece of paper. She took it from me and read it, hands trembling, though I wondered if they always did by now. She shook her head.

"Ancient history," she said.

"Why did you give me the letter?"

"I don't know. To see if you'd notice what book the words were from. As a kind of joke. I didn't know you had crossed paths with ... Hines. I don't know. I couldn't stand to keep it. I couldn't stand to see it destroyed. I knew that you would guard it with your life. And you were involved. Your life was affected by that letter, too — "

"Not like yours was — "

Fielding shrugged.

"What was his real name?" I said.

"You can find out if you want to," she said.

"What happened at Bishop Feild?" I said. "Don't you think you've kept this secret long enough?"

As if she had been asked to do so a thousand times and was at last relenting, she got up and went to the closet at the foot of

her bed, opened the door, reached up and took a box down from
the shelf. She put it on the table, rummaged around for a while,
then extracted a yellowed edition of the *History*. It was so tantalizingly close I almost grabbed it from her hands. I changed my
mind again. She *was* guilty. But Hines had been involved. How
satisfying it would be to see at last those little windows in the
pages, ellipses where the words had been.

She sat there, staring at the book's outer cover.

"There should be a word missing from the title page," I said.
She ignored me, went on staring at the book.

"For God's sake, Fielding," I said, "just open the damn book
to the title page."

Fielding stood up and hurled the book across the room,
barely missing the window, all but falling down in the process. She
collapsed into her chair and sat back, breathing heavily, her eyes
closed. She reached out for her glass, felt for it, picked it up before
I could help her and took a long swallow of Scotch, still breathing
hard as she swallowed.

"You look at the God-damned book," she said, pointing, eyes
still closed, to where it lay, open but face down, beneath the window. "You're the one who's so obsessed with the past, not me.
There it is, the literal past, Smallwood; the history of Newfoundland. Go take a peek."

If she thought to shame me out of it by recommending it to me
in this fashion, she had figured wrong. I crossed the room, picked
up the book and opened it to the title page ... from which were
missing the words and letters I had expected would be missing.

I closed the book and placed it on the table in front of Fielding.
She did not pick it up or even look at it, or at me. She slumped in her
chair, cradled her glass with both hands against her stomach.

"Turn the front cover," Fielding said, "and read aloud what
you see."

I picked up the book again and turned the front cover. In ink
that had run slightly, some lines had been carefully, painstakingly

written. I read them aloud. "'To Edward, on the day of your graduation from medical school. University of Edinburgh, May 9,
1901. Your loving parents, May and Richard Fielding.' Your
father's book."

"Keep reading," Fielding said. Below the first inscription,
there were several lines of illegible scrawl. And below those: "'For
Edward Fielding. My grandson tells me he and your daughter are
good friends. Friends as you and I might have been had we gone
to school together.'"

I felt myself reddening with resentment, embarrassment. I
fought not to let it show.

"Actually, that's not really from the judge," Fielding said. "It's
from his son, Prowse's father. Prowse took me to see the judge one
day to have him sign my father's copy of his book. He scrawled
something we couldn't make out, so Prowse took the book to his
father and he wrote that inscription, a decipherment of the
judge's, he said, but I'm not so sure. The old man seemed pretty
far gone to me. Prowse's father even wrote a note of explanation
to my father about how the judge had palsy or something and
only his family could make out what he wrote."

I suffered all the more keenly because I had to hide what I was
feeling. So Prowse had done exactly the same thing with Fielding.
Except he had not owned up to Fielding that the "translation"
was his. I had long since known what Prowse was like, but I felt
more betrayed by him now than I ever had. How many copies of
the judge's *History* were floating around with inscriptions forged
by Prowse to the fathers of his friends?

"I believe your father has one just like it," Fielding said.

I looked at her. She was not smiling. She was staring reflectively at her glass of Scotch. Prowse had told her. He would have
taken her to see the judge before he took me and might therefore
have convinced her that the inscription to her father was genuine,
while the one to mine was just a joke. How many jokes had she
and Prowse shared about me over the years?

"So where does Hines come into it?"

"Hines wrote the letter," Fielding said.

"How long have you known?" I said.

"I knew it all along," said Fielding.

"Why did he write it?" I said.

"The old Hines did things like that," she said, "just to keep himself amused. Drunks need more than booze to keep themselves amused, which you know as well as I do."

"Then why did you confess to writing the letter?" I said.

"I confessed because ... because I panicked. Because Hines said he was going to tell Reeves that Prowse did it."

"Prowse?" I said. She nodded.

"The past Hines put behind him," Fielding said. "The past he's always writing about. Prowse and I were part of that. We used to get Hines to buy booze for us. There was a whole other life outside the gates of Bishop Feild and Bishop Spencer, Smallwood. Hines told us, Prowse and me, about the letter. He had borrowed the book from me — I should have known he was up to something. We thought it was funny at first, a great trick. Until he told us who he planned to blame it on."

Fielding reached for her glass, but her hand was shaking so badly she could not pick it up.

"It would just have been Prowse's word against Hines," I said. "Reeves would have believed Prowse, not some drunk — "

"Hines knew about us," Fielding said.

"What do you mean?" I said.

"Exactly what you think I mean," said Fielding.

I felt myself turn crimson with hatred for Prowse. My face was burning. "*Us*? You and Prowse? While you were still in school?"

She said nothing.

"But so what if Hines knew about Prowse and you. He had no proof, it would still have been his word — "

"He was a photographer for the *Morning Post*," she said. "We let him take a picture of us once. Not doing anything. Just lying there. We thought that was pretty funny, too."

I could not look her in the eye.

"How did you know Hines wouldn't just go ahead and black-mail Prowse into confessing, too?"

"I took a chance," she said. "I figured at the worst I would save Prowse from having to take the blame all by himself."

"You were that determined to stick by him?"

"And at the best — Well, there was no point getting both of us in trouble."

"He should have confessed, too," I said.

"I know that now," Fielding said. "But Prowse is Prowse."

"I've sometimes thought you confessed for my sake — "

She said nothing, looked away.

"And all the while, when you and Prowse were supposedly on the outs, all the while Prowse was treating you like dirt at Bishop Feild — "

"As I said, Prowse is Prowse. It ended at some point. I can't remember exactly when."

"Well, I think I've got enough now to silence Hines," I said.

"And what if he won't be silenced? What if you threaten him him with going public with what you know and he says go ahead? I know men like Hines. They like nothing better than informing on the men they used to be, no matter what the crime."

"If he says go ahead," I said angrily, "then I go ahead."

"And then what happens to Prowse?" she said. "Have you thought of that? That picture of us may still exist, for all you know." I wanted to ask her why it should matter in the least to either of us what became of Prowse. But I was afraid of the answer. And I knew that if I got going about him, it would all come out. The night I watched him from outside her boarding-house. The light in her room. On, off. On, off. Our afternoon together.

"It won't come to that," I said. "Hines will back down."

"You're willing to take that chance? Would you be willing if *your* livelihood, *your* reputation was on the line?"

"I have nothing in my past — " I was going to say "to be ashamed of" and I could tell by the way she looked at me that she knew it. "I have nothing in my past that they can use against me that they haven't already used. They've said I flunked out of Bishop Feild; they've said a thousand times that my father is a drunkard. And don't forget, Prowse is a prominent confederate. Having him discredited could hurt our cause. If I thought there was any real chance of that — "

"Smallwood," Fielding said, "I've never asked you for anything before and I'll never ask for anything again. Please, don't confront Hines with this."

"I have to," I said. "Maybe even if I thought there was a risk, I'd do it. Confederation is too important. But there is no risk."

Her hand steady now, she sighed, raised the glass to her mouth and drank its contents. She turned away from me. "Then at least promise me you won't tell Prowse you know about all this."

"I'll promise you that. I have no reason to tell him anyway." I paused, my eyes full of spite-hot tears. "You've loved him all along," I said. "You've never stopped, never — "

She picked up the bottle of Scotch and hurled it with all her might against the wall. It smashed into tiny shards that went flying past my head and the Scotch sprayed out across the wallpaper in a map-like stain. The force of the throw carried Fielding to the floor, onto her hands and knees. I bent to help her up.

"GET OUT," she screamed. "GET OUT."

A column she must have written before my visit ran the next day, but the day after that the first panel on the third page of the *Telegram* was filled with something else.

It was soon going round that Fielding had "disappeared" without a word to anyone as to where she was going. I checked with her landlord, who told me that he did not know where she was but that he expected her back, for she was still paying the rent on her room, which contained all of her belongings. All that occurred to me at the time was that it seemed I now had one less worry, namely, that at some point Fielding would come out in favour of independence by making Confederation the sole target of her columns.

I went early the next morning to the boarding-house where, my mother had told me, Hines was staying. I was informed he had already checked out. It occurred to me he might be hiding from me, and perhaps he was, until the next ship sailed for the mainland. For it turned out that I was right, not Fielding, though I am sure Fielding attributed Hines's sudden departure from Newfoundland to my confronting him with what I knew.

Hines never spoke a word in Newfoundland against Confederation, nor was there any partisan mention of the subject in subsequent issues of the *Backhomer*. He had known, that afternoon in my mother's house, that I had blundered onto his secret. There were things, it seemed, that not even Hines could afford to have attributed to his former self, things for which he did not think his congregation would forgive him.

Fielding's Condensed
History of Newfoundland

Chapter Twenty-Nine:

THE ODE NOT TAKEN

Boyle develops a love/hate relationship with Newfoundland and, never able to resolve this ambivalence, writes two odes, which we here alternate, verse by verse.

> When sun rays crown thy pine-clad hills,
> And summer spreads her hands,
> When silvern voices tune thy rills,
> We love thee, smiling land.

> (When men do drown for lack of gills,
> And, dead, wash up on land,
> Their wives their silvern tears do spill,
> And keen and wring their hands.)

> When spreads thy cloak of shimm'ring white,
> At winter's stern command,

Thro' shortened day and star-lit night,
We love thee, frozen land.

(When shrouds of snow, beguiling white,
At winter's cold command,
Do shorten day and darken night,
Where art thou, frozen land?)

When blinding storm gusts fret thy shore,
And wild waves lash thy strand,
Thro' spindrift swirl and tempest roar,
We love thee, wind-swept land.

(When rotting sculpins line thy shore,
When capelin swarm thy strand,
The stench is such one hears men roar,
"Thou reekest, wind-swept land.")

As loved our fathers, so we love,
Where once they stood we stand,
Their prayer we raise to heav'n above,
God guard thee, Newfoundland.

(As lived our fathers, we live not,
Where once they knelt, we stand.
With God nor King to guard our lot,
We'll guard thee, Newfoundland.)

As Loved Our Fathers

I T WAS ALL I COULD DO to keep myself from running to the basilica and kissing the feet of Archbishop Roche when he denounced Confederation in the *Monitor*, the official Catholic newsletter. The archbishop, in editorial after editorial, said that Confederation amounted to treason, a treason that would betray the men who built our country and cause the country itself to become "tarnished" by the Canadian, royalist, socialistic, dole-dependent way of life against which we could protect ourselves only through continued independence. The baby bonus, he said, was "an incentive to fornication."

I knew these editorials would galvanize support for Confederation among fence-sitting Protestants, who outnumbered fence-sitting Catholics two to one. The Orange Lodge distributed to all its members a letter denouncing the Catholic Church for denouncing Confederation. I myself called the Catholic Church the tail that wags the dog.

What had seemed like just another election now began to seem more like civil war. It was as if only with the entry of the churches into the campaign did people finally realize what was at stake, only then were they convinced, or fooled into believing, that *everything* was. The Catholic appeal to patriotism and the Protestant call to "bring to naught" the attempt of the Catholic Church to "dominate Newfoundland" did more than just stir up sectarianism. It forced us to face our long-buried demon of identity.

We confederates took out on the independents the shame and guilt we could not admit, even to ourselves, to feeling, and the independents were all the more fanatically for independence the more they doubted, the more tempted to join our side, they felt.

In St. John's, days before the second referendum, flags of every kind flew everywhere, as if bunting week had been declared. The raising of the pink, white and green on one side of a street provoked the raising of the Union Jack on the other, though it was by this time no longer clear which faction was favoured by which flag. No longer did neighbourhood vie with neighbourhood, or street with street, or even house with house. The population was as atomized as it could get. It was not uncommon to see, on the same house, one window with a poster exhorting passers-by to vote Confederation and another exhorting them to vote for independence. In houses all over the city, mealtimes were like that scene in Joyce's book where Stephen's aunt and Stephen's father argue bitterly about Parnell.

Grown-ups who knew that, unlike them, children could travel unmolested through the streets, put them up to marching in parades, beating drums and blowing horns, stalling traffic.

One such parade in support of independence went right past our offices. There was a child on each sidewalk and one in the middle holding aloft a street-wide, slogan-bearing banner that blocked my view of the chanting horde behind them. In the rows of houses on either side of the street, grown-ups leaned from upper-storey windows, looking down as if some sort of coup by children that they were powerless to stop was under way. The children sang a verse from a song written by the "antis" in 1869:

Would you barter the rights that your fathers have won?
No! Let them descend from father to son.
For a few thousand dollars' Canadian gold,
Don't let it be said that our birthright was sold.

They sang, to the air of "A Mother's Love's a Blessing," a song called "The Hero of 1948."

Our skies above look brighter, our paper mills now hum,
There's iron ore in Labrador, enough till Kingdom come;
The U.S.A. she wants our fish, the long dark night is o'er,
So don't surrender, Newfoundland, don't give up, Labrador.

A country-wide grudge match had been declared, an arbitrary means of settling old scores, old grievances that had nothing to do with politics.

Ostensibly the wager was the future of the country. But really it was the question of who for all time could claim that they had "won." What it was they'd won seemed not to matter, as long as the winners could feel they had been vindicated. Here was a contest that you could never live down losing and that over winning you could gloat forever.

Spouses, brothers, sisters, parents, children, churches, unions were divided, not along religious lines and not, though they would have told you otherwise, because their politics were different.

Throughout the second campaign there prevailed a kind of anarchic, atavistic party, like a Mardi Gras or mummer's festival without the masks. Under the exemption, the amnesty conferred by such occasions, anything was permitted. No one gave any mind to how things would be afterwards, when this exemption had been lifted, when the issue had been settled, for it seemed at the time that the fight, having become an end in itself, would last forever.

It is hard to convey to someone who knows how things turned out what it was like back then, when no one knew how a victory by one side would be received by the other, or what margin of victory would be acceptable.

I went out with my bodyguards and my revolver in my pocket on those last few summer nights before the vote, got up in some disguise, a pulled-down hat, an up-turned collar, clothing of the sort I was never known to wear. Out of every door left open to let a cooling breeze blow through, the same din of contending voices carried into the streets. Every bar we passed was in an uproar. When the bars were shut and those men who lingered outside on the street after closing time had drifted off, we walked, the three of us, through a city that was eerily quiet.

It was inevitable, what with me being the leader of the confederates and my parents being independents, that there would occur in the Smallwood house just such a bloodletting as occurred in houses throughout the country.

Ours took place during a Sunday dinner just days before the second referendum. My father had recently made a point of being out whenever I came by but was ominously present on this occasion.

I saw his toting pole in the corner of the porch and prepared myself for what I knew was coming and because of the possibility of which I had left Clara and the children home. The only other member of the family on hand was my brother David.

We managed to get through dinner without talking much, but then my father went out on the deck that overlooked the city. We could see him through the sitting-room window. It was a warm day. The doors to both decks were open to let a breeze blow through the house. I could see my bodyguards standing on the ocean-facing deck, smoking cigarettes. My mother looked at me beseechingly, begging me to draw upon all the reserves of forbearance that I possessed.

My father raised his arms as if to address a multitude. It was years since I had heard him hold forth on the deck. I had many times since I moved out cut short a visit the second he went out there, determined that I would never again be a part of his captive audience.

"OLD LOST LAND," he roared, in a voice that would have drowned out Hines's from a hundred yards away. My mother closed her eyes, blessed herself, clasped her hands so tightly that her fingertips went white.

"A country that might have been but may never be because of one of mine. ONE OF MINE," he roared, smacking the rail of the deck with both hands. "One of Charlie Smallwood's. It galls me, Minnie May, it galls me to know that in the history books, they will record me as his father, that when they look for explanations they will point to me, as if I made him what he was. The sins of the son will be visited upon the father."

I stood up, stepped aside from David, who tried to block my way.

"Whatever I am, I am in spite of you," I said, standing in the doorway, addressing his back. He did not turn round. He was facing the setting sun and the tiered row houses of St. John's across the harbour, the whole city looking as if it had been arranged to show off to best effect the towering basilica of St. John the Baptist, shaped like an about-to-take-flight dove with wings outspread.

"Better to be an honourable failure," he said to his imaginary multitude, "than a treacherous success. Better to accept what you were born to than sell your soul to get ahead."

"If you had accepted what you were born to," I said, "you might have made something of yourself."

"I could have done great things," he said, "had I been unscrupulous. All that ever stood between me and the big time was my conscience, which would not let me compromise myself. I bypassed many opportunities rather than betray myself or someone else."

I was about to reply when he turned around, strode past me and went upstairs, taking the steps two at a time as if to assure me that he was coming back. I looked at my mother, who sat there exactly as before, eyes closed, hands clasped.

"Joe," David said pleadingly, but before he could finish, my father came running down the stairs with the two volumes of my failed encyclopedia, *The Book of Newfoundland*, tucked beneath his arm. He had not spoken a word to me about the book until this moment. He put one volume on the coffee table.

"What have we here?" he said, holding the other out in front of him, as if the better to identify it. "*The Book of Newfoundland*," he said. He turned to the title page. "Edited by Joseph R. Smallwood." He read the dedication out loud, "To my parents, Charles and Minnie May Smallwood," then cocked his head as if to say, "Now isn't that something?" He thumbed through the book, scornfully reciting the names he saw inside, those of famous Newfoundlanders, as if I had been taken in by them, fooled by them into thinking anyone would want to read about them.

"Why didn't you get one of your editorial board members to sign it for me? Sir Richard, for instance. "'To Charlie. Your son and I are friends. Friends as you and I might have been had you kissed my arse.'"

My mother ran upstairs to her room. While my father paused, we heard her pacing overhead, convinced, I had no doubt, that all this was her fault, that this was what came of vainglorious books.

"I'm not in here," he said. "The old man and Freddie and you, my first born, and God knows how many other Smallwoods are in here, but not me. Except in the dedication. 'Dedicated to my parents, Charles and Minnie May Smallwood.' I have thought about that a lot. Oh, yes. At night, out there on that deck all by myself, I have pondered on it. A dedication is the only way I could ever get my name into a book like this. He seeks to appease me for deeming me unworthy of inclusion in his book by working my name into the dedication. I am honoured, deeply honoured, and not at all offended as some men might be."

The fact that what he said about my trying to appease him was not entirely untrue did not make it any easier to take.

"Under what heading would I have put you?" I shouted. "Noted drunks of Newfoundland? Noted good-for-nothings? Noted ne'er-do-wells? I should walk out of here and never speak to you again. I would if I didn't think it would break my mother's heart."

David tried to intervene, but my father waved him off. "Charlie Smallwood," he said. "Noted for nothing and therefore not noted. But you haven't outdone the judge, if that was your intention, as I'm sure it was. What would the judge make of your book, I wonder? What would old Prowse think if he saw it on the shelf beside his own? How would the judge judge you? I believe he would tell you that people will still be reading his book long after they've forgotten yours."

"He's ... he's drunk," David said. My mother had stopped pacing overhead. I knew she must be listening. Her ear to the door, or even the floor perhaps.

"He's always drunk," I said, looking at him but talking to David in low tones, as if my father could not hear me. "If that's an excuse, then he's not to blame for anything he's ever done. He's been drunk since before I was born."

I turned to him. "I'll never speak to you again. You are no longer my father. I am no longer your son."

My father hurried to the sofa, and with the book still in his hand, huddled side-on into the cushions, his face averted in the manner of someone about to receive a beating that he knows he deserves, or that he provoked so his attacker would come off looking shameful.

I stared at my father for a full minute, but he did not look back. His eyes opened and closed as if he were on the verge of sleep or collapse, suddenly sober and exhausted. He had provoked it. This confrontation was something he had long been contemplating.

I felt a surge of perverse affection for him. Ridiculous, fearful, helpless old man. I suddenly realized how old he was, how drained of energy he was from having held forth on the deck for but a few minutes, he who had once done it all night long.

The one thing he feared more than life was death. How he had trembled, how terrified he seemed when I threatened to disown him, as if this was the first casting off, the first severance of many that, when they ended, would end him.

"I'm sorry, Joe," he said, beginning to cry. "Don't mind me, boy. You know me, boy. You know what I can get like when I'm drinking."

I looked at David, looked upstairs when I heard the floorboards creak.

"It's all right," I said. I held out my hand to him and, smiling up at me appealingly, he took it. Though he looked as if he was putting everything he could into it, his whole arm shaking, there was no strength in his grasp. He was an old man, my father. An old man who had never had his day.

"Don't worry," I said. "It's forgotten."

But of course, it was not forgotten, as such things never are. I had disowned him in spirit and retracted only for pity's sake, form's sake, my mother's sake. Not out of love, and we both knew it. And it was always there between us after that.

Second Referendum Night, July 22, 1948

I had done my share of celebrating. I did not trust myself to drive. Everyone I knew who owned a car was roaring drunk, even my bodyguards.

I dared not call a cab. The driver would be as likely to kill me as to kiss me. Twice as likely, here in St. John's. On this night, even a confederate cabbie might not want to chance having Joe Smallwood in his car.

It did not matter; I felt like walking anyway. It was between three and four in the morning when I went outside, alone, my bodyguards let me think, or believed they had, for as I walked I knew they were behind me somewhere, I could hear them, laughing, probably too drunk to do me any good, more likely to draw attention to me than anything else. I decided I would lose them if I could.

A few brave souls walked, arms linked, through the streets with bottles in their hands, confederates who walked right past me without giving me a second look. The streets, strewn with confetti, were otherwise deserted.

I heard, from somewhere in the east end, a solitary, punctuating shotgun blast that echoed back and forth between the harbour hills. Earlier, guns had fired almost constantly for hours, not so much in celebration, it seemed, as in symbolic execution of the losers.

I felt the weight of my revolver in the pocket of my jacket, and the iron ingot I had worn in the other pocket for three months now as a counterweight, so my jacket would hang evenly. I felt the pull of both weights on my shoulders. They caused me to hunch slightly and I wondered if I would ever walk upright again. And how much longer I would need the gun.

Everywhere, it seemed, the pink, white and green flew at halfmast. Let the old flag fall. The anti-confederates, looking out their windows the next day, must have wondered how they lost; there were so many more of them than us.

But only in the city. Not in the outports where the antis had never been. They had been to London and they had been to New York, but they had never been to Bonavista or La Poile, and that was why they lost. Here and there the Union Jack flew at full mast.

I knew my father was still up, though the southside hills were dark. I didn't have to write about others any more. From now on, others would write about me. I would make history, had made it.

I no longer had to write it. Yes, I knew that my father was out on the deck and that he knew that his son was somewhere in the city down below.

I tried to imagine what the city must look like from the Brow. A couple of hours ago, it would have looked like a relief map, the confederate one-third lit up, the rest dark. But there were just a few lights now. Anti-confederates, I suspected, though I was not sure why. Keeping bitter vigil. I knew that my mother had voted for the losing side and that my father, if he voted, had done so, too, each for their different reasons.

I walked down Bonaventure, past Fort Townshend, turned left where Harvey Road met Military Road. I walked past the Colonial Building, Government House, hurried across Cavendish Square in front of the Newfoundland Hotel, outside of which huddled a knot of men I knew were anti-confederates because of the aggrieved, subdued way they stood there, smoking cigarettes. It did not occur to them I might be *him*. Though I was wearing no disguise, they paid me no attention.

By the time I reached Battery Road, I was sure I had lost my bodyguards. I felt safer here among the houses of the city poor, the fishermen who I knew had voted for Confederation.

I walked to the end of the road, and though it was so dark I could barely see, I followed the trail that led down towards the Narrows, felt my way with my left hand on the cliff-face, grateful I could not see the precipice that I knew was on my right.

The boat was there when I arrived, anchored within a few feet of the Boot. Instead of tearing down the Boot, the anti-confederates had shot it as though it were an effigy of me, so it was only just still boot-shaped, ragged-edged, and you could only just make out the splintered, perforated letters that spelled Smallwood.

The man on board threw me the mooring line, and I pulled the boat in closer to the shore and to the Boot until the man put up his hand. I threaded a line through a hole drilled in the rock and tied a knot.

It took the man, using a steel saw, ten minutes to cut through the iron bar drilled into the cliff, ten minutes to bring down the Boot, which landed with a thud on the prow of his boat. At a nod from the man in the boat, I untied the mooring line and threw it to him. I turned, and as I headed back up the trail, the cliff-face on my right now, I heard the boat, in low throttle, pull away from shore.

VI

——◆——

TWO
HEMISPHERES

On the morning of the 24th June 1897, four hundred years will have rolled away since John Cabot first sighted the green cape of Bonavista; four centuries will have elapsed since the stem of the *Mathew's* boat grated on the gravelly shore.... May we not confidently hope that when the morning sun shines out again on the anniversary of the great Baptist's day in 1897, evil times will have passed, and our Island, closely united with her prosperous younger sisters, will once again become a happy and contented New-found-land?

— D. W. PROWSE, *A History of Newfoundland*

Fielding's Condensed
History of Newfoundland

Chapter Thirty:

BOND: SCOUNDREL, SCOURGE

A name never spoken by Newfoundlanders except as part of an expletive is that of Sir Robert Bond. As colonial secretary under Whiteway in 1889, Bond almost effected a reciprocity agreement between Newfoundland and the United States without consulting Canada. This was clearly in contravention of Clause 6(b) of the British North America Act, which states that "the interests of one part of British North America may not be sacrificed to those of another except when the phrase 'one part of British North America' is defined as 'Newfoundland.'" Luckily, the Canadians heard of it in time to complain to Britain, which vetoed the agreement as it was obliged to do under the above-mentioned clause.

In the colony, Bond managed to convince Newfoundlanders that their interests had, for the umpteenth time, been sacrificed by Britain to those of the Canadians. It was because Bond was among its members that the delegation of 1894 pulled a Whiteway and turned its back on the generous terms of u   nion offered by Canada to Newfoundland — and because of the failure of that delegation that for the next fifty years Confederation was as dirty a word in the colony as Bond is today.

It is nearly twenty years before Newfoundlanders realize what a scoundrel Bond has been, before they realize he was almost single-handedly responsible for hardening the terms of the already granite-like agreement with the railway-building Reid family.

Bond so fools his countrymen in 1900 that they elect him prime minister by the largest majority in Newfoundland history and re-elect him in 1904.

We Let the Old Flag Fall

FIELDING'S JOURNAL, MARCH 31, 1949.
TWELVE MILE HOUSE.

Dear Smallwood:

There are not as many sectionmen on the Bonavista as there were in 1925. Soon the branch lines will be closed. They tell me no one has lived in Twelve Mile House for seven years. It's mine for as long as I want it. I haven't decided yet how long that will be.

I dare say you are celebrating somewhere now. Discreetly celebrating in St. John's while your bodyguards keep watch outside your house. It said in the Telegram *that at midnight, you planned to have a glass of rare champagne. What is there to do tonight but write to you and every few lines look up at the clock? I measure time in sentences, counting down the page. I dare say the whole country is clock-watching. People who would otherwise be asleep at this hour are up and waiting for the moment to arrive.*

The moment. "Immediately before the expiration of March 31, 1949." A phrase added to the terms of union at the last minute, when someone noticed that otherwise our transformation would take place on April Fool's Day. How immediately? How small a fraction of a second? That which we are we were. Though the moment of our transformation never comes, we are transformed.

Someone out there is playing the "Ode to Newfoundland" on the bagpipes. In protest or in celebration? I can only faintly hear it. It sounds like it's coming, not from anywhere along the line, but from far out on the barrens. Perhaps he thinks he's out of earshot and is playing only for himself. Which makes the gesture no less inscrutable. Someone who voted against Confederation bidding Newfoundland goodbye? Or some confederate piping her into the promised land? Impossible to tell, the ode being what it is.

The bagpipes. A single instrument but it sounds like fifty. I didn't know that anyone along the line had a set of pipes. I'll ask the sectionmen tomorrow if they know who it was. It rained today but now it has stopped. There is still snow on the ground, snow with the texture of ground glass, which would not bear a man's weight. What a walk he must have had across the barrens. He must have a light with him to see his way and his watch, but I can't see one, and a light out here on a night like this should be visible for miles.

"As loved our fathers, so we love." But not you, Smallwood. You did nothing as your father did it. Nor did I, when I could help it.

It all began here, Smallwood, on the Bonavista. This is your district, and you were the first confederate. They still remember that you walked across the island for them or their fathers in 1925. And Cabot made his landfall twenty miles from here.

I like to think that Cabot came ashore at what for me is bedtime, the sun just up. June 24. Three days past the summer

solstice. The Mathew *at anchor, he rowed into Keel's Cove in
a dory that he dragged up on the beach, having reserved to him-
self the right to first set foot on any land that he "discovered."
Nineteen forty-nine. Your name will be paired with that year as
Cabot's is with 1497. Your year. You have brought about Judge
Prowse's devoutly-to-be-wished-for consummation.*

*The piper is into the last verse now, unless he plans to play
all night. "It was patriotism versus pragmatism," Cashin said,
"and God help us, but pragmatism won." I don't know. I still
don't know. I could not bring myself to vote. Me and more
than twenty thousand others. And the margin was just seven
thousand votes. Since that day you came to my room to
confront me about Hines, that day I fooled you into thinking
that at last you knew who sent that stupid letter, I have felt even
more unresolved than usual. Unresolved about everything.*

*We have been in limbo for the past nine months, neither
country nor province. Only a few would understand that this is
just the old abiding limbo made manifest, that we have always
been in limbo and perhaps always will.*

*I wished, on referendum night, that it could be all over
with by morning. I wished your side had no time to gloat, the
other side no time to brood. It was the nine-month interval,
which ends tonight, the interval between the referendum and
actual Confederation, that I dreaded most, not because I
thought bad things would happen, but because I knew that
nothing would. Nothing. A step had been taken that could
never be retraced.*

*For months, I thought, even the winners, knowing that
nothing new can happen now, will think about the past. And
though they will deny it, even to themselves, and though they
will not understand it, they will feel guilty, as I do.*

*Nationality, for Newfoundlanders a nebulous attribute at
best, will become obsolete, and the word* country *will be even
more meaningless than it was before. The question that has been*

*there from the start, unasked, unanswered, unacknowledged,
will still be there.*

*We have lost something we would have lost no matter
which side won.*

*The bagpipes have stopped. The ode is over. On the clock
midnight passed while I was looking out the window.*

*The piping came from the east. Somewhere out there, five
hundred miles away perhaps, the sun is up already; a line of
light is making its slow way across the water, encroaching
slowly; daylight's journey across the ocean from the Old World
to the New is nearly done, while behind me, westward, the
island, the gulf, the continent that will always be that far away,
are dark.*

———————

I COULD NOT STOP looking at the old constable, standing at
the back of the drawing room of Government House with tears
streaming down his cheeks. It was April Fool's Day, 1949. The old
man, who, for decades, had worked at Government House, stood
rigidly at attention, fists clenched. In the huge marble fireplace, a
heap of white birch blazed. Beneath the chandelier, on a table
spread with cloth of blue and gold, scrolls tied with red ribbon were
unrolled and signed. I was sworn in as interim premier, an office I
would hold until the first election. The new lieutenant-governor
was given by the secretary of state a mahogany-framed certificate
of Canadian citizenship. Newfoundland the country ceased to be.

There was something splendidly sad about it, as there was
about the placard at the base of a flagpole I saw later that day that
read We Let the Old Flag Fall, something that had nothing to do
with partisanship or bitterness. By contrast, there was a man who
on the same day, in a gesture of protest so excessive that it did not
ring true, hung his whole house in black crêpe.

Weatherwise, April 1, 1949, was exactly the kind of day it should have been, it seemed to me. Cold. Foggy. Light rain. The kind of day that makes you forget St. John's ever looked otherwise and that makes you prone to pointless reflection.

I could tell by looking at them that the people on the streets understood at last. I met with a lot of people that day, some for the first time, and tried for their sake, and the sake of appearances, to seem exultant, anticipatory. "It's a great day for Newfoundland," I said, and meant it. But I grew tired of saying it.

Nine months it had been, with half the population acting as if it were under sentence of death and the other half, for all their outward bluster, not much better. I tried not to dwell on my part in it all. I was unsure how significant a part I had played. Britain had found in old Mackenzie King a face-saving way to cut us loose. He had put on his career the final flourish of Confederation and completed the long-dreamed-of dominion that would truly run from sea to sea. Perhaps it would have happened, sooner or later, with or without me.

I lunched in a restaurant from which I could see the city, opposite my father's deck-house on the Brow. Everything seemed unbearably detailed. I remember the row houses, the grain of the wood beneath the paint on the clapboard of the house across the street, the wood wet through with rain. The street signs bearing the names of governors all born and buried elsewhere.

There were no protest demonstrations, no parades, though many had been planned. By late afternoon, the streets were all but empty.

There lay over everything the guilt that accompanies the doing of a terrible but necessary thing.

We moved into Canada House, the former residence of the Canadian high commissioner, a now obsolete office, and the former home of Peter Cashin's father, Sir Michael Cashin, who for a short time had been prime minister of Newfoundland. It was on Circular

Road, two houses down from the house in which Fielding grew up. From it, you could see Government House and the Colonial Building and Bannerman Park, where for years I had given speeches while standing on a kitchen chair and once while hoisted on the shoulders of two fishermen.

It was a large white wooden house with three wings and six chimneys with two pipes apiece. With all fires going, twelve columns of smoke rose from the house. There was a stone fence and a large iron gate made of two halves that opened inward like the gate of Sir Richard's house. "Canada" was written on one gate and "House" on the other.

The house came fully, lavishly, furnished, which was fortunate, for we could not, with all our belongings, have filled a single room. There was a threesome of housekeepers who vacuumed sofas never sat upon, aired out rooms never occupied, beat rugs that, had they been stolen from us and recovered, I could not have sworn were ours. There were mahogany desks and dining tables, gleaming chandeliers, theatre-curtain-like drapes with drawstrings as fat as belfry ropes. Our bed was elevated so far from the floor I felt while lying in it that I was levitating.

For a while, I basked in the glory of having done what Reeves at Bishop Feild had assured us all could not be done. I had not only climbed to the top of my little ladder, I had leapt across to the larger one beside it and climbed to the top of that as well.

Or so I hoped it seemed to outsiders, anyway, for though I could see the point of having and wielding power, I could not see the point of wealth. My new house had thirty-two rooms, twenty-five more than any other house I had ever lived in, that many more than I knew what to do with.

Fielding came back not long after the first provincial election, which occurred just months after I was acclaimed premier. I opened the *Telegram* one morning in my office in the Colonial Building and there, on page three, was her column, Field Day, with not so much as a note of explanation about her eighteen-month absence. Nor did she allude to it in her column.

She had either not left Newfoundland, or she had been getting newspapers sent to her abroad, for in that first column she showed herself to be not only fully up to date, but also attuned to the mood of what I was calling the new Newfoundland.

I had won the election by a landslide. I was already ruling the province with such an iron fist that most people were afraid to speak out against me. Newspapers especially were under my thumb. I blacklisted newspapers that criticized my administration, refusing them government advertising and refusing any companies who advertised in them government contracts. Squires, Alderdice, the Commission of Government had all done this; it was legitimized by tradition as far as I was concerned.

But Fielding vowed she would be "an atom of dissent beneath my mattress," and I knew she meant it. I could imagine her brooding at a distance for eighteen months about all the wrongs, real and imagined, I had done her through the years. That was a long time to brood. That she had come back after so long was the measure of just how resolved, how determined she must be.

There was no one close to Fielding whose job or reputation I could threaten. She put forward in her column so unflattering an image of herself that no rumours I could leak could make it worse. It would hardly do her any damage for me to reveal that she was the reprobate she claimed to be.

I knew I could silence her if I could silence the Telegram, which was the only hold-out, all the other papers having fallen into line, but there were just enough businesses owned by Roman Catholics and with Roman Catholic clientele, and just enough townies whose bitterness at losing the referendum and hatred of me were still at fever pitch, to keep the Telegram in advertising.

The Telegram's main rival newspaper, the Daily News, quoted me at such length that I practically had a column of my own with which to counter Fielding's.

I said that at a time when her readers had needed her most, she had deserted them, first by not having had the courage to take a stand on Confederation and second by literally running away. I challenged her to explain her sudden disappearance. I said that she had spent her time "brooding and sulking somewhere." It was obvious, I said, that now that she knew nothing could come of it, now that she knew the cause was forever lost, she had decided she was an independent and obviously intended to carry out against me some sort of personal vendetta.

Fielding wrote in her next column: "The number of Josef Stalin's enemies who still draw breath and the number of Joey Smallwood's who still draw pay cheques is about the same."

It was understandable that I be enraged but stupid of me to let it show. I phoned the publisher of the *Telegram*, threatening to sue him for libel and slander if he published one more word from the "poisoned pen of Fielding."

Fielding's next column included a mock "editor's explanation."

"Miss Fielding," Fielding wrote, "was not directly comparing Mr. Smallwood with Josef Stalin, who murdered twenty million of his countrymen just to keep himself in power, an act of which Mr. Smallwood is obviously incapable, since his countrymen number only sixteen million. Rather, the foregoing is a simile in which irony is — we hope you will agree — wittily employed to make a point. If we may say, for one too modest to do so on her own behalf, how clever."

"Is this how it will be from now on?" I countered. "I for one don't plan to spend my time decoding Miss Fielding's columns. If she has something to say, she should come right out and say it. She can try to hide behind that cleverness of hers all she likes, but we see through it, we plain-speaking Newfoundlanders who say what we mean and mean what we say. We see through it."

My colleagues assured me that Fielding was harmless and ought to be ignored. I tried to ignore her, but the constant sight of Prowse would not let me, Prowse whom I had for a while thought of banishing from my administration altogether, but who, as a prominent confederate, had important allies whom I was not yet certain I could rule without. And so I appointed him deputy minister of finance.

Whenever we met, I tried to rub it in that, unlikely as it would have seemed to either one of us ten years ago, he was my subordinate, working for me, taking orders from me. But there was always in his eyes, in his manner, something subversive of my authority, as if we both knew that I was not the premier but the "premier," both knew how I had come by the position and how long I was likely to retain it. I wished Prowse had not been in the room with me that day I met MacDonald at Government House. MacDonald, of course, had needed a witness in case I had more scruples than anyone who knew my history had reason to expect.

And I was unsure of how Fielding would react if I treated Prowse shabbily. It might, I supposed, be one way to get at her, but how close they were or had ever been I was not exactly sure, despite what I had said to her when we last met about her having loved him all along. She had certainly seemed worried that I would do something that would damage his reputation. But I doubted her affection for him because the more I thought about the explanation she had given me for confessing to writing the letter to the *Morning Post*, the more it nagged at me that there was something wrong with it. I had only her word that she was telling the truth. The supposedly Hines-incriminating book proved nothing. That Hines had been involved I had no doubt, but his hasty departure from Newfoundland shed no light on exactly *how* he had been involved.

It unsettled me that she seemed to have contrived a way to exist outside my world, not only beyond my influence, but also beyond my comphrehension. I had no idea if anything she said was true. And she did not seem to want anything. She had no ambition, she had nothing she would find intolerable to lose, Prowse included, I suspected, telling myself that this was not just wishful thinking. It was not just her criticism of me that rankled, it was the mere unaccountable fact of her relentlessly being there, dogging me without apparent motive and with what ultimate purpose I doubted even she could say.

I pretended to be unable to "get" her columns, knowing that most people did not "get" them. I could not understand, I said, the popularity of a writer so given to "romancing," which in Newfoundland simply meant not talking or writing about things as they really were.

"It's all very clever, I suppose," I said. "At least, I'm told that some people think so, but the fact is that none of it is true. And if it's not true, then what's it worth?"

I phoned her once and dismissed her work as "booze-inspired cant," her as "booze-befogged," "booze-hazy," "Scotch-besotted."

"There's no analysis here, Fielding," I said. "There's no constructive criticism. I suppose you have to be sober to analyse and criticize."

She let me have my say, saving hers for her column, I supposed. She said little more to me than hello and goodbye, but, ridiculous as it made me feel to admit it, it was good to hear her voice.

We are on a different footing now, her silence seemed to say, not just because of the station you have risen to in life, but for other reasons, too. But it seemed to me her relentless attacks were out of all proportion to what I had ever done to her, or even what she thought I had done, namely, put Prowse at risk by threatening Hines.

Field Day, September 19, 1950

"Got a phone call from himself yesterday. I made a suggestion. He made, and offered to help me carry out, a suggestion of his own. Said on the record I was off my rocker. Off the record a good deal more. The words *Scotch* and *bitch* came up a lot."

(Editor's explanation: Miss Fielding and Mr. Smallwood, though they have never met, chat frequently by phone, often sharing a chuckle over the unaccountable rumours that there exists between them some sort of animosity. The words Scotch and bitch came up frequently in their most recent conversation because Mr. Smallwood had phoned Miss Fielding with the happy news that his terrier had just had a litter of puppies, three of whom were female. Miss Fielding, who had been promised the pick of the litter and who has followed with much interest and concern the course of Pokey's pregnancy these past few months, could not have been more pleased. As for the exchange of suggestions, it demonstrates perfectly the deep-seated friendship that exists between these two, which no amount of professional rivalry can undermine.)

She began calling me by a variety of nicknames in her column: himself and, because my initials were J. R. and I was still so small, so scrawny (130 pounds at the age of fifty), Junior. She even resurrected the nickname she had coined for me at Bishop Feild and referred to me as "Splits."

I worked too long, too hard, too frenetically to gain weight, never putting in less than eighteen hours a day, weekends and holidays included. I was like a one-man company whose business was running Newfoundland.

This was partly because I trusted no one, believing that the quality, the first chance they got, would try to edge me out and put one of their own in my place, if not Prowse then someone like him. I could not delegate responsibility without also dispensing power, and I was therefore unwilling to trust any task of any importance to someone else. I was unofficially a minister of all portfolios.

How could I not have made mistakes? Fielding devoted a column to the four men who, at the height of a blizzard, knocked on my door and explained that they were "Icelandic herring fishermen" who had come, they cryptically said, because "Iceland is going down and Newfoundland is coming up." Newfoundland could go "high up," they said, if I were to buy herring boats for them. I think I did it because I could, because of the sheer novelty of being able to fulfil such a ridiculous request. I had only to say yes and the boats were bought.

The Icelanders left Newfoundland weeks later with a contract, came back the following spring with four dilapidated boats that were not worth a fraction of the $400,000 I had doled out, spent nine months fishing (during which time they caught six barrels of herring), then disappeared and were never seen again. When I worked this out, I found that each single fish cost the province seven hundred dollars, or about fourteen hundred times what it was worth.

Someone convinced me there was no better place in the world to manufacture gloves made entirely from the skins of gazelles than Newfoundland. Into this scheme went half a million dollars; out of it came not so much as a single pair of gloves.

There was the International Basic Economy Corporation, which charged my government $240,000 to assess the prospects for a third pulp-and-paper mill in Newfoundland, almost instantly on payment declared that there were no such prospects, then disappeared.

Fielding wrote about all these blunders, for which I otherwise escaped chastisement, in her column.

I replied with a press release.

"How are we to attract the great businessmen and industrialists of the world to Newfoundland when people like Miss Fielding are casting doubts in their minds about everything we say and do? Perhaps Miss Fielding does not understand the effect these columns of hers have on potential investors who come here. How much money, I would like to know, has Miss Fielding scared away from Newfoundland? Perhaps her readers should ask themselves that question."

Fielding replied that far from scaring "investors" away, her columns, which showed what an easy mark I was, were in all likelihood what attracted them to Newfoundland in the first place.

I decided that what I needed, what Newfoundland needed, was a specialist in economic development, a one-man brain-trust, someone who would not be a mere consultant, but a civil servant, a member of my staff.

I phoned Ottawa for advice on the matter and, after speaking to several dozen persons, had recommended to me a man who sounded like the very thing I was looking for, a professor and a consultant for the federal government on immigration and economic development.

His name was Dr. Alfred Valdmanis. At a press conference, I introduced him as someone to whom we would one day build a monument.

Fielding's Condensed
History of Newfoundland

Chapter Thirty-One:

THE PEOPLE'S PARTY

In 1907, Bond's lieutenant, Sir Edward Morris, crosses the House to sit as a Conservative. In 1908, invited to lead the Conservatives against Bond in the election, Morris, to whom the Reids lend their moral support (having by this time been so Wintered by Bond they have no other kind to lend), declines.

Instead, he converts the Conservative Party to the People's Party. Bond absurdly suggests that it is clear from what he calls the Pee Pee's manifesto that the People's Party differs from the Liberal Party only in having Morris as its leader instead of him. In other words, says Bond, the election is a contest between the Liberals and the Liberals and he claims to be unsurprised when it ends in a deadlock, with both parties winning eighteen seats.

Governor William MacGregor calls on Morris to form an administration. Morris accepts. MacGregor dissolves the House. Another election is called. Morris campaigns this time as the leader of the ruling party rather than the leader of the opposition; it is only his confidence that is enhanced by this distinction, not, as Bond asserts, his ability to dispense patronage at will.

Confidence and Morris win the day. Shortly thereafter, the Railway Extension Act is passed. The Reids, by way of token reparation, are asked to build six new branch lines, thereafter known as "the olive branch lines."

Defeated again in 1913, Bond resigns, spends the rest of his life in sulking seclusion and, in 1918, when there is a bid to bring him back to lead the Liberals, declares: "I have had a surfeit of Newfoundland politics, and I turn from the dirty business with contempt and loathing."

Despite the, alas, too-numerous-to-mention ways that Morris improves the lives of Newfoundlanders, it is not until the ascension to the prime ministership in 1919 of Sir Richard Squires that Newfoundland turns the corner to prosperity and self-respect.

As we intend to end our history with a postscript selection from *Quodlibets*, we would like here to thank Sir Richard Squires for the commendation that begins our book. We can think of no one more appropriate, or by whose kindness we could be more flattered, than Sir Richard to commend to the public a book that his record in office has inspired us to write and whose virtues, if any there be, are animated by his own.

We have said "end our history." But this is in fact but its beginning, the start of its maiden voyage. That it will still be afloat when its rivals are with barnacles encrusted at the bottom of the sea we have no doubt. Nor do we doubt that she will have put in to every port before her day is done.

There, the bottle of champagne smashed against her hull, the blocks removed, she goes sliding down the slip — and Lo, is Launched!

Junket

I TOLD THE NEWFOUNDLAND people that Valdmanis was so highly qualified that I was going to pay him more than three times what I paid myself. I was making about seven thousand dollars a year; Valdmanis I would pay twenty-five thousand.

Valdmanis was a Latvian economist with an obscure past who gave everyone he met a different version of his life story. He told me that as a schoolboy, he was recruited into some sort of elite education corps whose purpose was to turn out the future leaders of Latvia; that during the war he had been a leader of his country's resistance movement; that sometime between leaving Latvia and coming to Canada, he had been given the highest award the Swedish government could give, the Stella Polaris.

Though rumours flew about that his doctorate was self-conferred; that he had not received the Stella Polaris but some citation that could be had from the Swedish government for the equivalent of box-tops; that far from leading his country's resistance movement, he had been a Nazi collaborator or quisling during the war, I said I had not the slightest doubt that Valdmanis was the real thing, "a man of honour."

Valdmanis gave himself the title of director general of economic development, telling me that it would "impress the Europeans."

I picked him up at the airport myself in the Chrysler Imperial my cabinet insisted I own and drive, as it was more befitting a premier than my battered Dodge, which I had hated to part with.

He was about five foot seven, slightly, compactly built, with a full head of tightly curled black hair, a very high forehead and intense green eyes. His most distinctive physical characteristic was one he brought to my attention, floating irises, he called it, explaining, only hours after we had first met, what he meant by this.

"In most people," he said, bringing his face to within about six inches of mine so I could get a better look, "the iris" — he pointed, all but touched his eye with his forefinger — "the coloured part of the eye, extends from the upper eyelid to the lower eyelid. In a person with floating irises, people who generally have larger than usual eyes, the iris does not extend all the way to the lids, a portion of the eyeball is visible above and below the iris, so the iris appears to be, and is said to be, 'floating.' Only about 2 per cent of the population have floating irises."

The effect of his floating irises, as I had no doubt he knew, was to focus his stare, to give you the impression that you were being looked at from behind his eyes, as though through a pair of peepholes.

"Where are your wife and children?" I said.

"They're staying in Montreal for the time being," he said. "The children have travelled a lot. My wife doesn't think I'll last more than a few months in Newfoundland because of what she's heard about the weather. Once she sees that I'm here to stay, she and the children will join me." It seemed odd to me that a wife and mother would base such an important decision on weather rumours, but I said nothing.

He quickly took my measure, I suppose, and the measure of Newfoundland — its historical measure, that is. I saw this and did not mind. Perhaps he had some charm or charisma he could turn on or off at will, for though I was greatly taken with him, it soon became clear that my ministers were not. He affected with them a humility and courtesy whose insincerity was meant to be transparent, to offend. He referred to each of them as "your excellency" and whenever he met them bowed in what to me seemed a playfully unctuous manner, like a send-up of some Old World court tradition.

Perhaps, to others, his flattery of me, his devotion to me, was just as transparently insincere. To me, it was as if he believed it was merely a happy coincidence that the one man of real ability in Newfoundland happened to be the man in charge, the elected leader. I convinced myself that it was because of my ability, not because of my office and power, that he took to me.

His belittlement of others I took as an indirect compliment. I thought his contempt of so many demonstrated, not arrogance, but high standards and discriminating judgment, and I was flattered that he should be so impressed with me.

I saw Valdmanis as a kindred spirit together with whom I could accomplish more than I could with all the members of my Cabinet. I also saw him as harmless. He was an outsider and so would never be a political rival.

Five minutes after we met, he said he believed that in Newfoundland, he had found his "spiritual home." I did not think this was insincere, because I could not imagine that anyone would try in so guileless a manner to curry favour.

Perhaps what appealed to me most about him was that he seemed not only so lonely, but also isolated, enisled, as if the world within which he had been designed to excel had ceased to exist or had never come about in the first place. Enisled.

We were no less enisled for having joined Canada, not yet, at least. Perhaps that is why it seemed to me that Newfoundland, this world apart, was just the place for Valdmanis, and he for it. Enisled, a Newfoundlander by predilection if not by birth.

In his first few months in Newfoundland, he revealed his social and cultural talents one by one until it seemed he would never run out of ways of surprising us. At a Christmas party, he sang Christmas carols in what was obviously a trained voice. A month later, at a Government House ball, he waltzed about the floor, as if their feet were melded to his, women who had no more idea than I did how to waltz. He was a multi-linguist who charmed visitors from other countries by conversing with them in their language while the rest of us stood by in open-mouthed, astonished silence. He played half a dozen musical instruments — the piano, the violin, the flute — flawlessly. But the question was always, faintly comically, what for? For he seemed to take no pleasure in his talents, seemed more to be saddled with them than anything else.

It was at the suggestion of Valdmanis that I switched tactics where Fielding was concerned. Unlike my Cabinet ministers, he did not try to convince me of her insignificance or recommend that I ignore her. He assured me that I was right in thinking that her criticisms of me must somehow be "neutralized."

He urged me to invite her to travel with us, at government expense. She would, if she agreed, join Valdmanis and me and our retinue of civil servants as we travelled throughout the countries of Europe on what I called, when I announced it to the press, a trade mission, the purpose of which would be to entice "world-class investors" to Newfoundland.

"What would be the point?" I said. "If you think Fielding is going to tone down her attacks on us in exchange for a trip abroad — "

"I want to get to know Miss Fielding," Valdmanis said. "I cannot think of any other way of contriving to spend time with her than to invite her on such a trip."

"She'll write about everything we do," I said.

Valdmanis shrugged. "She'll write about us if she comes along or not."

In the end I agreed, though I foresaw a fiasco. Valdmanis told me how I should extend the invitation. I rang Fielding up on the telephone.

"We want you to come along with us, Fielding," I said. "We want you to see just how hard we work. Once you get to know Dr. Valdmanis and see close up what he is trying to do on behalf of Newfoundland, once you see the sort of obstacles that we are up against, once you have a feel for what it is really like to be a leader, a premier, a politician, I believe you will see us both in a different light."

"Smallwood, tell me something," she said, "aren't you at all worried by how eager all these people of his seem to be to 'invest' in Newfoundland?" (There had been a piece in the *Daily News* about the scores of potential investors Valdmanis had arranged for us to meet.)

"Not a bit," I said. "After all, you don't say no to Santa Claus."

"And you want me to come along so that once I see how hard it is to run a province, I'll become a more — what? — a more responsible reporter? Come on, Smallwood, what's this really all about? I'm not going to mysteriously disappear on this trip or something, am I?"

I laughed. In the end, unable, I suppose, to resist finding out what our ulterior motive might be, she accepted our invitation.

I announced it at the junket press conference as a kind of coup. "Would I invite Miss Fielding along," I said, "Miss Fielding of all people, if, as the leader of the opposition claims, I had something to hide?"

"It will be interesting to see," one *Telegram* reader wrote in a letter to the editor a few days later, "if after being wined and dined and God knows what else for a month throughout the principalities of Europe, our Miss Fielding will ever be the same."

We flew to London and gathered ourselves there for a tour of the major European cities at the rate of two or three a week. We spent our days in offices and factories and our evenings at the opera, the ballet, the theatre, after which we were wined and dined by people who, in Valdmanis's obscure former life, had been, as he described them, "associates" of his. Wherever he took us, he seemed not only to know everyone but also to be held in high esteem. "What do you expect?" Fielding said. "If you were showing visitors around Newfoundland, how many Catholics would you introduce them to?"

Fielding's columns ran daily throughout this month-long junket, filed one day from London, the next from Paris, the next from Hamburg. By three days into the trip, I was receiving word about the columns Fielding was filing, which were appearing in the *Telegram* back home. She knew I knew about her columns, but I pretended to think that she would eventually come round.

We let her accompany us almost everywhere we went, Valdmanis acting as if he thought the sheer splendour and luxury of her surroundings would win her over.

"I want her to think that this is our strategy," he said. As for me, I was as interested as Fielding to know what our ulterior motive might be, but whenever I questioned Valdmanis, all he said was that he merely wanted "to get to know" Fielding, and that to do so would take time.

Valdmanis, using his old diplomatic contacts, got us a brief audience with Pope Pius XII at Castel Gandolfo, the pope's "home away from Rome," as Fielding called it in her column. I kept looking at Fielding to see if she was suitably impressed — I was starting to think we really had brought her along in the hopes of winning her over to our side.

I introduced her. "Your Holiness," I said, "this is Miss Fielding, a prominent journalist in Newfoundland. She writes for the *Evening Telegram*, one of the great small newspapers in the world." My God, Fielding's expression seemed to say as she looked at me, why don't you just have me killed if it means that much to you to shut me up? I was surprised myself that I did not choke on the words.

I had with me a suitcase full of prayer beads and holy medals, which Valdmanis had bought in shops near the Vatican, and the pope agreed to bless them after I told him of my plan to distribute them to Catholics back home.

"He plans to hand them out with pictures of himself in Catholic ridings in the next election," Fielding said. The pope smiled, assuming, I suppose, that she was joking, though that was exactly what I planned to do. I felt myself blushing deep red and I tried to smile as if I too thought it was a joke. Valdmanis remained expressionless, as if Vatican protocol forbade levity in the presence of the pope, which for all I know it did.

Valdmanis was especially well-connected in Germany, where we spent two full weeks, but that, I told myself, was only natural, since, by his own admission, he had spent most of the war there, where he had been sent, as he put it, for "defying the Nazis" while in German-occupied Latvia.

This, I knew, was not the whole truth. He had been chief public prosecutor and director-general of justice in occupied Latvia. He assured me his duties had not entailed what such titles might lead one to believe.

On Valdmanis's instructions, I frequently pointed out to the Germans that their country was much like Newfoundland, in a state of transition and rebuilding, and I told them they had better rebuild it fast before they were overrun by the Communists.

We negotiated with Alfred Krupp, the steel magnate, to set up a mill in Newfoundland. As Krupp had been jailed by the Allies since 1945 for war crimes, this proved difficult and, as Fielding wrote in her column, "might have been impossible if not for the invaluable A.V., who spent an entire day acting as go-between for Krupp and Smallwood, running messages back and forth between our hotel and the prison where Herr Krupp is being held."

At times, the junket took on an almost surreal quality. In Bavaria, on the lawn of some penniless aristocrat, we were treated to a command performance by a troupe of ballet dancers; when the dancers left the lawn, a display of fireworks began while somewhere offstage a choir half-sang, half-recited a heavily accented version of the "Ode to Newfoundland": "As luft our fodders, so ve luff / vere vonce dey stoot, ve stant. / Our prayers ve raise to heaven abuff, / Got guard thee, Newfoundlant." Later, by way of justifying my promise to give our host for this event a large "loan" to start up some business in Newfoundland, I told the Newfoundland legislature that he was "a great figure in industry" who, though he had "no money in actual dollars," had in his house "two-quarters of a million dollars' worth of famous paintings."

It is all there, in that phrase. Not half a million dollars' worth of paintings, but two-quarters of a million dollars, as if two of anything were better than one of anything else. "Famous" paintings, that was important, too; that had helped carry the day, in my mind. The mere fact that he owned something whose quality and value were acknowledged outside of Newfoundland made him a worthwhile risk.

"Newfoundland," I had said, before becoming a confederate, "can be one of the great small nations of the earth." That oxymoron, "great small," seems to me now to sum up my view of Newfoundland quite well. Fielding once devoted a column to my habit of using the construction, "one of the great small ... of the world." She quoted me as having said that the *Telegram* was one of the great small papers of the world. She reported, accurately, that I had pledged to make the newly established Memorial University one of the great small universities in the world. She said I said that the Long Range Mountains were among the great small mountains in the world, that Churchill Falls was among the great small wonders of the world, that the Humber River was one of the great small rivers in the world.

She wrote:

In one of the great small hours of the morning, it occurred to me that our forests were among the great small woods in the world, as is our premier one of the great Smallwoods in the world, not to mention one of the great small Smallwoods in the world, for which we ought to reward him with one of the great small dogs of the world, a Pekingese, perhaps.

I boasted often of how I had met with Truman, been photographed with Gandhi and shaken Churchill's hand. "Those are great men," I said to my audiences in an almost chastening tone, "great men" seeming to imply that they were great in a way that neither they nor I could ever hope to be by virtue of our being Newfoundlanders. I acted as if, for a Newfoundlander, there was no greater accomplishment than to be judged by some great man to be a credit to your people.

I never addressed Valdmanis directly as anything but "Doctor," and Valdmanis never called me anything except "my premier." This formality was never dropped. Even when we talked among ourselves, it was "Doctor" and "my premier."

I was infatuated, not so much with Valdmanis, as with the man he was impersonating, who had all those qualities that I felt the lack of in myself — worldliness, sophistication, business savvy, education, culture, taste, refinement.

In Zurich, I wound up, because of some sort of a mix-up in reservations, having to share a hotel room with Valdmanis.

Field Day, May 6, 1951

Rather than saddle the Newfoundland tax-payer with the cost of two, we all ride in the same Mercedes. We stay only at the best hotels, but it is also true that only the best hotels have beds big enough to sleep three.

Mr. Smallwood and Mr. Valdmanis are of sufficiently modest stature that there is plenty of room for me between their feet and the foot of the bed, where I lie crosswise, my journalistic objectivity inviolate.

As for your premier and your director-general of economic development, dear reader, they will often lie awake, late into the night, side by side in their pyjamas, their hands behind their heads, talking, planning strategies, devising schemes. To think that their most masterful of which to date may have had their origins in pillow talk!

"We will dot Conception Bay with factories," your premier said the other night. I, too, lay there, listening, wondering if perhaps I had misjudged them.

They are a lively, fun-loving pair who betimes will wile away the hours playing "pedals," a Latvian children's game in which two participants lying flat on their backs at opposite ends of a bed, with their hands behind their heads, place the soles of their bare feet together and "pedal" each other like bicycles, the object of the game being to pedal one's opponent off the bed, though my premier and the Latvian are so evenly matched that neither can budge the other and they pedal themselves into a state of mutual exhaustion, then fall asleep.

I was, after seeing this column, no longer able to keep up the pretence of having invited Fielding along in the hope that she would see the light.

"I am familiar with most of the great newspapers of the world," I said to Fielding when a copy of the column was sent to me, "and I can tell you with certainty that none of them would publish this sort of drivel. Two men and a woman in one bed, two men playing 'bicycles' or something, what is that supposed to mean? It is the worst sort of trash...."

Valdmanis managed to calm me down somewhat.

"My premier is tired, Miss Fielding," he said. "This has been a long trip, a great strain on all of us."

It became an even greater strain as more of Fielding's columns began to arrive. For the first time since I had hired him, I berated Valdmanis for committing "a blunder of monumental proportions."

"My premier," he said, "you must trust me. I cannot explain to you now, but it will soon become obvious to you why it was necessary to invite Miss Fielding along. I cannot tell you now. Most of it I will never be able to tell you, for it will be best if you do not know."

"You're doing things without my authorization?" I said.

"You must trust me, my premier," he said. "There are things that must be done that you are better off not authorizing."

"Something had better come of this," I said. "Something worthwhile, something worth the stupid risks that we are taking."

"There are no risks for you," he said. I threw up my hands and we spoke no more about it.

Field Day, May 21, 1951: The Foot of the Bed, Room 346, Hotel Hamburg

I have taken to writing my columns at night, while lying in bed. At this moment, my premier and the Latvian are sound asleep, tired out as usual from playing "pedals." Tonight's bout was yet another stalemate, though it ended in some animosity when the Latvian accused Mr. Smallwood of cheating by removing his hands from the back of his head, which Mr. Smallwood admitted to doing, though only long enough, he said, to adjust his glasses, which were slipping off.

"It doesn't matter," said the Latvian. "You used your hands." Mr. Smallwood's plea that pedals is a Latvian game, the rules of which he is still learning and couldn't possibly know as well as someone who grew up playing it, fell on deaf ears, however, and the Latvian told him that next time, he would be disqualified. They went to sleep in a pout and one can only hope that for the sake of Newfoundland, they make up in the morning.

Valdmanis could not keep up with the pace I set. I was energized by sheer rage, unable to look at Fielding, though I knew that it was out of the question to send her home at this point, that if we did we would look ridiculous. Fielding would not have been able to keep up the pace either, but she was free to beg off whenever she wished and spent a fair amount of time alone in her hotel rooms, recuperating from, or laying the groundwork for, hangovers or writing her columns while Valdmanis and I continued our endless rounds of meetings and official functions, often leaving at eight in the morning and not returning to our rooms until midnight.

In Hamburg, during our second trip to Germany, while the three of us were riding in the backseat of a gleaming chauffeur-driven burgundy Mercedes, which I assured Fielding was not being paid for by the people of Newfoundland, Valdmanis, mopping his brow with a handkerchief, seemed on the verge of hyperventilation.

"My premier, I cannot continue," he said. "Don't you ever get tired? Don't you ever need to rest?"

"Not much," I said. "That is what comes from clean living, Dr. Valdmanis. I do not smoke, I do not drink" — I looked meaningfully at Fielding, who looked away — "I do not chase women."

Valdmanis advised me to play my mock "trump card" a few days before we left for home. Throughout the trip, I had, at Valdmanis's suggestion, been promising Fielding a "scoop" and finally I told her what it was.

Field Day, May 25, 1951: The Foot of the Bed, Room 346, Hotel Hamburg

Never was their pedalling more vigorous than it was last night. It was all I could do to keep from being bounced right off the bed. I held on to one of the bedposts and watched with astonishment the blur of their four ever-accelerating legs.

"My premier, I cannot continue," A. V. protested at last. "I cannot, I am winded, I must rest."

"I've beaten him at his own game," said the premier gleefully, not even breathing hard as the Latvian flopped down exhausted on his pillow. "I have out-pedalled a Latvian. There are not many who can make that claim. That is what comes from clean living. I do not smoke. I do not drink. I do not chase women. I am easily able to outrun those who chase me."

His hands still behind his head, he stretched out full-length, showing off his five-foot-six-inch pin-stripe-pyjamaed form to best advantage. He eyed me craftily, the lights from the chandelier reflecting in his glasses, the thick black rims of which had never seemed more becoming.

"I will give you something to write about, Miss Fielding," he said. He chuckled when I told him I was shocked. "I will give you something you can really sink your teeth into."

"What?" I said.

"An election," he said.

"A WHAT?" I said.

"An election," he said, "an election. You know what an election is, don't you?"

"Yes, yes, of course I do," I said. "I thought you said — but never mind."

"I'm calling an election as soon as we get back to Newfoundland," he said. "I just decided it, right here in bed. I can't tell you the date yet, but you can say in your column that

I'm calling an election as soon as we get home. How's that for a scoop?"

A. V. was overjoyed. "You will win by a landslide, my premier," he said. "You cannot lose. You will never lose. You will win this election, and the next one, and the next one after that. Our partnership will last forever. Together, we will make Newfoundland great. We will, we will, we will." He stood up on the bed and began jumping up and down, spinning around in mid-air. Mr. Smallwood lay there, smiling, regarding reflectively his size-six feet, which he wiggled back and forth.

We flew back to Newfoundland.

Fielding's Condensed
History of Newfoundland

Chapter Thirty-Two:

THE HERMIT

We here present the last and most ambitious of Robert Hayman's rhymes, "The Hermit," in which a fisherman of Bristol's Hope, relieved of his possessions by the pirate Peter Easton, addresses that now absent personage and, because of his misfortune, meditates on Newfoundland and casts upon the island and all its inhabitants an everlasting curse — then runs away.

> Easton, bastard, plundering whore,
> You sank my boat, you burned my store.
> "But look ye on the bright side now,
> Men there are worse off than thou,"
> You said as you did sail away.
> If such there be for them I pray.
> "I leave and leave you with your life,
> I leave and with me leaves your wife.
> To her 'tis nothing new, I'm told.
> She has with all your friends made bold,

And all the men from down the shore
And back again, and many more."
My friends did swear this was a lie
And some of them with me did cry,
And swore that they would miss her, too,
"As much, or even more, than you."
"I never will see her again.
She's gone with Easton and his men,"
I said to them who laughed at me,
"But you at rest will never be.
Smallpox and scurvy, wind and cold,
Because of these you'll ne'er grow old.
Red men, pirates, storms, starvation:
Death will seem like consolation.
Now on your heads this curse I place,
On you and yours and all your race
And those of other races, too.
Who sets foot here the day will rue."
I then strode off into the wood,
The Hope behind me left for good,
And by myself from then did live,
To those back home no thought did give.
I slept according to the sun,
And for a spear forswore my gun,
And tried to live as Red Men did,
Though from the Red Men too I hid.
My days in solitude I spent,
My nights the same, inside my tent.
I lay there in my little room,
Upon my thoughts a cast of gloom.
"This land should not have settled been,
Its shores should have remained unseen.
Its woods should not have been traversed
Not e'en by those who got here first.

They'll soon be gone, the ochre-men
Who number fewer now than when
John Cabot landed on the Cape
Or on them old John Guy did gape."
I then did drowse and close my eyes
Of Red Men dreamed and their demise.
Whereas the Hopers still did come
And plagued though by my curse their sum
Despite the French and English crown,
Did ne'er to nothing dwindle down.
I stirred and soon was wide awake,
Too late discovered my mistake.
When on the Hope the curse I hung,
It was my own death knell I rung.
I, like the Red Men, soon would be
Consigned unto eternity.
I wished this Newfoundland could be
Unlooked at except by me,
And when I died looked at by none.
Then out of time this place would run.
The land again would be the same
As before the people came.
It would not be empty, lonely
Or forlorn. It simply would not be.

Hotel Newfoundland, New York, 1920
The San, St. John's, 1922
Twelve Mile House, June 1923

Revelations

LIKE THE CARPETBAGGER Yankees who, after the American civil war, went south to cash in on reconstruction, their ilk, after Confederation, came to Newfoundland.

In the year following our trip abroad, they came from England, from France, from Lichtenstein and Luxembourg, from Switzerland and Sweden, from Holland, Belgium, Italy, Spain and especially from Germany. They came to stake their claims to a piece of Newfoundland, to loans, to licences, to grants, to exploration rights and tender contracts, to mineral rights, water rights and real estate.

It was mostly Germans who were successful in securing deals with us.

Valdmanis and I were forever announcing agreements between the Newfoundland government and Herr Someone or Other: Herr Grube of Hamburg, Herr Moaser of Hamburg, Herr Hohlbrock of Hamelin, Herr Braun-Wogan of Berlin. In her column, Fielding called them all collectively Herr Humbug of Hamburg.

Frauds, shady businessmen, scam artists, shysters, impostors, opportunists, eccentrics, mountebanks, they proposed, and were given government grants for, the most unlikely, far-fetched, bizarre schemes for the economic development of Newfoundland, almost all of which flopped or never got off the ground.

It was enough for me that they came from far away; this to me was their collateral, their foreign-sounding names were their credentials. I was exasperated with, I dismissed as provincial, ignorant, bigoted and small-minded, anyone who wanted to know who these people were or where they came from.

I cited as a reason to give a character named Dr. Luther Sennewalde a hundred thousand dollars the fact that he had "nearly" won the Nobel Prize for physics. Sennewalde's proposal? To set up in Newfoundland a factory that, he said, would employ a "secret optical process" to manufacture, per year, several hundred thousand pairs of eye glasses.

"There is a guaranteed market," I said, parroting Valdmanis, "one in every five Canadians wears glasses." Far from cornering the eye-glasses market, Sennewalde, who was found to have shipped to Newfoundland, not secret optical equipment, but scrap metal and rocks, made off with his hundred thousand dollars to Montreal, where he was caught and found to have in his possession a one-way ticket to South America.

A. Adler and Sons of London, England, received from me a "loan" of half a million dollars to make chocolate, chocolate of which I said at a press conference: "It is the genuine thing. It is real English chocolate. You can be the most bigoted, the most prejudiced person alive on earth, but if you eat Adler's chocolate, you must say that it is good." In spite of my pitch, opinion in Newfoundland was almost unanimous that it was bad. Adler's went under two years later.

Herr Grube of Hamburg convinced me to invest in a plant that would import natural rubber from the Far East to make rubber boots and seamen's clothing. I described him to the legislature as a man of "dynamism, energy, push and ability." I did not know until he arrived in Newfoundland that he was also a man who spoke not a word of English.

Within a year highlighted by a bizarre series of miscommunications, he was gone, but by that time I was on to a Herr Braun-Wogan, in whom I professed a confidence that turned out to be as justified as that which I had placed in Herr Grube.

Valdmanis-negotiated, Newfoundland-funded, German-owned businesses were forever starting up and shutting down, their German owners disappearing overnight, leaving us to dispose of their enterprises.

I rose one day and told the legislature we had sold an abandoned cement mill for nearly $4.5 million. A company bought it with, as the auditor-general put it in his annual report, "money that was advanced to them by the government of Newfoundland." In other words, we gave them the money so they could give it back to us to "buy" our plant.

Valdmanis did not seem especially distressed by these debacles, nor did he seem to feel responsible for them or worried that I might place the blame on him.

"Germany is still our best bet," he kept assuring me. "This is how it is with economic development," as if he saw in me signs that I was beginning to doubt, not his abilities, but my own, and as if, contrary to how it might seem to an economic neophyte like me, things were going exactly as they ought to have been at this point in what he called the program.

In December 1953, with most of the $45 million surplus we had carried with us into Confederation gone, and with the embarrassing failures mounting day by day, Valdmanis came to me and told me his wife had insisted that he return to Montreal.

"She does not want me to live here all the time," he said. "I cannot convince her. She thinks the weather here is worse than it was in Latvia. I cannot reason with her. But there is no reason why I cannot do my job just as well from there for a while, better in fact, for I will be within easier reach of investors and promoters."

I thought he was just suffering a temporary loss of nerve, and it actually seemed plausible to me — such was my own frantic state at the time — that he would do his job better if he was not under such close scrutiny as he had to endure in Newfoundland. And so Valdmanis left for Montreal.

Not long after he left, I realized that he had no intention of coming back and would go on collecting his exorbitant salary for doing next to nothing as long as I allowed him to. I decided to fire him, using as my excuse the supposed "revelation" that he had padded his expense account, which he had, although so had everyone who worked for me. But I was determined to get rid of him, hoping that by doing so, I would convince the Opposition party that I had at last come to my senses.

I fired him on one of the rare visits he made to Newfoundland, fired him face to face. I called him to my office, and he came in as he always did, smiling broadly, with his hand outstretched.

"You're going to resign," I said. "And you're going to do it right away. You're going to say it's because of pressures in your private life and that's all you're going to say."

Only days later, a Latvian engineer who lived in Newfoundland came to see me. He told me, on condition of anonymity, that each time Valdmanis negotiated a contract with a German company, he charged them what he told them was a "standard 10 per cent commission," which he said would go to the Newfoundland Liberal Party, though he insisted that my name would be kept out of it. Such arrangements and stipulations were, it seemed, nothing new to the Germans, who readily agreed to them.

I had not the slightest doubt, even before I had the RCMP investigate them, that these allegations were true. Valdmanis alone of those of us who, at various times, had gone to Europe had been able to speak German and understand the engineering technicalities that were involved in proposed development projects. And so he had always done the negotiating, the presence at the table of people like me who would not have understood a word of what was going on having been deemed, by me, to be superfluous.

I assured the RCMP that any crimes had been committed without my knowledge and implored them to trace down the missing money, since, if every cent was not accounted for, it would be assumed to have gone not only into Valdmanis's pocket, but also into mine, or into the coffers of the Liberal Party, and in either case I would be ruined.

The money, $470,000, though never recovered, was eventually traced to bank accounts in New York City that were held in the name of Valdmanis's sister-in-law. Most of it Valdmanis had paid out to a pair of refugees, a Latvian and a Rumanian who were living in New York. In exchange, they had signed over to him a fish plant in New Brunswick, which he must have known was worthless. It was suspected that this was just a paper transaction, and that Valdmanis, in paying the refugees, had in fact been paying himself. Valdmanis later claimed he had given the money to blackmailers, but refused to elaborate.

He was arrested and brought back to Newfoundland to stand trial. He had been in St. John's two days, awaiting his preliminary hearing, when one of his lawyers hand-delivered a note to me that read:

"It is urgent that I see you. I have information regarding Fielding which I am sure you will find very interesting — more interesting than you can possibly imagine!"

It was out of the question that I visit him, for word of it was sure to get out no matter how circumspect I was. Suspicions and allegations that I had been in collusion with Valdmanis were rampant enough. But I could foresee no harm in speaking to him on the telephone and had Prowse arrange for him to call me at my home at eight in the evening.

I was sitting alone in my study when the phone rang. I picked up the receiver and held it to my ear, but said nothing. "Hello, my premier," Valdmanis said in a cravenly jaunty way that made me feel embarrassed for him, but I said nothing. When next he spoke, his voice was weak and quavering. I wished I could see his face to see if he was acting. I wondered if even then I would have known.

"I have information," he said. "While we were in Europe, I had some my of associates procure some things from Miss Fielding's room. I only did it thinking I could help you — "

"What information do you have?" I said.

"I know who wrote that letter," Valdmanis said, his voice formal now as if he had gathered strength from the coldness of my tone. "I also know some other things about Fielding. Everything you could ever want. And more." I did not, until that moment, even know that he had heard about the letter, but I did my best not to sound surprised.

"And what do *you* want?" I said.

"Complete immunity from prosecution," Valdmanis said, though it was a plea, almost a question.

I hung up and sat there at my desk, thinking, waiting for the phone to ring again, which it soon did. I let it ring until it stopped. Again I waited, again the phone rang, again I let it ring. This went on for about an hour until at last I picked up the receiver.

"My premier," Valdmanis said, weeping freely now. "I must get *something* in return."

"If you plead guilty," I said, "and spare me the embarrassment of having to testify against you in open court, I will do what I can to get you a reduced sentence."

There was a long pause, complete silence from the other end as if Valdmanis had his hand over the receiver and was consulting with someone. Finally he spoke again.

"My premier," he said, "there are two main charges of fraud against me. If I plead guilty to one, could you see to it that the other charge is dropped?"

"I'm not promising anything," I said, "until I hear what you have to say about Fielding."

"I have nothing to say," Valdmanis said. "A package will be delivered to your house just after midnight tonight. Do we have an agreement?"

"That," I said, "depends on how satisfied I am with the package."

"You will be satisfied," Valdmanis said.

"If I am, you will not hear from me, ever again," I said. "If I'm not, you will." I hung up.

The doorbell rang just after midnight, not a sufficiently unusual time to rouse my wife and children from their beds. I went to the front door, opened it. On the step was a large package wrapped in brown paper. There was no sign of anyone, no sound of a car pulling away. I picked up the package and went inside.

I testified, *in camera*, at the preliminary hearing in August 1954, as did half a dozen German businessmen.

Valdmanis was escorted into the courtroom by two policemen, who flanked him as he stood before the bar. He had Bradley-like black dewlaps beneath his eyes, as if he had not slept since his arrest, but he at least was well-dressed and so, I hoped, might seem to be deserving of the diminished sentence I had arranged for him to get — or rather, to not be so obviously undeserving of it that it would be impossible for us to pretend that no deal involving me had been made.

He pleaded guilty to one charge of fraud and the other charge was dropped. He was sentenced to four years at Her Majesty's Penitentiary, the only structure in Newfoundland named after her. He was released after serving sixteen months. Who he really was, what he had been through and what he had put other people through during the occupation of his homeland by the Nazis none of us would ever know.

I had been taken in by him, as I would be by a succession of other men who followed him and his example, men who wound up much as he did, all but destroying the country I had sought them out to save.

I drove to Fielding's boarding-house, parked my car around the corner, got out, duffel bag in hand, and hurried up the steps, up two flights of stairs, then down to the end of the hallway to her room. The day's papers were, as usual, piled up outside her door, the last-to-be-delivered *Telegram* on top. I knocked. There was the customary frantic commotion from within, which I no longer suspected might be done just for effect, for now I knew what she was hiding.

Finally, unconcernedly, as if it was not unusual for someone to come knocking on her door after midnight, she said, "Who is it?"

The time was long past when, in the hallway of a boarding-house at night, I could shout my name.

"It's me," I said. She opened the door. She was wearing a white, open-necked blouse outside a pair of black slacks, and her feet were bare.

"Oh, God," she said, her cigarette shunted to one side of her mouth. "A midnight visit from the premier." I was about to speak, but she beat me to it. "What's that?" she said, "a bag of money? You can just leave it with all the others if you like. First door on your left as you leave the building."

"Can I come in?" I said. She motioned me inside with a waiter-like flourish of her hand.

"You were working?" I said.

"I was," she said, mock-sighing, "so many scandals, so little column space. A woman's work these days is never done. We're starting something new this weekend, the Valdmanis supplement — "

"I'm not here about all that," I said. She glanced at the duffel bag again.

"Sit down," she said, "sit down."

We sat at the only table in the room, the one on which she worked, ate, read, drank, and slumped over some nights and slept,

I had no doubt. Now that I lived where and how I did, her accommodations seemed unbelievably shabby. There was a bottle of Scotch in its usual place, the back right corner of the desk. I was so accustomed to seeing it there, it looked like a knick-knack. For her, since Confederation, nothing much had changed.

We sat at right angles, me side-on to the narrow end of the table. I put the bag on the floor beside my feet. She poured herself a glass of Scotch from the bottle, offered me one, but I declined.

"All right," she said, "I'll bite, what's in the bag? The head of someone you're not as fond of as you used to be? The — "

"Copies of your journals," I said. "All of them, or most of them, I'm sure, since you were in the San. Valdmanis had them made while the three of us were travelling abroad. That's why he suggested I invite you along, to get you away from here long enough to give the place a thorough going over."

Fielding slumped back in her chair, fingered and stared at her glass, sighed.

"I don't understand," she said, "I don't pose that much of a threat to you, do I?"

"No. But I convinced him that you did," I said. "After I convinced myself. Not so much a threat as a — distraction. A lifelong distraction. But I didn't know about" — I indicated the bag — "about this. I didn't know he had — people in here while the three of us were on that junket. He wanted something on you, you see, not something he could use against you, but something he could use to get a favour from me, should the need ever arise, which he had every reason to think it might."

Fielding looked away from me, waiting, I was sure, to see how much I knew, how much I had deduced from the journals in which, though she must have intended that no one else would ever read them, she had been inscrutably secretive about some things until after Confederation, constantly referring to "it" or the "something" that had happened. Early in my reading of the journals, I thought Valdmanis was trying to trick me; I had to read so much before I found what I was looking for. In fact, there were still some things I did not know, and other things I was convinced were true but could not prove. I believed I knew who the writer of the letter was, but I was still not sure of his motivation. That seemed as good a place as any to start.

"Your father sent that letter — "

"Don't be ridiculous — "

"You confessed for him, to protect him."

"Does that seem like the sort of thing that he would have done?" she said. She stood up, however, grabbed her cane, which was leaned against the wall, and hobbled to the window, her back to me. For a long time neither of us spoke. She turned and came back to the table, turned her chair to face mine, one arm resting on the table, cupping her cheek. She closed her eyes.

"Yes," she said at last, nodding her head. "It seems that things are not always exactly what they seem to be. My father knew that you were the only townie in the dorm and that, because the letter was postmarked St. John's during Christmas, when all the bayboys were away, Reeves would assume or at least suspect that you wrote it."

"So who was the father?" I said.

She looked startled and glanced at the duffel bag again.

"I told my father you were," she said.

"Why?"

"Because you were too young to marry me. And I didn't want to marry — him."

"Hines?" I said.

She sniffed. "All Hines ever did was take pictures of me."

I winced, knitted my eyebrows in puzzlement. She tried to look unfazed. "Then who was the father? It doesn't say in your journals. You just refer to him as 'he.'"

"It was who you think it was."

"Prowse."

"We used to go to the judge's house. It was a big house; the judge lived there by himself and sat all day in his study. Oblivious. We did what we pleased where and when we pleased."

"But what about Hines?" I said. "Where does he come into it?"

"One thing I told you about him was true. He worked for the *Morning Post*, remember. He was the 'friend of the school' that Reeves referred to when he interrogated all you boys. My father paid Hines to intercept the letter after it arrived at the *Post*. He had to make sure it wound up in Reeves's hands so Reeves could see the postmark."

I remembered how Hines, in his sermon, had seemed to know so much about my days at Bishop Feild. *The way the masters treated you at school and laughed at your ambition. You will never live down the mark they gave you for character.* He must have found out about me from Fielding's father, who perhaps found out from Fielding. I did not want to know.

"Why did Hines leave Newfoundland in such a hurry after I confronted him? You had no way of proving he was involved."

"Actually, I did," she said. "I found the *History* at the back of my father's closet one day. I was always snooping around. Prowse said once that because my father wasn't married any more, he must have dirty pictures somewhere. If he did, I never found them. But when I was looking for them, I found the book. I knew about the letter by then; Prowse had told me about it. I'd read the judge's book a hundred times. I knew what words were missing. I pieced the letter together, realized it was my father who had written it. I also found in the *History* a letter from Hines demanding money from my father to buy his silence. I don't know if my father ever paid him anything. Anyway, after you came here and told me about Hines, I tracked him down and told him I still had the blackmail letter. He denied knowing anything about it. But the next day he was gone."

"And Prowse never knew anything?" Fielding shook her head. "When did you tell your father you were pregnant?"

"I never did. He found out himself. He used to give me semi-annual check-ups. When I was due my next one, I told him I would feel embarrassed having him examine me, now that I was — growing up. Nothing to be embarrassed about, he said. Which was true. By that time, I'd been leaving my clothes on for years while he examined me. He heard the heartbeat when he was listening to mine. Heard it through my dress. He insisted on knowing who the father was."

"And you told him it was me. But I was *almost* old enough to marry you. Who would have been the wiser?"

"In a situation like that, every month makes a difference."

"That's not it, Fielding," I said. "Why don't you tell the truth at last? Forty years later and you still can't tell the truth about it."

"And what truth might that be?" she said, twirling her glass about on the table.

"You know," I said. "Just like I knew who the father was."

"My father wouldn't have wanted me to marry you," she said. "Under any circumstances."

"Someone like me, you mean."

"I knew if I told my father it was Prowse, there would be a confrontation. He would talk to Prowse's father and demand marriage. He thought very highly of the Prowses. Prowse and I would have been marrying younger than people in our set usually did, of course, but only by a few years. I was four months pregnant. My father would have considered it a good marriage. He and Prowse's family would have made sure that the baby and I were well cared for until Prowse finished his education. People would certainly have guessed what was up, but with everyone doing the honourable thing, there would have been only one of those modest, short-lived, everyone-pretending-to-look-the-other-way sort of scandals, the sort that two families acting in consort could easily have faced down. It would in time have been forgotten. Or at least never talked about. Like my father's divorce. I knew of a similar arrangement that had been made between two other families in our circle. On the other hand, perhaps I was wrong, perhaps I panicked, perhaps even if I had told him Prowse was the father — who knows? But anyway, I told him it was you. I had no reason to think you would ever find out, or would ever be harmed by it. Maybe it was not just marriage to Prowse but marriage altogether I was trying to avoid. I chose you because of the store my father put by social standing, money, all of that. Not because of the store I put by it. I hope you won't confuse his world-view with mine."

"A convenient distinction," I said. "There's more of the snob in you than you'll ever admit to or even understand, Fielding. You say you were sure there was no risk and yet there was, wasn't there? And you were quite happy to risk me. You didn't know for sure what he would do."

"I'm sorry," she said.

"Tell me something," I said. "When you were in the Harbour Light, why did you give me that letter?"

Fielding shrugged. "I know what you're thinking, that I wanted you to find out. Maybe I did."

"And your confession about writing the letter to the *Morning Post*?" I said.

"You may not believe it, but it was partly to spare you being punished for something I knew you hadn't done."

"But mainly to protect your father."

"Yes. He didn't know I knew. At least, I never told him. I was afraid that if I did, he would tell Reeves what he'd done and he'd be ruined. Even after I was expelled, I said nothing. I thought he might confess to me. Just to me, I mean. I thought it could be our secret. But he never did."

"Didn't your father, when he heard why you'd been expelled, ask you why you confessed?"

She nodded. "I told him I did it because they suspected you of writing the letter and I wanted to keep you out of trouble. We said nothing more about it."

"Why did you want to protect someone who didn't have the courage to protect you?"

"I was pregnant; I was going to have to leave school anyway."

"Not the way you did, not like that. In disgrace for something he did — "

"Was provoked by me into doing — "

"Why didn't he come forward?"

"It would have been pointless for him to ruin his reputation — "

"Better to ruin mine and yours — "

"I didn't have one to ruin. And I didn't want to acquire one. I didn't care about being expelled. I knew what I wanted to do with my life, I knew I wanted to be some sort of writer — "

"You cared," I said.

"All right, Smallwood, I cared. My mother abandoned me. I was planning to renounce my child. I knew that Prowse was — Prowse. All I had left was my father. When I left Bishop Spencer, he sent me away to the States, to New York, where my mother hid me in her house until the babies were born. She pretended they were hers, faked a pregnancy, padded her dress more and more as the weeks went by. Not as unusual as it sounds. Quite a lot of mothers have done it through the ages. She had married another doctor, a man my father had gone to medical school with. He helped us hush it up, delivered the babies in his house. My mother and her husband raised them. David, my son. Sarah, my daughter. Who is nearly forty now. They thought it was best that I not see them. Took them away until after I went home. Alone. As alone as I have ever been.

"After you left for New York in 1920, I wrote my mother, using a pseudonym on the envelope, and asked if I could see the children. That's why I couldn't go with you right away, remember? When you told me where you were going?"

"I was foolish enough to think," I said, "that you were sad that I was leaving."

She smiled. "I would have been," she said, "if I hadn't known that I was going, too, which I did right from the start, I really did." I looked away from her.

"I knew I couldn't make that trip again and not see them. So I wrote my mother. She wrote back saying, 'David and Sarah believe that I am their mother. It would be unthinkable to tell them the truth at this point in their lives.' I wrote back and said she could introduce me to them as someone she once knew in Newfoundland, not as their mother or even their half-sister. They were barely five years old. They would never have guessed or suspected anything. But my mother refused again. She didn't trust me not to say anything, not to cry and make a scene. I wouldn't have done either, but she had no way of knowing that.

"So when I got to New York, I went to her street. All day one Saturday I watched my mother's house, half-hiding, walking back and forth, first on one side of the street, then on the other. I wore a hat pulled down low, a scarf. I doubt my mother would have recognized me anyway. I had changed a lot in five years. Finally, about three in the afternoon, this was in October, she and Sarah and David came out of the house and walked hand in hand, Sarah on one side of her, David on the other, down the street towards me. I crossed over to the other side and walked along far enough behind them that they wouldn't notice. My mother and my children, holding hands. My mother with my children, pretending they were hers.

"I crossed the street again, followed behind them until they stopped at an intersection. I stood directly behind them. Close enough that I could see Sarah's face. More like Prowse than me. Blond and blue-eyed. They were both dressed in little blazers — I wanted so much to touch them. Hold them in my arms. You can't imagine what living in New York was like for me after that, Smallwood. Always knowing they were in the same city. A thousand times, every time I saw a woman with two children, I thought it might be them. A few other times, as you know, I watched them from outside the playground at their school."

"What about Prowse?" I said.

"He knows about that," she said.

"But you said — "

"He hasn't known all along."

She put her elbows on the table, her face in her hands.

"I told him not long after David died," she said, her voice muffled. She lowered her hands. She looked as if she had been crying for hours. "David named me as one of the people who should be informed in case anything happened to him. He never knew I was his mother. He thought I was just his half-sister. 'My son. You are my son.' The words were on my lips, Smallwood, all the time he was here. That night in the movie-house. Sitting next to you is the woman in whose body you began. I wondered if he might somehow sense it." She cried, the heel of her palm on her forehead, tears dripping onto the table.

"That's enough," I said. But she shook her head.

"Two officers from Fort Pepperrell came to the door one day and handed me a telegram. 'We regret to inform you ...' That's when I went back on the bottle. I think I would have anyway, I was so worried about him. I couldn't sleep. He wrote to me a few times from France. I wrote to him. 'P.S. I'm your mother,' I always felt like writing. Three months after we first met, he was killed."

"I'm sorry," I said.

She nodded, bit her lip. Blinked back a sudden surge of tears. "Oh, my poor boy. My poor, sweet, darling boy." She slumped over the table, her head between her arms, shoulders heaving. I put out my hand and touched her hair, brushed it back from her forehead.

"I told Prowse about two weeks later," she said. "Maybe I shouldn't have. To find out, on the occasion of his death, that you had a son you never knew you had, never met."

She straightened, not caring now that I could see her face. "He didn't believe me at first. At least, he said he didn't. I assured

him that no one but him could be the father. I asked him what reason I would have to lie. He begged me never to tell anyone that he
was the children's father. He was more concerned that I keep it a
secret than anything else. But maybe that's not fair. Who knows
what he went through later when he was alone, what he's been
through since? I told him not to worry. I wouldn't tell anyone."

I had to ask. "Did you tell Prowse about David the day ... the
day I met you at the Press Club, the day we came back here — "

"The day I tried to get you into bed," she said, laughing and
crying at the same time. "Yes," she said. "I called him at his house
when I woke up. It took some doing to convince him to meet me
here. I must have sounded like I was in no shape to meet him somewhere else. But how did you know that?"

"I drove around for hours that night," I said. "I drove by here a
hundred times wondering if I should — see how you were doing."
Fielding put her hand over her mouth to suppress a smile, a generous, even-keeled smile. "I saw Prowse leave. He stopped by his car
and looked up at your window. You turned the lights on, then off.
Then on, then off again. I thought it must be some sort of signal."

"And you jumped to certain conclusions."

"Yes," I said. "Yes, I suppose I did."

"Prowse and I have hardly spoken since our school days,"
Fielding said. "Not even when I told him about David could he
bring himself to touch me. Especially not then, perhaps."

"Then why? Why did you do that with the light?"

"When we were — going together," she said, "when we were
at the judge's house, I would always leave first, by the back door,
which you couldn't see from the street. I would stand in the back-
yard and wait for Prowse to flash the upstairs light, to signal that
the coast was clear, that there was no one on the street and I could
leave. It all seemed so exciting. Our secret signal. Our way of saying goodbye. The night I told him about David, I said I would flick
the lights after he left. I didn't know until now that he waited for
the signal. But I'm glad to hear he did."

I remembered Prowse skipping jauntily down the steps of Fielding's boarding-house. Having just been told his son was dead. Trying to convince himself, perhaps. Nothing has happened that I cannot control. My life need not change. A son I did not know I had is dead. He did not exist for me yesterday, he does not exist today. A daughter I will never meet lives a thousand miles away. Nothing has changed. For a moment there I thought it had, but I was wrong. No one but Fielding will ever know. Fielding's life and mine are still far apart and they always will be. Nothing has happened that makes it more likely that I will ever have to live like Fielding. I will never live like Fielding. I have nothing new to fear.

But he waited for that signal, and when he saw it, threw aside his cigarette as if hoping with that gesture to dismiss the past, the notion that anything that happened then could matter to him now. But even for Prowse, as Fielding said, other moments were still to come, perhaps. At times, when he is by himself, the name some stranger gave his son will come to mind. David. The son whose picture and whose gravestone he has never seen. The daughter he has never seen and knows he never will.

"That night at the movie-house — " I said.

"My mother had told David when she thought he was old enough to understand such things that he had a half-sister in St. John's. From her first marriage. He looked me up. I don't know why I was so nervous when we saw you. Maybe I thought you would know from looking at him who his father was, see Prowse in David's face. Maybe I felt guilty. I couldn't bear to introduce him to you as what he thought he was, my half-brother. Also, I could see that you were jealous and the idea of leaving you in your misery appealed to me.

"Oh, Smallwood. Three days we had, three days. Every spare minute he had we spent together. The whole time I wondered if I should tell him who I really was, who he really was. He called me sis. He's going to war, I thought. This might be your only chance.

He might not come back. But then I thought, He's going to war, he'll need all his wits about him, this is no time to turn his whole world inside out. So I didn't tell him. I spent three days with him, pretending to be his half-sister, biting my tongue while he introduced me as that to all his friends. Though he never said 'half-sister,' just 'sister.' 'This is my sister, Sheilagh Fielding.'

"He told me all about Sarah, gave me a picture of her. 'Here she is,' he said, 'your sister.' On the back, he'd had her write, 'To Sheilagh, from Sarah.'

"Sometimes, I think that if I had told him who I was, he would not have died. He would have been nudged onto a path far enough from the one he followed that it would have led him safely home. I know it makes no sense — "

I pulled my chair over beside hers. She raised her head and looked at me. I kissed her on the lips; she kissed me back. And then she all but pulled me from the chair and held me to her, her arms beneath mine, which were crossed around her neck, her arms enfolding me completely, hugging me twice as hard as I hugged her, or was able to, for I was hugging her with all my might.

I thought of what she had said about David, how it tortured her to think that if she had told him who she was, he might have made it safely home. A nudge here, a nudge there. Had any one of a thousand things been different, the two of us — But I had no sooner thought it than I knew that I was wrong, that I had freely chosen to remain apart. And though the past was not lost to us, though it was there with us in that room while we held each other, I would not have changed it if I could.

Forty years of love were consummated with one hug. With my face pressed against her neck, I smelled her skin, a smell whose distinctiveness made me realize I had never held anyone this close, this fervently, before. Not even my wife. I felt or heard, I could not tell which, the beating of her heart, felt her cheek, wet and warm, against mine, tears from her face dripping onto mine as if both of us were crying.

We could not have stayed that way for long. Had she hugged me any harder, my bones would not have held. And soon she was out of what breath her old illness begrudged her at the age of fifty-five. We pulled apart.

Fielding. If I had ever met her father, I would have had to call her Sheilagh. And she, if she had ever met my family, would have had to call me Joe. Our one moment, our one point of intersection, had just come and gone. We had for years been moving closer together and from now on we would move apart. She had left the feel of her body on mine but already she was fading like water drying on my skin.

"Where does Sarah live?" I said.

"Still in New York," Fielding said. "She's married, has a little girl named Karen. I keep track of her by subscribing to her alumni newsletter. I'm fairly certain I'm the only person in this boarding-house getting mail from Columbia University."

"You should have got married, Fielding. After I asked you, I mean. Since then, I mean. You should stop drinking, live somewhere more ... You should see your daughter and your grand-daughter; you should see Sarah, that's something you can do."

"What would I tell her? The woman you think was your mother, the man you think was your father, on whose headstones you are named as their daughter, were not really your parents. I am your mother and the man you think was your father was not re-lated to you by blood at all. What good would that do her now?"

"You're so alone, Fielding," I said. "Don't you mind?"

"I'm afraid to write Sarah," she said. "I'm afraid that she won't answer, or that she will and she'll say that she never wants to see me."

I thought of the Lost Newfoundlanders page in the *Backhomer*.

"The day might come when you lose track of Sarah," I said. "When you don't know where she is or even if she's still alive. What then? Imagine her and Karen never knowing you existed."

Fielding sobbed again, one hand over her mouth. "You've got to write to her," I said. "You've got to."

June 17, 1955. St. John's

Dear Sarah:

Perhaps David wrote to you about meeting me in St. John's while he was on his way to France in 1943. He gave me a picture of you, which I have often looked at since he died. David died not knowing who I was. And perhaps because of that I felt his death even more keenly than I would have had he known. I can think of no better way to say this than simply to say it. I am your mother — that is, I gave birth to you and David. You have a right to know who your father is, and I will tell you should you ever ask.

I have only lately been able to admit to myself that my father did not love me as much as I have all my life been pretending that he did. He loved me as much as his heart and his circumstances let him, I am sure. I tell you this, not in the hope of making you feel sorry for me, but to help you understand why I would so much like to meet you.

You owe me nothing, Sarah. I have done nothing yet to earn your affection or respect. Any silly, giddy girl can have a baby, even two at once. I was happy when I was sixteen to be shipped off to New York before my pregnancy began to show, and to let my mother pretend that she was pregnant while I went about my lying-in for five months in her house; happy to let her pretend, to save my reputation and my father's, that the babies, when I had them, were her own. But I have not often been happy since.

My mother was a woman who was capable of great courage. I am sure that if she could have, she would have taken me with her when she left my father — for which, knowing my father as I did, I bear her no more ill will than can be helped. I would like to have had her as my mother. But she was and always will be yours. I would not expect you to ever call me Mother, or think of me as that. I would not expect you to introduce me to anyone as such. Our secret can remain our secret, if you like. You can call me Fielding. Everybody does.

I cannot imagine how strange it must be for you to receive such a letter — even stranger, I am sure, than it seems to me to be writing it so late in life. It may seem to you that you have nothing to gain from meeting me, or that I have no way of proving that what I say is true. As to the latter, I have since I was twelve faithfully kept a journal of my life, which now fills many volumes and in which all that I have told you is set out in more detail. As for the former, I can tell you only that I have felt your absence, yours and David's, all my life. I was for a time, many years ago, confined to a sanatorium with an illness that left me unable to conceive more children. I thought about you often while I was in the San.

Perhaps if I had never met David, I would not be writing to you now. I know it is foolish, but I sometimes cannot help thinking that if I had told David I was his mother, he might have made it through the war.

I believe that when David looked me up, it was with the intention of paying a brief and dutiful visit. I remember opening the door to find him standing there, in uniform, his hat removed, as if he had come to the wrong address bearing bad news. He did not expect to be greeted so fervently by a half-sister who had never been to visit him, but I couldn't help myself. When I saw his name on his lapel, I threw my arms around him and hugged him until he hugged me back. Three days later, when we were saying goodbye, I cried and made such a fuss that I embarrassed him. I told him I loved him and, perhaps because he knew I wanted him to, he told me he loved me too.

Three months later, when they told me he was dead, it seemed strange that I hadn't sensed or felt his death the moment it occurred, which had been weeks before. His death was for me only a dreaded possibility until I opened my door and saw the two officers. Perhaps others who were joined to him by something more important than mere blood sensed it when it happened. Perhaps my mother did, perhaps you did. I don't know. I don't know if such things can be felt. I didn't know until I was told that my father was dead, or until her brother wrote me that my mother was.

But blood must count for something, Sarah. It did when I met David and held him in my arms. I look at your picture every day and wonder what you look like now and imagine meeting you. I wonder what your daughter looks like and imagine meeting her.

Blood is a place to start from, I think, for you and me, and for Karen, should you choose to tell her who I am. Only rarely in my life have I been joined to others by something more important than mere blood. I hope that you will write to me and that we will see each other soon.

Sheilagh Fielding

———

October 9, 1955. New York

Dear Miss Fielding:

Your letter seemed sincere, which makes it all the more difficult for me to assure you that you must be mistaken. I have checked the hospital records here in New York and with everyone who knew my mother, including two of her brothers. They confirmed what I have always known — that I have a half-sister in St. John's — but they were as mystified by your letter as I was. Although it would not further your purpose any, I would like to meet with you — we are half-sisters, after all. If you can make your way to New York, we could meet at the address below, which you will notice is not mine. I'm sure you will understand why, under the circumstances, I would prefer that our first meeting not be at my home.

Yours truly,
Sarah Taylor

"Did you tell her everything?" I said.

"Everything," Fielding said. "I even told her I'd kept journals — "

"You should have sent them," I said. "She doesn't mention them in her letter."

"No," said Fielding. "She doesn't."

"She wants you to come see her, anyway; that's a good first step. She must know, or half know, that what you say is true."

There was a long silence.

"Maybe," Fielding said at last. "Or maybe she thinks that if she doesn't agree to meet me, I'll just show up on her doorstep someday and scare the life out of Karen. I should never have written her. She doesn't want it to be true, and I don't blame her. It's not as if she or Karen knew about this all their lives, like me. And she'll want to know who her father is. What will I tell her?"

"Tell her the truth. If she ever meets Prowse, she'll know that you're telling the truth, even if he denies it. You'll go and you'll bring the journals with you," I said. "And I'll go with you. I don't mean I'll meet her with you. I'll just make sure that you get there."

Something More Important Than Mere Blood

Dear David:

I have decided that I will go and see Sarah. But before that, I have to stop doing something I went back to doing when they told me you were gone. I stopped once before, when I was in my thirties, but I am in my fifties now, not as strong and more afraid. I start tomorrow. I will write all night and go to bed when the sun comes up, but no amount of Scotch will make me sleep. And at three o'clock in the afternoon, I will pack a bag and, with my cane in hand, walk down the hill to a place they call the Harbour Light. It will be a long walk. And a long time before I write to you again.

TWO YEARS LATER — it took her that long to make up her mind and work up the nerve to quit the booze again — an aide drove me to her boarding-house at six in the morning. She came down the steps, stopping with both feet on each step, stepping always with her right foot first, then bringing down the left, holding a bag of luggage in each hand. She let my aide take one bag and lugged the other one, the one that contained her journals, to the car.

With her luggage in the trunk, she stood with her arms tightly at her sides, rounded shoulders slightly hunched, holding her cane at the middle with one hand, not in front of her as she usually did. She looked vulnerably hopeful.

"I still think we should have flown," I said, but she shook her head.

"I haven't thought it all through yet," she said. "I reserve the right to change my mind."

My aide drove us to Riverhead Station, where we boarded the train. We had reserved two berths and one compartment, in which, after we had stowed our luggage, we sat facing forwards.

Fielding said nothing from the moment the train began to move to when we reached the Bog of Avalon.

"I've never seen the whole island before, you know," she said. "I went both times by boat from St. John's. I've never been farther west in Newfoundland than where the Bonavista branch begins."

I remembered my own first cross-island journey in 1920. I was almost able to summon up how first seeing Newfoundland had felt. I resisted the urge to tell her what sights she had in store. She was the closer to the window and she leaned her forehead against it and for a few seconds closed her eyes. It was going to be a sunny day once the morning fog burned off.

We saw, far off in the distance, the headlands of Conception Bay and from time to time the bay itself in alternating shades of blue depending on the sky.

"All David ever saw of Newfoundland was St. John's. Maybe — " She wiped her eyes. "We'll see," she said. "We'll see."

I tried to busy myself with work but could not concentrate. "Fielding, " I said. "Why, in your journals, is it only *after* Confederation that you spell things out? Before that, you wrote as if someone was looking over your shoulder."

"It had to do with deciding to come back to St. John's, deciding to be an atom of dissent beneath your mattress. For Newfoundlanders after 1949, the past was literally another country. It was for me. I finally realized I had more to fear from the future than the past."

"I wonder why your father picked Prowse's *History* to compose the letter," I said. "The first book that came to hand, I suppose?"

Fielding shook her head. "I told my father that Prowse took you to see the judge to have your father's book signed, just like he took me. Told him the inscriptions were exactly the same. And he sensed, without knowing the details, that Prowse had hurt me in some way. For my father, there would have been a certain symmetry in choosing that book.

"You know, my father blamed you for everything, not just for getting me pregnant, but for everything I did after I had Sarah and David, even things I would have done anyway. He wanted me to finish school somewhere, then go to university, but I refused. I had been a recluse for so long I wanted to go on being one. But I came out of it and talked the publisher of the *Telegram* into letting me have the reporting job that was least popular among the men. My father didn't think it proper, of course, my being a reporter — and spending all my time in the courts, at that — but when he found out you were working the courts, too … He had already made me swear that you didn't know about the baby and that I would never tell you, but he made me do it all over again. Of course, I didn't tell him about you converting me to socialism, which by the way you never did, I just pretended so I could be with you — My God, Smallwood, how many shades of purple are you capable of turning? I've never seen that one before."

She had spoken so offhandedly she had caught me off guard.

"I'm sure he blamed you when I came down with TB. A little over a year later, I was in the San. A year after that, the doctors told him what, as a doctor himself, he must have known already: that I wouldn't last another month. He blamed you for my death, even though it didn't happen. He blamed himself, too. Even after I was well again."

She stopped talking, but still I could not settle down. It was not the country we were passing through that kept distracting me, but Fielding seeing Newfoundland for the first time at the age of sixty.

"When I asked if you would marry me — " I said. She did not look away from the window.

"I was going to tell you everything that night," she said. "And then see if you still wanted me."

"You mean — " I said. "You mean you would have said yes?"

"*Would* you have still wanted me, knowing then what you know now?"

She knew the answer was no, or she would not have asked. She had known that night in New York thirty years ago, because of how I acted when she paused to think and when, instead of yes, she said my name. My last name. And because of the way I misread her expression and intentions, and the way that, to spare myself, I retracted my proposal and pretended I was joking. Such a man, had he known then what he knew now, would have withdrawn his proposal. I would have run; I would have done what I wound up doing anyway, would have tried to convince myself that I had never really loved her and that it therefore did not matter that she was not what I had imagined her to be. She loved me then, as absurd, vain, pompous, strutting and ambitious as I was, and perhaps she loved me now.

I had that. And I had loved her, I had at least once in my life been capable of that, able to escape my self long enough to love. Suddenly, the unacknowledged sorrows and blunders of my life surged up in me all at once. I thought I would be sick. I gasped, put my hand over my mouth until tears began collecting on my fingers. I took my hand away and looked at it as if I had just discovered I was bleeding.

Fielding turned away from the window.

"Thank you," I said. She nodded, smiled, turned back to the window.

When we were just outside of Port aux Basques, she knocked on the door of my berth, waking me. Still lying in bed, I opened the door. She was fully dressed.

"Would you mind if I went by myself from here?" she said. "It's not because of you. I've thought about it. It's best if I make the trip from Port aux Basques to New York by myself."

I saw her off. I caused quite a stir when I was spotted on the dock. I was cheered and patted on the back like some national mascot. People waving goodbye to passengers looking down from the ship pointed to me.

"It's Joey," they said excitedly. "It's Joey," as if I often appeared thus to punctuate the visits to Newfoundland of people from away, or to bid goodbye to Newfoundlanders leaving home. They allowed me to make my way to the edge of the dock. Fielding stood at the railing as the boat slowly pulled away from shore. None of the people gathered there knew who it was that I was seeing off, but they were curious.

Fielding blankly surveyed the crowd, the receding dock, as if she could not find me or was not trying to, her mind, perhaps, already on her destination.

She raised her cane in a general, faintly benedictory way, as if she were dismissing an apology or resisting the urge to make one.

She would, of course, be coming back. But not to me. I thought of my wife, my two sons and my daughter. To whom I had never been a husband or a father. If it was not too late for Fielding to start again, it might not be too late for me. I decided I would drive to the nearest airport and fly back to St. John's.

This time, I really had crossed the country by train for the last time. Soon there would be no more trains in Newfoundland, no way to cross the core except by bus or car. Even sooner than that, I would win my last election.

I did not solve the paradox of Newfoundland or fathom the effect on me of its peculiar beauty. It stirred in me, as all great things did, a longing to accomplish or create something commensurate with it. I thought Confederation might be it, but I was wrong.

Perhaps only an artist can measure up to such a place or come to terms with the impossibility of doing so. Absence, deprivation, bleakness, even despair are more likely than their opposites to be the subject of great art, but they otherwise work against greatness. Or the sort of self-sacrificing, love-driven person who Sir Richard said did not exist.

Or Fielding, who is both. Fielding to whom no monuments will be raised, after whom no streets or buildings will be named. Unlike me, in whose name books have been written, plaques placed, statues erected.

She loves me, but not just me. But I love only her.

I tried, for the fifteen years of public life I still had left after I rode the train with her to Port aux Basques, to camouflage by great accomplishments my broken heart.

I could not admit to myself that what I was attempting was impossible. Having gained power so late in life, and having no way to console myself for losing it, I could not renounce it. I no longer had the luxury of patience, was no longer able to disbelieve in my own mortality. If I was going to live to see Newfoundland transformed and live to take the credit, that transformation would have to happen soon and therefore as the result of some grand, unprecedented scheme.

I went to Labrador, was flown inland to where, ten thousand years ago, the earth dropped out from beneath the Churchill River. Suddenly, as suddenly as when the earth beneath the water first gave way, the falls were there, the mist from them billowing about the plane, while visible through it was that great plummeting convergence of white water. Below me, said the man whose dream it was to harness it, was the power to make turbines ten storeys high spin like toy propellers.

By a corridor of conveyance that would carry this power from the wilderness of Labrador to the cities of the south, the gulf between Newfoundland and the New World would at last be bridged.

FIELDING'S JOURNAL, MARCH 17, 1989

Dear Smallwood:

I was there the night in '72 when you made your farewell speech, in the drill hall in Pleasantville, a huge arching shell of a place that, because the Americans once owned it, reminded me of David. How cold it was that night. It would have been cold inside if not for the number of people who came to hear you say goodbye, two thousand of them crammed into a hall meant to hold six hundred. I stood by the wall as usual, to have something to lean against, though the metal was so icy to the touch I could feel it through my coat. There was a part near the top that buckled whenever the wind blew especially hard. I remember looking up and wondering if it would hold.

Seventeen years ago. Others spoke on your behalf, telegrams were read. One, from Louis St. Laurent, with whom you signed the terms of union, made you cry. Then you spoke. For an hour you spoke. Embellished your accomplishments, made light of your failures or ignored them altogether. But it was exactly what they expected you to do. When you finished, they rose to their feet, cheering, crying, clamouring to see you or touch you as you left the stage, relieved that after hanging on too long, you were letting go at last.

You were carried from the drill hall on the shoulders of two men. Raised above the crowd, you took the full force of the wind when you got outside. You turned your face away, held your hat up to your ear to shield yourself.

They carried you to the new car they had bought you as a farewell gift and set you down. You waved one last time from inside the car, then drove off, moving slowly through the crowd that followed you to the gates of Pleasantville. Then you drove off up the boulevard beside the lake.

When your car passed out of sight, the cheering stopped. There was an interval of silence, hesitation, a collective revery that lasted until the next great gust of wind sent everyone running back the way they came, laughing and joking as people will who are commonly afflicted by the weather.

I walked back with the help of a man who did not introduce himself and called me Missus, and clearly wondered what I was doing out alone on such a night. "Here, Missus, take my arm," he said when he saw me picking my way gingerly across the ice. He walked me to my car.

I'm told that on the night of your last election, you had your chauffeur drive you around the city while you listened to the radio, as if you were still campaigning, as if you thought your chances of winning were somehow better as long as you kept moving. You almost, but not quite, outran defeat. Not until the next day was it certain you had lost, and not until weeks later did you admit it to yourself.

You tried everything to stave it off. Ordered recounts where none were needed. That you offered to appoint to the Cabinet any member of the opposition who would cross the House was the worst-kept secret in St. John's.

You resigned at Government House in the drawing room where you were first sworn in as premier. That night, Tories, and no doubt independents who hated you then as much as they had in 1949, went out on their back steps and, in a celebration

*mocking that of referendum night, fired shotguns in the air. The
pink, white and green appeared on flagpoles from which, for
twenty-three years, no flags had flown.*

*I always thought of you when I drove along the isthmus
of Avalon. You can see the ocean there from both sides of the
highway. And the ruins of the refinery at Come by Chance, the
smokestacks like the skyline of some long-abandoned city.
Failed and mothballed except for the token banner of flame that
they tell me still flutters from one stack. It was that little flag of
flame, its unwarranted cheerfulness and optimism, that reminded
me of you.*

*The country is strewn with Come by Chance–like monoliths,
the masterpieces of some sculptor who worked on a grand scale
and whose medium was rust. Quarries, mines, mills, plants,
smelters, airports, shipyards, refineries and factories, to all of
which paved roads still lead, though no one travels on them
any more.*

*You all but gave away Churchill Falls, which you had hoped
would crown your career as Confederation had crowned
Mackenzie King's.*

*They tell me you cannot read, write or speak, but can only
understand the spoken word. You whose life was one long
holding-forth have no choice now but to listen. You are a
captive audience. Stroke-stricken. Struck. "He was always
having strokes," Prowse said, but he meant the judge, not you.
You nod or shake your head, point to what you want. Your
grandchildren read to you, letters, books.*

*They made you a recording of the judge's History, took
turns reading it. Old Prowse speaking to you in dozens of
different voices. I would love to hear it. I imagine you thinking,
When the voices out there stop making sense, the voice in here
will, too. Perhaps, after the next, you will be like a man my
father once described to me, who knew the names of things
but was unable to think in sentences. Your mind an inventory*

of the world. Like your Encyclopedia of Newfoundland and Labrador, *which I have heard is almost finished.*

I made you a tape, too, which by now you will have heard:

Dear Smallwood:

I am told that as neither of us can travel, this is the only way we can communicate. I have to confess I wrote this down and am reading to you now. It seems a shame we cannot see each other one last time. This is so one-sided, me talking to you, you not talking back, and me not even there to hear myself and to watch you listen. There was a time when I would have given anything to see you stuck for words. I still would, to tell you the truth.

I think often these days of what my father said when I asked him if he believed there was an afterlife: 'The grave's a fine and private spot / Where none I think do ought but rot.' It doesn't seem as funny now as it did down through the years. It is unfortunately true that we cannot make the sun stand still, nor can we any longer make him run.

I consider myself hugged and kissed by you, Smallwood, and am thinking now of you bidding me goodnight. You may, if it pleases you, do likewise with me.

———————

Field Day, June 6, 1959

On this day 130 years ago a woman who was known to the people of this city as Nancy April and to herself as Shawnawdithit died in St. John's. She was the last Beothuk Indian.

When I was in my early twenties, I came down with tuberculosis and was confined for two years to the San. There was little to do but read and one of the books I read was Howley's book about the Beothuks.

Nancy was named April after the month that she was captured, as her sister was named Easter Eve after the day that *she* was captured and her mother Betty Decker after the boat on which she was transported from her place of capture to St. John's.

In 1823, the three of them were often seen walking the streets of St. John's together, wearing deerskin shawls over the dresses they were given by the whites with whom they lived.

When curious children gathered around them, Nancy made as if to chase them, which caused them all to scatter, at the sight of which she laughed out loud. Everywhere they went, people gathered round to gape. Of the three of them, only Nancy seemed unafraid. She sometimes went so far as to mimic the looks of wonderment on the faces of the people that they passed. She was perhaps too young to understand; or perhaps she was feigning unconcern to reassure her mother and her sister, who were sick.

People reported seeing them so laden down with iron-mongery, which they planned to take home with them, that they could barely move. I have often, since reading Howley, thought of those three women, not two months removed from their world, wandering around in one full of things they had no names for, laden down with bits of iron that they found discarded on the ground but that in their world, if only they could make their way back to it, could be put to precious use.

After a failed attempt to reunite them with their tribe, of whom there were by this time not more than two dozen left, they were sent to live with magistrate John Peyton and his wife in the town of Exploits, near the river of that name on which, for no one knows how long, the Beothuk depended for their livelihood, and where Nancy's mother and her sister died in the fall of 1823.

Nancy was for several years a servant in the Peyton household, where she learned very little English, but enough to tease
Mrs. Peyton about how hard she worked her servants.

A society to prevent the extinction of the Beothuks was
created in 1828 by William Cormack, who brought Nancy
back to St. John's to live with him. Cormack suggested that she
learn English and, in turn, teach him her language and way of
life. She could not read, but she could draw quite well and
name what she drew and some of what she saw. Cormack introduced her to people as "my interesting protégé."

She drew many sketches for Cormack, some depicting
Beothuk dwellings, clothing, weapons and burial practices, and
narrative maps showing where certain members of her tribe
were killed or captured and the path of what is thought to have
been their final expedition. When Cormack left Newfoundland,
Nancy was sent to live with Attorney-General James Simms.

I think often, too, of Cormack leaving Newfoundland in
the spring of 1829, when it was certain that she would soon
die, unwilling to wait a few weeks more. It is not recorded why
he left, though as he was single and quite well off, it seems
likely that, if he had wanted to, he could have stayed.

She knew she was the last Beothuk. How, other than sad,
this made her feel, she was unable to communicate. Nor can I
imagine it, any more than I can a world that would seem as
alien to me as ours must have seemed to her. "As for beds,"
Cormack said, "she did not understand their use," and instead
slept on the floor beside them.

I am not much better able to imagine the point of view
of the men at whose hands so many of her people died. I like
to think that in their place, I would not have done what they
did, but that is something I can never know.

But when I was in the San, I was drawn, morbidly drawn
perhaps, to read and re-read Howley's book, and I was young
enough to think that Nancy and I had a lot in common.

It was said of her that "she could not look into a mirror without grimacing at what she saw." That sentence would not be out of place in my obituary. She was described as having been "stout but shapely before she fell ill." Some people might say the same of me. We contracted tuberculosis at about the same age. I survived, for no other reason I can think of than because I understood the use of beds.

My father could not bear to watch me die. When he was told my death was certain, he stopped coming to the San to see me. I had very few other visitors. It was partly my father's abandonment of me that made me identify with Nancy. I fancied that Cormack had been in love with her and had gone away because he could not bear to watch her die. There are times when I still think it might be so.

She made a great impression on people long before they knew that she would be the last Beothuk. But it is hard not to think of her as that, "the last Beothuk," perhaps presumptuous to try in what is, after all, an address to absence, silence.

She was buried on the south side of St. John's, below the Brow, not with those whose graves she drew, not with those whose beads she wore, but with the Church of England dead, the Church of England poor, her grave unmarked. Her remains lie somewhere near the Church of St. Mary the Virgin, but where exactly no one knows.

According to one person who knew her while she stayed with Peyton, she had left behind her in the interior two children about whom she "fretted constantly." Nowhere else except in this one account are these children mentioned, so I am almost able now to persuade myself that they did not exist.

When I was in the San, I liked to think otherwise, however, because I had two lost children of my own.

I had a son and have a daughter who were conceived in St. John's and born in New York. I met my daughter and my granddaughter for the first time two years ago.

I met my son for the first and last time three months before he died in France in the Second World War in 1943. I saw him before that when he was five years old. Once, I stood behind him on a sidewalk in New York, without him knowing I was there, without my mother knowing. From time to time, even though they were holding hands, my son looked up at my mother as if to make sure that she was still there. That was the last time I saw my mother.

I made the trip to New York by train and by boat, as I did when I first left Newfoundland in 1917 and again in 1920. The island looks the same now as it did back then.

It doesn't matter to the mountains that we joined Confederation, nor to the bogs, the barrens, the rivers or the rocks. Or the Brow or Mundy Pond, or the land on which St. John's and all the cities, towns and settlements of Newfoundland are built. It wouldn't have mattered to them if we hadn't joined.

I gave my granddaughter a copy of Judge Prowse's *A History of Newfoundland*, a book that is not as easy to find as it used to be. Prowse, boomer that he was, was also a confederate. He presides throughout the History with his gavel and his Bible, calling Confederation with Canada "a consummation devoutly to be wished." Consummation has come and jarred one hemisphere.

We have joined a nation that we do not know, a nation that does not know us.

The river of what might have been still runs and there will never come a time when we do not hear it.

My life for forty years was a pair of rivers, the river that might have been beside the one that was.

On the day this country joined Confederation, I was hiding out from history, mine, yours, ours. I went back to a section shack on the Bonavista branch line that I once fled to years ago to write a book that I hope will one day be published. I stayed there for months, wondering, waiting — about what, for what, I hardly knew.

I thought a lot about my parents: my American mother, who came to Newfoundland but went back home, without me or my father, when I was five; my father, who didn't know I knew that he betrayed me and thought that if I found out, I would no longer love him. He was wrong about that, as he was about so many things.

I sat alone in the section shack the night of the second referendum and listened as the results from each region were announced. The signal was weak, the numbers barely audible through a drone of static as if they were coming from a remote country I had heard of but had never seen.

When I was certain that the issue had been decided, I turned off the radio and went outdoors. There was a ladder on the side of the shack that led up to the roof, where I kept a rocking chair and where I liked to sit on nights when it was clear, as it was that night, to look at the stars and to watch the trains go by.

There was no wind. The moon, nearly full, was reflected in the ponds around the shack. I could see the glint of other ponds from what I guessed must have been ten miles away.

It was July, but it was cool enough that I could see my breath, and a sheen of condensation lay on everything. I sat in the chair, rocking slightly, imagining, as it was almost impossible not to do on such a night in such a place, that I was the sole person on the planet.

And then I heard the train, long before I usually did, long before it passed the shack, for the conductor, who was obviously a confederate, was blowing the whistle constantly. I saw the locomotive light far off in the distance. For a while, it looked as though nothing but a light was coming, but then I saw the dark shape of the train.

It was not a passenger train. Perhaps it was a freight train with some cargo as oblivious to politics as the ponds that it was passing. Or perhaps this was a run purely for the sake of celebration, not so much of victory as the enemy's defeat.

For a few seconds there was nothing in the world but sound, the continuous blare of the whistle, the chugging of the train. The conductor saw me and waved his hat as he went by, grinning gleefully, as if he hoped I was an independent. To spite him, I waved back. I saw his mouth form the words *We won*.

What did he imagine we had won? What, had he "lost," would he have imagined he had lost?

I watched the train until it disappeared from view, the sound of the whistle receding. Something abiding, something prevailing, was restored.

I have often thought of that train hurtling down the Bonavista like the victory express. And all around it the northern night, the barrens, the bogs, the rocks and ponds and hills of Newfoundland. The Straits of Belle Isle, from the island side of which I have seen the coast of Labrador.

These things, finally, primarily, are Newfoundland.

From a mind divesting itself of images, those of the land would be the last to go.

We are a people on whose minds these images have been imprinted.

We are a people in whose bodies old sea-seeking rivers roar with blood.

During the writing of this novel, I consulted many books, far too many to list here, but I acknowledge a special debt to D. W. Prowse's *A History of Newfoundland* (London, 1895), and to Richard Gwyn's *Smallwood: The Unlikely Revolutionary* (Toronto, 1972).

I would like to thank Anne Hart of The Center for Newfoundland Studies at Memorial University of Newfoundland in St. John's, and Ingeborg Marshall, an independent scholar and authority on, among many other subjects, the Beothuk and William Cormack.

I owe personal notes of thanks to my tireless and supportive agent, Anne McDermid, and to my editor at Knopf Canada, Diane Martin, whose guidance, patience and advice helped immeasurably in the founding of *The Colony of Unrequited Dreams*.

Finally, I would like to thank Gerry Howard, Editor-in-Chief at Anchor, Doubleday in New York, for his friendship and enthusiasm, and for giving *Colony* a home in what my father used to call "the country north of Mexico."

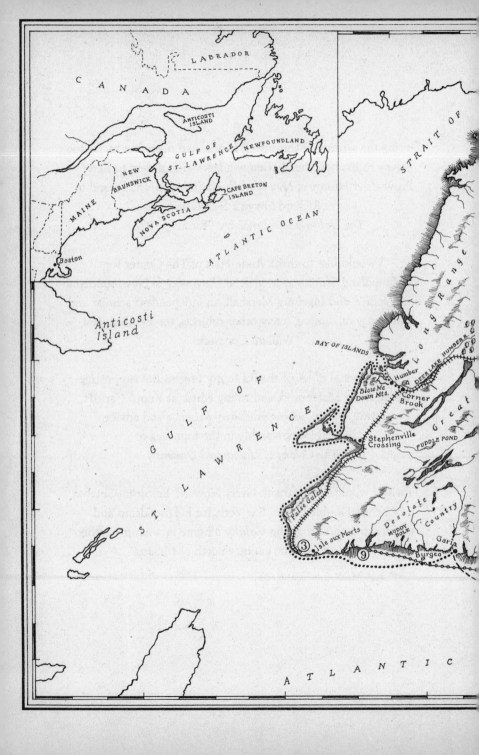

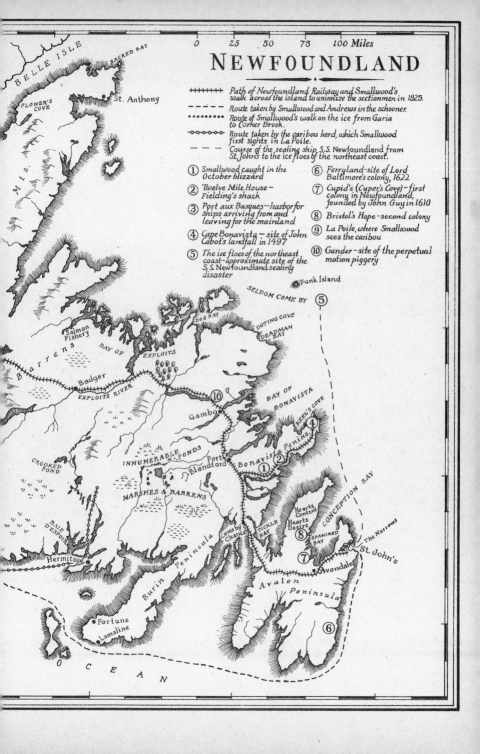

NEWFOUNDLAND

0 25 50 75 100 Miles

++++++++ Path of Newfoundland Railway and Smallwood's
walk across the island to unionize the sectionmen in 1925.

– – – – – Route taken by Smallwood and Andrews in the schooner.

•••••••• Route of Smallwood's walk on the ice from Garia
to Corner Brook.

-o-o-o-o- Route taken by the caribou herd, which Smallwood
first sights in La Poile.

– – – – Course of the sealing ship, S.S. Newfoundland from
St. John's to the ice floes of the northeast coast.

① Smallwood caught in the October blizzard

② Twelve Mile House – Fielding's shack

③ Port aux Basques – harbor for ships arriving from and leaving for the mainland

④ Cape Bonavista – site of John Cabot's landfall in 1497

⑤ The ice floes of the northeast coast-approximate site of the S.S. Newfoundland sealing disaster

⑥ Ferryland – site of Lord Baltimore's colony, 1622

⑦ Cupid's (Cuper's Cove) – first colony in Newfoundland, founded by John Guy in 1610

⑧ Bristol's Hope – second colony

⑨ La Poile, where Smallwood sees the caribou

⑩ Gander – site of the perpetual motion piggery

BELLE ISLE

SACRED BAY

FLOWER'S COVE

St. Anthony

Mts.

Barrens

Salmon Fishery

BAY OF EXPLOITS

DOG BAY

SELDOM COME BY

DOTING COVE

DEADMAN BAY

Funk Island

⑤

Badger

EXPLOITS RIVER

⑩

Gambo

BAY OF BONAVISTA

KEEL'S COVE

④

Bonavista Penins.

CROOKED POND

INNUMERABLE PONDS

Port Blandford

②

①

MARSHES & BARRENS

Hearts Content

Hearts Desire

⑧

CONCEPTION BAY

BAIE D'ESPOIR

Come by Chance

TICKLE BAY

SPANIARD BAY

The Narrows

Hermitage

Burin Peninsula

Avalon Peninsula

⑦

Avondale

St. John's

Fortune

Lamaline

⑥

O C E A N